I0662627

The Earthborn Series: Book 1

Empyreal

By Spencer Helsel

Empyreal

Copyright © 2016 Spencer Helsel

All rights reserved • Printed in the United States of America

Cover design by Jessica Helsel

Book design by CreateSpace

ISBN: 978-0-692-84232-4

For my wife Jessica. You're my favorite.

<u>Acknowledgements</u>

This book wouldn't exist without so many people. First and foremost, I want to thank my wife who created the amazing cover art. To my family, especially my sister who has shown such strength and courage, thank you for all the encouragement. A special thanks goes to David Robinson for the editing services and feedback to make this novel better.

Appreciation also goes to some of my students: Jennifer Thompson, Sabrina Bernedt, Jaime Periquet, Zoe Robinson, Skye Fricke and Daija Brascom who encouraged me to pursue my writing and spent time reading rough drafts. I am forever thankful to have been your teacher.

And thank you to whomever bought this book. It's hopefully the first of many to come.

Part I
Earthborn

Chapter One

"Seven minutes of darkness," the host of 115 JHN Los Angeles crooned through Dani's headphones as she lay on her bed. "That's how long the solar eclipse is expected last as the sun slips behind the moon. For seven minutes there will be no daylight, but wear protective eyewear. It's going to be one hell of a sight. You won't want to miss it."

The station switched to a song and soothed her back into her quiet, meditative state. She sighed, one hand resting on her stomach, the other flung out above her head; another nothing day in a long stream of nothing weeks. Summer was ending but unlike her classmates, she wasn't trying to get in one last trip to the beach or see the newest movie. Dani was anticipating school starting again for one infuriating reason.

She heard him despite her music. His scream was muffled by her headphones. She wished it blocked him out completely.

"Daniella! Get out here!"

Ricky's voice grated her nerves. She ground her teeth together.

"Daniella!"

"For the love of God," she muttered, pulling off her headphones, "what Ricky?"

"Get out here!"

"Why?"

"Because I said so!"

Her door was closed, but without the headphones she couldn't block out the party in the living room or the dozen raucous voices.

Or him pounding on her door. "Open up!"

"Go away!"

Ricky didn't like being shut out of any part of—as he put it—his house. There wasn't any lock on the knob, but Dani found a way to jam it when she wanted privacy. Unfortunately, the thin walls didn't stop his yelling.

"Yvette!" Ricky screamed. "Get your daughter to open the door!"

Her mother's voice joined in. "Daniella del Lucio! Will you please get out here?"

"Listen to your mother!" Ricky echoed, as if somehow that helped.

Groaning, Dani sat up and dropped her feet to the floor. There was no way to get out of this. Whisking back the strands of her black hair into a loose ponytail, she slipped her feet into her sneakers. Ricky was her mom's most-recent and most-worthless boyfriend. They moved into his house a couple months ago. Her mother, Yvette, lost their old place. They needed a roof and he had one. Dani hated him, roof or not.

Hanging from a nick in her headboard, she picked up a necklace and looped it around herself. It was a simple silver chain with a ring, but it was special to her.

She was almost to the door when Ricky barked from the other side, "Daniella! Now!"

"*Ya voy!* Jeez!" She was never one to back down from argument, especially with Ricky. He yelled. A lot. It made living here tough. Her mom got by, but that was only because she didn't argue with him as much as Dani. When her mom did argue, it was ugly. Dani lay awake at night, hearing them fight in the living room or their bedroom or pretty much wherever he felt like screaming. Which was everywhere.

Her mom always tried to smooth things over. She was real quick to come to his defense. Dani used to ask why she stuck up for him. But now? She didn't bother. Yvette played it off like it was no big deal and after a while, Dani stopped asking.

And she pretended to not notice the bruises.

She threw open the door. "What do you want?"

The hallway was full of people. There were always people over. Music thrummed noisily from the living room. The thick, chalky air mixed with the stench of cigarettes. Dani hated cigarettes.

One hung half-burned from Ricky's mouth. He was a hefty guy with a scowl to match his seemingly-constant sunburn-red face. He worked as a used-car dealer, but if the past was any indication, he wouldn't be there long. He'd gone through two jobs since he and her mom hooked up.

Trash, ash trays and empty bottles covered every surface of the house. It stunk like a dive bar, but that was probably because on any given day, at least five people came over to party.

"I need cigs." He sipped from a nearly-empty bottle, ash falling into the murky, foul-smelling liquid. "And we need more beer."

"So?"

"So run down the street and get some." He grinned at her with cracked, dry lips under his bushy mustache. She never knew what her mother saw in him. He was as attractive as a zit.

"You yelled at me to come out to get you cigarettes and beer? Did you forget? I'm sixteen, Ricky. I can't buy that."

"Quit being a brat and go to the store. They won't card you."

"With what money?" Dani asked.

"You got money."

"It's my money."

"It's my house." His lip curled back angrily from his yellow teeth. She swore she could see his breath like a cloud of putrid green. "Or do I have to remind you?"

Not after the other half a million times, she didn't say.

Her mom hurried from the living room, dressed in sweats and a tank top. Her mess of blonde-highlighted hair fell loosely around her eyes and she smiled, but it did little to cover up her look of dread. Dani could tell when her mom faked a smile. Usually, it was around him.

She handed out beers to the guests and quickly flew to Ricky's side. "Is everything okay?"

"I'm trying to get your daughter to help out around here," Ricky snarled, "but like usual, she's being a pest."

"Only to piss you off, Ricky." Dani smiled sweetly at him.

His frown deepened. Lately, it was difficult to hold her tongue. Dani usually got herself into trouble with a snarky comment.

Yvette jumped in, putting herself between her boyfriend and her daughter. "Oh honey, it'll be fine. Here." She pulled out several bills from her purse and handed them to Dani. "Get some drinks for Ricky and me. I could use a smoke, too. Then buy yourself a soda."

Dani stared at the money. She knew it was from her mom's shift at the clinic. Since it was a free-clinic, it didn't pay very well. Her mom hadn't had a job that paid well for some time. The reason for that was the beer in her hand. At almost noon, it probably wasn't her first. Or second for that matter.

"What about him paying for it?" Dani asked. "It's his ugly habit. And all these *arrimados* around here are his friends."

Ricky made something between a grunt and a growl. "Don't speak that Spanish crap around here. You know I don't know it."

Dani couldn't help herself. "*El burro sabe mas que tu.*" *A donkey knows more than you.*

"Honey, relax. Its fine, its fine." That was her mother's line when Ricky got angry. *Its fine, its fine.* It never was. "Just do this for me, sweetie." She braved a smile. "It's an eclipse party! Everyone needs to have a good time. Maybe you should invite someone." Yvette giggled. "You could always invite Nathaniel. He's such a cutie."

"Oh God Mom! Eww!" Dani rolled her eyes. "We're *just* friends. That's it. Nathaniel is like my brother."

"Well, he certainly doesn't look at you in a brotherly way."

Ricky shoved Yvette out of the way. His sweaty, musky face was suddenly in hers, scowling. "Look kid, you and your mom can gossip all you want later, but I need cigs and beer now. Go get 'em," he grabbed her arm, shoving her back, "you useless waste of space."

That was her breaking point. She didn't like him, she didn't like the way he treated her mother and she certainly didn't like him touching her.

She angrily stuffed the money back in her mom's hand. "No." She retreated back inside, grabbed her gym bag from the bed and shoved past them.

"Where the hell do you think you're going?" Ricky demanded.

"Out!"

"Like hell! I need stuff!"

"Get your own stuff, *lamecharcos!*"

The house was full of people as she stormed through. She heard Ricky behind her and her mother talking him down, but Dani didn't bother looking back. She slammed open the front door and marched out into the hot California morning.

Screw him.

Ricky's house was in a suburb of Sun Valley. Hot and dry, it deserved its name. On hotter days, it felt as if they were two miles from the sun. You could cook on the sidewalk.

But Dani didn't mind. Anything was better than being stuck inside that house.

"Dani!" Her mom followed. "Dani! Stop!"

She heard Ricky yelling inside. *Big surprise.* Dani distinctly made out her name, plus a few adjectives she wished she hadn't.

"Dani, wait!"

"What the hell are we doing here, mom?" Dani spun on her heel, confronting her mother. Her disheveled appearance, the running mascara, the beer still in her hand; Dani fumed. And she wasn't about to bite her tongue. Not after that pig touched her. "Why the hell are we living with that jerk? He treats you like trash and me worse!"

"Honey—!"

"No, mom, no! Ever since we moved in, he's made me feel like he owns me. He'd rather yell than talk. And now I'm buying him cigarettes and beer? I won't do that."

"It's for everyone." Her mom brushed back strands of her messy hair nervously, finishing her drink. "Honey, we have people over."

"We always have people over!" Dani screamed at the house full of party-goers. "Do any of you actually live anywhere else?"

She could see a few staring out the window.

"Daniella! You hush this instant!" her mother hissed. "They're our friends."

"No, they're *his* friends!" Dani shouted. "I haven't seen anybody we used to know. I haven't seen one, single person from the old neighborhood since we moved here."

"That's not true."

"Really? Who? Who have we seen?"

"Well, there's Nathaniel—."

"Who I'm embarrassed to bring here!" She glared at her mom. "And cigarettes? You never smoked before."

"It helps me relax. You of all people should know I'm under a lot of stress at work."

Months of frustration spilled out. "At work? Where do you work mom? The free-clinic?"

"It helps people."

"You don't work there because it helps people. You work there because it's the only place that'll take you."

"They didn't have space for me at my old job."

Dani snatched the empty bottle from her mother, holding it up angrily. "They didn't have space for a drunk!" Dani chucked the bottle at the sidewalk, shattering it. "You moved in with Ricky and now you're drinking before noon."

"It's a party."

"It's disgusting."

Dani stormed down to the sidewalk. She was too angry to talk anymore. Her mother yelled after her. "Where are you going?"

But that was it. No more. Dani headed down the street. She hated Ricky. She hated living there. It felt more like prison than home.

Ricky's house, like quite a few others on the block, was a squat, one story bungalow on the corner of the street. It had almost no grass left in the yard and the recent drought in California killed all of the remaining plants. Any more days like today and it would spontaneously catch fire, or at least Dani entertained herself with the idea it would.

Dani needed time. She needed to clear her head. And she had an idea of where to go.

Hey. She snapped off a quick text. Can we meet up?

She crossed the street at a jog. A few seconds later, his response came back. Yeah. Where?

Meet me at the Wreck Center?

10

Sure. What's up? Nathaniel texted.

I need to get out. You know where to find me.

Nathaniel was a friend from her old school, Lightpoint Academy; before she moved in with Ricky and had to transfer. He lived in one of those foster homes with way too many kids and not enough adults. At sixteen, he was the eldest of four other kids, with no chance of adoption or the need to be. From what he said about his foster parents, it wasn't a pleasant experience going home. They had that in common.

The only reason he went to Lightpoint, a charter school, was because the foster system secured him a scholarship. Though being a foster kid put a scarlet F on his chest, he wore it like a badge of honor. He was an outsider like her. He and Dani hung out after school, since neither of them wanted to go back to where they lived.

Not home; just where they lived. Neither saw it as home.

On days like today, they went to the Sun Valley Recreation Center. They referred to it at the "Wreck Center" because they felt like their lives were wrecks; their social lives were wrecks, their home lives were wrecks, their school lives were wrecks. They commiserated. He was the brother she never had.

Well, he certainly doesn't look at you in a brotherly way...

Dani rolled her eyes. *Thanks Mom.*

The Rec Center had one great thing: a punching bag. Usually, if she wasn't at the house, she was here; more than usual, lately. And the only thing that soothed her soul was to hit something.

She crossed Strathern, then Lorne, arriving at the squat beige building. The Rec Center was a community spot for parents and kids. It had baseball fields, a jungle-gym and wide open spaces shaded by trees.

As Dani crossed the street, she heard flapping wings. Slowing down, she looked up and spotted a snow-white bird. The animal reminded her of a dove, but looked more like a hawk. It was larger than the average hawk, with a spread of feathers around the top of its head like it a crown. The bird landed on the branch of a tree overlooking the sidewalk.

She smirked. "Hi there. What zoo did you escape from?"

The bird cocked its head, watching her curiously.

"Don't look at me in that tone of voice." She said playfully. "I'm not your food."

The bird ruffled its feathers.

"Yeah, that's right, be intimidated birdie."

She toyed with the idea of calling animal control—the bird was way too exotic to be local—but because she was looking up, Dani wasn't paying attention and ran headlong into someone. He was a grimy-faced man; a homeless vagrant with sweat-stained clothes and reeking of something dead. Dani normally didn't pay the homeless much mind. They hung out near the Rec Center, though usually they didn't bother anyone. She even gave them a few dollars here and there.

This guy, though, didn't ask for money. He just glared at her.

"Sorry." She mumbled, stepping around him.

Or she tried to, at least. He stepped in front of her, blocking her.

"Excuse me." She said, trying to side-step him again. Again, he followed. "Hey! Get out of my way!"

The man leaned in to her. He reeked. Dani never really made fun of anyone for the way they smelled, especially a homeless person. It wasn't their fault. But this man smelled of something so horrible she actually gagged a little.

She backed away. He took a step forward. What the hell was he doing? And then, he did something really weird:

He sniffed her!

He's smelling me? What a perv! She jumped around him, spinning and not letting her back to him. He creeped her out. The man followed, continuing to inhale deeply again and again as if she was the first good thing he smelled in years.

"Get away from me!" She warned. She was backpedaling so fast she didn't notice another vagrant behind her. She bumped into him. This one was larger, but equally as filthy. He also gave her a curtesy whiff, piquing his interest. "Jeez! Back off!"

She fled from the group, shaking. She kept up the pace, not running but certainly not taking her time. Thankfully, when she glanced back, the pair of homeless men did not follow her, though they did watch her from where they stood.

What the hell was their problem?

The encounter freaked her out, but shaking it off, she slipped inside and checked in. She was happy to be here. Here, she felt safe. Here, there was a chance to hit something.

She changed into a pair of athletic shorts and top before heading to one of the spare rooms. Stepping inside the hushed, air-conditioned space, she smiled widely. In front of her was a punching bag.

Dani never took self-defense classes. Most of what she learned was trial-and-error. She'd been coming for the past couple of months. She was never the violent type, but something about hitting the bag helped calm her down. She was such a regular the people at the center usually kept a room open for her.

Slipping on a pair of clean gloves from the rack, she loosened up and stretched. When she was ready, she approached the bag.

The first punch was solid. It took nearly breaking her wrist to learn to keep her arm straight. Dani swung her body into the blow. The bag bounced. All the power came from her hips. She hit it again, gritting her teeth. After nearly passing out a couple of times, she learned to not hold her breath; instead exhaling when she struck.

Smack! Smack! Smack! Her knuckles collided off the surface of the bag. *Smack! Smack! Smack!* She came at it hard, first quick punches and then power strikes.

And then kicks. She liked kicks.

Her leg swung, coming around with practiced precision. The key to kicking was striking with your shin and swinging your hips. Everything else was balance.

Dani's blow thrashed the bag. She struck again. Her hands burned. In her mind, all she saw was Ricky's face. Her anger flared. *Smack! Smack! Smack!* Two blows and then a kick. She landed back on her heels, then spun and kicked out behind her. Her heel connected.

Wow. Never done that before. She kept it up. Her breathing came fast. Her hands still hurt but it motivated her all the more. It felt great. *Smack! Smack! Smack!* Her anger grew. The bag bounced harder.

Smack! Smack! Smack! Grabbing the bag, she laid in a few body blows. She wished it was Ricky.

The door behind her opened as her strikes and kicks got faster. She moved around it, hitting it with everything she had.

"Wow. Angry much?" she heard Nathaniel ask.

Dani jumped. Her leg arched up and around. She screamed as she struck. The chain snapped. The bag summersaulted off the attachment and landed on the floor, skidding about a foot before rolling to a stop. Dani landed on her feet and stared.

So did Nathaniel. "So," he asked slowly, "having a bad day?"

Chapter Two

Nathaniel and Dani left together, though not before Dani apologized for breaking the bag. No one knew why the chain snapped so easily. Dani weighed maybe a hundred forty pounds. The chain had to be old. That was the only explanation.

The sun was still high and families were out and about. Some played in the baseball field behind the Center. More than a dozen kids crawled on the jungle gym next to the entrance.

"So Rocky, what's the matter?" he asked.

"Rocky?" She gave him a withering sideways glare.

"Do you prefer Rambo?"

"I don't like getting compared to Stallone at all. And shut up."

Nathaniel smirked. He was tall, lanky, and carried a book under one arm. He always had a book. It was his escape. His brown hair was short, not exactly clean cut since he never had money for a haircut. He either did it himself or let someone at the house do it, which meant it was a disaster half the time. His copper wire-frames sat awkwardly on his nose, one side a little higher than the other. Likewise, there wasn't money for new prescription glasses. His California tan was not beach-perfect—more farmer's tan than surfer dude—but it wasn't much lighter than she was naturally.

"So what's up?" He asked casually. "What's wrong?"

She crossed her arms. "What makes you think anything's wrong?"

"Um..." he cocked a thumb over his shoulder. "The beat-down you just gave the that bag in there and the fact you texted me to meet you. And you're playing with your necklace again."

Dani absently looped her thumb into the necklace and played it across her lips; a nervous tick of hers. The necklace was from her mother; or rather, the person her mother used to be.

"So what is it?" he asked.

She ignored the question. "Whatcha reading?"

He glanced down at his book. "Tolstoy. You didn't answer my question."

"Nothing's wrong."

He took a seat at a picnic table. "And I'll believe that when Hell freezes over."

She rolled her eyes, tucking the chain away. "There's no such thing as Hell," then murmured to herself, "worse than this."

"Was it Ricky? Your mom?"

"I don't want to talk about it, okay? I just want to chill." she huffed, sitting quietly for a moment. "So, Tolstoy: any good?"

"I highly doubt it'll be on our summer reading list, so you don't have to worry."

Dani smiled, but the mention of school made her nauseated. She missed Lightpoint. She was comfortable there. Her new high school felt like another planet. But at least she could spend her days away from Ricky.

Nathaniel noticed the look. "Dani, what's wrong? You can pretend all you want, but like hell you're okay. I know you. Something's up. What is it?"

Nathaniel had a habit of spotting her tells. "Nate, just drop it, okay?"

She only called him 'Nate' when she wanted to tease him, or in this case, distract him.

But, "Dani?"

His concern made her cringe. Dani didn't like people prying into her personal life, even Nathaniel. Some would think having a guy best friend was impossible. Dani found the idea of having girl friends impossible. Nathaniel didn't gossip behind her back, or anyone's back for that matter.

Of course, his concern came with something else; something that made her squirm. There was something a lot more than friendship there. She pretended not to notice.

Instead she stared over at a little girl playing by herself; picking grass and putting it into a pile. She was alone. She wore a simple yellow sundress clashing with her brown skin and black hair. She reminded her of herself.

Alone.

"Fine." Nathaniel sighed after a minute of silence, knowing full well Dani was a nut that wouldn't crack. "You don't want to tell me? How about we talk about something else?"

"Like?"

"I don't know. The future? I started looking at colleges."

"Really? Which ones?"

Nathaniel lit up. He rambled on about each school he applied to for next year, as he was graduating early. Each school sounded like Heaven. Dani listened, smiling, imagining the different places he could go. Nathaniel always wanted to go to college. She even talked about visiting him once he got in somewhere. She'd come by, see his dorm room, meet his friends.

But, of course, she knew that was a lie. He had no money to pay for college and no way to get a loan. He knew that. She knew that, too. That's why she said she'd visit him. Likewise, it was a fantasy. Dani knew that as soon as he left Los Angeles, she'd never see him again.

Her mind left her body, swirling into the dark depression she went to when things got bad; a place she visited often. She didn't have a home. Not really. Ricky's house wasn't home. Sometime soon, she wouldn't be there anymore. She wouldn't go back to school, either. Like Nathaniel's fictional college future, Dani knew deep down it wasn't going to happen.

She accepted it the moment she thought of it. Her time at Ricky's was ending.

"...and you've got to see the museum there." Nathaniel told her. "As soon as I get enough money, I'm getting a flight or a bus or something to UC Berkeley and—." He stopped talking. "Dani?"

"Hm?" she snapped out of her daydream. "What?"

"You look like you checked out there for a second. What's up?"

"Nothing." She said. She grabbed her gym bag. "I just realized I've got to get going."

"Seriously? I just got here."

"Yeah. I, um, I'll be back. I just have to run back to the house to get something."

"You want me to stick around? The eclipse'll be in a few hours. Want to watch it here?"

"Sure." She smiled tightly and stood. "That'll be great."

"Okay."

She got walking. Only when she was a few feet away did he call out to her. "Dani!"

"What?"

She could see that concern on her face again. "Are you sure you're alright? You're not going to do something stupid, are you?"

"Nah." She waved it off. "I'll be good Nate."

His nickname should have told him otherwise.

She was running away.

Dani's heart thudded in her chest as she ran back to Ricky's house. Somehow, just thinking it brought everything into focus. Ricky. Her mom. That house. She'd been unhappy for a while. She thought the idea of running away with no place to go would terrify her, but it didn't. Terrifying would be staying there.

Her mom wasn't going to stop drinking. Ricky wasn't going to stop being Ricky. She wouldn't stick around and watch them implode.

16

The party was rowdy when Dani arrived. Ricky and two of his buddies were outside, beers in hand.

"Look who's back." He sneered drunkenly.

Dani strode past him without a word.

"Hey! Where're you going?" he shouted at her back.

She kept walking.

Inside, the music blared deafeningly. Dani didn't bother with anyone, even the creep inside who cooed in her direction, "Hey sweetness. Why don't you park yourself over here?"

She ignored him, weaving around drunks to her room. She threw down her bag on the bed and started packing.

Clothes—just the bare essentials—some things she might be able to sell like her MP3, computer, a few DVDS; what money she had; toiletries; she stuffed all of it into her bag.

Her mom found her as she was zipping it up.

"Daniella?" She looked even more disheveled than when Dani left. Her black mascara streaked down her face. Her ponytail was loose. And, if Dani wasn't mistaken, a fresh hand-shape bruise encircled her right wrist. She slurred a little, "Honey, what're you doing?"

"Leaving."

"Leaving where?"

"This place! This hellhole!" She said. "I'm tired of doing this, mama."

"Honey, we live here."

"No, we don't. Whatever this is, it isn't living." She snatched up her bag, but stopped in front of her mom. She reeked of cigarettes and beer, but even then, she was her mother. She had to try. "Mama, come with me."

"Come where?"

"Anywhere but here." She looped her necklace out of her shirt. "Let's just go. You and me; like before. Like when you gave me this."

Her mom grimaced. Instead of saying anything, she took a huge swig from her cup. Then, with a plastic smile, she said, "Don't be silly, honey. Why would we leave?"

She wouldn't try anymore. Dani loved her mother, but there was no way she was doing this again. She stepped around her and marched back out into the hall. Yvette called after her.

As if like some demented re-run, Dani walked back out of the house like she did earlier; mom yelling for her to stop, Dani with her bag, and even Ricky adding to the chorus.

"Where the hell are you going now?" he demanded. "First you don't buy cigs and beer. Now what—?"

"Just shut up, you worthless piece of trash!" Dani snarled.

"Hey! Don't talk to me like that!" He snatched her elbow in his steely grip. Way to close to her now, his foul breath was hot against her cheek. "This is my house."

"Don't touch me!"

"I'll touch you if I want." He seethed lewdly, spittle flying from his mouth. His hand squeezed around her elbow. "Anything under this roof belongs to me."

People were gawking; partygoers, neighbors across the street. Some came out and formed a crowd on the front lawn. Not a single one of them would stop him. They were here for the spectacle.

"You should learn your place around here." Ricky growled. "What the hell do you do but eat my food, take up space and complain? I gave you a home! It'd be nice to be thanked for it."

"Well don't worry!" she shouted back. "I'm not staying!"

The statement was enough to shock him and for her to pull free. She could see her mom's face. She was terrified.

"You can keep your house!" Dani screamed. "It's all yours! I'm leaving!"

Her screams turned the front-lawn crowd quiet. Ricky glanced over his shoulder. The shock quickly evaporated. She yelled at him in front of his friends. And very quickly, the shock was replaced by anger.

"No." he seethed.

"What?"

"You're not leaving. You mouth off and you think you can just leave whenever you want?"

He reached for her again. Dani ducked back. "I said don't touch me!"

"You think you can tell me what to do?"

He caught her, but that was the last time he would. She twisted away from him and with a scream, kicked squarely to his knee. Ricky dropped. He hit the dirt. His beer slipped from his hand and sloshed out onto his shirt.

Groaning in pain, he sat up; his expression changing from confusion, to pain, to anger. When his eyes fell on Dani, his glare became a fierce bearing of teeth.

Ricky clambered to his feet and charged like an animal. Dani had never been in a fight; not a real one. Luckily, Ricky was drunk. He clumsily barreled right at her and she easily dodged. Dani instinctively grabbed and

18

spun, throwing him. Somehow, she launched him past her and slammed him head-long into the top of the fence bordering the property. His momentum sent him over, the chain-link clinking as he tumbled onto his head with a loud *smack* on the sidewalk. He finished toppling, feet flopping stupidly to the ground.

"Oh my God! Ricky!" Dani's mother shot past her and through the fence door. She slid down next to him. "Ricky, sweetie, are you okay?"

Ricky groaned, sitting up. Blood gushed from a gash in his scalp.

"You—You ungrateful waste of space!" he screamed at Dani, stumbling to his feet again and nearly falling. A small red river ran down his forehead into one eye. "Look what you did to me!"

"Stay back!" Dani warned, though despite just thrashing him, she didn't have a lot of confidence she could take him if he came at her again.

Yvette stepped between her speechless daughter and her boyfriend, "Ricky, are you okay?"

"Of course I'm not okay! Do you see what your ungrateful kid did to me? I'm bleeding!"

"Ricky, I'm sorry!"

He hit her. Ricky's hand shot out and backhanded Yvette across the jaw. She shrieked, grabbing the side of her face.

"Don't hit her!"

Ricky clambered over the fence, headed straight for Dani. "I'm going to teach you the same lesson you little—!"

His hand came back to punch. It never got there. Dani's arm came up as if on its own, knocking it aside. With her other fist she struck directly to the bridge of Ricky's nose. Her practice with the bag at the Center kicked in. Her hand burned. Luck or anger or both was enough to break the cartilage with a soft, wet crack. His head snapped back and he dropped to the ground again.

"Ugh! My nose!" Blood blossomed in a spout of red. "You broke my nose!"

Dani was over him. Her anger flared to life. Her hand radiated pure heat. She hit him again. And again. Two swift strikes and he went down harder than before.

"Dani! Stop!" her mom screamed.

But she wanted to hurt him! He hit her mother. He attacked her. Why the hell not? She hit him again viciously. She felt strong; stronger than ever. She felt his cheek shatter under her knuckles.

"Dani! No! I said stop!"

She raised her foot to kick him in the face.

"LEAVE HIM ALONE!"

Yvette shoved her backwards frantically. Her mom dropped to her knees in the dirt beside the abusive drunk, cradling his face in her hands. He moaned in pain, mewling over his broken nose and bloody, gashed face. Dani's other punches opened cuts on his cheek and jaw, yet her hands were untouched. It was like she hit him with bricks. Could she do that? Did she? He looked like he'd gone ten rounds in a UFC octagon. She couldn't believe she'd done it.

And she couldn't believe who her mother cried over.

"Are you okay?" Yvette whimpered, streams of tears and mascara running down her cheeks. "Ricky, honey, baby, talk to me!"

Ricky only moaned in pain.

She was crying over him? *Him?* "Mom!"

Yvette ignored her, wiping away some of the blood on Ricky's face. "Somebody call an ambulance!"

Dani took a step forward, tears in her eyes. *Isn't she worried about me? Isn't she worried about her own daughter?* "Mom, please—!"

"Get away from us!" Yvette screamed at her.

"Mom, it's not my fault!"

"I said get away!" Yvette screamed. "Just leave! You want to go? Go! Get out! Leave if you want! I don't care!"

Ricky sputtered blood, trying to simultaneously push Yvette off and swipe at Dani. "Get the hell out of my house and don't come back! I'm not putting up with this! As long as I own this place, you can sleep on the streets!"

Even though Dani planned to run away all along, her mother screaming at her—defending him no less!—sent tears streaming down her cheeks. "Mom, please, I—!"

But Yvette wouldn't look at her daughter anymore. "Dani, just go! Get your stuff and go!" She sniffed, the mark on her cheek from Ricky's knuckles still bright red while she lovingly caressed his face. Her voice was so quiet Dani could barely hear her, "You're not my daughter. I don't want to see you anymore. I don't want to ever see you ever again."

Dani opened her mouth to say something, anything, but closed it. It was no use. Yvette wouldn't even look at her.

"Mama..." she choked. "Mama...please..."

Yvette helped get Ricky up. They hobbled inside with the rest of the crowd. Dani stood there helplessly. Her hands hurt. Her eyes stung with tears. Through blurred vision, Ricky, her mom and everyone else disappeared.

Still crying, Dani snatched up her bag and ran.

Chapter Three

Dani didn't stop running until she was four blocks from Ricky's house. Her shoes clapped along the sidewalk, echoing in the early afternoon heat, accompanying her heavy sobs. Her tears ran out at block one; her doubts about running away at block two. By block four, she slowed down and doubled over, sucking in ragged sobs.

Her mother's voice repeated in her head. *Go! Get out!*

She stifled her tears and straightened up. She couldn't stay there. If she did, she'd turn around and go back. She couldn't do that.

Wiping her red, puffy eyes, she crossed towards the Sun Valley Rec Center. The bleating California sun was still up, meaning the pavement—and her for that matter—were cooking.

She spotted Nathaniel swinging back and forth on one of the swing sets, book nestled in his lap. The park was mostly empty. When he looked up, he saw her tears and jumped up to wrap her in a hug.

"What happened?" he asked.

She cried. She cried and cried until she could finally say it.

"I ran away."

She explained everything. They took a stroll through the trees to the baseball fields while Dani told him what happened at Ricky's. He didn't pressure her for more info or say empty platitudes. He listened, one arm around her shoulders for comfort.

Somehow she got through the story without crying. They ended up against one of the fences to the baseball diamonds. Once she finished, Nathaniel pensively thought for a moment about what to say.

Finally, "You know what this means, right?"

She sniffed. "What's that?"

"I can never say a Your-Mom-Joke again." He shook his head. "It's a travesty."

Dani barked out a laugh and covered her mouth. That was the last thing she expected, and because of that, it was the best thing. "You're such a punk, Nate."

"You want me to be serious?"

"Hell no." She wiped her red cheeks. "I could use a little humor."

"I got that in spades, babe."

Dani rolled her eyes. Nathaniel knew how to be funny at just the right time. If anyone else tried to joke like that with her, she would have hit them.

"So what do I do?"

"Well, I was thinking we watch the eclipse." He checked his watch and then the sky. "It should start soon."

The Rec Center had mostly cleared out, with a few stragglers moving to open ground to see the sky. Nathaniel and Dani did the same. He handed her a pair of homemade cardboard with pinholes in the middle.

It was still pretty bright out, but as they watched the moon—now nothing more than a dark circle—it began to cover the orange ball of the sun. She slipped on the glasses with the two pinholes so she could stare directly at the eclipse.

"You know," Nathaniel mentioned, "they used to say that an eclipse was an omen. They saw it as the heavens aligning."

"Uh-huh. And I'm sure that you could tell me just what kind of eclipse this is going to be." The moon was now almost over the sun.

"A total eclipse."

She giggled at her own private joke. "Of the heart?"

"No, the sun dummy."

"Let me guess: it's called a total eclipse because it's totally going to cover the sun?"

"Wow, you're so smart."

"Shut your cakehole."

The moon fell into place. As it covered the sun, a ring of light poured outward from behind it. Dani had to admit: it was impressive. She even felt moved by the sight. She felt different. She was watching the heavens align.

The sky darkened, and soft, flare-like beams danced from behind the moon like a heavenly light show. All they needed was music.

"Cool." She commented.

"Cool?" Nathaniel chuckled. "Total eclipses are rare. This is epic!"

"Way to make it geeky, Nate."

The eclipse lasted for a few minutes before the moon shifted and the light poured out the other side. Sunlight returned. Day became bright again. Dani winced, lowering her gaze, taking off the glasses and blinking. Even a little bit of sun for too long was hard on the eyes.

"So, epic?" Nathaniel asked, grinning.

"Epic." She agreed.

At least one of them had a reason to smile today.

———————————

"I'm not sure what I'm going to do." Dani mused, swinging gently on the swing. The sun dipped below the horizon, bathing the remaining sky with oranges, blues and purples. The lights of L.A. glittered in the distance. "Where am I supposed to go? I don't have anyone."

"You have me." He reminded her, swinging beside her.

"You live in a foster home, Nathaniel." He frowned for a second. If she didn't know him so well, she wouldn't have seen it. "I'm sorry. I shouldn't have said that."

"No, you're right." He sighed. "My foster mom would never let me bring anyone to the house. If I did, she'd call the cops. But maybe there's a place we can find for you tonight. A lot of the foster kids talk about halfway houses and shelters for runaways."

She couldn't believe those were her only two options: halfway house or a shelter. Or she could sleep on the streets. The third option was not any better than the first two.

She put her face in her hands. How could this be happening?

"We'll figure it out." He assured her.

They sat for a little while longer, not really saying anything. She checked her watch. It was past seven thirty. Normally, she'd worry about getting home. Ricky didn't like her coming in late. Now, well...

She stared across the park. There were a few people still out. Los Angeles was alive with light, but most of Sun Valley had gone home.

There was one group cutting across the Rec Center's lawn from Cantara Street to Lorne; three of them, all huddled together. Silent. None of them spoke, which was odd, but not because silence was odd on its own. It was the way they walked. They weren't just ambling around; out for a good time after dark. They moved like a pack of animals in formation. They moved with a purpose.

Then she smelled something. She knew that smell. Where did she remember it from?

"Nathaniel, how about we get out of here?" she suggested, grabbing her bag.

"Where?"

"Anywhere."

The group was almost to them. She recognized them. They were the same vagrants from earlier. And she could see their eyes. They were looking right at them. They came towards them through the shadows.

"Come on, let's go."

She and Nathaniel looped through the playground to Lorne Street. They could cross over and disappear between the buildings. At least, Dani hoped.

The homeless men picked up the pace at a lopping jog.

"Dani, what's going on?"

"Just keep walking." She told him, moving faster, but trying not to run.

"Why?"

"I don't know. Just go."

They crossed the open grass towards the street. But just as they got clear of the playground, two figures emerged from behind some cars. She could see that they, too, had the same soiled, disheveled appearance as the three behind them. And, like the other three, they didn't bother looking anywhere else but at them.

She and Nathaniel halted.

Behind them, the three homeless drifters spread out, blocking any chance of going back. And the two in front blocked the way across the street.

They were surrounded.

Chapter Four

"Dani? Who are they?"

"I don't know."

She could hear something behind her. The three beggars that chased them were sniffing, just like before.

"If we have to run," she told Nathaniel, "we try to run past the two in front of us."

"Why would we run?"

"Just run if I tell you." She didn't know why, but every nerve in her body told her to bolt.

"It's just a couple of bums. Half the time they're looking for money." He stepped forward. "We don't have any money. Okay? We're just trying to get home."

More sniffing; deeper, louder.

Their silence unnerved him. "Just back off. Get out of our way."

The heavy breathing kept up, their heads turning from Nathaniel to Dani and back. What did they want? They were so loud. So... animalistic.

Nathaniel attempted to intimidate them. "We'll call the cops."

And then, all at once, they inhaled together; one long, loud drag. Their bodies tensed, heads back, breathing in. And then they stopped.

Nathaniel glanced at Dani, shrugging.

Someone tackled Dani from behind, throwing her face first into the dirt. She screamed. The awful stench of the homeless man filled her nostrils as he shoved her to the ground. He screamed, something more animal than human. One hand seized her shoulder and another her hair, pinning her down so hard it hurt. She tried to push him off, but he was too strong.

Nathaniel took his book in both hands and swung, beating him across the face. But it didn't work. Another vagrant leapt forward and tackled him, too.

He leapt almost five or six feet in a single lunge to do it.

Dani threw her elbow back and connected with the eye socket of the man on top of her. It was desperate, but it worked. He shrieked in pain, but his voice wasn't that of a man. The scream sounded like it belonged to some kind of creature.

She rolled onto her back, shimmying away on hands and feet. The filthy vagrant, tall and gangly as if he hadn't eaten in months, scrambled up to his feet. His lips pulled back and he hissed.

Dani's heart leapt into her throat. His teeth weren't normal. They were all canines. Like a shark, each one was a stout, jagged point. And as she watched, the teeth stretched from his gums, elongating like a row of switchblades. The vagrant's jaws stretched a way they shouldn't like a mouth full of daggers. His hiss turned into a rumbling growl and he scrambled forward on all fours.

Dani rolled as he launched at her. He shot past. She came up onto her feet, but heard one coming at her from behind. She rolled again and a wave of stench and a howling street beggar charged past.

Her heart pounded in her chest. Nathaniel screamed. One of the men—or whatever these things were—picked him up and pinned him by the throat to a lightpost as if he weighed nothing.

"Nathaniel!"

Arms wrapped around her and lifted her off her feet; the first drifter again. Hot, foul breath huffed on the back of her neck. When she turned over her shoulder, she came face to face with him—with *it*. Its eyes were milky white, completely empty of anything resembling human. It made a sound like a laugh, but no human voice sounded like that. Its mouth opened impossibly wide, jaw unhinging, and reared back to tear into her. And now instead of one row, there were two rows of long, jagged teeth.

She screamed.

Then something happened. One moment, the arms of the putrid man clenched around her body. The next, he was gone. The top of his head separating from the rest. He dissolved into a cloud of dust. His arms evaporated. Dani dropped to the ground in a shower of grey. She coughed, inhaling something awful and chalky. She almost vomited, but she was free.

Then she heard a scream. It was one of those things. The creature-man stormed through the ash towards her. Then abruptly, the scream stopped and it disappeared, too.

The man holding up Nathaniel turned towards her, hissing. Dani struggled back up and ran at him. She grabbed the vagrant's arm, trying to pry him off of her friend. Nathaniel choked and struggled and flailed his legs.

"Get off him!" she screamed. "Get off him!"

He shoved her back. She tried again. This time she grabbed his wrist and pulled. Her hands felt hot. She thought she could hear hissing when she touched his skin. He howled in pain and his grip loosened.

Then he hit her with a backhand.

Dani saw stars. The ground rolled up at her as she fell hard into it. The vagrant-thing, whatever it was, opened its jaws to sink his knife-like teeth into Nathaniel's throat.

But in the split second it took, something stopped him.

27

She almost didn't see it. It happened in a fraction of a moment. Someone melted out of the shadows, a streak of silver flashing in the overhead light. Nathaniel dropped. The vagrant's arm disappeared, disintegrating below the elbow. He fell to his feet, inhaling gratefully. Whatever or whoever freed Nathaniel moved fluidly through the dark, spinning with another silver flash, slicing across the open air. Then the vagrant's head went missing. His body disappeared in a cloud of thick grey-black dust that cascaded to the ground. Then the figure vanished.

"Nathaniel!" Dani ran to him. "Are you okay?"

He sputtered, clutching his throat, croaking, "What happened?"

Around them the homeless creatures screamed. There were still two of them. They howled, talking in a mixture of hisses and grunts as they circled them.

"Come on!" she grabbed his arm and pulled him up. "Run!"

Bag over her shoulder, Nathaniel's book long since left behind, the two of them took off. Instead of running for the Rec Center, or towards the buildings across the street, or even trying to cross Lorne like they originally planned, Dani and Nathaniel bolted behind the Center. They ran at a dead sprint, leaping over a table. Behind the Center, the floodlights were still on at the baseball fields. They sprinted towards them.

They could hear inhuman snarls behind them, but neither dared look back.

"Who the hell are those guys?" Nathaniel cried.

"You mean _what_ are they!" Dani shot back, legs flying.

She reached the fence for the first baseball diamond, throwing open a gate and shooting through with Nathaniel close on her heels. He yanked the door closed, flipped the lock and the two of them ran again. The floodlights were so bright they could barely see. She squinted, for the first time chancing a look back as they crossed.

And she wished she hadn't.

One of the vagrants dashed from the shadows on the other side of the fence. For a moment, she hoped the boundary would slow him down. Instead, he leapt onto it and with only a few pulls, he was over. The burly man with a beard of molted hair didn't look at all like he could move fast, but he climbed over and leapt from the top. He—no, it—launched itself across the open, landing on its hands and feet an impossible distance from the fence. Then, like some kind of mutant dog, it scampered after them on all fours.

Nathaniel cursed. "Run faster!"

"I am!"

The two of them cut across from the field into the open park, but with nothing to put between them, there was no way they'd make it to the next cross street. Behind them, the large drifter huffed like an animal, its jaws oozing with saliva as it scuttled; bones shifting in ways they shouldn't. The nightmare from hell was gaining on them.

Nathaniel stopped. He skidded to a halt, turned and sprinted back towards the creature.

"Nathaniel! What are you doing?"

"Run!" he told her. "Run Dani! Get out of here!"

"Nathaniel! No!"

The pair of them charged at one another. Dani couldn't keep going; not if Nathaniel risked his life for her. She turned and ran after him. No way was he going to die for her.

"Nathaniel!" She screamed, but it was too late. They were less than half a football field apart. The thing on all fours picked up speed, eager to run Nathaniel down. Even if Nathaniel changed his mind now, the vagrant would be all over him. "Nathaniel!"

Just as the beast closed to only a few dozen feet, it leapt into the air. Vaulting off the ground, arms outstretched, Dani could see long, blade-like claws extended from the tips of its fingers. It aimed directly for Nathaniel; descending for the kill.

And then he appeared. As if materializing between them, someone was suddenly there. He stood calmly in the path of the monster; the silvery, long object in both hands. She couldn't see his face because he wore a hood over his head, but he moved with near-impossible speed. His arms came up, the silver object swung and in one motion he cut the homeless man-creature apart.

The vagrant exploded into a shower of grey dust. The filthy cascade washed over Nathaniel and his protector, the force of it spreading into a cloud that Dani ran headlong into. Then she ran into Nathaniel, both of them choking on the ashy filth.

It took a few seconds before the smoke cleared and revealed their rescuer. Dani blinked away ash. Not only did he have a hood up, but what he held wasn't silver and wasn't just an object. It was straight steel sword, almost four or five feet long, gripped between his two hands. The blade was almost as long as he was tall, widening at the bottom near the hilt. The surface glinted with an unnatural sheen in places not covered in tar-like ooze and ash. He held it loosely, looking for other threats before turning towards them.

29

That's when he—because in fact it was a he—cast back his hood. "Are you alright?"

He was a few years older than them and only a few inches taller than Dani; mid-five-foot. His hair was untamed, bent about his ears in little cherub-like curls the color of dark chocolate. His clean-shaven face and eyes paired with his locks; light-brown irises the color of honey and tan skin. They narrowed with concern. His face was serious, as if what he'd just done wasn't enough to drive home that this wasn't a social call.

"I—I'm fine." She stammered.

He seemed to forget her, shifting his eyes to her friend. "Nathaniel? Are you alright?"

"I'm fine. I mean, I'm fine too." Nathaniel babbled.

He re-sheathed the massive sword—Dani was still having trouble wrapping her head around that thing—into a scabbard that hung from a two-tonged strap connected to a belt. For the first time she noticed that he wasn't wearing a hoodie or a jacket. Whatever it was, it didn't even look to be from this century. His clothes were composed of some kind of tunic top, or other loose-fitted cloth with a straight collar and ties across his chest. The material looked heavy and woven, but shone in the dim light. He wore a leather buckle-belt, slacks and boots, with both forearms inserted into some sort of metal braces and two others on his shins. The whole outfit was black, which was probably why she hadn't noticed it before. The only ornate part was a symbol on his back, embroidered across his shoulders: concentric circles, one inside the other, each flaring like fire outward around a central ring.

"We have to go." He told them. "More wraiths will be coming." He jogged off the way they came. "Come on!"

Dani and Nathaniel shared the same bewildered look. He just expected them to follow? After what just happened?

He noticed they weren't coming and paused, turning back with an irritated frown, which deepened into a scowl. He re-crossed the distance back to them.

"Look," he said seriously, "normally this is where someone like me would tell you that 'you should come with me if you want to live' and I would explain why, but we don't have time for that. We're exposed out here. If you stay, you die. If you come with me, you might live long enough to see sunrise."

"You expect us to follow you?" Dani demanded. "Why?"

"Did you not just see me save you from a pack of wraiths?"

Nathaniel had mind enough to ask, "What's a wraith?"

The boy pointed to the grey dust around them. "That."

"That doesn't answer the question." Dani told him. "Why should we follow you? We don't know who the hell you are."

"I just explained that it's not important. Now let's go."

"You need to explain better."

His jaw tensed. "Well, I'm not going to and I'm not talking to you." He shot back. "I'm talking to Nathaniel."

He was bad-tempered, on-edge and—from what Dani could tell—rude, but he saved their lives. That earned him the right not to be cussed out, but she wasn't one to simply follow.

"You said Nathaniel's name." She pointed out, trying to get him to tell her at least something. "You know him, but does he know you?"

"I've never seen him." Nathaniel said.

The man with the sword murmured tersely. "Quit asking questions and come with me before more of those things find us."

"No." she folded her arms. "I'm not going anywhere."

"I'm trying to save your life. Don't make it difficult."

"No, not until you tell me what is going on."

He didn't like her. She could tell and she didn't care. He shifted his eyes to Nathaniel. "Are you coming with me or not?"

Nathaniel took one look at Dani and shook his head. "I'm with her. I'm not going unless you tell us what is going on. Who are you? What were those things?"

The brunette-haired warrior sighed heavily, shaking his head. He muttered to himself, "Consarn it, why do they have to be so difficult?" Then, as if it were the most normal thing in the world, he said, "My name is Ethan. I'm a Guardian Numen and that thing," he thumbed over his shoulder at the grey dirt, "is what remains of a demon called a wraith that tried to kill you. Now, I've answered your questions, so can we walk and talk? I really don't want to be eaten alive trying to save you."

Chapter Five

Ethan No-Last-Name walked fast for a guy holding a very large sword. Dani and Nathaniel were out of breath from their encounter with the vagrants, but he walked as if he was a machine that wouldn't wear out. He was fit. Even Dani could tell that through the black get-up he wore. He swung that sword like he knew what to do with it. He carried himself like it, too. He was, if anything, prepared.

He led them out of the park, his hand never leaving the weapon strapped to his belt. He kept looking back and forth from them to his surroundings, simultaneously making sure they weren't and that they still followed him. Whatever his reason for showing up, he wasn't letting them out of his sight.

They followed, but neither of them spoke.

Wraiths? Demons? Dani couldn't wrap her head around it. She knew what she saw was real, no matter how unbelievable. She saw their teeth. She heard their growls. She watched them do things no human being could do. But demons? Demons were real? How did someone even start to come to grips with that?

Dani wasn't particularly religious. She never really went to church. Most girls she knew went part of the time, at least for their *quinceañera* or Christmas Mass. Dani never felt the need. And though she wasn't particularly religious, she definitely didn't remember anything about _that_ in Sunday school.

Her world had gone upside down.

They crossed into the neighborhood after a few minutes. Ethan glanced back at them again, staring suspiciously at her.

"I don't like this." Dani whispered to Nathaniel.

"Tell me about it. Did you see those things?"

"No, I mean him." She tipped her chin at Ethan. "I don't trust him."

"Why? He saved our lives."

"I'm not so sure. You're telling me it's a coincidence that this guy just happens to be walking by when we get attacked? That's not at all too convenient?"

The thought hadn't occurred to him. "Maybe we ask him what he was doing there. He could give us some answers."

"We tried, remember? He's not in a very talkative mood."

"He might talk to me. He knew my name."

That was true. He knew Nathaniel, but Nathaniel didn't know him. Why? Was he there for him? It fit her theory that Ethan hadn't simply been in the neighborhood with a five-foot-long demon-slaying sword, but it didn't explain who the hell he was, what was going on, or why the hell he dressed like that.

Nathaniel picked up his pace, walking ahead of her. "Hey, Ethan, slow down!" The man with the sword ignored him. "Hey! Slow down a second!"

"We don't have a second." He snapped, crossing the street. They followed. "We've got to keep moving. If they have your scent, more will be on the hunt."

"More wraiths, you mean?"

"Yes."

"More demons?"

He nodded, not looking back. "That is what I said."

"And they're after us?" Dani asked, joining Nathaniel's side.

Ethan didn't answer her. He just kept walking.

"Hey, I'm talking to you!" Ethan reached the street corner. She snatched him by the arm, spinning him around. "I said I'm talking to you!"

"And I'm not talking to you." He shot back.

What's his problem? "If I'm in danger, then I deserve to be told why. Why were they after us? Why did they try to kill us?"

Ethan's jaw tensed visibly, his eyes flicking to Nathaniel and then back.

"And why the hell do you keep talking just to him? You won't speak to me. What's going on?"

"It doesn't concern you."

"Those things concern me. They tried to kill me!"

"No, they tried to kill him!" He angrily pointed to Nathaniel. "You were just in the way. My job is to make sure they don't kill him, which means I don't have time to explain myself to some mundanus!"

She blinked "What is that supposed to mean?"

Ethan sighed heavily, shaking his head. "Nothing."

"No, not nothing. Mun-what? What's that supposed to mean?"

"It's not an insult." Ethan told her. "It's what we call people like you."

"People like me?"

"Mundani. Normal people. That's what I mean by people like you: a mundanus. It's your average, every day, run-of-the-mill human being." He looked at Nathaniel, completely ignoring her. "Look, I don't want to do this here. It's not my job to babysit. I could tell she was a friend and I didn't want her to die, so I saved you both. I couldn't wait until you were alone like

33

I planned. The wraiths forced my hand. But the truth is I came to get you. And now we have to go." Finally, he looked back at Dani. "I did you a favor. I got you away from the wraiths and their hunting ground. Once we leave, his scent won't be on you and they won't come after you anymore. You're safe and you're welcome. Now go home."

Rude, she thought, but didn't get up in his face again. He earned that much from her.

"'We leave'?" Nathaniel was confused. "You mean me and you?"

"Wait, wait, you're taking him?" She looked at Nathaniel. "You're taking Nathaniel? Why? Where?"

"It's none of your concern."

"Stop telling me what's my concern!" she snapped.

Nathaniel stepped in beside her. "Dani is my friend, which means it is her concern. At least, it is about this."

"Nathaniel, you don't understand. Not yet. If you did, you'd know that what I'm doing is what's best for you both." He stepped past Dani. Nathaniel was taller, but Ethan was such a powerful presence. When he spoke, his voice was magnetic. "There is more to you than you know; more than you could possibly realize. You're not just some kid living in a hell-hole of a foster home."

"You know about my foster home?"

Ethan nodded. "Yes. You weren't born to be just another statistic that the human race failed to help. Even before you were born, your name— like so many others—was written in a book that holds thousands of special people. You are destined to live in a place far brighter than this one. You were meant to join us: the Numen. The Earthborn. We've been waiting for your powers to manifest and for you to see the world as it truly is; to be able to come to us. Now you have. And it is time."

Ethan placed a hand on his shoulder.

"You have power, Nathaniel. You may not understand it, but you've started to show it." He held up Nathaniel's right wrist. "Do you see this?"

"What? My arm? I don't see—." He stopped.

Just below his wrist, on his forearm, a small band of skin changed color. It was darker, starting at the joint and lacing up his forearm. It was like a birthmark, but Nathaniel didn't have a birthmark. And this was much more intricate. The skin looked tattooed with Henna; dozens of interlocking marks creating a band up to his elbow and back.

"I've never seen that."

"It's your mark." He told him. "We call it a halo. Every one of us, every Numen, has one. It manifests with our powers as a sign of who we really are."

"But I don't have powers."

"You do. Or at least you will, with training." He insisted. "That's why those wraiths came after you. They can sense what you really are. They can smell your Numen side. You saw them, didn't you? You saw them for what they really were? It's called seeing through the veil. No mundanus could ever see their true forms."

Nathaniel shook his head, unable to take it all in. Dani could see the billions of questions in his eyes; too many to ask and too many to answer.

"You're part of a greater destiny." Ethan told him. "You can't stay here. You will never be safe in Los Angeles or any city on Earth, but I can take you to a place where you will be. I can help you to understand and teach you to fight back."

Nathaniel traced the mark on his skin with his thumb. He shook his head and looked to Dani. "What about her? They'll come after her."

"They don't want her." Ethan assured him, giving Dani the first sympathetic look. "No offense. And they're dead. They couldn't tell a soul if they wanted to, so she's safe. And like I said, once we leave, your scent will disappear. Then the veil between the worlds will affect her mind like it has countless others. She will forget what happened."

"Like hell I will!"

"It's inevitable." Ethan promised. "The veil keeps the supernatural hidden from humans. Even those that have seen monsters rarely, if ever, believe what they've seen. Once Nathaniel is gone, you won't remember this. You'll convince yourself that it's all a fantasy. You will tell yourself something to explain his disappearance and you will never question it. That's the power the veil has on mundani."

"I could never do that." She insisted. Nathaniel was the only friend she had. "I wouldn't."

"It doesn't matter. He can't stay. If he's going to survive, he has to leave."

Nathaniel didn't like the idea any more than Dani. "I have to leave?"

"Yes." Ethan pursed his lips, nodding. "I'm sorry, but for people like us, it is how our destiny plays out. We can see the monsters. Dani can't. We don't belong in this world, but she belongs here, living her normal life. You have to accept that."

Nathaniel shook his head. He didn't want to leave her. "But she's my friend."

35

Ethan put a hand on his shoulder again. "It's for the best."

This was insane. There was no way it could be true, could it? But those things—wraiths, whatever—came after Nathaniel. They attacked him. They tried to kill him and they would have if Ethan didn't show up with his sword. Nathaniel was the target. Monsters and demons and whatever else were after him. He could see what they really were—.

"I could see them." She said.

Ethan turned back to her. "What?"

"The wraiths—those homeless guys—I saw them turn into freaks. They had sharp teeth, white eyes, and ran like dogs. I thought you said mun-whatevers can't see them."

"Mundani can't." Ethan frowned, dropping his hand from Nathaniel's shoulder. "No mundanus can see a wraith's true form. The veil stops them."

"Then why could I?"

His frown deepencd. For the first time, he actually really looked at her. His honey-brown eyes narrowed in suspicion. "You couldn't have seen them. That's impossible."

"I did."

"Then you saw through the veil briefly. It'll become difficult remember them. The details should start becoming blurry." The last part sounded like he was trying to convince her, not explain to her.

She shook her head. "Nope. Trust me: something like that is hard to forget."

"Describe them again."

"Long teeth growing out of their mouths like something straight out of Hell, puss-white eyes, and they growled like dogs. They could run like them, too."

"How did they smell?"

"Smell?"

"Yes. How did they smell?"

Dani thought about it. "They stunk, but not like people do. I don't know. They smelled like...like rotten eggs or something. It was disgusting."

Ethan's eyes weren't narrow. They were wide. "Impossible."

"What's wrong?"

But he didn't answer. Instead, he shook his head. "Zounds!"

"I'm sorry?"

He snatched Dani's right arm, pushing back the sleeve. "Impossible!" he stuttered over his words. "That's sarding impossible! There is nothing...it has never happened...your name wasn't in the book!"

"What? Ow! Hey! Stop! You're hurting me!"

Ethan shoved her shirt sleeve up to her elbow. Dani realized what he was looking for: the same mark Nathaniel had. A halo.

But her forearm was bare. Just normal brown skin. He visibly relaxed when he saw her arm. He stopped rambling. Shaking his head, he took a calming breath and dropped her arm.

"Is everything okay?" Nathaniel asked, unsure of what just happened. "What's going on?"

"I can't explain." Ethan said slowly, unsure. His brown eyes met Dani's. "You're not gifted, that's for sure. I don't know how you saw them."

"Gifted?"

But he wasn't answering. He kept talking to himself. "I thought maybe you might be a Tuatha De Dannan or Fomorian or something, but clearly you're a mandanus..."

"Um, hello?" she waved her hand in his face. "You're rambling."

He shook it off, as if it were silly. "Sorry. I was talking to myself. I can't explain it. You shouldn't have been able to see them or remember them. And you definitely shouldn't be able to smell the brimstone."

"Brimstone?"

"Rock sulfur." He explained. "We call it brimstone. Hell is caked in the stuff. All demons smell like sulfur."

"But I could smell them." Dani insisted.

"I know. I can't explain. Only a Numen should see them, but you're a—."

He stopped. He'd been staring at the ground, trying to think, but something caught his attention mid-sentence.

Dani took a step back. The last time he got that look, he raved like a lunatic. "What is it?"

Ethan reached out and, gently this time, took her left arm. He raised it up and pulled back the sleeve. Dani looked down.

There, clear as could be under the street lamp, was a dark-brown, intricately woven ring on her arm; starting right below the wrist and looping up her forearm.

Her eyes narrowed. "Is that a...?"

He dropped her hand. "A halo." He stuttered. "You—You have a halo."

"What does that mean?" She caressed the mark on her skin. It was smooth to the touch, as if it'd always been part of her, but she had never seen it before. "Why do I have this?"

Ethan didn't speak. He wasn't relieved like with Nathaniel; explaining her destiny and about her greater purpose. He was silent. Speechless.

Even Nathaniel was confused. "Ethan? What does that mean?"

He rubbed his jaw, walking away in a dazed trance. She could hear him muttering to himself, but she couldn't understand it. They were words she never heard.

"Zounds..." he murmured, "...what in bloody hellfires...?" It was like cussing, but they weren't words she recognized.

"Ethan, what does that mean?" Nathaniel demanded again. "Talk. Speak English!"

He finally turned back, shaking his head, but at least now he spoke to them. "It means," he paused, unable to put into words what he was thinking. He repeated himself, "It means that Dani...that Dani," he finally looked her in the eye, "is a Numen."

She and Nathaniel exchanged looks. He smiled. "You mean, she's like me?"

Ethan shook his head. "No, that would be impossible."

"You keep saying that. Why? Why is that impossible?" Dani asked.

"Because," he spoke lowly, as if afraid, "it's never happened before."

She scoffed. "What? A female...whatever you call it? Numen? Like I'm the first one of those?" She meant it as a joke.

But to her surprise, Ethan nodded. "Actually, yes," he met her gaze, "you'd be the first ever in existence."

Her smile dropped. "You mean...?"

Ethan nodded again. "There's never been a female Numen before."

Chapter Six

It was a mostly silent walk. The trio continued together, the plan to drop her off not an option anymore. Dani's presence clearly disturbed Ethan. He wouldn't look at her except to double-check she was still with them. And when he did, there was no longer an indifference in his eyes. If she had to guess, there was something a little closer to fear. He was afraid.

Afraid of her.

You'd be the first ever in existence. There's never been a female Numen.

No females. No girls. Dani touched the mark on her left arm. She didn't cover it up. It seemed weird to, even though her skin felt no different. What magically tattooed her when she wasn't looking? What was a Numen? How was she chosen? Why was she chosen? Was it odd her halo or whatever wasn't on her right arm?

By Ethan's expression, the last answer was pretty easy to guess, but it didn't help with the others. There was too much she didn't know.

"Where are we going?" Nathaniel asked. "You said there might be more wraiths. Where can we go that's safe?"

"I know a place for people like us."

They'd been walking awhile. It took Dani a second to realize they were near her house. Or rather, Ricky's house. She checked her watch. It was almost nine p.m.; only hours since she ran away from home. She was only a few blocks away, but it felt like another world out of reach.

Ethan stopped. "Where we're going is a place no one outside of our people," he paused, looking at Dani hesitantly before continuing, "and a select few others can go. We don't allow Earthly possessions of any kind. So the bag can't come."

Dani glanced at her pack. It was literally everything she owned and he wanted her to leave it?

"I'm sorry," he said, as if reading her mind, "but you won't need it."

Could she really leave everything she owned? Slowly, she shifted it off her shoulder and walked to the edge of the street. Dense bushes lined one of the buildings near the sidewalk. Dani tucked the bag back behind them. If she had to, maybe she could come back for it. If not...

"The necklace, too." He told her.

She paused, touching the chain around her neck. "It's important to me."

"You can't take it. The watch either. Or yours." He told Nathaniel. "It all has to go."

"Can I take my glasses?" he asked. "I'm blind without them."

"No you're not."

Dani scoffed. "I've known him almost my whole life. He's almost as blind as a bat."

Instead of arguing, Ethan snatched the glasses off Nathaniel's face and held them away. "Well?" he asked.

"Hey!" Nathaniel blinked, but after a second, he grinned. "I...uh...I can see."

Ethan tossed the glasses on the ground, forgetting them. "Becoming a Numen changes you physically. You'll be stronger, faster and any impairments disappear." He glanced at her. "For both of you." Then he quickly left them to finish discarding their things.

Dani and Nathaniel removed their jewelry, placing them in the bag. She zipped it up and left it without looking back.

"How do we get to this place?" she asked. "This place you say is safe for us, I mean?"

"We take a bus." He told her, continuing on.

"A magic bus?" Dani half-joked. Stranger things had happened tonight.

"No, a normal bus."

On schedule, the public transit pulled into the stop. Ethan jogged, calling for them to catch up. He moved abnormally fast, as if his legs held more power than they should.

"Wait!" Dani called after him. "They're not going to let you take that freaking sword on with you!"

But Ethan ran to the front, sword plainly in the open. If the driver was concerned by his new fare's armament, he didn't show it. As Dani and Nathaniel joined him, he boarded without a problem. The driver, instead of collecting a fare, waved him on. No money needed. Puzzled, Dani and Nathaniel followed. Likewise, he allowed them to board, sans payment.

Confused, they took seats near front; him in one, the pair of them across the aisle. The bus hissed and pulled onto the street. Ethan stretched out, arm on the backrest and leg across the open seat next to him with his sword.

"How'd you do that?" Dani asked.

"Do what?"

"How did you get on here with that?" she pointed at his weapon. "And how did you get on without money? Did you Obi-Wan him?"

"You mean with the driver? He can't see my sword. I told you: mundani can't see through the veil."

40

"Explain that." Nathaniel asked. "What's the veil you keep talking about?"

Ethan shrugged, "It's the thing that separates the supernatural from the natural world. It's like a curtain that keeps us hidden."

"They can't see you?"

"They see only what they want to see. It convinces mundani that what they are seeing they aren't actually seeing. See?"

The pair of them blinked, confused.

He sighed, thinking of a better way to explain. "Ever spot something out of the corner of your eye, but when you looked nothing was there? But you could have sworn it was? Then you told yourself it must have been a figment of your imagination?"

"Yeah."

"That was you partially seeing past the veil. Something or someone was behind it, using it to remain hidden. Humans can see through it from time to time, but it's usually by chance or by magic, and it hardly ever lasts. It's not that they can't see us or can't see what we actually are; it's just that our abilities convince them to forget us."

"So you're saying you're supernatural?" Dani asked.

"I'm human, but yes. We can do more than most. Numen are," he hesitated again, as if about to say something but then not, "supernaturally empowered humans. And we can use the veil on purpose, even against other supernatural creatures."

"No way."

"Way." And then Ethan disappeared, suddenly not in his seat. A second later, he appeared in the row behind them. "See?"

Dani flinched. "All of us can do that?"

The 'us' made Ethan wince, but he nodded.

"And you can make normal people see things?"

He shrugged again. "It's more we can make them _not_ see things. And some supernatural objects, like my sword or my clothes, naturally do the same. We don't have to concentrate that hard to cover them up. What the driver probably sees is a boy wearing a hoodie. That's about it."

Dani shook her head.

"Is something wrong?" Ethan asked.

"These aren't the droids you're looking for."

"What?"

"Nothing. So we learn how to do all of that where we're going?"

He didn't answer. He got very uncomfortable around her; like he forgot who she was until she asked questions. Then he remembered and

41

became uneasy. She didn't know what that was about, but suspected he wasn't going to tell her. Not yet, anyway.

They rode the bus route, making its stops for passengers. No one paid them any mind. Ethan rested his head against the window. Dani and Nathaniel talked a little bit, but mostly stared out the window. The bus pulled onto the Five and headed into Los Angeles.

The lights of the city glistened in the night. It was very beautiful; like a star-spangled city in Heaven. As they rode, Dani peeled her eyes from the city skyline to the passengers sitting behind them. There were two, a guy and girl, all of twenty or thirty. They smiled back at her when they noticed her staring. Cute couple.

Until their eyes melted. Dani swallowed a scream as their eyes disintegrated and the sockets filled with what looked like burning, orange coal-embers.

Ethan's hand slapped down her shoulder, quieting her. "Don't scream."

"Did you see?" she was hyperventilating. "Did—Did you see them?"

"Yes. Don't worry. They're not demons."

"They're not?"

"No."

"What are they?"

"Just a couple of jinn out for a night on the town. Relax."

Jinn? What the hell was a jinn? She looked back at the couple, who talked in low voices with smiles like any other boyfriend/girlfriend. No one else on the bus noticed periodic cracks in their skin which spouted small gouts of fire. Their clothes never burned. The fire leaked through them, leaving them unscathed.

"You're seeing through the veil." Ethan told her calmly, his eyes still shut and head tipped back. "It's scary at first. Just relax. Everyone freaks out the first time."

He kept his hand on her shoulder, which made her feel a bit better. Nathaniel was equally disturbed by the two creatures posing as humans in the next booth. He took Dani's hand and squeezed.

They continued their ride into town.

"A construction site?" Dani stared at the empty lot in front of them. "This is safe ground?"

Ethan nodded.

The lot was across from the Citadel Outlets, a fancy tourist trap for L.A. The lot was nothing more than a large dirt-and-gravel space, with some spare rebar and a trailer.

"And how is this safe?"

He headed off down the sidewalk to the main gate, following the chain-link fence bordering the property. Instead of passing through, Ethan stopped at the entrance. A sign with large lettering stating NO TRESSPASSERS hung right in front of them.

"This place is abandoned." Dani pointed out.

Ethan smirked. "Is it?"

"What does that mean?"

"I mean," he said, "that we—and a few others—can use the veil, even against ourselves. Objects can be clothed in it. That goes for buildings, too. So, look again, but actually look."

Dani and Nathaniel did. She didn't know what she was supposed to be looking at or for, though. And then, as she looked, the plastic sign began to glow. And the longer she looked, the more things changed.

As if erecting itself out of the rubble, a building formed in the empty space right in front of them. The sign moved higher. The chain-fence melted together and filled in with bricks from thin air, until it wasn't a fence but a wall. The gate transformed from a simple lock-and-chain gateway into a pair of large, polished oak double-doors. The sign became neon as it centered atop the door. Burning orange tube-lights created a symbol of a fire and within that, red tube-lights melted into lettering, spelling out the name of the large, two-story building that hadn't been there a moment ago.

"Welcome to the Hellfire Club." Ethan told them, knocking.

A panel on the right door slid open. A pair of oddly-colored, greyish-brown eyes stared back out at them.

"Password?" a deep voice demanded.

"Open the sarding door, Rudolf." Ethan told him.

Dani glanced sideways at him. *Sarding?*

The panel slid back in place and a lock clicked. The door swung wide and a man, who was easily over six feet tall and wide as a bus, stepped out. He had no hair on either his scalp or chin and wore a dark black shirt with the Hellfire Club symbol emblazoned on his right muscular peck. On the left it said SECURITY. From behind him, they could hear the thrum of music.

"You talk like that and one day soon, boy, you'll end up six feet under."

Ethan smirked, the first smile she ever saw from him. It looked out of place. "Sard yourself, Rudolf."

Sard yourself? Ethan was so normal, but then he said strange stuff like that. What was it? A weird slang from where he was from?

The big man ignored him and turned his gaze on Nathaniel. "Is that him?"

Ethan nodded. "Yes. That's him."

Then he noticed Dani, too. "Uh...Ethan?"

He already knew what the man wanted to know. "Is Judah here?"

"He's at the bar." He thumbed over his shoulder.

"Good. Have him call us a cab and come see me." Ethan slid by him and into the building. "Come on, guys...er, guy and girl."

Nathaniel and Dani followed. As they moved past the big behemoth, she noticed his "skin" didn't look like skin at all. It was grey, smooth, and sculpted. She realized why he looked so funny: he wasn't a --man, but something made out of mud. What the hell?

The door shut and both of them stuck close to Ethan as they walked down a short, dark corridor into the building.

Dani didn't even get through her first question. "Ethan, what—?"

"Rudolf is a golem." He explained.

"A golem?"

"A creature made out of clay and brought to life by magic. Judah, Hellfire's owner, makes them and uses them as his security and staff. Usually, they aren't the smartest creatures, but Rudolf's been around as long as I have so he's smarter than most."

"And how long is that?" Dani asked.

Ethan didn't answer.

"What is this place?" Nathaniel looked around. The hallway was lined with burning lanterns inside glass and brass encasings. "Some kind of fortress? Sanctuary? Church? School?"

"Better." Ethan smirked again. "It's a night club."

He opened a set of doors at the end of the hall and the music magnified. They stepped out onto a small raised landing of a dark-lit bar, which swarmed with people. Whatever Hellfire looked like on the outside, it was somehow twice that size inside. Lights strobed through the darkness, moving with the beat of the music that bounced from the DJ's platform. The club was draped in reds and golds. Curtains and paintings, with walls covered in mosaics, seemed at odds with the packed dance floor and booths of modern deco. There were compartments along the walls on both levels ringing the room. A single bar took up the middle of the space, illuminated by multicolored lights and a massive neon chandelier. It was both like and unlike any other bar in LA.

And staffed by golems.

Pouring drinks, walking the crowd as security, serving customers; the large clay creatures were everywhere. Their skin reflected palely in the dim light, like sand under moonlight.

"I have never been in a place like this." Nathaniel murmured to her over the music.

Dani agreed. "Like modern chic meets...I don't know."

"The term is baroque." Ethan explained. "Judah is a fan of that century. Let's get a booth. We need privacy."

They followed him into the crowd, which appeared to be human, but Dani already knew that the chances of that were slim to none. Several people similarly dressed to Ethan waved as they passed; same tunic-like hoodie but different colors, and all men. They greeted him as they passed with a strange bow, pressing two fingers to their forehead. More than once she spotted an ember-eyed jinn like the ones on the bus. There were other human-like people, but their eyes were colors no human had; greens and purples that glowed in the dark. Golem security and staff paid them no mind. She heard what sounded like a wolf howl over the music.

They found an empty booth on the first floor, pushing aside a privacy curtain and taking their seats around a table. Ethan unclipped his sword, sliding it into the seat next to him and raised his hand for service. A golem appeared to take their order.

"Galenical," Ethan ordered, "straight and no belladonna. You guys want anything?"

The pair of them just stared at him.

"Right. Just for me then."

"Two Corinth." The golem responded.

He reached into his tunic and removed two coins. He placed them into the golem's hand and it departed.

"So," Ethan sat back, relaxed for the first time Dani had seen him, "I'm guessing you have questions."

"About a billion." Nathaniel said.

"Well, I got my own." His eyes fixed on Dani. "I don't want to lie to you: I wasn't expecting two of you, let alone a girl. I have no idea what that will mean, but I want to say I'm sorry. I didn't mean to mistreat you. I assumed you were a mundanus and that made me careless."

"I'll say." She grumbled, but nodded. "And though you were being a jerk, I think I can put that behind me if you tell us what's going on. So we're both Numen? You called us Earthborn, too. Why?"

"That's part of why we're here. Judah, the owner, knows a lot more about this than I do. His club is safe ground for people like us and he can explain things better than I can. Suffice to say: Earthborn, or Numen as we call ourselves, are special individuals with gifts."

"Who can kill demons?"

"Yes."

"And there aren't any girls?" she asked. "At all?"

"No. There's never been, at least as far as I know."

"Then how do you all—?" she stopped herself and burned with embarrassment. Did she actually almost ask him how they have sex? "Um...how do you all...make baby Numen?"

His mouth twitched with a smile. "We don't."

"So, what, no Netflix and chill? Who the hell made that rule? It sucks."

"I didn't make the rules. There are women," he shrugged a bit, "but they aren't Numen. And there are rules against fraternization."

"Sucks." She confirmed. "So why do you want to talk to this Judah guy?"

Ethan sighed, folding his hands on the table. "It's a little hard to explain. I want to ask him about you and hopefully get some answers. He's kind of the expert at all things weird."

"Is there anything you can tell us?"

"Well, I can tell you that all Numen, at least all of them so far, have their names in a book."

"A book?"

"Yes. It's called the Book of Metatron. Please don't ask me about the name. It's a long, long story, but the book always contains the names of the one hundred and forty-four Numen who appear every eclipse."

"Every eclipse?" Nathaniel asked. "You mean like the one today?"

"Yes. Every solar eclipse, which is every couple of years, one hundred and forty-four Numen manifest their powers. Before then, they're just human. Wraiths and other demons don't sense what they are until the time is close. After the eclipse, they can smell you. That's why they attacked you."

Dani remembered the homeless men at the Rec Center; smelling her, circling around her as if she were meat. If Ethan was right, they thought they smelled Numen. She shuddered to think what could have happened if they knew for sure.

"When the eclipse happens, you also get your halo."

"So you have one?" she asked.

46

"I have several."

He untied a strap that kept his shirt knotted close to his wrist. Then, as he raised his forearm underside-up, he unbuckled the long metal brace around it. It came apart and clattered thickly onto the table. He pulled back his sleeve and showed that not only did he have a halo, but more than a dozen twisting up his arm, interlocking and weaving in an intricate pattern of symbols. It was like a tattoo from the universe. The symbols were so strange she couldn't begin to understand what they meant, but at the same time it seemed familiar; like a language she forgot.

"What are they?" she asked. "I've never seen a language like that."

"It's an ancient, dead language." He told her. "You've never heard it or spoke it."

"They look familiar." Nathaniel mused, echoing Dani's thoughts.

"Everyone says that. It's a mystery. New halos appear every eclipse. The marks on the halo tell a story of what we've done, down to every deed. They remind us of our accomplishments," he pushed his sleeve back and put on the brace, "and failures."

Dani couldn't help but notice, "So if they appear every eclipse, then according to your halos you've been a Numen for, what, twenty six years? You aren't twenty six. You look barely seventeen."

"You're right." He told her. "I look seventeen. I've actually been a Numen for thirty six years. Solar eclipses aren't regular."

"Are you trying to tell us you don't age? You expect us to believe that?"

"We age." He assured her. "Let's just say that's it's slower than normal. A lot slower."

Thirty six. Ethan was thirty six—or rather in his fifties since he was seventeen when he became a Numen. One of many things tonight making her head spin.

"So we won't age as fast either? We're going to stay young?"

"Not young per se. Nothing on Earth can stop aging. It's one of those laws of nature nothing can break. But as long as you live you will grow older slower."

"Is everyone as young as you?"

"Most." He synched the tie at his wrist and fastened on his metal armor. "Like I said, the older ones are older; centuries older. We also used to be chosen younger. I've heard of Numen being called as early as thirteen on an eclipse. It seems that whatever society accepts as the age of maturity, that's the age a boy is called to be a Numen. In America, it's usually between sixteen and eighteen. But consarn it if I know whether that's true or not. It's just a theory."

Dani's eyes narrowed. "Consarn it? You talk funny."

"Most Numen think you talk funny. We don't age that fast and people live longer, so slang where I'm from changes as slow as we do. Don't worry, you'll get used to it."

"What are the metal cylinders?" Nathaniel asked, switching subjects. "You wear them on your arms and legs. Why?"

"They're bracers and greaves. They're standard armor for Guardians while out on mission, since half the time we're running from demons to keep you lot safe."

"So you were sent to get us?" Dani asked, and then remembered. "You were sent to get Nathaniel, I mean? His name was in the book?"

Ethan nodded. "Yes. It's been there for almost four eclipse cycles, or what most of us just call cycles. That is about seven years. When their name appears in the book, a Guardian is assigned to them. We watch them grow up; protect them if need be without their knowledge. It forms a bond for us. Every Guardian must care for his charge."

Nathaniel looked uncomfortable. "You've been watching me? Creepy."

Ethan shrugged. "Maybe. Then again, aren't you glad I was tonight?"

He didn't have an argument for that.

"But my name wasn't there." She made it a statement.

Ethan nodded once more, frowning. "No, it wasn't. As I said, there's never been a female Numen."

"Which means I never had a Guardian."

"Yes. It was lucky you were with Nathaniel tonight. I won't lie: this will disturb some people, especially the Elder Council."

"The Elder Council?"

"Our bosses, you could say."

The golem waiter appeared, handing him a large, frosted glass of something green. Ethan took a long swig. He coughed, shaking his head. "Every time—EVERY TIME—those mudbags put belladonna in it!"

"Well, I'm sorry Ethan," said a voice over the music, "but they are made of clay. You can only expect so much."

A man as big as a golem appeared at their table side. He had large, rosy cheeks poking over his thick, black beard that hung over the top of his wide chest. His happy complexion matched his almost instantaneous ability to put them at ease; not something easily done for someone so large. His belly was as wide as a delivery truck and his arms were like tree trunks. He

48

was as tall as his clay waiting staff, and yet his demeanor made Dani comfortable without even speaking a word to her.

His huge beefy hand slapped Ethan on the back. "And if you don't like the drink, don't order it."

"Judah," he gestured for the big man across the table, "this is Nathaniel, my newest charge. And this is Dani."

Judah chuckled, but it was somewhat more bemused than happy. His smile widened a fraction. "Yes. Rudolf informed me: a female Numen. That, in and of itself, brings the owner to your table." He extended his hand to both of them. "A pleasure to make your acquaintances. As my rude friend here said, my name is Ben Judah. Most call me Judah. I am the owner of this fine establishment."

Nathaniel shook his hand. Dani smiled her best. "Thanks."

"Oh don't thank me, young lady." Judah said with the gentlest of voices. "I'm afraid that your existence is going to make quite a stir in our community. I'd chance to say that by the end of the day, the very people who saved you will probably put you to death."

Chapter Seven

Judah took the thick red curtain, undid the holds and let it fall to seal off the booth. As the curtain fell into place, the music died. Dani suspected that even the cloth in this place was not what it seemed. Judah squeezed himself into the booth next to Ethan, which was no small feat given his size.

The big man smiled at her. "Now, let us look at that halo of yours."

He didn't grab her arm like Ethan. Instead, he patiently held out his large palm, waiting. After a second, Dani extended her left. Judah's eyes widened a fraction.

"The left arm, eh?" He didn't explain the significance. Using his large thumbs, he tenderly rubbed the halo. He turned her arm over, examining it on both sides, before returning it to the table. Laying it flat, he patted her hand sweetly. "My lady, I have to say, this is quite a shock."

"What does it mean? Is it real?"

"It is quite real. She is a Numen. But I haven't the foggiest notion what it means."

Dani glared at Ethan. "I thought you said he had answers."

He shifted uncomfortably. "I thought he might."

Judah chuckled, his whole big body bouncing around like some demented, drink-serving Santa Claus. "My dear, Ethan is right. I do know a fair more than most, but what you have there," he pointed to her arm, "is something no Numen has ever seen. Neither have I."

"Are you a Numen?" Nathaniel asked him.

"Heavens and Hells no!" Judah told him. "I wouldn't fit in with the ranks of the all-boys choir. No, I am a gifted man of sorts and very happy to just run my club. It affords me a great life. A long life, too."

"How long?" Nathaniel asked.

"Give or take a few centuries." He shrugged. "I forget. Time passes me by."

"You look good for over a hundred." Dani commented slyly.

"Thank you." He made a small bow with hands clasped. "I do try to look my best. This fine specimen you see sitting before you takes time before it can be brought into public. But, that's not why you are here, is it?" His smile faded. "You're here because of your situation. I take it Ethan hasn't informed you fully of what it means to be Numen?"

"He told us a little. Numen are, like, demon hunters?"

Judah laughed; not a chuckle, but a loud, thunderous boom that shook the table.

Ethan scowled. "It's not funny."

"My boy, it most certainly is!" Judah's laughing subsided as he wiped a teardrop from his eye. "You really didn't tell them, did you?"

"I thought you could explain better." He muttered out the side of his mouth, finishing his drink.

"Nathaniel, Daniella—it is Daniella, correct?—yes, you are partially right. Numen do hunt demons, amongst many other things. I'm sure by now Ethan has shown you the skill by which he dispatches beings of Hell. And before you ask, yes, Hell is for real. Though," He smirked at his own practical joke, "thankfully *that* won't ever be a book. What a terrible book that would be!"

He laughed and laughed, but no one else did.

"Anyway, yes, Numen hunt demons. They protect the natural and supernatural world from them, but they are much more than a mere human with a sword. By now I assume Ethan's called you Earthborn?"

"What does that mean?" Nathaniel asked.

"It means, my boy, Earth born angels."

Any follow-up questions Nathaniel or Dani had evaporated the moment Judah laid that on them.

"Angels? As in, *angel* angels?"

"Yes. Shocking, no doubt." He waggled his eyebrows playfully. "I'm sure you know what angels are."

Both nodded.

"Well, you may not know fully, I wager. Most people think of angels as winged, benevolent beings who bestow joy and blessings kindly upon humanity; appearing as loving fairy-godfathers who grant wishes and crap rainbows."

"Unicorns crap rainbows." Ethan reminded him.

"Of course. Contrary to that, however, angels are not and were not anything of the sort. They were warriors, similar to Ethan here." He gestured to the brooding boy next to him. "Angels were God's army."

Nathaniel shook his head. "There's a God?"

"Yes. Why?"

He grinned sheepishly, "I've never been a big believer in God."

Judah chuckled again, though less thunderously. "Well, given your new destiny, I'd work on that."

"Why? Are we going to meet Him?" Dani asked wryly.

"I'd say not, since most of Creation hasn't seen or heard from God in quite some time." Judah said, now very serious. "He disappeared after His angels went to war."

"War?" Dani shook her head. "They fought a war? Against who?"

"Each other." The gigantic barkeep informed her. "A few millenniums ago, probably close to the beginning of time as we know it, the angels had a civil war. We refer to it as The War in Heaven."

"They fought one another? Why?"

"Well, there's a matter of debate on that topic," Judah gave Ethan a sideways glance, "but let's just say it was over some divisive differences. Differences of opinion, if you will. At any rate, the angels slaughtered each other into near extinction."

"And that created Numen?" Nathaniel asked, better able to think through the mountain of what Judah just said.

"Oh, Heavens no, no, no! That came later." Judah told him. "Many centuries later, demonkind emerged. From where is also a matter of debate, but they were there. They threated humanity. And around that time, the first of the Numen became a Numen. And again how that happened—."

Dani finished for him. "Is a matter of debate."

Judah pointed at her, grinning beneath his beard. "Smart girl. Yes. Not much is known of how or why. Many say it was the Will of God Himself—or Herself, since technically God is neither male nor female...or He is both. I'm unsure. I think He was played by Alanis Morissette in a movie once."

Ethan rolled his eyes. "And by Morgan Freeman."

"I did so enjoy that movie. I treasure that man."

"Get on with it, Judah. You're getting off topic."

"Right." He shifted in his seat. "That's a habit. I do apologize. As I was saying, the very first Numen was a man named Enoch. Once he became what he was, he went by the name Metatron, meaning 'the first guardian.' And after him, another one hundred and forty-four became the second generation of Numen. Most of them have long since died off, as well as Metatron himself, but his legacy lives on. Every solar eclipse, one hundred and forty-four more are chosen. Ethan explained about the book?"

They both nodded.

"The book has become the Numen's sacred text. Where it came from is a matter of—." He stopped, realizing he was about to repeat 'is a matter of debate.' Instead, he said, "It is a mystery. But it names each human who will be called to be one of the Earthborn. They have become Earth's protectors. They even created seven societies—seven celestial cities—which guard humanity against demonkind."

"Cities?" Dani shook her head. "As in, cities full of Numen?"

"Amongst other creatures."

"Where are these cities? I've never heard of them. I've never seen them."

"You probably wouldn't, considering you've never seen this place, either." Judah waved to the club. "The veil keeps the supernatural invisible and separate from the natural. And these seven cities have never existed in the same location. They move around the world from place to place, country to country. Any center of human authority has a city protecting it."

"I'm taking you to one." Ethan told them.

"Where is this city?" Nathaniel asked. "Nearby?"

Judah's eyes rolled up to the ceiling.

"What? You mean there's some kind of city above California?"

"Above Los Angeles." Judah corrected. "Why do you think it's called 'the city of angels?' There was a whole movie dedicated to the idea. They got it mostly right, though I'm not a particular fan of Nicolas Cage. Except Con Air; tremendous film..."

"It's called Empyrean." Ethan ignored Judah's off-topic musings. "It's where I'm taking you. Our Elder Council is there. They are twenty-four of the most intelligent men I've ever known."

"Which is not saying much." Judah grumbled.

"Hey!"

"I am merely speaking the truth." He held up his hands.

"They'll know what to do," Ethan told Dani, "about you."

"About me?"

"About how to help you, I mean."

"My boy, I think you are overestimating their abilities." Judah told him.

"Snails, Judah, what is that supposed to mean?"

"It means that the Council has never been good about breaking tradition. It took them centuries to acknowledge some supernatural creatures weren't inherently evil; longer to protect them from demons. They hate most human civilization, including this one."

"They do not."

"They all call it New Babylon. I would say that is pretty prejudiced."

Ethan sighed heavily. "I have to take her. I can't just leave her here." Then, thinking, he asked, "Can I?"

Judah frowned, the first unfriendly gesture he made. He looked at Dani and shook his head, "I'm sorry, my dear, but my club is my life. I have a business to protect. And sooner or later, the Council will hear of you. Hiding you here would only mean incurring their anger and I could lose everything. My golems would offer you poor protection."

53

"Protection? I need to be protected from them?" Dani felt a sickening, sinking feeling in her gut. She didn't like what Judah implied. "So, I have to go?"

"It is the best option." He advised. "Plead your case before them."

She hated that idea. "I don't like begging people for anything."

"I said plead your case, not plead." He corrected. "I wouldn't give those old, stogy malignancies of existence any concession. Like many bureaucracies, they get in their own way as much as their enemies. Their society is secluded; one that looks down on," he glanced sideways at Ethan, "it's members frequenting establishments such as mine. They may help prevent the darkness from killing off humanity, but it does not mean I look fondly on them."

"You're not giving me much hope here."

Judah smiled kindly at her. "But there are a few among them who could be brought to reason. It would be enough to protect you. One in particular, Jeduthun, I know personally. He's a sensible Elder. He may help the others see the light." He chuckled as if the last word was a joke. "Light. Very funny if I do say so myself."

"Why is that funny?" Nathaniel asked.

"You'll see when you arrive in Empyrean." Judah promised, rising. "Go there. They will not kill you outright. Show them that you are more than just a lovely young lady." He took her hand in earnest. "Show them you are more than a mere girl to fear, for that is what they will do: fear you. People fear what they do not understand. And fear drives many awful things."

"What do I show them, then?" she asked.

He smiled, leaning over and kissing the back of her palm. "Show them your strength. Show them your humanity. Show them you are not some boogeyman in the dark. Anyone who sits with you for more than a few minutes sees your good heart. Make them see." He released her hand. "I wish you luck, Daniella del Lucio, Judge of Light."

"Judge of Light?"

"The meaning of your first and last name." he told her with a smile. "Farewell." He turned to Ethan before pulling back the curtain. "It will take some time for your, uh, cab to arrive. Apparently you were not the only Guardian to have troubles this evening."

"Who else?" Ethan asked, his voice pained with worry. "Kleos?"

"He is fine. I already heard from him. Mastema did not go, of course. He wouldn't have been trusted by the Council, even though his skill is unmatched. One Guardian did not return, though all charges have been accounted for. I'm sorry for your loss." And with that, the big man departed, letting some music filter through the curtain before disappearing.

Ethan's scowl deepened. His mouth turn down; a flash of anguish. *One Guardian did not return.* Someone died. Someone Ethan knew.

"Are you okay?" she asked.

He got up from the table, knocking over his empty glass and clattering it to the floor. He left the two of them at the table, cursing under his breath.

Apparently not.

Chapter Eight

"Should we go find him?" Nathaniel asked after Ethan didn't return.

"And do what?"

"I don't know...something...?"

Dani pushed the curtain aside. The song that thrummed through was a strange mix of club music and what sounded like medieval classical. The club had dozens of patrons dancing in the strobes and neon lights. More than one looked questionably human, while others seemed no different than anyone she knew—with the exception of partying in a club that didn't exist.

"He's the only person we know here." She conceded. "I'll look for him. Stay here."

"What am I supposed to do?"

She gave him a look. "Do you really want to go wandering around this place?"

He shook his head.

"You stay here in case he comes back. I don't want both of us getting lost in," she sidled out warily into the bar, "that. If I'm not back in five minutes...!"

"Do what?"

Good question.

She could feel the music in her bones as she made her way into the crowd. The enthralled throng of party-goers coursed together, moving and swaying to the beat. As she passed, one woman turned in the arms of another, her eyes like burning coals. A gout of fire burst from her mouth into the air, startling Dani. She stumbled into someone behind her.

"Sorry!"

She turned and screamed. A creature with black skin and red eyes, covered by a hooded cape, screeched savagely at her. Dani jumped, stumbling into more strangers who heckled her. The unearthly bar guest hissed and turned in a huff, it's back moving as if beneath the cowl it had more than arms. Maybe wings? It disappeared into the crowd.

The DJ in the booth switched songs, changing to something mellower. People fanned off the floor, allowing her through. Shaken, she made her way to the bar.

Unfortunately, Ethan wasn't there. Neither was Judah. The golem behind the bar with a block-like head shaped cartoonishly like a buzz-cut asked, "Do you want a drink?"

"Uh, I'm okay."

The golem replied. "I have wines, beers, liquors, distilled spirits, unnatural spirits, evil spirits—"

"What?"

It blinked, and then repeated robotically, "Do you want a drink?"

"I said I'm okay."

"Yes, you did." It replied. "Do you want a drink?"

Dani just stared. "No, I do not want a drink."

It finally nodded and walked away. She heard a soft laughing, or something that sounded like laughing, and turned to the person at the bar next to her. The man sitting in the stool to her right looked almost normal.

You know, except for the dog head.

The creature was like a man in a business suit from the neck down, except he had a mixture of hairy paw-hands. But from the neck up, he was a black Labrador with glasses.

"You got to talk straight to 'em." It, or rather he, said. It had a male voice but in this place? Anything was possible. "They're kind of stupid when they're first made. That one's new. You said 'I'm okay' and not just 'no.' It got confused."

"Oh...well, thanks."

"Sure, sure. Come here often?" His jowls pulled back into an unmistakable dog grin.

Dani grimaced. "Uh, no. First time."

"Can I get you something, sweetness? It's on my dime. A girl cute as you should have a drink in her hand."

Dear God, he's hitting on me! "No thanks."

"I'm a lawyer." He said out of the blue. "Yep. Started my own firm."

"Cool story, Fido." *What the hell? A dog lawyer?* Interested as she was by that, she didn't feel like getting hit on by Rover. "I don't really want to talk. I'm just looking for a friend."

The dog frowned, or in a way dogs did. "You don't have to mean. I was just offering you a drink. Prude."

"Hey!"

"Whatever." The dogman returned to his drink, lowering his head and lapping it directly out of the glass on the bar.

Dani shook her head. Hit on by half-dog freaks in a bar, and then getting told off when she turned him down. Was this her life now?

She slid off the stool and ran into Ethan. He looked annoyed. "Where'd you go? I went back to look for you."

"I was looking for you!" She snapped. "You left us at that booth alone!"

"I did since, you know, you were safe. Forgive me." His tone wasn't apologetic. He glanced past her at the dog-person. "Of all the cynocephali you talk to in this place, you talk to the one that's a sleazy lawyer?"

"Hey!" the dog behind her barked. Literally.

"Quit hitting on anything that walks on two legs, or four for that matter, Dogmund." He shook his head. "Forget him. Our cab is here."

"Cab? You're serious?"

He pulled her away from the bar.

As they wove through the crowd, Dani grumbled. "I didn't need you to stick up for me with that...that dog-thing."

Ethan smirked. "You think you could take on a cynocephali? Be my guest. Even the tame ones like that are animals."

"Yeah they are." She grumbled.

"Don't take what they say personally, though. They're all dogs. Take it as a compliment and try to be nice."

Take it as a compliment? Seriously? Dani shrugged his arm off and turned back. "Mr. Dogmund?"

His ears perked up and grinned, "Yeah sweetness?"

She smiled, and not nicely. "Believe me: if you ever, _ever_, call me sweetness again I will neuter you."

Apparently, she looked like she meant it. The canine lawyer made a high-pitched whine like man's best friend when he got caught peeing on the carpet. Dani had a glare in her eyes like rolled up newspaper.

Dani turned back to Ethan. "Nice enough?"

"Subtle."

"Thank you. Now where's this cab?"

Sure enough, outside idling on the curb was a bright yellow cab.

It glowed under the dim street lights. Emblazoned in neat black lettering across the side was PSYCHOPOMP CABS and leaning against the hood was the driver. Right off the bat Dani could tell he wasn't a cabbie, which meant that wasn't actually a cab.

The kid, who looked all of twelve, leaning against the cab fit right into the weirdness of her night. The first thing she noticed was the wide-brimmed, floppy hat. In and of itself, that wasn't very odd. Except that two small feathery wings sprouted from the top, which flapped when he saw them come out. He wore no shirt, his bare upper body wiry and muscular, and wore a robe-like shawl over his shoulders. His pants and boots were a medieval-chic similar to Ethan's. In one hand he carried some kind of long stick with a pair slithering snakes wrapped around it. His almost elf-like smile was mildly mischievous.

"I heard you needed a'fetching." He shrugged off the hood. "Good to see you made it safely, Ethan. I heard through the Dionysus vine that you ran into a couple of wraiths."

"It wasn't anything I couldn't handle." Ethan bit his lower lip nervously. "You heard?"

The cab-driver's own grimace matched his. "I did. It wasn't my ferry, but I heard."

"Do you know who?"

"Titus."

Ethan's shoulders sagged. "Damnation."

"Aye, 'snails to it all," the driver agreed, "but every charge is safe. That's a small blessing." The driver tipped his chin at Nathaniel. "Is he your new charge?"

"Nathaniel, meet Hermes."

They shook hands. "Like the Greek god?"

He chuckled. "Exactly like."

Nathaniel's eyebrows perked. Ethan nodded. "Hermes is a god. Lower case 'g.' He works for us."

"With you." Hermes shot back playfully, and then explained, "I'm a psychopomp."

"A what?"

"A ferryman." Ethan told him. "He and his kind, they're a group of gods and spirits called psychopomps. They ferry people across magical borders. He's the one that gets us where we need to go."

"No worries. I'm a lot kinder than some of the other gods. I at least earn the title of a lower case g; unlike some. Let me tell you: Zeus isn't a god. He's a douche."

Ethan gestured to Dani. "This is Dani."

Hermes eyes flicked to her, noticing her for the first time. She'd gotten used to being overlooked, but it didn't make it any less annoying. Instead of explaining, she just held up her left arm and pulled back her sleeve to show him the halo mark. His eyes widened.

"Yeah, I know." Ethan told him. "This is going to be complicated."

"Complicated?" Hermes gaped. "You need a stronger word for it."

"We need to take her with us." Ethan told him. "She has a halo. I've already had Judah look at it. It's real."

"But—!" Hermes was at a loss for words. He pulled Ethan closer. "Ethan, she's female."

"Uh-huh."

"And all the other charges have been collected. They're already on their way to Empyrean. Your charge makes one forty-four. You know what that means."

"It means we have one hundred and forty-five." Ethan said calmly. "It doesn't change the fact that Dani is a Numen. The wraiths attacked her the same way they attacked Nathaniel and I. She can see through the veil."

"Could she be something else?"

"Like what?"

"I don't know. Gifted, jinn," he licked his lips, "demon?"

"I'm not a demon, a-hole." Dani folded her arms.

He glanced back at Ethan. "Prove it."

"You mean other than just coming out from the Hellfire Club?" he turned to Dani. "Look at the cab. What do you see?"

Dani sighed exasperatedly, but did as he asked. Other than the ethereal golden glow, it looked like any other taxi. But just like the club forming from a construction site, Dani watched the yellow car change, too. The tires and hubcaps melted, transforming into spoked carriage wheels. The front seat moved forward, changing into a bench attached to the front of a large, Victorian coach. The back seat formed into a carriage compartment. A frame expanded from the front and four golden horses made of brilliant sunlight materialized from thin air, filling the frame. The taxi was no longer a taxi. It was a flaming, chariot-like carriage.

"A golden carriage ride?" She asked.

Hermes gaped. "God's nails!"

It was another one of those weird swears. Ethan smacked his arm. "If the Elders hear you talk like that—never mind. Satisfied?"

He nodded.

"Good. Then let's get the hell out of here." Ethan opened the door to the carriage. "Everyone in."

Nathaniel and Dani climbed up. Inside, two benches faced one another for them to sit. Hermes, still staring at Dani, closed the door behind them and then, with a flap of his tiny wings, floated to the bench up front.

Hermes called through a window up front. "Everyone ready?"

"Ready." Dani called back.

"No worries, I've flown this thing hundreds of times since I stole it from another god! I'm an excellent driver!" He called out to the horses. "Gitty'up!"

The horses spouted fire from their noses and neighed. Their hoofs clapped on the asphalt, leaving melted imprints, and hurtled forward. Dani and Nathaniel tossed back against the seat like in a 747 going from zero to a hundred. Ethan was ready. He hung onto his seat across from them to keep upright. Outside, the world blurred and the carriage took off from the ground, curling up skyward.

Dani screamed. Nathaniel screamed louder. The carriage climbed straight into the sky, keeping Dani and Nathaniel pinned to the back. The horses, as if still running across ground, spouted embers and smoke from their hooves as they galloped. Somehow, Ethan barely felt it, calmly drumming his fingers on the windowsill. Outside, fiery cast-off obscured the view as the ground slowly shrank away.

Over the sound of deafening wind whipping past, he yelled, "Try not to vomit! Hermes hates cleaning it off the seats!"

And then, for the first time Dani knew him, he laughed.

It was disturbing.

They kept climbing. She didn't know how long it took. Los Angeles faded into the night below. She never felt a pressure change, nor felt lightheaded as they soared into thinner air, but she swore she saw the lights of a commercial airliner as they passed. Then they hit the clouds.

White filled the void around them. The carriage shuddered. Ethan rolled his head back, silently whispering to himself.

"What are you doing?" Dani asked.

He held up a hand, still murmuring. A little louder, he counted, "Five... four... three... two... one..."

Suddenly, Dani didn't feel like she was climbing. Instead, it was as if they leveled out. The clouds around them lightened from the dark blue-greys of night to the white of day. The air lightened. She swore it even smelled different; pleasant and soothing.

And then there was light.

It filtered through the clouds, illuminating the cab. Around them, the clouds took on a crystal-like shimmer. Dew collected on the windowsills of the coach. Dani touched the droplets. It was cool. She rolled the liquid between her fingers.

When she glanced at Ethan, he watched her. She couldn't read his expression, but it was as if he wanted to see what would happen when they crossed into these clouds. Before either of them could speak, though, the skies cleared. From her window, she saw exactly why Judah made the light joke at the Hellfire Club.

"Welcome to Empyrean, the realm of light."

Hermes' flying carriage broke from a bowl-funnel of clouds that surrounded a massive, monolithic mountain. Overhead, the sapphire blue sky was perfection. The sun bathed the surface of the large peak. The sheer cliffs and rocky outcroppings all shot heavenward in a long race into the sky. She couldn't see the base in the gloom below where the funnel met. Pouring down the rock face, a raging waterfall churned from inside the crags, spilling from a river-gate built into a stony outcropping.

As the cliffs rose from the clouds, about halfway up vegetation began; the reverse of anything natural. Larger and larger trees grew out of the mountain the higher it went. At the peak, the mountain came to an end. As if a massive hand scooped out the top, a gigantic crater capped the enormous crag. An enormous green forest with trees taller than the Redwoods of California filled the inside of the crater from which the waterfall flowed.

When Dani squinted, she could see the unmistakable outlines of buildings; not skyscrapers like L.A., but definitely buildings. Large, gleaming towers and pure, snow-white stone structures like marble or ivory dotted between the trees. And when she looked closer, there also appeared to be buildings built *into* the trees themselves; parapets of stone and wood, windows jutting from tree-trunks, terraces on spread branches, walkways and skylines interwoven between one of more of the colossal oaks. There were roads, open squares, fields and gardens. It was a city, but it was a city unlike any she'd ever seen.

A single building dwarfed Empyrean at the center. At first she thought 'castle,' but palace seemed to be more appropriate. It took up a fourth of the town and the only part of the city not dominated by trees. Long, wide steps ascended to the entrance of the grand castle. The palace's walls stretched along a cliffside overlooking a forest valley and river, with battlements and more war-like fortifications. The final building, a large tower rising far above the rest, dominated the whole landscape; taller than any building inside the crater.

The carriage angled down like a roller coaster out of sky towards the mountainside. Large, shining gates jutted from the side of the cliffs below the city, interlaced into the battlements along rocky splits. They were almost a milky white, as if marble mixed with steel. Silvery steel molded around light pink stone.

"The Gates of Pearl." Ethan told them. "They're the entrance to Empyrean. There are a set facing North, South, East and West to defend the cardinal directions. Those are the West Gates."

As the carriage approached, they spotted platforms built on the hinges of each gate like the world's highest high-dives. Standing guard on the parapets were men dressed in shining armor. Unlike Ethan, their tunics were a color of deep, burnish red. They reminded Dani of Roman centurions; armored from head to foot, holding spears and shields. One snapped the butt of his spear on his pedestal. Behind him, the massive center gate swung open.

"Gatekeepers." Ethan said. "One of the duties here in Empyrean."

"That job must suck." Dani commented. "Does anyone fall off?"

He shrugged. "Some, but they can fly so it's not an issue."

She wondered if he was kidding, but couldn't tell.

As they approached, she noticed the pedestals weren't the only defenses. A row of archers lined battlements above the gates.

They sailed through the large yawning. The fiery chariot fell towards a filled, open square of various things; a large ball of light, a horse with six legs and man in a floppy wide-brimmed hat, even a large raven the size of an elephant. More psychopomps, Dani assumed.

"Hang on." Ethan advised. "Hermes comes in hot."

The carriage hit wheels-down brutally, nearly sending Dani and Nathaniel into the roof. Hermes bellowed from up front and the horses braked, their hooves sparking up embers along the stone floor. The creatures brayed loudly, skittering to halt. The whole coach lurched sideways, with its passengers screaming bloody murder. They slid a few dozen feet and finally came to a stop with a hard lurch. Behind them, twin burn marks scorched across the bricks where they touched down.

Hermes smiled through the window. "Houston, the eagle has landed!"

"Don't be impressed." Ethan opened the door. "He says that every time. He's just upset that the mission was named after Apollo."

Dani never before wanted to be out of a vehicle so badly. Around them, high cliff walls formed a kind of entry cloister behind the pearl gates, with steps leading up to a large stone archway and heavy wood-and-steel-braced doors.

Gatekeepers helped the guides with new arrivals. Hermes stood by, offering to help her out. His head wings, which upon further look were not coming from the hat but his actual head, flapped as she took his hand. She didn't say no, since she was so wobbly she might fall on her face.

63

The gates swung shut with a loud, resounding clang. Through the clouds beyond, she could see that despite the glowing daylight above, the lights of L.A. dotted the dark world below; somehow impossibly hidden from this amazing mountain in the sky.

Ethan argued with Hermes in low voices.

"What's that?" Dani asked.

"Nothing." Ethan responded automatically.

Hermes shook his head. "Stop lying. She deserves to know. And no, I won't do that." He told him, before addressing Dani. "Ethan wants me to tell the Gatekeepers that he forced me to take you here."

"Why?"

"Because when they see you, they're going to arrest us all and he wants to protect me."

She almost asked why again, but a trumpet groaned in the distance. All at once, everyone was in motion. Gatekeepers turned towards them, swords and spears coming to bear. The archers at the top of the battlements turned and faced inward, bows drawn.

A small contingent of heavily armored Numen appeared from the archway and darted down the steps. Most were Gatekeepers. The exception was the man in front. His tunic was snow-white. He wore silvery armor, a helmet adorn and laced with gold, and a visor down over his eyes. In his hand was a long, curved blade. A scimitar. He pointed it at her as he came to the bottom, the soldiers at his back fanning out.

"Hold there!" he demanded. His skin was olive colored and his black beard fanned down his jaw but didn't meet at the chin. Other than that, Dani could see none of his face. "Hold there! Declare yourself!"

Ethan held his hands raised. So did Hermes. Nathaniel followed. But everyone looked at Dani.

Slowly, she raised hers, but she was unsure why she had to do it.

"I said declare yourself!" the man in white demanded.

"Elder Asaph—" Ethan began.

"Silence Guardian! Protect your charge!" the man named Asaph ordered. "Guide, what is the meaning of this? Who is this outsider? We do not allow gifted or any beings in without permission."

Hermes wings flickered nervously. He glanced at Ethan. "Do you want to take this one?"

"Elder Asaph," Ethan said louder, "please, put up your weapons. She is not a threat."

But the man didn't listen. He took two long strides, separating from his men, sword still held towards Dani. "I demand you declare yourself, or I will strike you down where you stand! Do it now, girl!"

Dani knew better than to mouth off. After all, only a lunatic would be stupid enough to get mouthy with men pointing swords, spears and arrows at her. No sense in getting everyone riled up.

"My name is Dani," she said, "and I'd really appreciate it if you stopped calling me girl and outsider, your ignorant morons."

Yeah, that was better.

Chapter Nine

She was in shackles. Shackles! At least, that was what Elder Asaph called them; a pair of polished steel-like handcuffs that went around her wrists and linked by chain to a belt they strapped around her waist. Not like *that* was demeaning or anything.

Ethan looked helpless. Nathaniel looked worse. Hermes was sympathetic, especially since Asaph ordered him placed in shackles as well for bringing her to Empyrean. They took his serpent staff. It hissed and nipped at the Numen who tried to hold it.

Six armed guards surrounded her and lead her into the city like some kind of criminal. Numen in black, red, purple, green, and blue all stared as she passed. Others in more modern clothes, all teenagers, stood beside them. Some looked confused, others smirked, and others just stared, but no one helped her.

With three soldiers on either side, hands on their swords, they led her up the steps through the massive stone archway past the large doors. Hermes followed up behind. Asaph himself stood with Ethan and Nathaniel, barking orders to one of his men to run to the Throne Room to gather the Council.

"Inform them that an intruder has been brought to the city." He warned.

Intruder. Outsider. Girl. Sweetness. She'd been in the supernatural world less than a day and the names were getting old, fast.

The city was much bigger than she thought from the air. The trees towered over her. Steps would trace around the trunks, each of which went at least six or seven stories up. Their foliage create green, luminescent streams of light. Buildings made of white stone bled into them. Stone walkways connected buildings or oaks dozens of feet above Dani's head. Numen drew water from aqueducts and fountains, gathered food from the very trees they lived in, or assembled on platforms above the street. Where the forest ended and where civilization blurred.

The buildings themselves were strange. There weren't steps or entryways to all the upper levels, as if people didn't need to climb stairs to get to them. She spotted pod-like rooms through the upper branches. How did they get up there?

As they walked, Dani noticed it wasn't just men in the crowd. There were women; little girls and boys even. Hadn't Ethan said there were no women here? Yet, there they were. Their eyes looked different; like some of the patrons of the Hellfire Club. Dani didn't ask why she was arrested, when clearly women existed in Empyrean. She kept her mouth shut.

The city stretched to the rim of the crater. Even from here, she could see what looked like a drop-off to the left, with the huge river valley she had seen expanding outward. Waterfalls, sheer cliffs, and untamed woods filled it to the edge.

The soldiers led her quickly through the throngs of gawking Numen. *Take a picture. It'll last longer*, she thought wryly. Then she realized cameras might not exist up here.

They took her to the large building she'd seen from the sky; the palatial castle. The massive tower stretched into the sky above it and from the peak, Dani could see what looked like shimmers of air wisping out over the clouds. The soldiers led the way up the massive steps towards large double-doors. More red clad soldiers formed a line and blocked the way of the pursuing gawkers. Just under the overhang, double two-story high polished wooden doors opened and they pushed her inside.

If Empyrean was impressive from the outside, the Throne Room dazzled.

The first thing Dani saw was the pool. It took up most of the massive chamber. Like a sea of glass, it's mirror surface reflected the many torches and sun from the skylight above. It didn't move or ripple, perfectly reflecting its mirror image. Rows of chairs and balconies rose up the sides of the main floor like box seats to the weirdest show on Earth. Or, rather, not on Earth.

And then, opposite the double doors, were thrones. They sat back from the mirror pond with seven large bowls, each one the size of a car and blazing brightly with fire, in front of them. The thrones themselves were not anything impressive; twenty-four of them, situated on a raised dais in two rows with one above the rest. A man dressed in white robes filled each seat. They didn't wear tunics like other Numen; not even like Asaph's under armor. Not soldiers. Instead, they looked more like priests. Each man was in their mid-to-late years; some elderly in their sixties or so, some as young as thirty. They each wore a floor-length robe and what looked like a crown around his head. Not kingly crowns, but simple bands of silver and gold, drawn with the same strange symbols as Ethan's tattoos.

But she couldn't focus on them. Instead, her eyes went to the rainbow. Like a glittering, solid wall, it surrounded the empty throne above the rest; hanging in the air like a magic barrier. Dani didn't have to guess whoever sat there was someone important, but the throne remained empty as her escorts led her up to the seated men.

Asaph moved to the front as they came to stand before the seven fires. Dani could feel their heat. The men waited. Asaph approached and bowed.

"Elder Asaph," said a man with a grey and white beard, "what is the meaning of this? Why did you summon us?"

He removed his helm. Asaph looked all of forty or less, with lines of grey leaking into his black beard. Strangely, he looked kinder with the helmet on.

"Fellow Elders, our borders were breached." He announced. To his men, he ordered, "Bring her forth!"

Her guards pushed Dani to stand on the other side of the lit torches, revealing her to the men. Immediately, there was an intake of breath and a flurry of murmurs and whispers.

The one who'd spoken banged his hand on his armrest, his voice magnified somehow. "Fellow Elders! Order!"

One of the men, sitting next to the first, stood. His hair and beard all perfectly matched the pure-white color of his robe. His eyes were the strangest blue Dani had ever seen; the color of clear morning sky.

"Silence!" he called.

Immediately, every other white-robed man became quiet.

The Elder looked down to Dani. "I am Castus, Consul Lord of the Elder Council." He said it like it meant something to her, but since it didn't, she didn't speak. "Who are you? How did you get here?"

Dani swallowed down her sudden cottonmouth. "I, well, my name is Dani—Daniella. Daniella del Lucio. And I was brought here."

"By whom, young lady?"

She let the young lady comment go since the last time she got lippy, she got arrested. She glanced back at Hermes, who didn't at all shrink away from her.

"I did, Elders." He announced. "It is my sworn duty as guide to bring all Numen to Empyrean."

"She is not a Numen!" Announced one, a brown-haired man with olive skin. "She cannot be!"

"She is." This came from Ethan, who was silent until now. He advised Hermes to keep quiet, but apparently ignored his own advice. "I can verify that she is an Earthborn."

"That is impossible!" another Elder cried. "She is female. There has never been a female Earthborn in existence!"

"But is it possible?" asked a younger Elder.

The thrones erupted into louder conversations. Castus called for silence. Once he got it, he turned to the man on his right, the grey-bearded Elder who'd spoken first. "Jeduthun?"

Dani recognized the name. This was the Elder that Judah told her about. Unlike his fellow Elders, Jeduthun was not arguing or whispering to other Council members. He watched Dani, his hands folded in his lap. He rubbed his thick, bearded chin.

"Jeduthun?" Castus repeated.

Startled out of his reverie, the man grumbled. "Well, I certainly never heard of one. I do not believe one has ever existed, though I'd advise Elder Heman to consult the Book of Metatron before stating it as fact."

The one who said it was impossible reddened in shame.

"Still, quite curious is it not? A female Numen. Daniella," he leaned forward, "these people behind you say you are a Numen; an Earthborn. Elder Asaph calls you an intruder. Do you have any evidence to support which one you are?"

Dani couldn't think of any. She brought nothing with her, but remembered what she did have. "I'll need to be uncuffed to show you."

Asaph stifled a grunt of disgust, as if she'd suggested something lewd. She gave him the stink eye.

"It's my mark." She told them. "My halo."

Jeduthun nodded. "Asaph, unshackle her."

The Elder opened his mouth to protest, but shut it. Scowling, he took a key from his belt and went to undo the binding on her right wrist.

"My left one." She corrected.

He frowned. "Your left?"

"My halo is on my left arm."

Asaph didn't act disgusted now. Now he looked a little afraid, as if touching her bare skin might burn him.

He undid the binding and stepped back so she could show them. Peeling back her sleeve, she held out her left wrist. If being a woman made these guys get a knot in their shorts, the halo on her left arm made the knot twist. Immediately, they burst into whispering argument, some so loud they really weren't whispers at all. Only Castus and Jeduthun didn't join in.

"She is an abomination!" Cried one of the Elders. It was the same one, Heman, who spoke up before. A chorus of agreements joined him.

But Elder Castus brought them to silence again. "Elder Heman, I will not have outbursts like that in our Council!" The jab was enough to silence not only the man he was speaking with, but his supporters as well.

Castus returned to Dani. "Thank you, Daniella. You may lower your wrist." She did. "Can she see beyond the veil?"

Ethan spoke up again. "Yes, Council members. She was able to see the wraiths for what they were when they attacked her and my charge, Nathaniel. She could smell the brimstone."

"So she is not your charge?"

"No, Elders. Nathaniel Cadell is my charge, as was written in the Book of Metatron, for whom the first throne is left unfilled." The last part sounded like a recital of some kind. It also explained why, other than a seat for Asaph, the only empty chair was the rainbow throne.

"Again, I say," Heman called out, "that not only is it impossible for her to be one of us, but now we see that is the only explanation." He stood. "All one hundred and forty-four charges have been brought to Empyrean, with the addition of Nathaniel Cadell. All Novices are accounted for. Do we accept that a woman is somehow the one hundred forty-fifth? There hasn't been a gifted born on Earth for centuries. She clearly isn't a mandanus. This," he pointed at her, "is nothing but deception and lies! It is an evil omen and a bearing of ill tidings that should be destroyed!"

Some Elders gave another chorus of agreement.

Dani's stomach rolled in disgust. *This?* She didn't even have a name. She was an object to him. A _this_ or a _that_; not a person.

Plead your case, not plead. Judah's words.

"I am not some evil omen!" She yelled suddenly, stopping every man in attendance. She strode forward, keeping her chin up, staring them all down. If they expected her to keep quiet, they were going to be disappointed. "I am not an intruder and I am more than just a girl." She glared at Asaph. "And I am certainly more than a pronoun." She pointedly glared at Heman, who seemed more shocked she spoke than speaking to him. Then she turned to Castus defiantly. "I didn't ask to be brought here. I didn't ask for some kind of demon to try to kill me. I certainly didn't ask to be put into handcuffs from the last century," she held up her shackles, "because I'm a woman, left-handed and not on your enchanted guest list. But I'm here. I'm not evil. I'm not some imposter trying to sneak into your clubhouse. I'm me. I'm human, or Numen, or whatever that means. I was brought here for the same reason as everyone else. I was chosen. I don't know what that means. I don't care. So unless the person doing the choosing is here, which I gather he is not, then you'd better accept it."

The whole chamber went silent. Most were too stunned to speak. Jeduthun, however, seemed almost comically entertained. A soft smile hid in his whiskers.

"I don't know what you want from me." She announced. "I frankly don't care. I've lost my family, I've lost my home, and for some reason I've lost my own freedom, but I'm not going to stand here while you call me names. I'd rather die. So if you are going to kill me," she made sure to throw her best shade at both Asaph and Heman, "then get it over with. I've got stuff to do."

Judah said show them her humanity, but now she was just showing them where to stick it. Asaph looked ready to draw his sword again. Heman's face contorted with pure fury. She chanced a glance at Nathaniel who, despite being utterly terrified, looked somewhat proud of her. Hermes even smirked a little. Ethan gave his best poker face, or whatever the equivalent Numen expression, and waited.

Castus stood once more, clearing his throat. "Daniella, I must say, in the two millennium I have sat on this Council, I have never heard anyone speak that way to us." She didn't know whether to be proud or say her prayers, so she said nothing. And two millenniums? Two thousand years? He looked old, but not that old. "Showing respect for your Elders, pardon the expression, is essential here; however, you do call into question our judgment of you." He glanced at Heman. "I do not speak for everyone on this Council, but I do not see any darkness within you, other than youthful spite. I see no reason to question your position here."

"Elder Castus, I demand you reconsider!" Heman barked from his place.

"You may demand all you like." Castus dismissed. "I call for a vote of this Council. She has our mark, despite its location. She has our abilities, despite being not of our number. She is a woman; not mandanus, not gifted. We must decide her fate. Will you send someone to their death on suspicion alone? Or will you allow a person's actions to speak for themselves?"

Every Elder had a different expression, but no one spoke. Some avoided Dani's gaze. Some avoided Castus's. Jeduthun and a few others nodded in agreement.

Heman and his group, however, weren't done.

"Her presence will disrupt the order of our society." Another Elder further down the line proclaimed, seeming to ally with Heman and his group. "What will happen? There are unforeseen consequences to allowing this," he sneered the word, "woman to stay."

"Again with the names." She muttered to herself.

"How will our newest recruits—how will our veterans for that matter—be able to focus with her here? She is a distraction that could cost lives."

Jeduthun didn't even bother to look at the man when he said, "Are you saying that you allow others to determine what you do and how you act, Elder Berith?"

The man looked insulted. "I was speaking on behalf of our men."

"Are you saying we do not train them well enough to think for themselves?" This time Jeduthun did look at him and it was unfriendly. "That would call into question the soldiers that you have trained. That calls into question our very existence. One woman can undo the divine destiny of this city?"

"How dare you doubt my abilities!"

"How dare you allow doubt." Jeduthun shot back. "You say your men cannot control themselves? That one woman," he looked almost apologetic to Dani, "determines how someone would act? We do not train dumb animals here, Elder Berith. We train warriors. Warriors whose ranks dwindle of late. I would never question their abilities, or the abilities of our fellow Elders, but you seem to. Or do you wish to change your demands?"

Berith reddened to match Heman's shade, but he didn't dare speak. He sat, not looking at anyone, including Dani. Now she understood why Judah thought highly of him.

"I call for a vote." Castus declared. "Who concurs?"

Jeduthun was the first to raise his hand and with him, nearly every Elder. Heman, Berith and two others noticeably did not.

"We have majority." Castus announced. "Daniella, welcome to the city of light."

Chapter Ten

Released by the Elders, Dani, Ethan, Hermes and Nathaniel left the Throne Room. She chanced a glance back as the door shut and caught eyes with Elder Jeduthun, who gave a small nod in her direction.

"Well, that was exciting." Hermes grinned.

"Thank you for all you did." Ethan said.

"Quit thanking me or I will hit you." Hermes threatened lightly. "Or she will. And I have a feeling her patience is not as unending as mine."

"Thank you all the same." Ethan shook his hand.

"I'm sure I will see you later. Nathaniel, m'lady," he tipped his hat to them and then with a flap of his tiny wings, took off.

"So," Dani said, gaping at the unbelievable city around her, "what do we do now?"

"Like every other Novice: I take you across the Vale."

"The Vale?"

He pointed to the massive valley that bordered the city.

"Why?"

"Sanctuary Hills and Novice Village." He said. "It's time to see your new home."

———

"Empyrean is divided in two." Ethan explained, leading them across the massive bridge that stretched the distance of the wide valley. The tall, stone supports disappeared into the teeming gorge below. A raging river glistened in the light as it flowed underneath.

"For millennia, those hunted by demons have sought refuge in Empyrean and places like it. The Vale acts as a border and the bridge connects the Numen Citadel, and the Keep where the Throne Room is, with the Sanctuary Hills on the other side."

As they crossed, Dani passed two women on their way to the Citadel. They smiled tightly but avoided her gaze. When she glanced over her shoulder, they looked back at her, but then quickly looked away.

"You said there were no female Numen." She remarked.

"They're not. They're gifted."

"Gifted?"

"Those with special abilities—either by birth or by trade; seers, alchemists, vilas, Tuatha De Danaan."

"Am I supposed to know what those are?"

He smirked. "No. Just think of them as special. Demons are attracted to all manner of supernatural creatures. They kill them. That's why most gifted don't live on Earth anymore. They fled here and the other angelic cities for protection. The Council allows them to live," he pointed ahead, "in the Sanctuary Hills."

The opposite cliffs stretched up in either direction, dotted with homes. Some looked like old-century hovels or earthen mounds, while others appeared to be group homes made of the same white stone. There were sparse trees here; not the Redwoods of the Citadel, but she could see some that appeared to be tree homes. And as they got closer, she could see men, women, children.

"Novices live on this side of the Vale." He told her, pointing to a collection of buildings farther uphill. "That is Novice Village. Each Novice lives in one of the twelve barracks as part of an aerie. It's an old word for 'flock.' They live here until trained and brought into the city to join the different ranks of Numen."

"Flocks? Like, what, we're birds?"

He laughed. "I like to think of the Novices as little lost lambs in need of shepherds, actually. This is where Guardians come in. We live with and train our Novices. The training is overseen by the Elders. Once you're accepted, you become a full Numen warrior."

Dani understood. "And since I have no Guardian, I have no aerie. No flock."

Nathaniel attempted a half-hearted joke. "You're flocked. Or is it unflocked? Deflocked? Flocked up?"

"Shut up Nate."

"Twelve spots in each aerie," Ethan confirmed, "and there are twelve aeries. All aeries have every Novice they need. So, yes, that's what I'm saying."

"Great." Dani shook her head. "So even though I left Earth, I'm still homeless." Homeless and in a place that thought she was a monster. Awesome. "So there's no other place for me?"

"There's someone who lives over here in the Sanctuary Hills. Shea. He knows the area. We might be able to find you housing."

"I could live with someone?" she asked half-hopefully.

He shook his head. "Intermingling between Numen and gifted is strictly forbidden by the Elder Council."

"Has it ever happened?"

He avoided the question. Instead, he said, "Much of your training happens in the Hills, the Vale or the Citadel—specifically, the Keep. The

Vale stretches up towards those cliffs you see in the fog. It's the source of the Crystalline River."

"Where does the river come from?" she asked.

"Excuse me?"

"The Crystalline River: where does it come from?"

He pointed up river into the fog at the top of the Vale. "That area is called The Dalles. No one's ever been able to make it all the way up. The Vale is," he seemed not to want to say, "dangerous, so no Numen or gifted venture that way."

"So you don't know where it comes from?"

"Something about the Dalles limits our abilities. The fog you see is difficult to navigate. Crossing the terrain in that direction is nearly impossible."

"And if you all—I mean, Numen—built this city, then why don't you know more about it?"

Ethan shrugged, passing other traffickers. "Because we didn't build it."

"What?"

"The story goes that the angels built the city." He turned, walking backwards as he spoke. "This whole city isn't on the same plane of existence at the rest of the world. There are several places like it; the seven celestial cities and a few others. The same thing that stops mundani from seeing us is the same thing that makes it possible for a city to exist above Los Angeles."

"That's total bull."

"Ever heard of a seven-forty-seven colliding with a mountain in the sky?"

Obviously, she hadn't.

"It's the same with the Hellfire Club: it's not really there but it is. Don't think of it as being in the same place as everything else. Think of it as existing," he thought for a moment, "beside it; there but not there."

"So no one's explored parts of Empyrean?"

He shrugged. "As I said, Empyrean was built by angels, but the Dalles? No. I've heard stories of Numen running away up there, but I've never known any. And all the Numen since then have died."

"Died?"

"We live for many, many centuries but we can still die. A lot die in battle or on demon hunts. Those who aren't warriors like Naturals and Alchemists disappear; killed by demons when they travel to Earth on mission. Earth is dangerous for our kind. Our numbers are dwindling. Demons are more active now than ever before. The cities crawl with them."

Dani could tell Ethan wasn't ready to talk about it. Instead, she asked, "And all of this was possible because of angels?"

He nodded. "That's what our books say."

She glanced around at the entirety of the Vale and Empyrean. A celestial city in the clouds, wrapped up in its own mystery. "So were you kidding about flying?"

"No, it's real."

"And can you fly?"

Ethan grinned. With a single step, he floated forward about three feet from them in a single bound. "What do you think?"

At the other end of the Vale Bridge was a village comprised of a small marketplace and homes. Dani marveled at people with strange-colored eyes, fiery jinn and cynocephali mingling amongst one another while Numen guards acted as border security; stopping people at the bridge and checking to see if they could pass over into the Citadel. Above their heads, Dani spotted what looked like human-shaped wisps of air dancing in the air. Fairies?

"Sylphs." Ethan told her. "Empyrean is full of elementals."

"Elementals?"

"Sentient nature; sylphs in the air, gnomes in the ground, undines in the water and salamanders in the fire."

"Salamanders? Seriously?"

"If you think that's interesting," he smirked, "you should see the giants that live in the upper hills."

"No way."

His eyes sparkled like crystalized honey, chuckling. "Come on: I'll introduce you to Shea. And we'll get you some provisions for tonight at the market."

They passed a hairy creature that could have, for all she knew, been Bigfoot. The Chewbacca look-alike shopped at the market like anyone else. Ethan first stopped off at a vendor's tent, removing some coins from a pouch on his belt and trading them for some wrapped up meats, vegetables and a couple vials of different-colored liquids and put everything into a canvas bag.

"You can buy almost everything you need here." He told her. "Empyrean's markets trade all over the world. Numen do business with the gifted. You just have to find things of value."

"What are those?" she asked, pointing to the coins.

"Shekels." He held them out. Each coin was the size of a silver dollar and made from different colored metals. He pointed them out. "The gold-looking ones are Orichalcum—Atlantian gold—and the brass-looking ones are Corinthiacum—Corinthian brass. The silvery ones are Adamant. The black ones are Hepatizon. Orich, Corinth, Adamant and Hepa; traded metals in the supernatural world. You can trade gold and silver, too. Up here there isn't a set money system. You barter everything. The shekels just have to be officially stamped with Empyrean's seal, or the seal of any celestial city."

He showed her the coins, which were stamped with the concentric fiery rings of his uniform; seal of Empyrean.

"Who is this?" asked a voice.

A woman, maybe in her sixties, approached. She wore a simple, old-century dress with a shawl. Like many of the gifted, which Dani assumed she was, her eyes were the color of emeralds and she spoke with an Irish accent. The lines around her eyes crinkled when she smiled.

"Adare, this is Dani." Ethan introduced.

"Aye, I heard there was a female Numen." She said, taking Dani's hand kindly in both of hers. "You've caused quite a stir, young lady."

"I didn't mean to." Dani answered wryly. "And how did you hear about me? You got a cell phone in that dress?"

Adare laughed happily. "My dear, a cell phone wouldn't work here. And no. Our community has its own way of communicating."

"Magic?"

"Would that surprise you?"

"No."

"I like you. You are forthright."

"Is that good?"

She patted her hand and let it go, addressing Ethan. "This one, Ethan: she's a keeper. Have you found everything you want?"

"Your prices are always best, Adare. Is Shea here?"

"He's back at the house. You know him: always busy. He's trying to get some fern flower to replenish our stock. Why?"

As Ethan and Adare spoke, Dani spotted a pair of bright blue eyes peeking from behind a shelf. As soon as she looked, they disappeared. A second later, they popped back up. Dani looked again and again, they disappeared with a wave of blonde hair.

Dani wandered over, glancing around the shelf, but the owner of the eyes darted away. Weaving through the shelves, she eventually found the owner: a small girl in an ankle-length dress with blonde braids and blue eyes, all of six or seven. She grinned sheepishly.

"Hello there." Dani knelt. "What's your name?"

"That's Korë." A dark haired girl her age—a gifted with bright violet eyes—stood behind her with a basket of fruit.

"Nice name." Dani stood. "And yours?"

"Roxelana."

"I'm—."

"Daniella. Yes, I know." She extended her hand.

Dani shook it. "Word travels fast. And it's just Dani."

Roxelana fluttered her hand over the fruit basket. Some purple, apple-like produce—but what apples were purple?—floated from the basket and over to the shelf with a wave. Despite the amazing ability, she acted as if it were natural.

"How do you do that?" she asked.

"I'm a vila."

"A what?"

She shrugged. "Nymph, fairy; we get called all kinds of things. But we're human...sort of."

"You're gifted, you mean. And Korë?"

"She's adorable." Roxelana pointed.

When Dani turned, the little girl held out what looked like a doll made of grass. When Dani reached for it, the doll moved, making her jump. Korë giggled.

"Making friends?" asked a third voice. The next gifted, this one laying out a basket of fresh bread, looked more super-model than supernatural. Long, leggy, blonde, she had the perfect runway scowl. One hand on her hip, she asked, "Is that her?"

Dani never instantly disliked someone before. First time for everything.

"Adare wants us to make sure the new stock is out." The girl told Roxelana. "Maybe Korë could help. Earn her keep."

"I'll help." Roxelana told her. "Just a minute."

"Fine." The girl departed.

"Don't put too much stock in what Airlea says." Roxelana told Dani. "She's...she's just Airlea. Come on. Your Guardian friend wants to introduce you to someone."

Roxelana, basket in hand, led Korë up the hill. Dani followed. Away from the market was a grass-and-moss roofed home. Larger than most, the steps lead up to a garden around the entryway. Korë ran inside. Ethan, Adare and another man waited out front.

"Dani, this is Shea." Ethan introduced.

Shea shook with a steely grip; someone who worked with his hands. His eyes were emerald like Adare's. He was tall, muscular, bearded and smelled of fresh earth.

"I hear you need a place to stay." He said. "I may know somewhere."

"A house?" she asked hopefully.

His smile twitched. "Well..."

Chapter Eleven

"They called this place the Arn." Shea told her, standing in the courtyard. "Arn is an old word meaning 'eagle.' It's also the name of the people who used to live here—a group who could speak to birds called feathertongues—but as you can see that was a long time ago."

The Arn used to be a gifted village of some kind; rundown homes built of the same white stone as the rest of Empyrean, but they'd long since become little more than ruins. They bordered three sides of a brick square with a small fountain, while the fourth contained an open-air pavilion Shea brought her to see. It was spacious, but empty. The entire village was overgrown by moss and grass. Vines crept up the columns, with spreads of beautiful flowers decorating the remains.

Dani sighed. "I've lived in worse."

"You want her to live here by herself?" Nathaniel shook his head. "She's almost a mile from anyone. She'll be alone."

Dani murmured to herself, "I'm used to it."

"There isn't any other choice." Ethan pushed on the rim of the empty, moss-covered fountain. A fracture of stone fell loose. "She can't stay with the gifted. There's no room at Novice Village. Difficult circumstances or not, all Novices live on this side of the Vale. It's either here or she sleeps on the ground."

Dani grumbled under her breath, "No room at the inn for me, then."

"I've brought blankets and things to keep her warm." Shea said, holding them out to her.

"And I brought food." Ethan handed off the canvas bag. "Everything is ready to eat."

"Is there a cheeseburger?" she asked jokingly.

Ethan smiled and shook his head.

"Well, maybe I should stay." Nathaniel suggested. "She'll need someone here. There's plenty of space."

Surprisingly, Dani was the one to disagree. "No. Nathaniel."

"But—"

"No," she told him, "I'm not taking someone's pity."

She knew she couldn't rely on Nathaniel, or anyone for that matter. The place was a ghost town, but if the Elders were any indication, she may not be welcome anywhere else. Past the rubble of one building stood the cliff's edge and a pedestal jutting from it, as if daring someone to jump.

"I'll stay here. I'm not worried." She told them.

"I can check on her." Shea promised. "At least, as much as the Elder Council allows me."

Ethan rubbed his hands together slowly. "A Guardian will be assigned to you eventually. Someone will train you."

"Train me?"

"To use your powers." He told her. "To use elixirs, charms and other weapons, and to fight hand-to-hand; you'll need to learn to survive against the demonic."

"Based on what I've seen, I need to learn to survive this place."

"That too." He acknowledged. "I won't lie: the world is dangerous for us right now. For gifted and Numen. It's just rumors, but there's talk of something really bad prowling the Earth. It's been spotted near here. It's killed a lot of us."

His voice was bitter. She remembered someone named Titus died; someone close to him.

He saw their looks. "Don't worry. You're safe here. You, the gifted; nothing has breached Empyrean's borders for a long time."

Dani doubted _safe_ was the right word, but then again she was a cynical kind of person. "You mentioned someone being assigned to train me. Any idea which lucky guy gets that job?"

Ethan did, at least according to his secret smile. "I think I might. You'd be lucky to have him. He's a keen trainer, but he's," he seemed unsure how to say it, "well, we'll call him rough around the edges."

"Sounds like fun." She was not enthusiastic.

"You'll need these, as well." Ethan handed over one last bag. Inside were folded brown clothes; a tunic. "Raiments. It's our uniform. All Numen ranks are assigned a color to represents your status. Novices are brown."

"Great. Like dirt." Dani ran her hands over the material. It was firm under the touch, but light.

"The tunics are special. They're fashioned from a fiber called Arachne-weave. They're like armor; it'll stop a knife or a sword slash, but don't try to take a direct stab."

"I'll try not to."

"They'll keep your warm when you're cold, cool when you're hot, and they're enchanted to be hidden from mundani by the veil. They'll appear as normal clothes to anyone not supernatural."

"Where do I get them? Does Empyrean have some sort of laundry delivery service?"

He smirked. "I'll make sure they're waiting for you. For now, we should head uphill to Novice village."

81

"For what?"

"For dinner. It's tradition: meet your comrades in arms."

"Oh. Goodie."

Novice Village stood about a mile from the marketplace. As the sun set, homefires burned across Sanctuary Hills and across the Vale in Empyrean's Citadel.

Twelve whitestone barracks comprised Novice Village. A large bonfire blazed in the square. It was alive with activity. Boys in street clothes—Novices—mingled amongst one another. A party spilled from the square into a large pavilion like the one she would sleep in. Despite the strange circumstances the one hundred and forty-four boys found themselves in, the assembled crowd was happy. Chattering, laughing, they hung around as if this were just another party.

Dani very quickly noticed that not only had the gifted community heard about her, but the other Novices as well. All eyes turned her direction when she arrived with Ethan and Nathaniel. She felt like Carrie at prom.

"So," she murmured as the music skipped a little, the gifted entertainers losing their place, "I take it they've heard of me, too."

"You'll be fine." Ethan assured her.

The party continued, if but a little put off by Dani's presence. Black-clad Numen—Guardians, she assumed—stood with their charges. They regarded her less hostilely than the Novices, but with equal curiosity.

Nathaniel split off with Ethan while Dani went to eat from a lavishly prepared table. She spotted Airlea amongst the gifted working the party. She gave her an ugly glare before flirtatiously handing off a drink to a Guardian.

"Don't worry about the looks," said a boy, "I'm sure it's nothing."

The owner of the voice was a Novice. Dani almost didn't see him, on account he was short. He had beautiful dark skin the color of mocha, short frizzy hair and a wide grin. He looked maybe sixteen at most; short, holding out his hand. "I'm Dink."

"Dink?" she shook his hand.

"Yeah. My real name is Ailbe Dinklage, but people call me Dink."

"Ailbe? That's a really..." she didn't want to say.

"A weird, super-Irish name? Yeah." His cheeks turned a burnish red hue. "My dad's from the old country, as he likes to say. Or did, really." He shrugged. "He died last year."

"I'm sorry." She smiled tightly. "I'm Dani."

82

"Cool name. That's better than Ailbe."

"I like Dink; straight and to the point."

"Yeah." He rubbed the back of his neck. "Except for the fact that it means 'stupid' in some parts of the world."

"Well, I doubt you're stupid. Where are you from? You don't look or sound Irish."

"Colorado. That's where my stepmom and I lived before, you know, all of this. You?"

"Cali born and raised."

Dink nodded. "Cool. Cool. Are you an orphan like the rest of us?"

"Orphan?"

He waved to everyone around them. "Most Numen are orphans when we're chosen. Some of us are runaways. For some of us, our parents died."

"Everyone is like that?"

He shrugged. "It seems to be a thing for Numen; like we're destined to or something. Maybe it's just bad luck. Maybe it's destiny." *That's a crappy destiny*, she thought. Dink kept going, "At least, like I said, most of us. Some are just jerks that got kicked out of the house. Which are you?"

She didn't like the last choice. "Orphan." She lied.

"So what aerie are you?"

"Aerie?"

"You know: your flock. I'm Aether. Your friends with Nathaniel, right? The guy over there?" He tipped his chin towards Nathaniel and another boy talking. "He's in Aether, I hear. So what aerie?"

Dani didn't know whether to lie or whether to tell the truth. Either way, she didn't have to. Just out of earshot she heard it. It was the laughter she knew all too well; sneering, snide, and rude. She chanced a look over. A group of Novices stood off to one side, one in the middle looking right at her. The moment they locked eyes, he ducked his head and laughed.

They were talking about her.

"Seriously, you'd hit it?" The one asked his friend. "I mean, she's cute and all, if you're into that whole Latina vibe."

Another, a stocky guy with a goatee, chuckled. "Yeah, well, it's not like there's a lot to pick from up here."

"Back home, we had her kind coming out of the wood work." The first smirked. "You couldn't throw a rock without hitting something brown."

Dani felt her blood boil.

"I heard they almost killed her." The first said. "The Elder Council or whoever nearly had her executed. Instead, they keep her downhill somewhere."

"With the other trash." The second agreed.

She finally had enough and wheeled on them, getting into their faces. At first, she did nothing but glare, but after a minute she finally stalked over.

"You got something to say?" she asked.

The two exchanged looks.

"What? Don't like it when someone confronts you?"

"We were just talking."

"About me." She pointed out. "You don't even know me."

"Hey, we don't need you eavesdropping." The second stood up in front of her.

"And you are?"

"Andreas. That's Lester. And before you get on your high horse," he took a step forward, making her instinctively take a step back. She hated that, "you'd better realize: this isn't high school. This is a whole different world. You don't like it? Tough."

A few others started to notice. A small ring formed around them.

"I'll show you tough." She seethed.

"That right?" his hand clenched into a fist. "You want to bet?"

Before she could answer, a voice rang out through the crowd. "Aye! Novices!"

The knot of Novices and Guardians split apart. Striding into the open was another Guardian with a thick black beard and long black hair, tied into a short ponytail from his tinted-tan skin.

He stopped, glaring from Dani to the boys. "What is the meaning of this?"

"The girl is getting out of place." Andreas answered.

"Is that so?" he asked, looking at his friend. "You are...?"

"Lester, sir." He answered with a southern drawl. "And yeah, we weren't doin' nothin'."

"Interesting." The Guardian eyed Dani before continuing. "Let me ask you two then: what is a wraith?"

Lester stuttered over his next words. The question threw him off. Andreas spoke up. "It's a demon."

"Really?" Kleos turned on him. "How do you kill one?"

The bigger guy didn't answer. He clearly thought a Guardian, another man, would back him up. Now it appeared he wasn't.

84

"That's right. You don't know." The Guardian told him. "You don't know that cutting off the head or destroying the heart of a wraith is what destroys it. And if you don't do that, you're demonic lunchmeat." He glanced around.

"Not fair!" Andreas protested. "This doesn't have anything to do with that."

"It doesn't?"

Kleos extended his hand toward the fire. The flames suddenly burst outward in a loud explosion. Gifted and Novices screamed and ducked for cover.

From the flames, a figure emerged; forged out of the embers of the wood. Giant wings fanned outward, the creature glared with a dark semi-human face and fiery eyes, screeching at them.

"You think fair matters?" the Guardian demanded. "You think lives aren't on the line? You sit here, drinking," he smacked the cup out of Andrea's hand, "and believe this is some summer camp? Some school of magic where you learn spells and live in safety? It's isn't!"

Silence spread over the Novices. The Guardian waved his hand and the terrifying creature disappeared. The others now stood around them, arms folded, listening.

"Can any of you tell me anything about demons?" He demanded. "Any of you?"

Every Novice, including Dani, didn't meet his eyes. Then, as he was about to speak again, Nathaniel raised his hand. "They're demonic, so...Hell?"

He smirked wryly. "Good. But were they born there? Did they die as something else and go to Hell to become a wraith? Does anyone know?"

No one did.

"That's because no one knows. What we do know," he wheeled on Andreas and Lester, "is that they kill the living. Wraiths are responsible for many deaths in the natural world. They'll eat anything: jinn, gifted, human, cattle. But they love to eat Numen most. And do you know the only defense against them?" He specifically glared at the two boys next to Dani.

They shook their head.

"Strength in numbers. You can be skilled with swords and elixirs and charms, but at the end of the day no one can fight an army on their own. You come up against three or four, you might win. You come up against a whole pack alone and you are dog food. So the next time you want to cause animosity with your brethren—er, fellow Novices," realizing Dani

85

wasn't a brethren of any kind, he switched, "remember that someday you might have to rely on them. Is that clear?"

Both Andreas and Lester nodded.

"The celebration is over!" Ethan announced. "Gifted, please return to your homes with our thanks. Novices! To bed! Assemble at the bridge at Morning Lauds! Training begins!"

The party broke up. Dani stood by with Dink at her shoulder. Nathaniel and the other boy wandered over.

Nathaniel whistled. "What bee is in his bonnet?"

"Apparently, a Guardian died." The boy with Nathaniel said. "He got one of us here before the wraiths overran him. Guardians are pretty tight with one another. They took it hard." He waved at Dani. "Hi, I'm Bouden."

"Bo-den?" *What's with the names here?* "I'm Dani. Nice to meet you."

The Guardian interrupted them. "Time to go Novices!"

Ethan appeared at her side. "Thank you Kleos. I didn't think you'd be here."

The Guardian, Kleos, frowned. "I almost wasn't."

The gifted filtered by. Airlea peeled off, stopping by Ethan. "Ethan, are you coming to vespertide?"

Ethan's face twitched when she mentioned the word _vespertide_. "Not this evening, but soon Airlea."

"I look forward to it." She smiled lustfully in his direction, then gave Dani the stink eye before departing.

"You should go as well." Ethan told her. "Remember, tomorrow, Morning Lauds."

"What is that?"

"You'll hear six trumpet blasts. All Novices report to the Vale Bridge. You're the farthest so that means you have the farthest to go."

"Of course I do." She expected nothing less.

"The Novices will take a tour of Empyrean tomorrow, so be prepared. The person giving the tour is Elder Asaph, Head Gatekeeper."

"Awesome." Which it wasn't.

Waving to Nathaniel and two new boys, she headed downhill. Soon, she was away from the lights of Novice Village. She glanced back, feeling miles away in the gloom. With only a lantern to light her away, she immediately felt it:

Alone. She was well and truly alone. And if her encounter at the party was any indication, it wasn't going to get better.

The sun dipped low. Night was coming. "I hope this doesn't get any worse."

She was immediately answered by the distant rumble of thunder.

Dani took shelter in the pavilion. The roof kept off the massive downpour so she wasn't soaked to the bone, but with no walls, the wind gave her repeated little sprays of freezing water. She tucked herself under the pillow and warm blankets from Shea. They offered some shelter.

Empyrean was supposed to be a heavenly paradise. So far, it was hell. Darkness rolled in. With the one lantern, the rain lit up the trees and allowed her to see the forest dance menacingly around her.

That'll put me right to sleep, she said, lying flat on her back. *Like a Freddy Krueger lullaby.*

The rain continued. She could see the Citadel across the Vale. Lanterns shone brilliantly through the storm from the Keep and Numen homes. More fires burned in the Vale.

She finally settled back on her bed. She curled up to keep warm. Hopefully, sleep would come to her soon.

Then she heard it: *Rustle, rustle, rustle*; just above the pavilion.

She sat up. "Who's there?"

No answer, but more rustling.

"I said who's there!"

She got up from her bed, keeping the blanket close out of some strange hope it'd shield her. She crept forward. More rustling.

She walked to the edge of the pavilion and looked up.

No one. The courtyard was empty save for drizzled puddles. Beyond, the trees shifted in the rain, but there were no lurking visitors.

She let out a breath she didn't know she held and sagged against one of the supports. "What the hell is this? Ding-dong ditch?"

Something shot out of the trees. Dani screamed and flung herself to the floor. A flap of wings and a screech slashed past her ear as she fell on her shoulder. Scrambling up, she pressed herself against the nearest pillar and confronted her intruder:

A snow-white bird with a crown of feathers; the same freaking bird she'd seen in Los Angeles!

The bird landed on the floor at the base of her makeshift bed, folding back its wings. It cooed softly, turning with a click of its talons on the wood to stare at her. Dani took a few breaths to slow her heartbeat from heart-attack pace.

Then she shot to her feet. "What the hell? You scared me!"

It did nothing but stare.

"What are you doing here?" she asked, as if it would actually answer. "How did you get here?"

The bird clucked, or sort of did. Its hawk-like eyes never moved off her.

"Get out." She told it. The bird didn't move. "I said get out!"

She shooed at the bird, which did little to move it. After several tries, she gave up. She wasn't going to scare it off.

"This is where I sleep, bird-brain. Not you. So if you don't move, I am going to move you myself. Last warning."

The bird didn't move, but instead cocked its head to the side.

"Fine." She held up her hands, stepping cautiously towards it. "But if you nip me I will roast you into a turkey dinner."

She went to grab it, wrapping her hands around the wide, folded wings. The bird didn't bite or screech. When Dani tried to lift it, it didn't budge. She attempted to hoist the animal up, but it didn't come. Then she pulled with her back. Same result, except she heard a soft *crack!* The animal's talons dug into the wood to the point that they seared the floorboards apart as it held on.

She stared back up into its eyes. "What the—?"

The bird threw out its wings. Dani's hands shot off and something like a burst of wind exploded outward, sweeping her backward clean off her feet into one of the supports. She hit and stars exploded through her vision. Then she landed butt-first onto the floor. The pavilion shook with the force of the wind.

Dani groaned in pain, grabbing the back of her head, vision swimming. Her hair came loose from her tie, so when she looked up she could see the bird through her black locks.

It cocked its head to the side again, staring at her innocently.

"Okay," she murmured, slowly getting to her feet once more, "you are _so_ not a normal bird."

The white animal shifted, sidestepping back and forth. Despite throwing Dani across the room, it didn't look at all threatening.

"Nice demonic birdie. Please don't do that again."

The bird's head moved to the other side. It's beak snapped a little.

"Is that your bed?" she asked.

Amazingly, the bird dipped its head.

Did it just nod? "Was that a yes?"

Again, another head-dip.

"And I'm supposed to find somewhere else to sleep?"
It turned its head sideways. Once.
"Was that a no?"
It dipped its head.
"So...yes. I can still sleep here?"
Again, a dip of the head.
"Birds that understand English. Right. That's not weird at all."
She approached cautiously, retrieving her blanket from the floor.
She inched around to her pillow. The bird turned to follow her with its gaze.
Slowly, she lowered herself onto the floor. The white hawk turned to face
her as she lay down. She pulled the blanket up to her chin.
"Are you going to sleep?" she asked it.
The bird turned its head.
"Are you just going to stand there and watch me?"
It dipped its head.
"Awesome. That'll put me right to sleep."
Then she closed her eyes.

Chapter Twelve

An earth-shaking groan woke Dani. She shot straight up in bed. When she did, she came face to face with the hawk which kept its promise. It watched her.

She covered her ears when the second blow came.

"Jeez! What is that?" she demanded.

A third time and she climbed out of bed. The world glistened wet from the previous night's rainstorm. Sunlight streamed down from every dewdrop and the clear skies above Empyrean made the entire landscape so unreal she blinked to remember it wasn't. Unfortunately, the deafening blasts made it hard to appreciate.

A fourth sound issued from across the Vale. Trumpet blasts. A fifth sounded. She remembered as the sixth came what Ethan told her: she was supposed to meet Asaph at the bridge with the other Novices.

"Great. What the hell am I supposed to wear?" She looked down at her dingy, wrinkled jeans and shirt from LA. They were smeared with whatever putrid remnants wraiths left behind. She couldn't believe she slept in them.

Then she noticed a neat pile of brown clothes in one corner. She picked them up and examined them. They were similar to what Ethan wore. What had he called them? Raiments? There was a top, slacks, even boots and a belt. Someone had left her clothes while she was sleeping. That wasn't at all disturbing.

She looked around for whoever dropped them off. "Couldn't you have gotten them in a female cut?" she called out to no one.

———————————————

Dani redressed. She tucked the slacks into the calf-length boots and laced them up with the leather cords. The large leather belt synched her tunic in place. On her back was the same symbol of interlocking, fiery wheels that Ethan had emblazoned across his tunic. She used a tie to pull back her hair.

"Are you going to be here when I get back?" she asked the bird as she departed, which didn't move from its perch.

It dipped its head.

"Great. Stay frosty, cucumber."

She jogged. The boots were comfortable enough. She followed the path from last night, passing gifted houses on the way to the bridge. The countryside was beautiful. Gifted worked in the fields; tilling the ground with old tools or, in the case of a blue-skinned woman with long hair to her ankles, she sung and small vegetables grew in her garden. Dani kept up the pace until she crested the hill and saw the bridge.

Then frowned.

A large formation of brown-clad Novices stood with their aeries; two six-person rows for each. Behind them, black-clad Guardians waited. Dani could see Ethan and Kleos from last night among them. When Ethan saw her coming downhill, he frowned. Nathaniel, Bouden and Dink noticed her too, but very quickly turned their heads back forward.

Then she saw why. Or rather, she heard why.

"Each eclipse, one hundred and forty-four of the bravest and most courageous are selected by the will of God!" Cried Elder Asaph, standing in front of them in full military regalia. "Only those chosen to be the Earthborn, the only line of defense against the demonic—!"

He stopped mid-sentence as Dani trotted up. Every head turned her way. Most of the faces were stone-blank; Andreas and Lester sneered. The Guardians knew better than to speak, but some of the Novices whispered amongst themselves.

She ignored them, but Asaph did not.

"Quiet!" he barked. "Novice Daniella, where have you been? Formation began at thirty past Morning Lauds."

"What?"

Asaph's jaw tensed. His hand squeezed his sword hilt. "Morning Lauds are the call to rise. Did you not hear them?"

"You mean the trumpets? The entire universe could hear them."

A few Novices snickered. Even some of the Guardians smirked. Asaph quickly brought them to silence with a glare.

From the back, Kleos spoke up. "Elder Asaph, if I may. It is not yet thirty past Morning Lauds. The Novice is not late. We are early."

Dani gratefully nodded towards him. He slightly dipped his head back.

Asaph grunted, "We do not stand on ceremony, Guardian Kleos."

"Well, Elder, we do if that's the standard by which we judge our newest recruits."

His jaw clenched so tight he might break his teeth. Lip curled, he turned to her. "Get into formation."

"Where?"

"Anywhere!"

Dani glanced at the twelve neat columns. There wasn't a spot for her. Asaph returned to the front of the formation, waiting. His glare could have melted the sun.

She wanted to say something, but she knew that antagonizing Asaph would only lead to more trouble. She needed to avoid it where possible.

But...

Dani walked over and stood at the very front of Nathaniel's column. She was almost directly in front of Asaph, who snapped his sword in its scabbard a little out of annoyance.

Okay, maybe she wasn't avoiding it entirely.

"The five *arche*." Elder Castus said from his throne of assembled Elders. "Do any of you know them?"

They stood in rows before them, the basins of fire blazing between them. Everyone was silent. Everyone except Bouden, who raised his hand.

"Yes, Novice...?"

"Bouden. Bouden Reese."

"Yes Novice Bouden?"

"The five *arche* are the five powers of the Numen, sir...er, Elder. They're the five classical elements: air, fire, earth, water and the veil. Though they're spelled weird."

"Yes." Castus nodded. "Weapons, resources, life; they are all. And they retain their classical spelling. Who knows the origin of the word?"

Again, every Novice, including Dani, found reasons not to look the Elder in the eye. Again, Bouden raised his hand.

"Novice Bouden?"

"It's Greek. It means 'the first powers.' It's the same as the origin of the word archangel. That's why they call them," he paused, blushing, "why Numen call them 'arcs.'"

"Correct. There are five arcs, as you say. There is Fyre."

With a wave of his hand, flames coursed from the basin and formed into a ball above his hand. Every Novice gasped.

"Water."

From the pool, a line of water whipped into the air and flowed across the fire, extinguishing it.

"Erthe."

The stones underneath the Novices' feet moved.

"Aer."

Castus levitated from his throne above them.

"And the veil: the Aether."

He disappeared, appearing again before them on the ground.

"These were the gifts of our forbearers: the angels. We will train you to use them; to better the world, to heal yourselves, and most of all to defend yourself from our enemies: the demons. Who knows of our history?" His eyes settled on Bouden again. "Novice? I'm sure by now you know."

Everyone looked at Bouden. He swallowed hard.

"The angels," Bouden said slowly, "they were the first defenders of Earth. Seven of them were known as the Archangels: the first angels to use the *arche* in war. Gabriel, the messenger of Heaven, built Empyrean. They say he blew the horn that sounded the battle against the demonic and that he'll blow the trumpet on Judgment Day; the last day of battle."

"Very well done, Novice." Castus nodded. "The room in which you stand is the Throne Room. All matters of importance, all things concerning Empyrean and the gifted we protect, are discussed here for the Council of Elders to decide."

"You are Novices. In the coming months, you will train to become the best warrior we can forge you into. You must become the successor to the angels of old. The world depends upon you."

Every Novice was quiet. Some looked afraid. Others, like Andreas, seemed confident.

Dani raised her hand.

"Yes?"

"I thought the angels didn't fight the demons?"

Castus blinked, as if he didn't understand. "Excuse me?"

"I thought the angels didn't fight the demons. I thought they fought each other. That's how they died, right?"

Castus' face went blank. Elder Jeduthun was more serious, as if Dani had stepped over the line. But it was Asaph and Heman that told her she made a mistake. Their expressions were pure fury.

Asaph growled, "How dare you speak—!"

Castus held up a hand, silencing him. "Daniella, where did you hear such a tale?"

It took all of her not to look at Ethan. "I—I think I read it." She wasn't sure if she should mention Judah. "I'm not sure where."

Castus' eyes narrowed. Jeduthun took over. "Yes, well, she is right, of course. Our ancestors did go to war with one another. And within that war demonkind came into existence."

Asaph seemed to boil in his armor. "But not by the hand our forefather nor the allies of Heaven! Questioning such thing is heresy!"

Dani didn't know what heresy was, but she assumed she didn't want to do it.

"True." Jeduthun nodded. "Those who fought against Heaven were those that created the very demons we face today. Their war spawned the darkness, but it is their war we continue in order to prevent humanity from dying by that dark force."

Spurred on by Dani's question, another Novice asked, "But how did angels create demons?"

"It is a question that has haunted us for ages." Jeduthun told him. "We do not know."

Another asked, "Then what happened to the angels?"

More questions. Jeduthun and Castus held up their hands for silence. Asaph shouted them down. "Silence!" Very quickly, everyone stopped. "You are not a gathering of children. You will not act as such!"

"Yes, yes, all will be answered." Castus agreed, eyeing Dani. "But some questions are better left for later. For now, there is much to see. Elder Asaph will take you through the Keep. Please, follow him."

Asaph led them off, but a gentle hand on her arm stopped Dani.

"Novice Daniella?" Jeduthun's smile was nearly invisible under the grey/white beard. "May I have a word?"

Jeduthun and she walked in the opposite direction from the others. They descended the outside staircase from the Throne Room. Some gifted passed them on the way inside. They bowed. He returned it.

"Being an Elder must be a big deal." She observed.

The older man chuckled. "Aye, quite. How are you finding Empyrean, Daniella?"

"I've been here less than a day and I've already been accused of being evil. So, you know, wonderful." She sighed. "And it's Dani."

He shook his head. "I would believe that much of this would be a shock. Many of us do not know what to make of such strange tidings. You've adapted quite well."

She shrugged. "I adapt."

"Yes, I see that is true. Tell me, where did you honestly hear the story of the Angels of Heaven?"

Any doubt that Jeduthun believed her lie went out the window. "Judah told me."

Jeduthun nodded. "Yes, I suspected as much. Not many of our Novices meet the proprietor of the Hellfire Club. Of course, not many are as unique as you, are they Dani?"

"Is unique a bad thing?"

"In a society such as ours? Maybe. I have lived a very long time, Dani." He folded his arms into his white robes. "One of the many things you learn is that in any society, change is not readily accepted. The longer a system is in place, the harder it is to change."

"You accepted me." She pointed out. "You spoke on my behalf."

"True. Why do you believe I did such a thing?"

She never met Jeduthun and she wasn't one to believe anyone was good out of the kindness of their heart. Experience taught her that.

"I don't know."

Jeduthun grinned, finger to his lips in a pensive smile. "Dani, I believe that everyone should be judged for their merits. I believe everyone should be held accountable for their actions. And I believe, most of all, that everyone should be vigilant and watchful. Which do you believe is the reason I wanted you spared and allowed entry?"

She already knew that answer. "The last one."

He nodded. "Make no mistake: I can see good-hearts and good-intentions, but I have also seen darkness and death come from the well-intentioned. I would never allow that to come to my city."

"Are you saying I'm a threat?"

"I am saying you are something." He told her seriously. "There are many things about you that are a mystery. There are things at work in our world—things of darkness—that threaten us. In recent years, that darkness has grown. Many would believe you a sheep amongst the wolves. Others, however, would see you as a wolf in sheep's clothing."

"Which do you believe I am? Good or evil?"

"I believe you simply are. Good, evil, these are labels for something that cannot be explained." He bowed briefly, touching his first two fingers to his forehead. "I enjoyed speaking with you, Dani. I caution you against public displays of defiance in the future. And I would discourage sharing much of what Judah has with others."

He parted, walking off, silent in thought. She stared at his back. If she ever thought of Jeduthun as some kind of ally or friend, any hope of that was gone. After that conversation, she even believed that he was more dangerous than Asaph or Heman. Time would tell.

––––––––––––––––––––––––

Asaph led them through the Keep to the large library known as the Anthenaeum. Several stories tall and located on the cliffside of the Keep, it had one entire wall that was nothing but glass that overlooked the lush green Vale. Shelves packed with tomes filled the walls from top to bottom.

Walkways and stairs wove around the massive chamber to platforms and tables, which themselves were surrounded by more stacks. Elder Atid, the Athenaeum's chief Chronicler, pointed to the many grimoires around them as if each one were all as unique and important as the next.

Asaph then took them deep into the bowels of the Keep to the Forge; the very heart of Empyrean. This chamber was windowless and dark. A deep pit vaulted down to the center of the room. A massive, molten boulder of steel filled the center. Liquid metal flowed down from an opening above and melded into a hunk the size of a Volkswagen. Numen in thick raiments stood at large forges arranged around the sides, smithing red-hot pieces of steel into weapons.

And it wasn't just Numen there. Gifted wove between the forges, helping. Sylphs soared around the chamber, cooling the air. And when Dani looked closely, what looked like fiery lizards—elementals? salamanders?—sparked fire in the forges to keep them hot. Hammer strikes pinged in the dark followed by the hiss of new steel. Small rivers flowed past the forges in aqueducts, which the metalsmiths used to quench the hot steel.

"This is the Forge." Asaph said from the doorway. "Our armor, weapons, and fortifications are created here."

"What kind of steel is that?" someone asked.

"Adamant. Celestial iron ore. Almost every weapon a Numen carries is forged from adamant. Once forged, it becomes adamantine steel. It can cut through wood, rock, flesh, and demon."

Nathaniel raised his hand. "Where does it come from?"

"It is found throughout Creation; Empyrean, the other celestial cities, any place the angels of old touched. It is Heaven's gift. The first mines were found below us in Empyrean. Now our smiths scour the world to find new veins to make more weapons."

"Why make new ones?" Dani asked. "Aren't there used weapons left over if someone dies?"

Asaph regarded her coolly. "Novice, how would you suppose we recover the weapons we lose?"

"You get them when you go back for anyone killed."

Asaph didn't say anything to that. The other Novices shifted uncomfortably next to her.

"You mean you don't recover the bodies?" She asked.

"You make the assumption there are always bodies left."

He led them out. As they did, two Metalsmiths with a newly forged sword placed it into a box and two sylphs took it, floating across the room. They disappeared through a vault door on the other end of the Forge.

Dani quickly ran to catch up with the Novices as they made their way to the Gardens.

"It is not just arcs and adamantine that keep us alive." Asaph told them. "Many species of plants are used for healing balms and elixirs, spells, magical wards, even protective charms woven into your clothing."

The Gardens were massive, like a public park, but instead of children at play, rows of flora dominated the open space. Gifted tended to the plants around them while Numen in green—Naturals, someone called them—clipped and collected them into baskets.

Somehow, though the Gardens were in the open air, swaths had different atmospheres. One step and you went from a tropical paradise to a cool, wintry landscape. The air shimmered between them; some kind of magic border.

Dani spotted a familiar face. She grinned and walked over. "Hey."

Roxelana, the girl from yesterday, looked surprised to see her. Or rather, that she was talking to her. "Hello."

"Is this where you and Korë spend your time?" she spotted the little girl as well and waved.

"Yes." Roxelana blushed. "We have abilities that suit us here. The Numen allow us to come and tend the Gardens. In exchange, we retrieve herbs for remedies."

"It's good to see you. It's been a bit lonely, being the only girl."

Roxelana was about to say something when Dani heard voices behind her. The tone and voice were familiar. Stuff like "kinda hot" and "man, gifted are even hotter than girls down on earth" filtered over; and that was the nicer things.

When she glared over her shoulder, Andreas and his minions crowded together like the high school boys they were. Chosen or not, becoming a Numen didn't cure you of being a jerk.

"It's nothing." Roxelana looked away. "You learn to deal with it."

"Deal with it?" Dani snorted. "Who said you had to? Do you want me to say something to them?"

"No." Her purple eyes widened.

"Why?"

"They are Numen. I'm not."

"I'm Numen." She reminded her. "That means I can say something." She turned and walked over despite Roxelana's protests, glaring at them defiantly. "Hey! You jerks got something to say?"

Andreas smirked. "You mean other than what I said last night?"

"You shut up pretty fast when Kleos put you in your place."

97

"That's because you need someone to fight your battles for you."

Dani's anger flared. But before she could retort, Asaph interrupted them. "Is there a problem?"

"This," she searched for the word Ethan used once, "sarding jerk won't leave that girl Roxelana over there alone."

"Who?"

Dani pointed. When she did, Roxelana looked away. Asaph's jaw tensed. He turned his attention back to Dani.

"Allow me to remind you of something." He growled to her. "You are Numen. She is gifted. They are not the same."

"So?"

He snorted in revulsion, "The men around you are your brethren," and then he added with disgust, "whether they like it or not. Do you feel the need to gossip about them to their superiors?"

She couldn't believe it. "Gossip?"

"I believe you call it 'tattling' on Earth."

Dani's jaw almost dropped.

"Your concern is the mission; nothing else." Asaph reminded her. "Get in line or get out of the way."

He stalked off. Dani was almost able to walk away before Andreas, emboldened by the Elder, added, "You know, we're gonna have to slow down for you keep up with us."

She paused. "What's that supposed to mean?"

"It means that yesterday," he said, "I saw a friend of mine killed by a wraith. He died right in front of me. I picked up real quick on our mission. You haven't, so let me remind you: we're warriors. We're supposed to fight. You can't."

Both her hands balled into fists.

"Guardians like Kleos protect you because they know you can't stand on your own. Or maybe, there's another reason a bunch of men always take your side." Andreas's voice wasn't just full of scorn, but something much filthier. "Either way, you piss off everyone around you. You don't belong on the battlefield."

Andreas took a step forward and instinctively, she took one back. She hated that, especially when his stupid grin widened.

"Do me and everyone else a favor: leave. You like the gifted so much? Go be one of them; safe behind the walls real men protect."

She was about to hit him, but she spotted Asaph over his shoulder. He heard. He stood too close not to, but all he did was stand and watch.

Andreas rolled his eyes and shoved past her. Lester and his lackeys followed. Dani stared at the ground, hands clenched so hard they hurt.

Dink and Bouden both stood quiet. Neither of them looked at her. Only Nathaniel asked, "Are you okay? Do you—?"

"Don't." She turned away, falling in with the crowd. "It's fine."

That's what her mom always said, anyway. *It's fine.*

Chapter Thirteen

She returned to her own little corner of the world alone and pissed off. She would have killed for some gel inserts. The whole walking-everywhere-thing was getting old.

She noticed it as soon as she arrived. She wasn't sure what it was, but something was wrong. The air felt different; something tugging at the back of her mind, giving her the wiggens. What was it?

When she turned her attention to the pavilion, she discovered she wasn't alone.

He sat facing her, sitting cross-legged with his forearms resting on his knees. He wore black raiments, which were only a few shades darker than his skin. His scalp and face were cleanly shaven, his eyes were closed, but as she approached they opened calmly. His irises were like coals. She stood on the stones, not daring to go near him.

"Who are you?" she demanded.

He said nothing. He just stared at her from his seated position. His black clothes suggested he was a Guardian, but she didn't have a Guardian. At least, not yet. Was he the guy Ethan told her about?

She stepped gingerly up onto the plank floor. "Did Ethan send you? Are you supposed to be my Guardian?"

He frowned, but made no other sign that he heard her.

"Can you hear me? Are you deaf or something?" she waved at his face. It would be just her luck that her Guardian was deaf. Were deaf people allowed to be a Numen? She didn't have anything against it, but she wouldn't put it past fate to give her a deaf trainer.

"Um, look, if this is some kind of game or something," she said, getting a little irked, "I really don't want to play. Do you speak English? *Hablas español? Entiendes?*"

Nothing. He just stared. It was annoying.

She gave up, walking over. "Great, look, this has been real but I'm starving. So if you want to sit there, sit there. I don't really care."

Then he moved. In one fluid motion, he leveraged up and one leg swept over. Dani walked right into his range all pissed off. His foot connected with her ankle and sent her sprawling onto her chest. Hard.

She hit the floorplanks and a painful burst of air shot out of her lungs. She couldn't breathe! She doubled in pain. Then he was over her, pressing a long, adamantine knife to her neck. There wasn't anything stopping him from slashing her throat open. She was a dead, dead girl.

"My name is Mastema." He said in a deep, rumbling voice. "And, aye, I am your Guardian."

She sucked in painful lungfuls of air. For a full minute she thought she'd choke to death on nothing. Her lungs didn't work.

She shuddered each breath as she tried to speak. "You...could have just...said so..."

The man over her narrowed his eyes. He removed the knife from her throat and sheathed it into his belt, standing. "I wanted to see how you would react to my presence."

"Why?" she croaked, finally able to breathe.

"You can tell a lot about someone in the first fifteen seconds." He told her, returning to his seated position, forearms on the knees.

Now that she could breathe like a normal human being, Dani was furious. He attacked her as some kind of test? She got to her feet slowly, this time staying as far away from him as possible. "You were, what, experimenting?"

He nodded once, curtly.

"You knocked me down, put a knife to my throat, and all to what? See what I would do?"

"No. I stayed silent to see what you would do. I wanted to learn about the girl I am to train by how you reacted to my silence. I knocked you down to see if you would get back up."

"I really hate being referred to as girl; you know, since you didn't ask." She grumbled. Standing up straight and brushing herself off, she huffed. "So, what did you learn?"

"You stand naturally well, which will help you fight." Mastema said matter-of-factly. "You're innately cautious, which will help you more. You're left-handed which most won't expect and you are strong-willed."

She didn't know how to take that. "Um, thanks?"

"You are also impatient, reckless when you are angry and from what I observed today, you like to speak out of turn to embarrass your superiors. Most of those negate any good qualities you have."

"I—hey! I'm not reckless and I wasn't trying to embarrass Asaph!" she said defensively. "He treated me like garbage. It was unfair."

"There is your first mistake." Mastema closed his eyes. "You expect fairness. Fairness implies that life is just, which it is not." He frowned. "And his title is Elder. Elder Asaph. He is your superior."

"You want to drop the snotty attitude?" she demanded. "I'm not going to treat someone with respect who acts like a child."

"Then you will fail. Failure comes to those who believe they are entitled."

"Are you saying I have an entitlement problem?"

"Are you saying you do not?"

This guy is pissing me off. "What business is it of yours what I do?"

His eyes opened again, frown still in place. "It is my responsibility. I am your Guardian."

"Yeah, well, don't act so happy about it."

Mastema evaporated into thin air. Dani jumped back. She knew he was there. He went behind the veil. Ethan did it on Earth, so she knew she shouldn't freak out. Well, shouldn't and wouldn't weren't the same thing.

She tried to calm herself, looking for any sign of him. It was unnerving. "Where are you?"

Silence. *What's with this guy?*

"Come out and face me!" she yelled. "I know you're there!"

She felt a breeze and swung blindly, but hit nothing but air. She took a few steps back, hands up defensively.

"Coward!"

"Coward," a voice from nowhere said, "is a word for those who do not understand war."

Something knocked her foot out. She landed hard on her other knee, howling in pain. She tottered back to her feet, swinging again but he was gone.

"You will learn." Mastema said calmly.

"Learn what? How to cheat?"

"How to survive."

Something hit her across the face. It wasn't hard, but it stung. She grabbed her jaw, staggering. Mastema materialized in front of her. His face was pitiless. He looked at her with the same compassion a kid with a magnifying glass did to ants. And she was the ant.

Dani swung with a practiced punch. He blocked it easily and hit her again. He didn't attack. He stood there waiting. Bored.

"You have fire. That is good. You will need it." He said. "But understand this, Novice: happiness, fairness, cowardice are for those with lives different from ours. I am your Guardian. I am your protector, but I am also your tutelary. It is my responsibility to train you, to teach you the ways of our society, and to help you understand what is needed to survive. The first lesson is to learn your place. And right now, you do not understand where that is."

She glared defiantly at him between her fists. "Tutelary? What does that mean?"

"Teacher." He turned away unconcerned she'd try to hit him again. "I will teach you, if you will listen. But you need to learn how to listen."

She kept her fighting stance, wary of any more of his lessons. "And what if I decide not to listen to you?"

"You will die."

He said it so simply that Dani didn't doubt it was true. "What's your damage?"

"Damage?"

"What the hell knocked you off the sanity bus and left you in Crazytown?"

"In some ways I am the most sane man you will ever meet." He reached down and retrieved a long, hook-curved sword from the floor; not a scimitar like Asaph's, but one with a flared, spear-like tip. He belted it to his side. "My 'damage' however, is none of your concern. I will return tomorrow. Evening training with your Guardian is always after Vespers. That's the evening trumpets at eight."

"Eight? As in, eight o'clock at night?"

"Yes. Is that a problem?"

She shook her head. "Aren't I training during the day, too?"

"Yes."

"That's crazy. I'll be exhausted."

"You would prefer a more lenient schedule?"

"Yeah!" His face was a blank slate. It took her a moment to understand. "Which isn't going to happen, is it?"

"No."

"Excellent. Eight it is. You report to the entrance to the Vale," he pointed away from the gifted village, "at Morning Lauds."

He strode to the edge of the cliff and the pedestal that protruded from the cliffside. Without pausing, he fell over the side and as Dani watched, ascended into the sky.

"I'm really not going to like that guy." She said to herself.

"I'm sorry about before." Roxelana said.

She and Shea came after dusk with some niceties Dani had gone without: more blankets, curtains to hang for privacy, a delicious soup and bread that tasted of honey.

Roxelana also showed her a way to braid her long black hair that kept it close to her head. It was tight, but easier to manage than a ponytail.

"What?" Dani asked, finishing her soup while she sat on the pavilion floor, watching Korë play near the fountain. "You mean at the Gardens? It's fine. Asaph was the jerk."

"Elder Asaph." Roxelana corrected.

"Yeah. That's what people tell me."

"You have to understand," she said, "there is a barrier between Numen and gifted. Numen are the immortal warriors of Heaven."

"Really? They seem like a'bunch of *pendejos* to me."

Shea snorted soup out of his nose.

"Besides," Dani put her bowl down and went to Korë, "there's no excuse for that *idioto* Andreas and his friends." She sat next to Korë on the rim of the fountain.

"The Elders don't let Numen fraternize with gifted girls." Roxelana told her.

"Fraternize? Is that what you call some guy being a pig to you? Besides, you can't sell me on the idea Numen don't find outlets for their wandering eyes."

Roxelana and Shea exchanged a look.

"What?"

"There is," Shea began slowly, "an unspoken custom. Vespertide."

"Vespertide?" she recognized the word. "Airlea mentioned that the other night."

"She regularly attends." Roxelana blushed. "That may be why she doesn't like you."

"I never did anything to her."

"Airlea grew up in Empyrean." Shea explained, as if apologizing. "She has always fancied Numen men. She's especially taken with Ethan. In her mind, you are competition."

Dani *pffted*, ignoring that. "So what's vespertide?"

"It means 'evening.'" Shea told her. "It's code for—."

But Roxelana stopped him. "Dani we both like you. You're nicer than most Numen, but you live in a different world than us. There are rules and breaking them means losing the protection the Numen provide."

"You mean they'd kick you out for being friends with me?"

Shea sighed. "Maybe. Sometimes the Elders have looked the other way. But with you...?"

He didn't have to finish. "I'm not very well liked. I get the impression I'm going to deal with a lot of things other Numen aren't."

He shrugged as if to say, *that's true.*

Roxelana put on a brave face, "It doesn't mean we can't talk. Just...not a lot."

Great. Dani turned her attention back to the girl sitting next to her. Instead of a dry, empty fountain, there was now clear, fresh water filling the basin. From the center, water bubbled up like a spring.

Korë beamed proudly.

"That's how she shows affection." Roxelana stood, gathering up their things. "Apparently, she likes you."

"She never talks?"

Roxelana shook her head. "Not to anyone."

"Why?"

She came over and took the girl's hand. "Some of the gifted didn't grow up in Empyrean's safety. Korë was one. Her family was gifted with powers over nature. It made them a target."

"For what?"

"For the things you're training to kill." She gave the girl a sad smile. "She was the only one of her family to make it here."

Dani looked at the small blonde girl with sapphire eyes. She smiled playfully, brushing Dani's cheek affectionately before Roxelana and Shea took her home.

Ethan called the gifted magical refugees. Suddenly, Dani didn't think her life was so bad. She may have lost her mother in a way, but Korë lost everyone.

Chapter Fourteen

Dani lay awake, unable to sleep; strange since there wasn't a storm raging around her this time. The night air was cool and buzzed with insects. The sky overhead filled with thousands of stars, all of them gazing over the mountain paradise.

Her bird companion stood vigilant, regarding her with an almost-concerned look. Eventually, she got up and padded across the pavilion to the edge. Leaning on one of the pillars, she looked out across the Vale. She could see torchlights in the Keep. A column of them marched from the mouth of the Keep into the streets, snaking and winding their way through an illuminated city. On a whim, she slid on her boots and quickly trotted out of the Arn.

At this time of night, the Numen Citadel should have been asleep, but when she arrived across the Bridge, Numen filled the streets. They reverently watched a procession of Numen who silently marched down the street. She could see that those on the road had their hoods raised with black masks covering their lower faces. Everyone did.

On the road, six Guardians carried a casket past her.

"Funeral procession."

She jumped. Ethan appeared next to her.

He didn't look at Dani, but watched as another casket proceeded past.

"This is a funeral?" she asked. "For who?"

"For those who gave their lives."

Dani remembered that a Guardian died. Titus, wasn't it? But now two caskets passed and more were coming. "All of these people...?"

"Some within the past week." He said. "Others more recently. We lose soldiers frequently. Sometimes it's only a few. This time, it was three Powers, a Natural, and," he paused, biting back a change in his voice, "a Guardian."

She felt terrible for him. The look on his face...

"Were you close?"

He frowned, nodding. "Titus was a Guardian when I arrived. He's one of the few left I knew when I first came here."

"Ethan, I'm so sorry."

He shook his head. "We lose people, Dani. It's the nature of who we are."

"Asaph told me they rarely get bodies back." She realized how callous it was to say that. "I'm sorry. I shouldn't've—."

"It's okay." He told her. "You're right: we don't always get their bodies back. We didn't get Titus. Instead, we retrieve their weapons or we bury all their personal belongings. The funerals aren't for them. They're for us. It's our way to let go."

"Where are they taking them?"

Waving for her to follow, he whispered, "Let me show you. You should see it for yourself."

Together, they followed the procession as the crowd dispersed. Those involved in the burial bore their dead through the streets until they passed into the Fane, looping around the statue of Gabriel and through a vault in the back. Ethan led her after them down the stairs.

The stairwell was wide; sloped downward dozens of flights. Ethan removed a torch from the wall, using it to light the way. They continued down into the mountain and the air became cool and damp against her skin. A light below grew as they neared the bottom, which opened into the mouth of a much larger chamber. Dani gasped.

A cavern large enough to fit a stadium was hollowed out underneath the city. Dani stared up at the stalactites the size of eighteen-wheelers hanging from the ceiling. Staircases cut cleanly into the floor wove down in between largely formed stalagmites and rock faces, some hollowed for lights. Lanterns glowed sapphire blue here, filling the space bright enough that she could see the funeral processions. It was almost beautiful.

But dotted throughout the subterranean catacombs were dozens upon dozens of tombs. Vaults of the dead lined the walls. Even as she watched, six bearers lifted from the ground and hovered up to place a casket into its resting place a hundred feet above the floor.

"We call it the Hypogeum." He said. "It's the resting place of our dead."

The Guardians who brought Titus' casket took it to the far side of the necropolis, laying him to rest within one of the vaults. As they enclosed him, the bearers removed their hoods and masks. She recognized one of them as Mastema. He spoke in soft, low tones with another. Kleos. His face was worn with grief.

Mastema comforted him, placing a hand on his shoulder sympathetically. Suddenly, Dani didn't dislike her Guardian half as much. Maybe he wasn't all bad, though she was sure that opinion would change.

"The caves over there lead to the adamant mines," he pointed, "but there's something else I want to show you."

The two of them took a staircase to the right, descending a separate set of steps away from the crypts. The stairs arched towards a wall, bringing them down to the floor in front of a section of the cave that had no tombs. Instead, it was flat, as if sanded down perfectly smooth. Dani faced what at first she thought were cave drawings. The wall section was covered in them. The blue lanterns illuminated the etched symbols she recognized as the angelic language magically tattooed on her skin. Except now, each symbol was the size of her hand and the script flowed across the surface in a never-ending stream. It went several stories up. She couldn't even see the top in the dark.

"What is this?"

"Something you should know." Ethan told her. "You asked Elder Castus about the angels and the War in Heaven. I brought you here to give you answers. Some, at least."

She stared at the wall. "This is, what, some kind of prehistoric history textbook? Is it about the angels?"

He smirked, shrugging. "In a way, yes. It tells their story."

"Who wrote it?"

"They did."

She pressed her hand against the symbols. Someone etched them into the stone and the sheer edges felt like they weren't just cut but stamped into it. Man-made tools couldn't do that. As her hands brushed across them, she realized that despite being inside the cool cavern, they were warm to the touch; as if someone just put them there.

"I can't read it." She said.

"Not many can. Even the Elders have a hard time. They periodically come down here to try to decipher it." He gestured upward. "But from what we can tell, they've been here since the first Numen set foot in Empyrean."

"This has been here for centuries?"

"More like millennia, maybe longer." Ethan commented. "We don't know."

"What does it say?"

He stared up at the hieroglyphs, a serious tone in his voice. "It tells us that before humanity came into existence, God created the Heavens and the Earth. He formed the universe out of the void of chaos. It was peaceful; that the angels would sing and the whole universe heard it."

"Sing?"

"They called it the eternal song; the symphony of the world. Whatever angels were, they would sing in a way that created things—bring them into existence—and then bring them to God to show their love. Every time the text talks about angels, it describes them singing everything into creation. Songs even created emotions: love, peace, happiness, friendship."

"Sounds nice." Dani murmured.

"But the story says that something went wrong." He pointed to another part. "There was a War. It was the very first war; the first act of violence in Creation. It pitted brother and sister against one another; angel against angel. It says the War waged between two sides. One side followed Heaven. The other side refers to the adversary."

"The adversary?"

"The Devil. Satan. When he was an angel, he was referred to as Lucifer, the Bringer of the First Dawn."

"The Devil is an angel?"

"Was an angel." He corrected. "He was God's greatest warrior; one of His very first creations. This tells us that Lucifer became angry with God. We don't know why. We can't understand that part. What we do know is Lucifer rebelled and with him, a third of the angels. The defiance was so great it shocked Heaven. The angels in response rallied around another: Lucifer's younger brother, Michael."

"The Archangel Michael from the Bible?"

"Yes. The Elders don't know at this point what the inscription says, but from what they told us, the two sides fought. It describes a different song sung by the angels, one that had never been before: a battle hymn. We think it refers here to Lucifer. From what we can tell, he called Heaven into war. And from there, the two sides clashed."

He kept going. "They fought across Creation. They destroyed one another. But, in the end, Lucifer was defeated. Michael and the other archangels, including Gabriel, cast him and his army down. They slaughtered most of them, but lost so many of their own angels became nearly extinct."

"And then Lucifer was punished. This part," he pointed high, "says that Michael created a place of torment and fire. He called it Hell and threw Lucifer into it. It's there that Lucifer dwells, trapped within a realm of fire and brimstone for eternity."

Dani marveled at the wall. She shook her head. "So all of that Sunday school stuff—the Devil and demons and angels—all of it's true?"

He shrugged, nodding. "Mostly. Think of religions like the coloring books of the actual story. How accurate your particular coloring book is leaves a wide margin of error."

"And demons? They come from Hell? Are they Lucifer's?"

"I've heard people say yes. They say Lucifer created them to torment humanity because we're God's chosen. Others think that the angels' war was so terrible that it sprung demonkind into existence from all the bloodshed and death."

"What do you think?"

"Me? I think they're monsters. It doesn't matter where they come from, but," he shrugged, glancing up at the wall, "if I had to guess I would say they come from us."

"Us?"

"Before I joined the Numen, people used the word 'demon' as a metaphor for the worst parts of ourselves; our personal demons. I think that's closer to the truth than anything else. Demons are manifestations created to be our worst fears and desires." He shrugged. "But I could be wrong."

Our worst fears and desires manifested into reality. Dani thought about the wraiths. It didn't seem far off.

"So what does the rest of it tell us?" she asked, indicating the wall. "What happened to the angels?"

"That's the part of the text that's most unclear. The angels wrote in a language that's never been fully spoken. We only know parts from what we've been able to gather."

"So you know some of it?"

"We know this: it speaks of God's anger. We're unsure of who He was angry with, but we do know He brought down some kind of punishment. And then," he stepped over, pointing, "they left."

"Left?"

He shrugged. "Like I said, this doesn't have all the answers. It says the angels left Earth, or left our reality, or something like that. Whatever it means, they disappeared. And before they left, they sang one last song."

"Song?"

"I told you: the angels sang. It was like their...I don't know...way of interacting with the world. Before they departed, they gathered together and sang. And that," he pointed, "is supposedly what made this. This entire story is identical to walls in the other six celestial cities. It appears in every single one. They called this record of the war the Song of Sacrifice. The angels sang a song of mourning over those they killed in their war. All of Creation wept. The inscription says this is how the emotion of grief was created. And inscribed here," he pointed to rows of list-like glyphs, "are the names of every angel who died. It counts the dead and stands as a monument of remembrance. It's why we built the Hypogeum around it. It is our place of remembrance."

"Then what happened?" she asked, trying to take it all in. "The angels just disappeared?"

"We haven't heard from them since. Not directly, anyway. Some have reported sightings of them over the centuries. They make appearances in people's lives and stories, but there's no proof they're real. I've never seen one and neither has anyone I know."

"And they allowed humanity to cope with the fallout from their war? Demons. Numen. We're inheriting their crap?"

"They couldn't deal with what they did. So that leaves it up to us."

Dani looked up at it one last time. She pointed to one section of wall, a part that stood on its own, "And that?"

"Prophecies, myths, legends; stuff the Elder Council hasn't shared much about. I wouldn't worry about that part much." But that was all he said about it. "So what do you think?"

She leaned against a large stone protruding at the edge of the landing. She couldn't understand it. When she looked up at the text, this massive record they could barely understand, she shook her head.

"This...this tells me almost nothing."

"Welcome to our world. Not exactly what you were expecting?" Ethan asked, leaning against the wall across from her. "You were expecting a holy mission? Guidance? Purpose? Destiny?"

"A little, yeah."

"I felt the same way when I found out. The gifted and others think our ancestors were some kind of angelic superheroes out to save the world; dying to protect us by going down in flames of glory. In the end," he look up over his shoulder at the Song, "they were nothing more than cowards who ran away."

They were silent for a long time. Dani stared at the wall, as if expecting to see something—anything—that might make Ethan's story add up. One angel became angry, fought his brothers and sisters, and effed up Creation. And then those that survived were so shell-shocked they left reality broken and infested with demons.

"It's not exactly the story you tell all the little Numen boys before bedtime." She grumbled.

"Still want to be a Numen? Because this," he thumbed over his shoulder, "is what we call our great forefathers."

"Do I have a choice?"

He shrugged once, non-committally. "Who's to say? You break all kinds of rules we used to think were unbreakable."

"Would you offer that to anyone else?"

111

"Would you be insulted if I said no?"

"A little." But looking at it again, she asked herself: *do I really want this?* So far she'd been accused of being a distraction to the entire male population of Empyrean, a weak link and a threat. And that was just the first day!

She sighed. "It's not like I have anywhere else to go."

"It's going to be difficult for you here."

"It's going to be difficult anywhere. At least here, people aren't trying to eat me alive."

The smallest of smiles tugged at the corners of Ethan's mouth. "Well, that's debatable. You've met the Elders."

"Do you think I should stay?"

"Do you care what I think?"

The question surprised her. Of course, 'no' was the obvious answer, but as she looked at him she sensed something much different about him; more so than the others. Jeduthun was kind, but pragmatic. Kleos stood up for her but who knew why? Most of her fellow Novices either hated her, didn't want to be associated with her, or at best wanted to help her with no way how. And then there was Mastema: a jerk.

But Ethan was different. He saved her life and brought her to Empyrean. Now he confided in her. Could she rely on him? She didn't know yet.

She blushed. "I think I should head back. I imagine being out after curfew is bad. Is there a curfew?"

"Not necessarily, but no Numen dared to question authority here before."

"Not one?"

"That surprises you?"

No, it didn't.

Chapter Fifteen

The night was warm as Ethan walked her back. It was nice to have company. He had a very serious expression almost all the time; like resting brooding face. But he didn't talk much about himself like most boys. In fact, most of his questions were about Dani.

"You never met your dad?" he asked.

"No." she shook her head. "He left before I was born. It's just been me and my mom all my life."

"Left? He just left?"

"Yeah. My mom raised me. We moved around a lot. When I was younger, I didn't notice that every time we moved to a new place, it was smaller than the one before. We were in an apartment when I was thirteen and lost that place last year when we couldn't pay. Then we moved in with Ricky. And after that...well, I'm here." She sighed and shook her head. "I never really thought much about my dad. Mom never talked about him. To tell the truth, I assumed I was mistake."

"A mistake?"

"She always acted as if I wasn't planned. If I did have another parent, I'm not sure he planned on being a father. But I'm just guessing."

"I'm sorry to hear that."

She shrugged, hugging herself. "It wasn't all bad. I have this necklace—well, used to have this necklace—that mom gave me. Real simple. Nothing special. She gave it to me when I was young. It sort of represented who she was before everything went downhill. I used to wear it all the time like I hoped she'd get better." She shrugged. "Doesn't matter now. She didn't. I had to leave it. It's gone."

Like her mom. Like her old life. Gone.

He nodded solemnly and then, for the first time, shared something. "I never knew my parents. They both died when I was young. I lived with my uncle for a while. As soon as I was seventeen, I moved out."

"Where?"

"Alaska, if you can believe it."

"*Por el amor de Dios*, why?"

He shrugged. "It was the Eighties. Seemed like the thing to do."

It was crazy to think that, despite looking a little older than her, Ethan was over thirty years old. Forty or fifty, if she did her math right.

"Anyway, I worked on a boat for a guy my uncle knew. We were at sea when it happened."

"Happened?"

113

"The solar eclipse. My Guardian took me off the ship in the middle of a storm. I guess everyone assumed I fell overboard and drown." He paused, eyes up to the sky in thought. "I always wondered if I hadn't been where the solar eclipse happened, would I have still become a Numen? Was it fate?"

He shrugged and kept going, walking her back to the pavilion. He stopped on the threshold.

"You didn't have to walk me, you know." She said. "I would have been fine without an escort."

"Who said I thought you needed one? Maybe I just wanted to."

Was he hitting on her? She didn't mind it, considering he was cute, resting brooding face or not. His cherub curls were endearing. He didn't have to be tall and imposing to be good looking.

"And though I didn't have to walk you, it made me feel better."

"Why's that?"

His frown deepened. "Dani, you're the only woman in this city; only Numen one, anyway. People will resent that. You're competition."

Competition. Gifted girls found her competition. Numen men found her competition. *Who said I want to compete with anyone?*

The mood broken, she frowned, too. "I thought all the Novices are supposed to be trained to fight as one? A family or something?"

"If you believe that, you're more naïve than I took you for."

Suddenly, Ethan wasn't a welcomed presence because of the inconvenient truth. "Good night Ethan. Thank you for the walk."

"You're welcome. Don't forget to be at the Vale tomorrow. It'll be," he devilishly smiled, "interesting." He bowed in that weird, formal way every Numen did—touching two fingers to his forehead—and then he departed.

Her bird waited by the bed; its judgey stare on her as she lay down, pulling the covers up to her chin.

"Nothing happened." She told it. "He just walked me home."

The bird cocked its head sideways, the stare much more intense.

"Don't look at me in that tone of voice."

Then she passed out.

Morning came. She snapped awake, shielding her eyes from the bright morning light. Her avian protector looked up from its perch as if to say *tisk-tisk, you were out late last night with a boy.*

"Don't judge me, Iago. I will flambé you Cajun-style."

A new set of brown raiments lay in a neat pile next to her. It was slightly creepy someone left her clothes, but it was also nice to have a fresh set. Was this an everyday thing? Who brought them? Elves?

Were there elves? She'd seen stranger things here.

She changed clothes, tied back her hair like Roxelana showed her, and laced her boots. It was odd, but she didn't hear the trumpets of Morning Lauds. Weren't they supposed to be sounded at six?

Unless they already did and I slept through them, she thought. *If I did that then—*

"Oh no!"

Bolting up, boots on, she ran across the dirty square and sprinted up the path. At first heading for the bridge, she remembered that they were supposed to meet at the entrance to the Vale, wherever that was. She found an off-shoot path that led away from the cliffs and scampered up it at a dead sprint. The path led uphill. As she crested, she could see the entrance to the Vale.

She'd never been here, but the sight wasn't as impressive as some of the other places in Empyrean. It was a simple open patch of grass without much fanfare. There were twelve columns arranged around it, with the usual overgrowth of vines and a single archway at the edge of the sheer cliff. Beyond it: nothing.

And standing in twelve neat groups were the other Novices. Late in two days. She cursed to herself and ran to join them.

Elder Heman stood at the front. Everyone turned as she huffed up, taking her place at the back of the nearest aerie. But her late arrival hadn't gone unnoticed.

"Novice Daniella!" Heman barked. The Novices in front of her parted and she came face to face with him. "Front and center!"

"Thanks guys." She mumbled, giving them ugly looks as she walked between them. Dani stopped in front of him. "Yes?"

"Yes, Elder." He corrected.

"Yes...Elder?" She bit her tongue. No use pissing him off.

"You are late, Novice."

"I woke up late."

"Is that an excuse or just stating a fact?"

She bit her tongue harder. "That's what happened. I was up late last night."

"Doing what?"

"I couldn't sleep."

"So you're late and up past curfew."

"There's a curfew? You all need to be clearer about that."

She said it before she thought about it. A few boys behind her giggled. Heman's glare twitched.

"Novice Daniella, I would expect someone who is about to take on the mantle of Heaven's warrior to be more serious." He said with unveiled anger. "I would expect someone who cares for their brethren to take that responsibility in a way befitting the destiny given to them. As I can see, that is too much to expect from you."

"It is apparent that you care very little for those you entrust with your protection and would likewise rely on you to protect them. Only someone as infantile as to show up late in two days would rely on others to fight their battles for them." He paced around, disregarding her. He spoke to the rest of the Novices. "Each of you accepted your place amongst us. Each of you is to be a guardian to humanity; gifted and mundani. Weakness has no place amongst you. Each of you," he proclaimed, "can only be as strong as the man on your left and right. Weakness won't just divide. It will kill." He turned back to Dani. "I can see you are not of the caliber as the rest of these men."

Her hands squeezed so tight she felt like the blood vessels might pop. They burned.

Heman turned away from her. "Get back in line, Novice."

Dismissed, she had a hard time not stomping back to her place. She wouldn't let this go, but this wasn't the time to make a stand.

"Weakness, strife, disloyalty; these are the means by which any army is broken. Your brothers are your strength. The man beside you is the one you must trust. Break that trust and you will break on the field of battle. You are strong. Rely on that strength."

He pointed to the Vale and the Citadel beyond.

"This is your first lesson. You will learn to use your gifts and work together. Those who learn survive."

Heman floated from the ground into the air. He hovered over them, speaking loudly.

"You are your worst enemy; your doubts, your fears. Those will kill you faster than a demon ever will. You must put that fear aside to become what you will be."

Heman waved with his hand. Just beyond the archway, the top edge of the cliff collapsed in upon itself. The stones fell and reformed, and where there had been a simple rock-face before was now the entrance to a switchback leading down the cliff into the valley.

"Your task is simple: survive." He told them. "To the west and the setting sun is the Vale Bridge and beyond that, the falls where the Crystalline River ends. Another entrance to the Vale into the Citadel lies on the other side of the river. Those that work together survive. Those that do not will die. This will not be just a trek into the woods. The Vale has its own perils. You have until the sun sets in the west over the river gate."

"Or what?" someone asked.

Heman's smile looked like he smelled the worse stench imaginable. "You do not want to be in the forest at night." Summoned out of thin air or hidden in the veil, dozens of crates appeared next to the Vale entrance, each one a different size and shape. "We would not send you unarmed. Your Guardian chose a weapon for you. Retrieve it. The box will only open by your hand."

Heman disappeared. The Novices rushed forward to grab a box. As Heman promised, they only opened for the right person. Some tried for the biggest boxes first, but they wouldn't open for them. Once someone found theirs, the lock came apart. There were dozens: silvery-bladed swords, axes, spears. Dink had a bow; Nathaniel a large broadsword. Andreas hefted a gigantic battle-axe from one of the largest crates. Forged from adamantine, each one shone in the sunlight.

In the mayhem, Dani couldn't get near a crate. It was like Christmas, but secret Santa played a practical joke on her. Novices tossed only empty containers her way. Once or twice she got her hands on a crate but it wouldn't open. It wasn't until the others were armed that she got in and searched through what was left. It was humiliating. Most were empty.

She still scoured the pile and heard laughing. Andreas, large axe over his shoulder, watched in amusement. She gave him a look that reflected a particular finger.

She finally found one unopened container. It was small, maybe a little bigger than a shoebox. Inside, she discovered a double-edged dagger in a sheath as long as her forearm from tip to pommel. In comparison to the other weapons, it wasn't much. She tucked it onto her belt.

Andreas assumed command. "Alright! We stay as a single group! Strength in numbers! We head down to the shores to the river and follow it. Straight shot. Any questions?"

She couldn't help it. Her hand went up.

"Questions that actually matter?" he clarified.

"Hey! *Idioto,*" she called from the back, "don't you think that following the river is just a tad bit too easy?"

A hundred and forty-four pair of eyes turned to look at her. Dani folded her arms in defiance.

"You got something to say?" Andreas demanded.

"Other than that's the stupidest plan I've ever heard of? Not really." She stared him down. "They gave us weapons and told us that the jungle down there is dangerous. Why? Just so we walk down to the river and follow it? You expect that to work?"

"Do you have a better plan?"

"Instead of blindly plunging into the Hundred Acre Wood from Hell without a real one? Yeah. How about we take time, use our vantage point here, and make a real plan."

Andreas scowled. "You know, we can sit here all day and bicker like a bunch of girls, but we're burning daylight. You heard Elder Heman: we don't want to be in there at night. So I'm going to ignore you and hope everyone else is smart enough to do the same." He started down the slope. "Anyone else coming or are you staying behind with this freak?"

Novices followed. Dink gave her a sad smile and followed with Bouden. Even Nathaniel didn't stay too long.

She took one last look at the Vale from the top, glancing upriver at the Dalles; the supposed place disgraced Numen fled to. Just below it, smoke trails billowed from the trees.

She followed. Strength in numbers. How long would that strength last?

The forest was unbelievably green. It had a canopy twelve stories up with tree trunks so thick you could drive a truck through them. Branches with leaves as broad as dinner plates cast green hues and sporadic sunbursts down around them. The forest was wet and mossy with trunks dark shades of brown. Boulders the size of houses and tree roots like monstrous snakes made the going slow. It quickly became obvious this wasn't going to be a simple hike.

Struggling to keep up the pace, those with the largest weapons tired out before they even got out of sight of the cliffs. The swords and spears weren't heavy unless you had to carry them for a while. And climbing made things worse. Even Dink struggled with his bow and quiver. Only about an hour or two in and this was a nightmare.

Andreas continued to lead but Dani could see their straight shot to the river wasn't so straight. They could hear it, but where the hell was it? Sound bounced off the trees, making it impossible to get a good direction.

"Are we lost?" Bouden asked, wiping his forehead matted with hair and sweat. He carried a single-edged saber, the scabbard catching on almost everything.

"No." Andreas said shortly, but looked around worriedly to get his bearings. "We should be near it."

"Should be?" Dani grumbled. She was doing better than most, but if anything bigger than a pigeon came their way she was done for. "Maybe we should have studied the forest before we started?"

Andreas scowled at her and pointed. "The sound is coming from this way. We'll get there soon."

And then more walking. A lot more. It was ungodly muggy. The Novices sweated, even with the enchanted raiments supposedly designed to keep them cool. Dani put up her hood. It gave some relief, at least.

Nathaniel sidled up beside her. "Nice braids. New look?"

She glared. "Shut up."

"How's it going?"

"How do you think it's going? I'm a leper."

"I think your skin is flawless."

"Shut up, Nate." She punched him in the shoulder. "How's it hanging with the boy band?"

"My aerie? Not bad. Andreas is...well..."

"A piece of *mierda* on rye?"

He laughed. "A diarrhea sandwich for sure, but he's alright."

She shook her head sadly. "You and your boys club."

"What does that mean?"

She didn't get a chance to answer. A Novice shuffled past her, but only a few steps ahead something hit him. He shot sideways off the ground and into a tree, pinned there. The force of the collision knocked him out. Behind her, Dani heard another yelp and a Novice fell out of sight.

"What the hell was that?" Andreas demanded, axe up.

Dink drew an arrow into his bow as if he knew what to do with it. Nathaniel's sword came up clumsily. Dani's knife was out, though she felt useless with such a small weapon.

Another cry. A Novice landed against a rock; out cold.

"Where are they coming fr—*uuhhhh!*" Someone yelled, and then he was gone.

The Novice on the tree was pinned to the trunk by thin, silvery cables no wider than a necklace chains; chains that thin shouldn't be able to hold him, but then again, they were made from the same silver substance as their weapons. Adamantine. The stuff was unbreakable.

She heard a whipping sound and watched as an arrow shot from the woods, struck another Novice and exploded into chains that bound him shoulder to ankles. He fell to the ground and struck his head.

They came through the trees. She couldn't see them clearly, but they fired arrows while in motion. One second they were there, then the next they were gone. Another arrow, another whip of adamantine cables, and another Novice was down.

"Archers!" she warned.

"Run!" Andreas screamed, taking off.

Everyone ran, fleeing the same way. And then arrows came from every direction.

It was a trap.

Dani grabbed Nathaniel and pulled him back. Instead of running with the group, they darted another way. She heard a *thunk* as an arrow bounced off the tree near them. The whipping chains sliced past. She ducked, looking back. Nearly a dozen Novices lay prone or pinned at the mercy of whatever shot at them. They couldn't leave them.

But a near miss forced her to abandon the idea. Helpless, she and Nathaniel took off.

More Novices hit the dirt or pinned to rocks and trees. Lester catapulted off his feet and was lashed upside down by his ankles against a trunk. He flailed, trying to free himself, screaming. A second shot got his upper body and there he hung.

Dink was ahead with Bouden. An arrow lanced out of the forest and latched Bouden's feet. He went down hard.

"Bouden!" Dani ran for him, even as another arrow whistled past. She slid across to him. "Bouden! You okay?"

"I can't get loose!" he failed to undo the chain. "It's got me hooked!"

Dani tried to cut the bindings. Unfortunately, unbreakable steel against unbreakable steel didn't work very well.

"We need to get him out!" Dani warned. "Dink! Use your bow!"

"And do what?"

"Shoot!"

"At what?"

"At anything! Buy us time!"

Dink drew an arrow, aimed and fired. The bolt sung through the trees. He fired again, this time in a different direction. Four arrows in random spacing, just hoping to throw off their attackers. His hand shook but he tried to keep steady.

Dani's fingers flew across the metal rope. It was designed with ball-bearings on the end that wrapped tightly on impact. Take one of them to the head and it was lights out. Or worse.

She got them loose as Dink let fly two more arrows. She heard a startled scream. He surprised someone. Dani pulled Bouden's feet loose as quickly as she could and when he was clear, he scrambled up.

"We got to move!" Nathaniel warned. "Now!"

"Where?"

They heard clashing blades and screams in the distance.

Bouden pointed. "Everyone ran that way!"

"So we don't run that way!" Dani was up, sprinting the other direction. "Come on!"

They joined in behind.

They ran towards the cliff she could see through the trees. Only a few dozen yards and Dani leapt over a large stone to crouch down. The three boys hid beside her, pressing their backs against the boulder.

"What the hell are we doing?" Dink demanded. "We should be running for our lives!"

"Shh!" She warned. "Those things are still out there!"

Quieter, he hissed. "Yeah! That's what I'm saying!"

"No, no, no!" She told them. "Whatever they are, I think there was more than one and," she glanced over the boulder, "I think they wanted everyone to run in the same direction. They attacked from one side and got everybody to stampede. They wanted to run us down."

Bouden groaned and shook his head. "We used to do that in Wyoming. It's how you herd cattle: keep them moving in one direction. They're easier to control that way."

Dani peeked again. She could see Lester still pinned to a tree. He was very much alive and conscious, but he couldn't free himself.

He started shouting. "Help me! Somebody help me!"

"Oh God." Nathaniel whimpered. "He's going to get himself killed!"

"Be quiet. I hear someone."

Something approached; moving fast. The sound of footfalls grew louder.

Lester screamed again. "Help me! Somebody! I can't get down!"

Dani heard what sounded not like footfalls, but horse hooves; someone on horseback. When she looked, she spotted them galloping up through the underbrush; silver breastplate and helm with faceguards down, obscuring the rider's face. He carried a bow and quiver as he spurred his horse out into the open in front of Lester. He was terrifying.

Especially since he wasn't riding a horse, but in fact was a horse. Or, rather, was half-horse.

When he came into the clearing, Dani saw that where a horse neck should start, the rider's upper body began. He galloped out, completely man from the waist up and equine from the waist down. He cantered around, aiming his bow in long and wide sweeps before targeting Lester.

His eyes widened. "Oh God! Don't kill me! I'm not with them! I swear!"

The man cantered closer, bow still aimed. From underneath the helm, he spoke in a deep voice. "You wear the brown of a Novice."

"I'm not! They forced me to come with them!"

Dani snorted in disgust. *Coward.* For all the crap he and Andreas gave her about being a man, he was screaming like a baby.

Nathaniel hissed. "Is that a...a centaur?"

The warrior turned in their direction. Everyone hunched out of sight. Apparently, centaurs had pretty good hearing. When they looked again, he lowered his bow, resheathed his arrow and drew a sword.

Lester screamed louder.

Dani couldn't just watch. Lester was a jerk, but he didn't deserve to die. She drew her knife and prepared to jump the rock. Maybe the four of them could take him on if they surprised him. It was a long way to run and he had a bow, but they had to try.

Bouden clamped a hand down on her shoulder. "Don't."

"He's going to kill him!"

"No, he won't. Trust me."

The centaur *clop-clop-clopped* closer to Lester. He screamed louder as the equine warrior raised his blade, but instead of decapitating him, he smashed the pommel down on Lester's temple. He went limp; unconscious, but very much alive.

"Hellfires, I hate Novices." The centaur snorted, then turned and whistled loudly. Other whistles came in response. To Lester's unconscious body, he grunted, "Hopefully, your companions present a more worthy challenge."

Two more centaurs in armor galloped into the clearing. They carried their own weapons—bows and quivers and swords so long they could cut down one of the trees. They galloped to Lester, undid the bindings, and lowered him down.

Dani whispered to Bouden. "How did you know?"

"They're Hellions." He explained, as if that actually explained anything.

"Hellions?"

"Non-human warriors that fight demons." He clarified. "I read some scrolls in Novice Village that say they're part of our army. They live all over the world. I heard rumors there are villages in the Vale; centaurs, other creatures, things that live here as opposed to the Hills."

Dani remembered the smoke signals she saw.

"Anyway, Hellions aren't Numen, but fight demons. Most of them are stationed on the frontlines in Hell. Hence the nickname. They fight there while we fight on Earth."

"So they're on our side?"

"Supposedly."

"Then what the hell is going on?"

"It's a test." Nathaniel said quietly, watching. "Don't you get it? They're supposed to capture us. It's a game to see who can make to the end of the river."

"So we're not in danger?"

"I didn't say that."

The two centaurs got Lester down and draped him over one's back. The pair galloped off while the original man-horse stayed.

"We need to find out what's going on." Dani said to them.

Dink shook his head. "You want to go over there and ask him? Be my guest."

"Actually, I was thinking of bringing him to us." She held up the cords that she took from Bouden's feet. "And I got an idea."

The centaur notched an arrow onto the bow; looking around, listening. Which meant when Dani stepped from hiding, she was easy to spot.

"Hey, Mr. Ed!" she called.

The centaur raised its bow and fired. Dani barely dodged when she flung herself sideways. The arrow passed, exploding into whipping chains that thankfully missed her.

Then she was up and running.

The centaur took off after her. It leapt a fallen log, trying to turn itself onto a path to intercept. It wasn't a fool. It knew where she was going, which she, of course, wanted.

As it galloped between two small trees to cut her off, it raised its bow to fire. Unfortunately, it didn't see the adamantine chain they suspended between the saplings at knee-height. The centaur hit it at full gallop and its front feet shot out from under it. The human upper body went face first into the dirt. Dani could hear the metal clang as the helmet connected with a rock. The centaur cried out in a mix of human and horse bray. Then it rolled, tumbling over itself to land on its side.

Nathaniel and Bouden dropped out of hiding, swords raised. They didn't know how to use them, but hopefully the centaur didn't know that.

Dink stood at the top of a rock, bow and arrow aimed. When the centaur went for its sword, he raised his weapon. "Uh, uh, uh Secretariat! I'll cut those derby-winner chances short if you go for it."

Whether it understood the insult or not, the centaur paused, fingertips at the sword hilt. It regarded them with tense unease.

"Take the sword and throw it away."

It did what he asked, removing the nearly five-foot-long blade and tossing it aside.

Dani trudged downhill, hands on her hips. "Hi. We'd like to talk."

Using two captured adamantine chains as restraints, they tied his hands to one front leg and removed his helmet. A large, brown beard dominated his face. His olive brown skin and hair were long and untamed. Underneath his armor they could see a normal human body, with the exception of his lower-half going equine. His face seemed a bit distorted; larger, with bigger teeth and jowls than a human's. His head was twice the size, too, but he was still handsome.

Once restrained, Dani took the lead. "I'm Dani. This is Dink, Nathaniel, and Bouden. We will be your captors today."

"I will not tell you where they took your friends." He warned in his deep, gravelly voice.

"Well, first off, they're not my friends," Dani told him, "but I think maybe you should tell us anyway since we're the ones with weapons."

"I made a vow." He said formally. "I accept death."

"Bully for you. We'd still like to know where you took them."

He didn't say anything.

Bouden cut in, lowering his weapon, "You're a Hellion, right? A non-human celestial warrior?"

The fact he knew that surprised the centaur. "I made my vows." *Was that a yes?*

"Okay, so we're on the same team." Bouden nodded eagerly, getting somewhere. "You won't tell us where you took the others because I'm guessing you're under orders not to, but I assume since we both work for Empyrean, that means they're safe. Can you at least tell us that?"

The centaur's eyes flicked quickly around the group, unsure, but he nodded slowly.

"Can you tell us your name?" Dani asked.

The centaur's eyes met hers. They were big, brown and afraid. He was brave, but he was fearful. "Nessus."

"Nice to meet you." She crouched down next to him. "So, this is a test, which means that you aren't going to kill us. It's sort of like capture the flag. Am I right?"

"I do not know of what you speak."

"It's a game. Not important. What's important is if the centaurs aren't going to kill us, we aren't going to kill you. Are we, guys?"

Everyone nodded.

"What we want to know is what else is out there," she waved to the woods, "and what direction we go to get to the river. Specifically, we'd like to know where the end is. Do you know?"

He shook his head.

"Are you lying to me?"

He shook his head again.

"How do I know that's the truth?"

"For it is. Our herds only patrol the centaur lands of the upper river." He explained. "We do not stray far from our villages south or into the Hills of the gifted. Once Novices are beyond our border, our duty ends. It ensures that if we are captured, which has not happened in many generations, we cannot reveal anything else."

Many generations. These guys had been doing this awhile. "How far do the centaurs go?"

"Only as far as the tall, fallen tree that bridges the river bend. Most cross the river there. We cannot."

"He could be lying." Nathaniel said.

"I have no reason to lie. My people's duty is to protect the river. No more and no less."

He had a point. A large tree that bridged the river; that was their target. "Are you sure you don't know what's across it?"

"I only hear the roars of the beast."

Roars of the beast. Awesome. "Thank you Nessus the Centaur."

"No thanks are required, Dani the Novice." He said formally. "I will die here. We will not meet again."

125

"Die? We aren't going to kill you. As soon as we leave, you can go. Though," she held up the quiver of arrows, "we're going to keep these." She tossed them to Dink.

He shook his head. "My leg will not allow me to stand."

There were deep gashes and ripped skin where his front legs hit the adamantine chain. She could see bone. What was it they said about horses with broken legs?

"Can't the others come get you?"

"The forest is wide. My fellow warriors may be too far away."

"Can't you whistle like you did before?"

"They will not hear it if they moved on. I am too far from my people."

Dead. Great. Like she needed *that* on her conscience. "How about I promise that if we meet another centaur, we tell them where you are." She pointed to her surroundings. "Near the cliffs, between two trees, next to a large rock shaped like an egg standing up. Can we do that?"

"Why would you?"

She blinked, not understanding the question. "Why wouldn't we?"

"You will put yourself in danger if you do."

"And I really don't give a crap."

Bouden hissed, pulling on her arm. "Dani, we don't owe him anything."

"You said he's on our side, right? That's the fight that matters. So maybe we just go ahead and do the right thing: save him."

He nodded, looking a bit ashamed he suggested leaving him to die.

"Until next time, Nessus the Centaur." She said, turning and walking off. Her friends joined her.

"Until next time, Dani the Novice."

Chapter Sixteen

They continued on. Dink took the arrows, which held bundles of whipping chains on the ends instead of arrowheads. Non-lethal. He added them to his quiver. They were much larger and heavier than the others. Apparently, centaurs weren't just good shots; they were incredibly strong. He didn't know if he could fire them.

Nathaniel suggested sticking to the large rocks for cover, keeping the cliffs on their right. That way they knew they were headed downriver.

"Centaurs are part horse." He said. "They have to stick to flat land."

"A-Plus." Bouden smirked. "Good idea."

So they stayed in the rocks. Periodically they heard screams or whistles; centaurs chasing Novices. But they didn't see anyone.

"What else do you know about Hellions?" Dani asked as they trudged through the forest.

Bouden shrugged. "Centaurs are the main force. There are a few other types—no gifted as far as I know. I read what I could last night, but like I said, they're stationed in Hell."

"So Hell is a place you can go?" she asked. "I mean, not as a dead person?"

"I guess. Some scrolls talk about a castle on the outskirts: the Fortress of Asphodel. Hellions get stationed there until they're sent to the front. But Centaurs live on earth or Empyrean, protected by the veil like all supernatural creatures."

As they made their way downriver, it got louder. It wasn't a straight shot downstream. The river curved. And as they walked, they could hear it more and more. The canopy broke. More light spilled in. And sure enough, after a few minutes they could see the bend ahead.

The reason they called it the Crystalline River became pretty clear. The waters churned down a winding, cascading mini-falls of rapids and rocks. As the water splashed into the air, it glistened like diamonds. Miniature rainbows burst from the frothing torrents. It was beautiful.

"Wow." Nathaniel murmured. "I've never seen water that clean."

"Me neither." Dani squatted behind cover. "I don't see any centaurs."

"That doesn't mean anything."

"What's that?" Dink pointed.

Through the trees farther down, they could see something lying across the river: a fallen tree lay bridging the water; wide, nearly as wide across as two cars parked together. The roots on their end formed a makeshift ladder to the top.

"You think it's guarded?" Dink asked.

"I bet." Nathaniel murmured. "Centaurs don't strike me as stupid."

"So do we just run for it?"

Dani shook her head. "They're faster. If there's any nearby, one arrow and we're done."

The rock face they used extended past the fallen log, ending at the water's edge farther downstream. They'd either have to cross the makeshift bridge or try crossing through the water. The river's rapids were moving too fast. No way could they swim.

"Maybe we could make it." Dink said hopefully.

Their hopes dashed. A centaur cantered into the open. He melted out of the forest, sweeping with his bow. More centaurs arrived. They carried fallen Novices; hog-tied and unconscious like sacks across their backs. They spoke quickly and a few departed. The original centaur and a companion remained, arrows notched and looking for more threats.

"Pholos," the first one called to the other, "scout the water's edge. A few got through but more are unaccounted for. Go!"

One departed, galloping father down to keep guard.

"There's no way around." Nathaniel observed. "He's standing in the way."

"True, but he's in the open." She hefted the adamantine chain. "I think I can swing this thing and Dink has the bow. Do you think you can hit the centaur from here?"

He gauged the distance and shrugged. "I used to do archery for fun. My crazy instructor was from Texas. She bow hunted and taught us how to shoot deer. This isn't much different. What about the other one?"

Dani moved to the other side. "You take down the one there. I'll handle the other."

"Are you crazy?"

"A little bit. You guys go. Do not worry about me. Get across and I'll follow."

Dani made her way down the rock face, changing her focus from the centaur near the fallen tree trunk to the one along the river's edge. This was crazy. She knew that, but she curled the adamantine coil in her hand and slowly approached. She'd seen these things spin through the air. The ball-bearings made them to twirl on their own. If she whipped them around and threw them using the center lash, it should work. *Should* being the operative word.

128

She crept down from the rocks. She flitted from one tree to the next. Crouching, she waited. The boys had to make the first move.

Seconds later, the other centaur screamed. An arrow hit him with a loud *thunk* and lashes flew out, binding his upper arms. He didn't fall, though; staying unsteadily on his hooves, he brayed loudly. A second arrow struck his lower horse-half. The chains took him in the center and the back leg. He went down.

"Buer!" the one called Pholos yelled, capering back towards him.

Dink, Nathaniel and Bouden descended from hiding. The centaur saw them, took aim and fired. His bolt nearly hit Bouden, but the boy was anything if not fast.

Pholos notched another arrow and took aim. He was standing still. He wouldn't miss.

It was now or never.

Dani sprinted, unraveling the cords and swinging them high. She had one. She had to make it count. She screamed to distract him.

He heard her and turned, shifting his aim. Dani loosed the adamantine lash and it sailed from her hand with unnatural speed. The silver chains flung through the air and with a satisfying clink they connected with the centaur's upper body, whipping around him. He grunted, bow and arrow dropping, nearly toppling sideways.

She pushed off a log and sprung upward, meant only to clear it, but instead she leapt into the air. As if the wind picked her up, she hurtled off the ground. Legs flying, she plowed headlong into the horse-man. Both toppled over.

She landed on her side. The centaur collapsed several saplings behind him with a *crack!* She rolled, groaning and sucking wind. When she turned over, the centaur was tangled, but definitely not down for good.

His horse hide flipped to its side, rising. Dani scrambled up. Knife in hand, she tackled his upper body and knocked him back to the dirt. She pressed the blade to his throat, point under the jaw.

"Yield!" he screamed, hands up. "I yield!"

"What?"

"I said I yield! I submit! Do not slay me!"

She blinked, shaking her head. "I—I'm not going to kill you." Which was ironic with what she held against his neck. "You surrender?"

"I surrender!" The centaur nodded. "I implore you not to kill me!"

"Dani!" Nathaniel called. He and the others were climbing the tangled roots to get onto the log. "Come on! They're coming!"

Dani glanced back at her prisoner, withdrawing the knife. "I won't kill you. Do you promise not to shoot at us once we're on the log?"

"We cannot." The centaur Pholos told her. "We are bound by our rules of engagement. If we cannot retrieve you, we cannot fire upon you."

"Good." She sheathed the knife, rising carefully in case he made a move. "There's another centaur, Nessus; he's upriver near the cliffs, between two trees next to a large boulder shaped like an egg. Do you think you can find him?"

The Hellion nodded. "Yes."

"Swear you will go get him and I will spare your life."

"I swear."

"Good." And she took off running.

More centaurs were coming. A lot more. She could hear the stampede. She reached the roots and began to climb. Nathaniel waited at the top.

"Go!" she told him. "They won't shoot you if you're over the river!"

He followed orders and ran. She climbed using the roots to the top. When she finally reached it and pulled herself over, she glanced back. More centaurs arrived; at least a dozen. They took aim but she was already moving across the fallen trunk. And true to his word, Pholos and his companions did not fire.

Below her, the diamond-like water rushed. Dani crossed to the opposite shore and jumped. It was high, but she landed easily. Dink, Bouden and Nathaniel were waiting.

"We made it!" Dink exclaimed. Across the river to the centaurs, he yelled, "Suck it glue factories!"

Dani punched him, hard.

"Ow! Hey! What, you're the only one who can crack jokes?"

"Only if they're funny and not completely offensive. They're on our team, remember? Be nicer."

He thought about it, then nodded. "Okay, okay. Sorry! I didn't mean that, Your Horsinesses!"

The centaurs made a gesture that, though Dani didn't know it, probably meant something close to the middle finger. They helped their brothers up, ignoring the four of them.

"So we made it." Nathaniel beamed, looking into the woods behind them. "Now what?"

"We keep going," she said, "toward whatever makes the roaring noises."

And just like that, their high spirits disappeared.

The woods were quieter. They stuck close to the riverline, keeping it visible, but below the rapids the water calmed. It followed in wide, open flats that made little or no noise. Instead, the chirping of birds and crickets accompanied their walk.

"So, Bouden," she said, making conversation in the unnerving quiet, "you've read a lot. Got any idea what might be down here?"

He shook his head. "No. It must be something natural to the Vale."

"Like?"

"There's tons of stuff." He murmured, gripping his saber tightly. "All kinds of things live here. I wouldn't be surprised to run into something more monstrous."

"Awesome. I love surprises." Pause. "Not."

After the excitement with the centaurs, it was kind of a boring walk. And the silence was unnerving. You couldn't anticipate silence.

Once in a while they spotted things; squirrels the size of house cats, a beaver making its home along the shoreline that yelled in a clearly human voice, "Buzz off!"

Talking beavers. What else did this forest have?

Something in the water poked its head out just offshore. Dani almost didn't spot it because the creature was made from the water itself; a woman with long hair made of churning water. She smiled before disappearing into the surface again without leaving a ripple.

A water elemental. An undine.

Overhead, a flock of bright, crimson-red birds flew in formation. The air around them shimmered like asphalt under the hot sun.

"Phoenixes." Bouden said. "Fire-birds."

"Wow." The flock was majestic. Each one of them was bigger than an eagle and made of oranges, reds and purples, with white feather plumage around their heads.

"Supposedly they create heat waves when they pass over in flocks like that."

"Anything else in this forest I should know about?" she smirked.

"Probably. A lot of supernatural creatures live in Empyrean; some of them are Hellions, others are just natural."

"And those?" Nathaniel pointed.

A pack of deer grazed on the grass and tree bark ahead. A few poked their mouths into the river, lapping up the glassy water. But not only were each of these deer about the size of a moose, each stag had a single antler made of intricate branches protruding from the top of their skulls. The antlers were ornate; curved, flowing, some so long that the deer could probably scratch its rear end by tilting its head back.

"Bouden? You're the expert." Dani nudged him. "What are they?"

He frowned. "I think...I think they're keresh."

"Keresh?"

"One-horned deer."

"Anything special about them?"

He shrugged. "They're sacred to a forest near Rome, I think. They're totally harmless, though."

"Oh good. I really wouldn't want to be eaten alive by cannibalistic deer."

Bouden chuckled. "Point of interest, there are cannibalistic horses out there. They're called—"

Dani held up her hand. "I don't want to know."

They approached the deer cautiously, admiring how beautiful the creatures' honey-colored coats looked; clean, silky to the touch. The deer didn't shrink away or try to run. As Dani approached the nearest stag with a horn long enough to hang ten coats on, it watched her with a tranquil expression. It chewed the grass between its teeth, regarding her with about as much care as one of its own.

She placed her hand gently on its side. The deer never flinched.

"They're so calm." Dink marveled. "It's like they don't fear anything."

"Yeah." Nathaniel pressed his ear against the side of a faun, a baby by keresh standards but normal adult-deer size. "This is so cool. Look how easy going they are."

Bouden, however, didn't join in. He mumbled to himself, "Don't fear anything..."

"I know, right?" Dani gushed, rubbing its fur. "Amazing."

"I thought I read something about keresh." His frowned deepened, trying to remember. "I remembered something from what I read..."

Dani stroked its hide, the pelt smooth to the touch. "Hey there, big guy." She said to it. "I bet you're—oh wow!"

The deer's powerful hind legs kicked off, darting sideways fast enough to cover the distance from her to the other side of the clearing in seconds and then off into the woods.

"Fast for something not predatory."

More deer took off. Their heads snapped up, alert, and then the entire herd dashed through the trees.

"Wonder where they're going in such a hurry."

"Such a hurry..." Bouden repeated to himself. Then, snapping his fingers, he realized what he was trying to remember. "Oh my God!"

"What is it?" Dani asked.

"Run!"

"What? Why?"

"Just run!"

To their left, something crashed through the trees. It wasn't a tranquil wind. Heavy footfalls, slow at first but now faster, shook the ground beneath their feet. The water rippled in the river. Then tree trunks started breaking.

"Run!" Bouden screamed.

Something roared. The sound shook Dani's teeth.

He grabbed Dani's and Nathaniel's arms, shoving them toward the nearest tree. "Dink! Hide!" he warned.

He was way ahead of them. He slid like a baseball player into home behind a large boulder. Dani and Bouden leapt behind one of the large trees along the shore. It was all-too-familiar to their fight with the centaurs.

But what came rumbling out of the woods was definitely not a centaur.

Dani's first thought was 'lion.' The big cat had the same mane of long black and gold hair, the same dusky brown color, same slinking walk of a lion as it padded from the trees. But this lion was over two stories tall from paw to head. Its feet were as wide as monster truck tires. When it opened its mouth they all would have been able to fit inside it; something she didn't want to try.

It let loose another roar.

"What the hell is that?" Dani hissed softly.

"Shh!" Bouden warned.

The Godzilla-sized cat meandered slowly to the water's edge. Slowly, the lion lowered its huge maw to the river's surface and lapped in loud, long pulls.

What the hell was this thing?

It drank. No one spoke. They didn't want to give it any reason to look their way.

Nathaniel slapped both their arms and pointed. On the other side of the lion, Dink crouched. He was completely visible to beast if it turned its head. If he moved, it would hear him, so he did his best not to.

"Oh my God!" She whispered. "It'll see him!"

"Shh!" Bouden hushed. "It'll hear you first if you keep talking!"

What could they do? There was no way they could kill it. The thing was ginormous. How the hell could something be that big?

Dink tried to move, scooting backward, but there was nowhere for him to go. There was only open ground around his hiding spot. And the thing was so big, outrunning it was impossible.

She sidled along the other side of the tree, staying low to the ground as she came around the other side. From this side, she was closer to Dink but that wasn't any better. His boulder was near its face.

But what else was there?

Dani waved silently, trying to get Dink's attention from the other side of the hind quarters. Dink crouch-walked behind the boulder. He spotted Dani. He understood what she wanted him to do. And he vehemently shook his head.

Come on, she pleaded silently. The lion continued to drink, probably slurping up the entire river. It was distracted. *Run this way.*

Dink shook his head like it would snap off his neck. Dani sighed. There wasn't anything she could do. Dink wasn't going to come to her.

So she sprinted into the open and ran towards him.

If Bouden or Nathaniel could yell at her, they would have. She sprinted past it's back paw, avoiding the long swinging tail straight to Dink. The sound of rustling grass made the loud slurping noises stop for a second, but the lion continued to keep its head down. Then, after a pause, it continued.

Grabbing him by the arm, she mouthed, *We're running. Follow me.* Dink shook his head again, paralyzed. *Run or I will smack the crap out of you*, she warned.

So they ran.

Together the pair took off at a dead sprint. They headed towards the other side of the tree. As they ran, Dani didn't think about the large lion. She just ran, holding Dink by the hand. Together, they sprinted. The tree was in sight. They were going to make it.

Then she looked at the lion. And over its shoulder, the lion was looking at her.

"Dani! Dink!"

She had seconds. The creature was so big, she was surprised how fast it moved. The lion turned and lunged. For it, that meant it was in front of them before they made it to the trees. Luckily, it overshot and smashed into the large oak, snapping it. Nathaniel and Bouden moved from hiding. Dani and Dink skidded to a stop.

The lion roared, which was deafening. It fell over the falling tree, tumbling in a resounding crash. Turning, Dani and Dink fled downriver in the opposite direction. Bouden and Nathaniel were after them.

"Go! Go! Go!" they were waving, screaming.

The lion rolled, the tree trunk falling off. It got to its feet slowly, but when it did, its massive head turned in their direction. And it let loose another powerful roar.

Then it sprinted.

The lion covered the ground in almost two leaps. They just made it to the tree line, dodging between two Redwood-size trunks. Screaming, the lion's jaws opened to bite.

Then its shoulders collided with the trunks. The beast smashed into them, jaws snapping. They could feel the force of its breath hit their backs. But they kept running.

They kept going until the sounds of it thrashing and snapping jaws faded into the distance. And then they ran some more.

"It's called Tigris."

It'd been almost an hour since they heard the creature. Even then, they didn't stop until their legs gave out. Everyone was exhausted. They took a rest on the edge of the river where they found the water pure as drinking from a bottle. So then they downed it faster than the lion.

"That was definitely not a tiger." Dink told Bouden. "That was a lion."

"No, they call it that because it was summoned to Rome by a rabbi." He said. "They named it Tigris since, well, the Tigris River. It lives in a mythical forest no one can find. I guess that's the Vale."

"Just our luck." Dani grumbled.

Bouden shrugged. "It hunts and eats keresh. They're faster than anything except the Tigris. I guess they're its main source of food."

"That and Novices." Dani joked, then the awful thought sunk in. "Do you think the others weren't as lucky as us?"

No one wanted to think about it.

Once sufficiently hydrated, the four of them continued downriver. Nathaniel lost his sword, which meant they were a weapon down, but they hadn't been very useful, anyway. They stayed near the water but now much more wary of cover in case something more awful waited for them.

Near death experiences seemed to be a part of Dani's life now; wraiths, the Elders, centaurs, dinosaur-sized lions. As the four of them made their way farther downriver, the Vale Bridge now in sight, she hoped the remaining part of the journey would be easier. What else could possibly be waiting for them in this valley?

Apparently, werewolves.

Chapter Seventeen

They spotted them as they rounded a bend towards a tall stone bridge support and they all dropped into cover.

"You have got to be kidding me." Dink cursed, checking from behind a shrub. "Werewolves?"

They gathered along the bank of the river in the shade of the bridge. The bridge support began at the shoreline and extended out into the water; algae covered a base wide enough to park several cars across. Surrounding it and using it as a camp, about six wolfmen milled about; shaggy grey fur, long snouts, pricked up ears, and pale eyes. Their lower bodies were covered in thick, disheveled fur tucked into chainmail and forest-colored tunics.

"Werewolves aren't real." Bouden muttered. "And shut up. You know dogs have a good sense of hearing and smell, right?"

"If they aren't werewolves, then what the hell are they?" Dink whispered.

"Cynocephali." Dani answered. "Dogmen."

Bouden looked surprised she knew the term. "How did you know?"

"One hit on me in a bar, once."

Bouden didn't even ask. "They're the origins of the some of the myths about werewolves, though they're born that way; not transformed. They're not lycanthropes."

"Lycan-what?"

"Shapeshifters. Cynocephali come in two distinct clans: houndlings and wolflings—the hound clan and the wolf clan."

"And someone brought a pack of wolves to play." Dink muttered. "Have I mentioned I'm a cat person?"

The wolfmen walked about aimlessly. They reminded Dani of dogs in a park; sniffing the air, sniffing one another, scampering around with their armor. They looked almost playful if they weren't dressed for battle and had vicious looking teeth.

"Are they Hellions?" Dani asked Bouden.

"Sometimes, but I've heard stories. Wolflings are definitely not herbivores."

She shrugged. "Then maybe if we can't get passed them, they just capture us."

"Uh, guys..." Nathaniel pointed.

It took a second to see where he was pointing, but just as he did one of the cynocephali scampered away playfully from its cohorts. It knelt and picked up an animal leg from a bloody carcass lying nearby. And though she thought it might be some kind of dead deer or a keresh, when the animal raised the bloody meat to its mouth, she saw that it wore what remained of brown trousers and a boot.

The rest of the body was difficult to recognize as a Novice.

Bouden swore. "Lumme! They freaking ate someone!"

"Still think they're on our side?" Nathaniel asked her.

She tried not to throw up.

There were six of them; taller than Dogmund from the bar, muscular and deadly looking. Their ears pricked up at the slightest sound from the woods and thankfully, they were too far away to be noticed.

The only way through, though, was through them and they were outnumbered.

"We find a new way around." Nathaniel suggested. "We go through the woods."

"Yeah, sure," Dink said sarcastically, "we just go trudging through the woods with animals that have super hearing."

"You could shoot them." Dani suggested. "You have the bow."

"I can't hit them with all that armor on unless I'm lucky." He said with a shake of his head. "And I'm not that lucky."

"What about the ones that explode into bindings?"

"The centaur arrows?" he checked. "I've got four left."

"Leaving two of them untied if he's lucky enough to hit with all four spot on." Bouden said with no enthusiasm.

"I did say I was unlucky." Dink said once more.

"Well, we need to get around them." Dani told them. "I'm open to ideas."

"And I have one." Said a voice from behind them. They turned. Andreas looked like hell.

They doubled back so they could be out of earshot. Dani had never thought cannibalistic dog-creatures would be preferable to a human being, but Andreas made that a reality.

His axe was gone; dropped in the run from the centaurs. He made it past the Tigris because it ate a keresh in preference to him. He scouted the cynocephali to find a way around, but found them instead. He didn't have good news.

"They're all over these woods. It's lucky they haven't found you. They're fast. I saw them take down a guy. Have you seen him?"

Dani shuddered, remembering the Novice leg in their camp.

"I did find one place we can get by them." He said hopefully.

That got everyone excited. "Where?"

"The bridge column where I found you." He rubbed his hands together. "It's the only place we can see them in the open. Their patrols are usually deep in the woods. They'll be too far away if we attack them by surprise."

Dani folded her arms. "There are six of them."

"Yeah, well, maybe we wait to see if some leave. Usually they go running off when they hear something. They're just dogs, after all."

"That kind of genius logic got us into this mess." She pointed out.

He shrugged, folding his own arms. "Got a better plan? I've seen those things run. They're fast, they're vicious and they hide really well. We never saw them coming."

"So your plan is to run out in the open?" she asked.

"Well, you all got weapons. If you lend me your knife, I can—."

"No freaking way." She spat. "You aren't touching my knife."

"I have more experience with weapons."

"And I have the knife."

"Guys!" Bouden cut in, stopping their argument. "It doesn't matter. Andreas, what's the actual plan? Even if there are less of them, we still have to fight."

"Well, yeah, that's a given, but it would allow some of us to get through."

"Some?" Nathaniel asked. "As in, some of us make it and some of us don't?"

"It's better than none of us making it."

Dani shook her head. It didn't surprise her that his plan sucked.

"I take it you want to be one of those?" She asked.

"You mean like you don't?"

"I don't want any of us to get left behind. Well," she looked him up and down, "mostly."

"Then you come up with a better idea."

"Guys." Bouden warned.

"You know what? Maybe I will." She got up in his face. "Maybe I could."

"Guys."

Andreas rolled his eyes. "Typical."

"What does that mean?"

"Guys!"

"It means you giving people hell and telling them what to do shouldn't surprise anyone."

"GUYS!"

Dani wheeled on him. "What Bouden?"

He didn't look at her. He looked past her. "I think we were talking too loud."

Dani turned. Standing at the edge of the clearing was a cynocephali. The dogman growled. All around them, the beasts melted out of the forest, their clothing helping to conceal them. Claws and teeth dangled dangerously from them. At least a dozen surrounded the clearing.

Dink drew an arrow and aimed, but it did little good.

In a very deep voice, one of the wolves commanded, "Drop your weapons or we will tear you to pieces."

They didn't need shackles. There were two creatures for each of them; one holding each arm. The wolves smelled like dirt and wet musk. They carried Dani along. Up front, Andreas was silent. Dink, Bouden and Nathaniel did their best to do the same, though wetting themselves seemed a likelier reaction. Even Dani felt a little pee-worthy between the large animal-men.

They walked them down to the riverbank. News of new meat traveled fast. More of them gathered. They dropped Dani, her friends and Andreas on their knees.

The leader was much taller than the rest. His fur was coal-colored and his lips drooled as he spoke.

"I am Remus." He snarled with a voice like gravel and teeth like steel. "I am the Alpha of this pack. We've been expecting a few more of you."

"Are you one of the Hellions?" Bouden asked, shaking. "You work for Empyrean, right?"

The creature called Remus tilted back and howled laughing. Others joined in.

"Do we look like we work for the Numen?" he demanded. "Do we look like servants to you?"

"Then who are you?" Dani demanded.

"Who are we?" the snout turned towards her. "We're the ones who weed out the weak. Elder Heman hires us to ensure that only the strong survive. He allows us to take the scraps of his table."

"What are you going to do with us?" Andreas asked.

"Kill you, of course. We're hungry. The last one of you," he glanced at the bloody pile of brown clothes, "tasted a little funny. But I'm sure one of you will be filling." He glanced at Dink and Bouden. "Well, maybe it'll be a two-course meal. Small portions being what they are."

More laughter from the wolfmen.

Remus's eyes returned to Dani. "I heard there was a female Numen. I've never had female. I bet you taste delicious."

She glared. The wolf at her back had a knife to her throat. Her knife. They were going to kill her with her own weapon and then eat her. This was not how she planned to go.

"Well, I'll tell you what," Remus told them happily, grinning, "I'll let you choose. You pick the one we eat first. If they're filling enough, then maybe you'll live because we're too full!"

The wolves cackled. Some snapped their jaws viciously.

"Of course, that just means leftovers for later, but who knows? Maybe we'll become compassionate before that happens."

Again, more laughter and howling.

"We won't choose." Nathaniel told him defiantly.

"Brave words, lunchmeat." Remus sneered. "Should you be first?"

Andreas glanced around at the other four. "You promise that who we choose is who you eat?"

"Andreas!" Bouden kicked him.

"What? What's the point in all of us dying?"

Dani shook her head. "You don't have any shame, do you?"

"What? Like you weren't about to throw me to the wolves?"

That got a lot of them laughing, and not in the good way.

Dani tried to think. How could they get out of this? Was there a way? There were too many to fight. Even if they could fight, they didn't have weapons anymore.

"So choose." Remus told them. "First come, first serve, so to speak."

Dani's hands felt hot, like they were boiling. Her whole body did. She wanted to fight. She'd rather die that way. But she couldn't get up.

"Choose." Remus commanded again. "Now."

"Don't." Nathaniel warned.

"Quiet!" the lead wolf barked. "Choose!"

The other wolves howled. Many of them crowded around. It was mealtime.

"Choose now!"

"I choose Dani!"

The wolves went silent. So did Dani. It didn't come from Andreas. Instead, it came from Dink. He knelt on the other side of her, his eyes wide, staring up at Remus. The moment he said it, the clearing went quiet. Then, shamefully, he looked at her. His face fell. He knew what he'd done.

Remus looked from him to Dani. His jowls curled into a smile. "Very well."

Dani couldn't stop glaring at Dink. He chose her? She helped save his life just an hour ago!

Both wolves behind her hauled her to her feet. Remus rubbed his man-paws together, licking his lips. "Thank you, Novice Ailbe. You made this quite easy for us." He chuckled thickly, sizing her up. "Not much on you. I'll bet you're lean meat. I need that in my diet."

"Bite me." She scowled.

"I plan to. Got any last requests?"

Did she? It amazed her that she never thought about dying until now. Did she have a request? *Tell Mom I love her?* Even that didn't fit. Her mother didn't care about her. The only other person who did was kneeling next to her. And Nathaniel was going to watch her die.

Remus snapped his jaws, making her jump. The other wolves laughed. "No? Too bad."

Strangely, she thought about Ethan. She thought about her walk with him the night before. He was kind to her. He was one of the few who called her Dani. He—

"How do you know my name?"

Remus stopped, his smile faltering. "What?"

"How do you know my name?" she asked him again. "Dink called me Dani."

"You are the only female." Remus said. "It wasn't difficult."

"Dani sounds like a boy's name. I should know. People pick on me for it. And you knew Dink's real name, too. Ailbe. You even called him Novice Ailbe." Her eyes narrowed. "You're pretending, aren't you?"

Remus snarled, snapping inches from her face. She didn't shrink back. The other creatures shifted uncomfortably behind her. They didn't laugh or play the part of cannibalistic monsters. Now they looked like she ruined their fun.

"You <u>are</u> Hellions." She said, not a question anymore. "You're like the centaurs upriver."

"We're nothing like those horse-mongers!"

"Aww, did I ruin your fun?" She smiled at her own joke.

Remus back-handed her hard enough to see stars. She tasted dirt and blood in her mouth. The wolf-leader pressed his claws against her throat.

"Do not mock me, Novice. I may swear my allegiance to Empyrean, but I do not let live those who question my dominance. I lead this pack. You are lucky I do not slay you where you stand and feed your bones to my young for marrow."

Her jaw felt slightly out of place. She stared the wolfman down. She didn't question whether he would kill her. She knew he would.

"Remus!" a voice reverberated through the valley. "Stay your weapon!"

Seven figures descended from above. Elder Heman floated in the middle, flanked by six Powers Numen. They levitated down around the Novices, weapons in hand. Remus snarled but bowed back.

Heman held a single-handed broadsword. He pointed it at him. "Stand back, Alpha. You are in our domain. Our word is law."

Remus's jaws snapped ferally, but he bowed back. So did the wolves. The Novices slowly stood.

"You have done your duty. These are the last. Be gone."

"You should speak with more respect, Elder." Remus warned. "We may owe our allegiance to On High, but that will not always keep my wolves to their oath."

"Then this blade will." Heman snarled back, almost equally animalistic. "It will run red with your blood if you speak to me in such a way again."

Remus bowed, his eyes flicking to Dani. Then, he smiled very cruelly. "I will always wonder what your flesh tastes like, girl. Until we meet again."

With a howl, Remus called his wolves away. They dashed into the woods, leaving Dani with Heman and his soldiers.

Heman and his soldiers flew out of the Vale with them in tow. He took them to the Citadel. A set of switchbacks, similar to the ones that brought them into the Vale, appeared at the edge of the Vale's cliff where the other aeries assembled. Everyone looked more or less disheveled, but alive. Even Lester was breathing, though he had a bruise where Nessus clonked him on the noggin.

Dani stood with Nathaniel and Bouden. Dink was there, head down, tears stinging his eyes. He couldn't look at her.

143

Heman floated down to the front of the formation. "You are failures! I told you that you would survive only by working together! You did not! At the first sign of trouble, you ran. And you ran together! I have never seen such a poorly-disciplined, idle-headed display of stupidity!"

"Elder," one spoke up from the front, "we aren't trained—."

"Exactly! That is the true point of this exercise: you will not— cannot—survive without training. You are useless. Many of you are unworthy to even say you are Earthborn. You couldn't hold a candle to a single, sarding one of the men who serve within our ranks. You are pathetic!"

Even Dani felt ashamed.

"Any skill you have, any achievement you make, comes from those who train you. Listen to them well. Only from them will you ever learn. Only from I and the rest of the Elders will you become what you are meant to be: truly Earthborn!"

Dani couldn't help it. She had to speak. "Elder Heman," she said from the back, "not all of us were failures."

She could feel every eye on her. She could almost feel several praying for her to shut up, but she'd come this far already.

"Novice Daniella," Heman spat, "care to explain how you were not an utter disappointment?"

"Did you not see us take down a centaur?" she demanded. Others shied away from her. "Did you see us avoid a two-ton lion on our own?"

Heman scowled. He looked as if he regretted taking her from Remus. "What I saw, Novice," he growled, "was you spare an enemy in the midst of combat. You hesitated to take a life. You want to know what that is in a real battle? Death. Death to you and anyone who follows you."

"He's a Hellion." She pointed out. "He's on our side. His name is Nessus and he didn't try to kill us."

"And you believe that demons will have compassion? You think they won't twist your emotions and make you doubt yourself? Feign friendship? Pretend to be on your side?" Heman yelled. "Your compassion will be the death of you. The enemy will know that. They'll use it to turn you traitor, or worse, kill you. This," he pointed to her for the rest of the Novices, "is what weakness is, men."

"How dare you!" She screamed so suddenly that Heman took a step back. "I did everything right!"

"Really?" he scowled again. "Then tell me why one of your companions offered you up to be killed first?"

Dink turned red with shame.

"They sent you to the wolves." Heman said, so close to her face she could smell his breath. "I never saw you plan or lead anything, but I saw one of your number use a bow with moderate skill. I saw one use his knowledge of creatures to save you. I saw one try to defend you." He glanced at Andreas. "And I saw one of you attempt to come up with a plan to get past the cynocephali, but all you did was argue with him until they discovered you. That is what I and the other Elders saw, Novice Daniella. I see no merit in you."

Her hand came up to hit him, but the air between them thickened into something like a shield, blasting her hand away. A blow to her stomach sent her to her knees.

"Do not speak that way to me, maggot." He strode back to the front of the columns. "You have forgotten where you are. You believe this city makes you safe. It does not. The centaurs and cynocephali are under our control. The great beast Tigris is ours to command. But do not suppose that this place is without danger."

A groan of pain turned everyone's head. Two Powers hauled a half-drowned Novice forward, his arm in a sling.

"You saw an illusion in the cynocephali camp. No Novice perished there. But one," Heman said bitterly, "nearly drowned crossing the river. He was alone. He was foolish. Had it not been for his Guardian, he would have perished. As it stands, that Guardian will be punished for allowing his charge to almost die. One day soon, even they will not be able to protect you."

"So let this be a lesson to you," he warned, "death awaits us all. You are dismissed. Tomorrow you report to the Training Grounds for your first day. Come back tomorrow better, or suffer a fate worse than your comrade."

Part III
Trials

Chapter Eighteen

The walk back was a lonely one. Nathaniel tried to talk to her, but Dani pushed him away. After what Heman did in front of everyone, all she wanted was something to hit. Bouden looked sympathetic, but he knew better than to try to talk to her. Dink was the one that looked anguished. He chose to sacrifice her to save himself. If he was sorry, she didn't care. He was at the top of her short list and that list was getting lengthy.

The sun dipped behind the rim as she trudged into the Arn. The Vale was a mixture of blue and black shadows. Lights ignited across the forest. She knew what they were now: centaur and cynocephali villages. The Vale was as much a home as Empyrean itself.

Exhausted, bruised, and cut up from the forest, she wanted to collapse in her crappy, makeshift bed.

Except it was gone, as was the pavilion.

"What the...?"

The pavilion had grown four walls. Or, at least, that's what it looked like. Someone created a shack out of the ramshackle building; a house-garden combo with new siding overgrown with flowering plants, fruits and vegetables. It was a house alive. Built into the side facing the fountain was a sliding panel door, which also had an extended porch roof to keep rain and sun off. The fountain and square were picked clean of weeds to look brand new. Someone erected torch-lanterns, which illuminated the square in soft, orange glow. And facing the cliffside was an extended covered-pavilion for training, complete with holds for weapons on the supports, weights and ropes, and an entrance into her home.

"Apparently, you have admirers." Mastema appeared on the other side of the square.

Dani jumped a little. "Seriously? Are you trying to imitate every horror film in history?"

"I do not understand."

"Of course you don't." She peeked inside the house. There was a bed against one wall, a large hot-tub like basin, and shelving for full sets of raiments. "Did you do this?"

"I did not."

"Maybe Shea and Roxelana?"

He extended a thick piece of yellowed paper, or whatever passed for paper up here. "I found this within your canteen."

She took it. "Canteen?"

"Your dining area."

"Someone built me a dining room?" She grinned. "Aww! Is there fine china?"

"Is that sarcasm?"

She rolled her eyes.

"With this dwelling, they have also given you a whole storeroom of food; enough to last you many weeks."

She unfolded the paper, scrawled with large, messy handwriting. "It's a note."

Danny,

I do not know if this is your true name. Danny is a very peculiar name for a female; however, your heart is the purest I have ever known and no name could change my sentiments of you. You spared me when you could have killed me and you sent my brethren to my aid when it would not benefit you. I am forever indebted. I bid you thanks for your kindness. As a way to show my gratitude, my people have delivered food and repaired your domicile. It was quite small and did not have walls. Do humans not live in homes with walls? I pray it is to your liking. This is a small gesture, but it conveys all the gratitude that I am able to give.

In your debt,
Nessus

"Nessus?" Mastema asked. "The centaur?"

"Yes." She folded the letter, smiling. "I met him today. Do you know him? He's sweet."

He nodded, frowning. "Sweetness is but another form of weakness."

"You must be a hit at parties."

"This is serious, Novice. Those who dwell within the Vale and those who dwell without are not meant to interact in such ways. I know you have befriended some gifted, but centaurs are forbidden from venturing beyond their borders unless allowed by the Elder Council."

Her mood soured, Dani walked past him into her new home. It smelled of fresh tree wood. She pressed her hand against the wall and flinched. "It feels warm. Alive."

"It may very well be. The planks of your home are amaranthine wood; a tree that grows in Empyrean. It's timber is some of the finest in the world. Centaurs are masters of construction. Their homes are as much alive as they are."

"Meaning?"

"There are almost no limits to what this house may provide."

"Amazing." She marveled, running her fingers across the wall.

He stepped inside. "Novice, friendship with non-Numen will cause you misery."

Even her new home couldn't brighten what Mastema dimmed. "I really don't have time for this."

"Make time."

"You're a pain in the ass. You know that, right?"

"Am I? I was unaware. For now, we must train."

She shook her head. "Train? I'm exhausted. Can we do this another day? I have a new house and I'd like to sleep in it."

He walked around to her new pavilion. Dani followed through the house.

"You survived the first test." He said. "That was a fluke, despite surprising me, Novice."

"I have a name, you know."

"Until such time you earn one, you will simply be Novice." He unhooked his sword from his belt and placed in a hold next to the door. "Your training is just beginning."

"Great. Super. Piss off." She wasn't going to take this from him.

Then Mastema, with a single move, drew something from the small of his back. He spun and threw. Dani flinched as something smacked into the wood inches from her head.

A knife nearly took her ear off.

"Are you insane?" she screamed. "You could have hit me!"

"You have a talking problem." He grunted. "Recognize it?"

The question caught her off guard. "What?"

"Do you recognize the blade that nearly took your life?" he came over and yanked it from the doorframe, holding it up to her eye. The dagger was nearly as long as her forearm, double-edged and made out of adamantine.

"It's my knife from the Vale." She said.

"Correction, it is the knife I chose for you to carry into the Vale. I had to retrieve it from a wolf that did not surrender it lightly. I would appreciate, in the future, that you not give my gifts to foes."

"Gift?" she got in his face, angry. "You gave me a knife to fight centaurs, werewolves and gigantic lions!"

"And you were better suited for it."

"How?"

149

"Did you not pay attention? I would have thought you were more observant. All Novices carried large weapons they eventually lost." Mastema pointed out. "It slowed them down. As a lesson, their Guardians purposefully put them at a disadvantage. I did not. I gave you the only weapon you could sensibly wield. If you had a sword, would it have done you any service?"

She wanted to argue, but couldn't. Truth was, nothing would have helped her.

"Exactly." Mastema saw her expression. "You did not need to learn about disadvantages. In that regard, you are already ahead of your peers. You understand living against the odds. It is your one advantage."

She huffed. "Am I supposed to thank you?"

"You are supposed to, but I do not expect it."

She hated this guy. She hated his guts. And he was supposed to be her teacher? "So the whole test was a set up? The Elders wanted us to nose-dive?"

"Failure, Novice, is the first step to victory."

"You sound like a fortune cookie." She clenched her hands into fists. "People laughed at me. They thought I was pathetic!"

"And you care what others think of you?"

She was angry with him. She was angry at herself. She was angry at the whole freaking mountain full of freaking misogynistic morons! And yet all she could do was argue with some unflappable, demented Obi-Wan.

"One of my friends," she grumbled, a bad taste in her mouth, "chose to sacrifice me when he thought the cynocephali would kill us."

Mastema dismissed it. "You think it reflects on you?"

"No."

"Lie. You believe it whole-heartedly. And you are a fool to believe it." He strode past her to a wooden chest in the corner. "What others believe is of no consequence to you."

"So I don't get to have friends?"

"You never did." He knelt and flipped the locks on the crate. "Accept this as truth now, or perish believing a lie. No one here will be your friend. They can be your ally, they can be a tool, but never a friend. Centaurs, gifted, Numen; no one stands by your side for long. The Elders branded you an outsider. You will remain an outsider. No amount of good deeds will change it."

Dani shook her head. "You are just all sunshine and rainbows, aren't you?"

Mastema said nothing and opened the crate.

"What kind of name is that, anyway? Mastema. Is it African?"

"I am a moor," he said, rummaging through the contents, "but it is not my given name. In life, before my ascension here, I was a marauder. I pillaged from childhood until the day I was taken." He indicated his sword on the hook. "I carried this weapon, the khopesh, and used it to bring death. So terrible was I that those I attacked gave me this name. Mastema."

"What does it mean?" she asked.

"It is the name of evil in their native tongue; a harbinger of disaster, destruction and persecution. They gave it to me as a symbol of what I had become. In penance, I have lived with it since to remind myself of what I am." He turned towards her, the dark glare in his eye like liquid, black fire. "We pretend to be of light, Novice. We are not. Understanding this is a gift. To have no illusions of goodness provides us a path, but a hard path. It is a path we do not choose, but are forced upon. You are on that path, as am I."

This was her Guardian? This was the guy they found to train her? His name literally meant evil and death.

"Why don't you have a Novice?"

"I have you."

"Why not before me?" she remembered Judah saying something about Mastema not being trusted. "Why were you the only one available?"

"There are other Guardians who do not have charges yet."

"*Yet* being the operative word. What's wrong with you?"

Instead of answering, Mastema reached into the crate and withdrew a long bowstaff taller than Dani. He tossed it to her and she barely caught it. "We begin training."

"What? Now?" she asked. "I can barely stand!"

"Perfect. Exhaustion breeds skill."

Then he attacked.

To say training didn't go well would be an understatement. To say Mastema beat her nearly senseless was an understatement. Hell, to say she learned nothing seemed to be the only accurate way to describe her training.

He instructed her how to plant her feet and face her opponent. With the bowstaff held like a spear, he attacked with the forward tip. Once or twice she connected hers to his and blocked a blow, but usually he swept out her legs or struck her in the ribs or hit her so hard across the face she saw stars. She ended up on her back so many times it was aggravating, then only to look up to find the man standing over her, demanding, "Get up. We go again."

He was a taskmaster. He was a Nazi. He was Hell on wheels.

His name suited him.

Night fell. Mastema lit torches for light. Dani moved, keeping her feet steady, never losing sight of him. He didn't use the veil. His staff hurtling around his arms and body, mastering the art of beating her into the floorboards effectively. More than once he struck her hard enough that when she blocked, the vibration was painful. Her palms ached. If she didn't block, she got bruises; body, arms, shoulders, everywhere. One decorated the back of her hand in black and purple and puke green.

For the umpteenth time, Mastema faced her. He attacked, point of the staff thrusting out towards her face. She deflected, dodging left. He struck again. Again, she dodged.

"Stand and fight!" he ordered.

"No way!" she cursed as his stave smacked her exposed thigh, nearly tumbling her to the ground.

"Coward."

He spun, gripping the bow by the end and whipping the other around high. She ducked and the wooden pole sliced past her head. She rolled across the pavilion against a support post. Mastema leapt after her.

Swinging, he sneered. "Many would see your gutless retreat as just another woman cowering in the face of men!"

Mid-twirl, the stick came up from under his arm in an upward strike. She bounced back, avoiding it again.

"Will you cower, Novice?"

"Forget you!" she struck back. Mastema blocked easily.

"Is that all you bring to this fight?" he struck again, missing but herding her against the column. He bared his teeth. "Try not to waste my time much more. This is tiring."

She glanced back over her shoulder at the column. Mastema continued to twirl the bow tauntingly. She got an idea, but didn't know if it would work.

"Ready to submit, Novice? Then I can tell the Elders what a pathetic waste of time you truly are."

She gripped the bow in both hands. She'd seen Mastema do this. Could she? "Well, come get some," she bared her teeth, "moor."

She knew the word was offensive. She halfway payed attention in ancient history class. The word was one step down from the n-word.

He stopped twirling, bringing the staff up and around, striking horizontally. Dani ducked, turning, bringing her own rod around as she spun in a wide arc. The long end arched out and using her momentum, she swung around the torch. As Mastema's bow connected with the support of the pavilion, smacking the wood and blocking his strike, her own came round and collided hard with the side of his knee.

He screamed in pain.

Dani felt a surge of satisfaction as he stumbled. She rose up, giddy to see the pain on his face.

"How about that?" she crowed.

Mastema's lip curled in disgust.

He flipped his weapon up to both hands and swung blindingly fast. He'd been holding back. This was too quick to block. The end of the rod connected with her temple and things went black.

She sputtered awake. Her head lay back against a folded piece of cloth on the edge of a tub; her tub. She was in her new house. She coughed, accidentally inhaling water that tasted like salt and iron.

She tried to wipe the flavor off her tongue. She was still dressed, but her raiments were soaked through and did little to wipe off the taste.

Kneeling next to her, Mastema frowned. "Do not splash me."

"What happened?"

"You fell unconscious."

"To hell with that! You knocked me out!"

"Yes." He replied calmly. "You are welcome."

"For almost putting me in the hospital?"

"For putting you in the bath of panacea."

The murky water's surface was a fine white film, as if he added something to it. It was tasted awful. "What is this stuff?"

"Panacea." He explained. "It is a universal healing elixir. It may be drunk or applied directly to wounds."

"Like hell it is—!" but then she saw her hands. The scrapes and bruises from today were gone. Nothing but unblemished skin remained. No cuts. She touched her temple. No pain.

"What is this?"

"I just explained."

"No you didn't." she stood, thankful to still be in her clothes but hating they were wet and stinky. "What is panacea?"

Mastema stood. He offered her a cloth towel, which she used to dab her face. "Panacea is a healing elixir made by our alchemists. Over time, it can heal almost any wound. It can be the difference between living and perishing in battle. It may even prevent death."

"You can bring the dead back to life?"

"It can bring you from the brink of death, but not death itself. Listen more carefully in the future, Novice." He turned on his heel and stalked out the door. "There are more raiments next to the basin for you. Inform me when you are redressed."

She peeled off her wet clothes and changed into fresher ones. Once dry, she felt cleaner than before. She hadn't showered in two days, which was gross, but panacea did more than heal, apparently.

She walked out into the square. Her Guardian sat on the rim of the fountain. He chewed something that looked like a cross between a gigantic cracker and bread.

He extended a piece to her. "Eat."

She accepted it and took a bite. It tasted delicious. She quickly devoured the whole wafer. "I'm so hungry." She said with her mouth full.

"Panacea speeds up your healing. You burn more calories that way and thus, become more hungry. I'm glad you have a source of food here, now."

"Ugh!" she grunted. "If only I had fish tacos!"

"Fish what?"

"Fish tacos! Come on! You've never had fish tacos?"

"No."

She accepted another piece and chewed slower this time. She might be living in a derelict village with ancient toiletries, but she didn't have to act like a caveman. Screw being lady-like, but she was going to be halfway-civilized. They silently ate for a bit. Dani smiled at Mastema, if nothing but to tease him.

"What?" he finally asked. "Cease your amusement. What do you smile at me for?"

"I got you." She told him, savoring the biscuit. "You got cocky and I got you with my staff. It was a nice trick, wasn't it?"

"You believe that after hundreds of years of combat, I did not see that attack coming?"

Now it was her turn to frown. "You let me hit you?"

"Of course."

"Liar."

"I would not expect a Novice with no training to stand against a warrior. No one should expect it of you."

"Heman does."

"*Elder* Heman." He corrected. "And he was proving a point."

"That he's got the conscience of a snake?"

"That failure is needed to understand reality. You'll face challenges and hardships. You must learn inner strength."

"You're sweet." She sneered.

"I see you choose wit instead of strength." He stood. "You did well today. I watched your progress."

"You watched me? How?"

He frowned again. "Is that not obvious?"

"Uh...how does no grab ya?" But she smiled. "But thank you. At least someone gives praise."

Then he ruined it. "You had luck on your side. You barely escaped the centaurs and if the Tigris wanted to devour you, it would have."

She frowned the Grand Canyon of frowns. "I was lucky? Forget that! I came up with a good plan. I got us through!"

"Only to be captured." Mastema reminded her. "And this time you were not in physical danger. The Hellions of the Vale fight for Empyrean. And the Tigris is trained not to devour human flesh."

"Trained? How do you train a twenty foot lion?"

Mastema lectured on, ignoring her. "Novice, you will understand one day that no amount of victories can free you of failure. Just as no amount of failure can keep you from victory. Situations are neither hopeless nor hopeful. They are what you make them. Be vigilant. You must learn to listen to guidance, whether it comes from a source you respect or not. Hated or not, your Elders do know how to train you. So do I."

"What? By whacking me with sticks?"

"Training cannot come from books." He told her. "It comes from experience. It comes from practice. We can provide both. If you listen, you will learn. If you learn, you will survive."

He marched back to the pavilion of her house with Dani following behind. Placing the staves inside the chest with other assorted training tools, he withdrew several large, dusty books. Elder Atid in the Anthenaeum called them tomes.

"What are those for?"

"For you to study."

Smartly, she said. "I thought you said training doesn't come from books?"

155

"No, but knowledge still does." He stacked them one at a time into her arms. "And I do not train brainless Novices."

"Jeez, what the hell are all these?"

"Ars Goetia." The first tome felt like a ton of bricks. The second was two tons. "The Infernal Dictionary. The Lesser Key of Solomon." That was one of the heaviest ones. "The Testament of Solomon. The works of Zoroaster. The Magical Papyrus. The Summoner's Guide. And the Malleus Maleficarum, though this is the real edition and not that nonsense passed around on Earth." He laid the scrolls on top. "And these are just light reading to help you along."

She struggled to hold them up. "Light reading?"

"They are the basics of demonology, summoning and magic that you will need."

"Magic?"

"Yes. Magic. Most of the other aeries have their own copies. You do not. I took these out of the Anthenaeum on my own. Try not to lose them."

"Why? Will they revoke my library card?"

"No. More than likely, they'll put you in stocks in the dungeon of the Keep and I along with you. I would rather that not happen."

At first she thought he was joking, but Vegas bets: probably not.

"Learn, study, succeed." He told her. He took his sword and walked off towards the far side of the village. "I shall return in the morning!"

"More stick fighting tomorrow?" she asked after him.

"Conditioning." He responded. Then he disappeared into shadows, either into the veil or just simply the dark of night. Either way she was alone.

Alone with her homework.

Chapter Nineteen

The following day Dani awoke to Mastema slapping her awake.
"What the hell!" She screamed, stumbling out of bed.
Her mentor frowned. "You were sleeping."
"Yes! That's what people do in the morning, you psychopath!"
"We need to train."
Outside, dawn hadn't even broke. "You woke me up early."
"An early dawn staves off the early grave." He called over his shoulder as he walked out the door.
She glowered at him from the floor. "Uh-huh. And do you have a saying for when your Novice murders you in your sleep?"
"No." His voice floated back.
Her bird friend took post at the footboard and stirred awake from under its wing, glaring at her like it was her fault they were up so early. Dani ignored it and got dressed.
Mastema waited for her in the pavilion.
"No weapons?" she asked, somewhat relieved. "Are we going to do some yoga?"
"No. Push-ups."
And so began the most grueling hour of Dani's life.
She went to the gym in Los Angeles twice a week. She hit the punching bag when she needed to relieve stress. She ran when she wanted to relax. But the workout Mastema put her through was neither relaxing or stress relieving. It was brutal.
Push-ups. Fifty of them. In quick succession.
Sit-ups. More than a hundred.
Knee strikes, burpees, hand-stand push-ups, cardio.
She threw up in the bushes by the time she was done.
"Well done, Novice." Mastema handed her a wooden goblet of water, which she chugged down to sponge the sting of vomit out of her mouth.
"I hate you." She croaked.
"Good training will make you feel that way. Come. You are late."
"For what?"
"The rest of your training."
Dani was already dressed. She grabbed some hair ties—the centaurs had actually left ties for her hair!—and Mastema handed her a bowl with some cooked chicken from an outdoor fire he started, with leaf-like veggies and an apple.
"Eat quickly."

"Why?"

He pointed. Uphill, just beyond her village, she spotted brown uniforms—Novices—trekking from Novice Village.

"Where are they going?"

"Combatives. Hand-to-hand training. Your first lessons of the day."

She nearly spit out her food. "I'm late?"

"Yes."

"But—But—!"

"I would run if I were you. Elder Azariah does not like his pupils to be tardy."

The bird made a sound. From its perch, it turned it's beak uphill. The Novices were gone, already ahead of her.

Awesome. Her enthusiasm would rival the lowest pits.

She took off at a sprint. The trek wasn't exactly short and she tried to keep up a good pace, but she was over running everywhere. She hoped that some kind of modern convenience like cars or magical horse-drawn carriages would exist here, but nope. She was stuck running. She ran past gifted homes after the Novices that disappeared over the crest of the hill. Overhead, small groups of black-clad Guardians soared past with their Novices in tow.

Of course they won't be late, she thought to herself. *Their Guardians actually like them.* Hers, on the other hand, stayed at her house. She couldn't believe Mastema was going to make her late AGAIN!

Groups of people passed her; gifted on their way to the bridge market, Gatekeepers coming off-duty, miners headed towards the bridge for work. Some stared as she passed, ever the sideshow freak.

The Training Grounds were towards the top of the hills, near the peaks where the clouds hung. In the distance, Dani thought she saw part of the peak move. When it did, she saw eyes. A giant?

But she pushed that aside and ran towards the Training Grounds. Cluttered with weapon racks, archery ranges and open rings, it was massive in size and cooler than down the slope. Dani, sweat ridden, shivered as the moisture frosted on her skin.

When she arrived, the Novices and Guardians had already assembled into groups. Each grouping of two aeries formed at different stations: archery, swords, the bowstaff she was all-too-familiar with. She spotted Nathaniel grouped to one side with his aerie and started that way, but he caught her eye and shook his head. Dani paused. He nudged his head towards the far side of the open space. Dani glanced over and saw an Elder looking pointedly at her from the front of the assembly.

Great.

Everyone waited. White banners hung on poles along the front of the columns. Emblazoned on the one in front of Nathaniel's group was a circle with a Z-like tail and a dot in the middle; a symbol she didn't recognize. Another had a D-like shape with a bolt through looking like a bow and arrow. A third showed a simple circle.

She trotted up and stood behind the nearest column, unsure of where to be. The Elder she didn't recognize wore no armor like Asaph or Heman, or a long flowing robe like Jeduthun. Instead it was short, simple and reminded her of a wrestler's uniform. He had grey at the temples of his jet-black hair, a thin beard that ran along his jawline into a goatee, and strange, piercing golden-brown eyes. His stern expression turned directly to Dani.

Once in line, she waited. The Elder continued to stare at her. It was silent; so much so she could hear the wind across the open plains around them. After a few seconds, the Elder cleared his throat. When no one responded, he did it again. Dani realized he grunted at her.

"Yes...Elder?"

The stocky man flicked his eyes right to another banner. It bore a drawn, bird-like stick figure. She remembered that the Arn, her home, supposedly stood for 'eagle.'

The Elder cleared his throat one more time. And once more, he gestured to the other banner. This time, he growled, "Find your guidon."

"My what?"

"The symbol of your aerie, Novice."

Dani got the message. The banner was for her. She moved over to stand in front of the eagle; the only one in her aerie.

"Thank you." He muttered.

Could have just said so, she didn't say.

"My name is Elder Azariah." His voice was hard. "I am one of eight Arbiters of the Elder Council. This means I, like Elder Heman and others you meet today, am one of those responsible for your training. I instruct in the ways of hand-to-hand combat and physical weapons. Today, every Novice begins their formal training here and the Keep. This marks not only your commencement into our ways, but serves as a fundamental for how you will train."

Dani raised her hand. Azariah's eyebrows shot up. "Yes Novice?"

"Will we have to continue to do morning training with our Guardians like today?"

Azariah looked confused. "As in, you have been training even before this session?"

"Yes. Hasn't everybody?"

"No."

His one-word response got a few chuckles down the line. Dani burned with embarrassment and anger. Only she had to get up at the butt-crack of dawn?

"Training is done in sessions." He continued. "You—the aeries Aether, Gylph, Corona, Meridian, Pinnacle, Ethereal, Crux, Nexus, Coronach, Halycon, Aerial and Jubilee—are the newest to receive training. This—." He stuttered to a stop, and then added, "I meant to say all aeries, including Arn."

A few people snickered.

"This is training. It is strict and structured. You will begin as one at the start of the morn and then split into groups. You received a scroll this morning with a schedule. You will follow it."

Dani hesitantly raised her hand again.

"Yes Novice?"

"I didn't receive a scroll."

Again, more laughter. Azariah grimaced in irritation, continuing. "Today will introduce you to the fundamentals of our society. The trumpets announce when new lessons begin. Everyone will gather together again for Studies in the Anthenaeum."

"You should rely upon your Guardian to learn, but also learn from one another and the twelve," he paused, glancing at Dani, "thirteen aeries present."

He reached down and retrieved a thick piece of wood. For the first time, Dani noticed what made this Elder much different than most. His hands looked large and broken, but what she mistook for cracked skin were in fact scars; jagged, fleshy scars. His hands were beat to hell and back. How could he still use them?

But when he flexed, the thick piece of wood splintered. They still had strength in them. Azariah wasn't just an Elder. He was a tough Elder.

"You will not always have a weapon." He told them. "You will need to rely upon your body to be your weapon. Break into partners with your Guardians."

Dani looked around. Mastema was nowhere to be seen. She raised her hand once more.

Azariah frowned for the third time. "Yes Novice?"

"I don't have my Guardian. Is he supposed to be here?"

She heard more than a few chuckles from the group.

Azariah was not amused. "Then you must train with other members of your aerie..." He quickly realized she was on her own.

"How am I supposed to train?"

Azariah frowned. "With no Guardian, there is very little you can do."

"So, what? I'm supposed to just stand here with my finger up my nose?"

More laughter, though now at both Dani and Elder Azariah. She silenced them with a glare.

Azariah's scowl went deep. "Your Guardian was to be here. He is not. As such, his choices have hampered you. Who is your Guardian?"

"Mastema."

The laughter died at the snap of the fingers. No one thought Mastema was funny. Even Azariah looked shocked.

"Mastema? The moor?"

"I think he just prefers Mastema, but yeah."

It was difficult to read Azariah's face. He looked afraid, or at least something close to it. Who the hell was this guy the Elders stuck her with?

Dani was about to give up when Kleos, the Guardian from the first day, stepped out of the crowd. "Elder Azariah? If I could, I would like to offer my services."

"Where is your charge, Guardian Kleos?"

"Absent, sir." Kleos glanced sidelong at Dani. "He was unwell."

"Unwell?"

"I apologize for Novice Ailbe's truancy."

Dink? Dani knew Ethan was Nathaniel's Guardian, but not that Kleos was Dink's.

"As my Novice and her Guardian are absent, I would like to offer my services." Kleos continued. "Unless you see anything wrong with aiding her?"

Elder Azariah was about to answer when she heard footsteps behind them. A Guardian trotted up the hill, but it wasn't Mastema. It was Ethan. He strode to the front and bowed, touching two fingers to his forehead. Azariah did the same.

"Yes Guardian Ethan?"

"I'm sorry for my lateness, Elder Azariah." He apologized, a little out of breath. "I would have been here sooner to inform you of Novice Dani's situation."

"Novice Dani?"

"Novice Daniella, I mean. Her Guardian was brought before the Elder Council," he bowed, "with your acquiescence, of course."

Azariah frowned. "The Council convened?"

"I thought you were aware."

"I was not."

"I apologize for bringing such ill tidings. I assumed the Council informed you. They must not be in need of you."

There was something about the way Ethan spoke; like he was baiting Azariah. The Elder looked upset.

"Novices," he declared, "there are tasks which require my attention. I leave you today in the hands of your Guardians. I will return once the Elder Council has concluded."

With that, he stalked away. Dani didn't know Azariah from Adam, but he was every bit as angry as someone on a murderous rampage.

Ethan joined Dani, with Nathaniel in tow, the slightest grin at the corner of his mouth. "Sorry I'm late."

"You did that on purpose."

"What?"

"You made it seem like the Council left him out of their meeting."

He shrugged. "I only told him the truth."

"The truth that made it sound like the Council didn't consider him important."

"I have no idea what you are talking about." Which, clearly, wasn't true.

Kleos didn't believe him either. "You will get yourself into trouble one of these days."

"One of them hopefully in the future and not today."

"Where is Mastema?" Kleos asked. "I haven't seen him in a spell. He does not strike me as someone who leaves his Novice destitute." Then, rethinking his words, he bit his lower lip, ashamed.

"What is with that guy?" Dani demanded, hands on her hips. "Why is everyone so afraid of him?"

"It's not fear." Kleos told her. "Not really."

"Then what? Is he some kind of outcast?"

Both Ethan and Kleos exchanged a look. Ethan said solemnly, "For right now, that's not your concern. What is your concern is training."

Kleos nodded. "Yes. Let's get to it. The other Guardians are beginning. So should we."

Guardians took over training. Ethan and Dani moved into an open space. Some around them began sparring, others learning how to stand or hold themselves.

"Ever fought before?" Ethan asked.

"Once. I broke the guy's nose."

"Good. You are a natural fighter. Has Mastema taught you anything yet?"

"How to take a beating."

"Also good." He stood next to her and Nathaniel. "Every fight can be broken down to three things: how to stand, how to attack, and how to—as you put it—take a beating. Now, the combat stance is important. Bend your knees. Place your dominant foot forward, the other behind and slightly to the left, toes pointed to your attacker."

Dani followed his instructions. Once she got the feet, they moved to the hands; up near her temples, elbows tucked tight to defend her sides. Ethan showed her how to move, how to dodge, and how to throw a punch. Kleos supplemented; explaining how to use her shins to deflect low shots and forearms for the upper body. It wasn't how Dani envisioned learning to fight, but it was simple and effective.

They moved into sparring for a few minutes. Dani noticed that each Guardian had his own style. Ethan's was something like boxing. Kleos was more fluid; striking with kicks and using hips to swing the legs. Once she started, it wasn't too difficult to repeat.

"Don't think about kicking an opponent in the face." Kleos told her after they were both breathing hard and Dani took a few practice punches. "Use your hands for that. With your feet, strike to the top of the foot," he pointed, "the side of the knee or the ribs."

"Do demons have feet, knees and ribs?"

"Don't worry about demons just yet. Practice on Ethan."

She faced him. Tensing, she kicked. It was slow and Ethan was able to shift his shin into a block, but he nodded. It was a good hit.

"And remember what I showed you." Kleos said, going back to an earlier move. "If an opponent charges, you put your foot in his sternum and fall back. Let his bodyweight and momentum carry him and toss him over your head."

"Right."

Before she could say anything else, someone shouted loudly, "So this is the girl?"

The voice belonged to a black-clothed Guardian. He looked older than Ethan or Kleos; Middle Eastern, with beard and hair trimmed into a continuous wrap around his head. Like all the Guardians, he was in fighting shape. Even in his raiments, he was clearly fit. His Novice—a burly, barrel-shaped boy of seventeen with dark skin and serious eyes—stood at his back.

"Nazir." Ethan bowed. "This is Dani."

"Yes. I have heard so much." Dani couldn't place his accent. He extended his hand. When she gripped it, it felt like iron. "Mastema's pupil. I'm surprised they gave him one."

"And why's that?"

He seemed shocked. "I'm surprised you haven't heard."

"Well, surprise, surprise, I haven't." More than a few Numen were complete buttholes. Nazir was no exception.

The Guardian showed nothing to her sarcasm. Showed, anyway. "I would think it was important for a Novice to know about their Guardian."

Ethan voice was a warning, "Nazir..."

"Not many would want the failure to be their teacher."

"Failure?"

Joking with her now, he sneered, "I will let him tell you. By the by Ethan, I noticed that you have not been attending vespertide recently. Why is that?"

Ethan's expression didn't change except the barest flick of his eyes in Dani's and Nathaniel's direction. "Should we really speak about this now?"

Nazir's smile widened. "Elder Azariah is not here. Why not?"

"Now is not the time."

"Vespertide?" Dani remembered Shea and Roxelana hinting it was how Numen and gifted mingled, but didn't know anything else.

The other Guardian sighed. "Another time, then. For now, why not a little sparing between Novices? Michael against Daniella? What about it, Novice? A sparring match?"

"I don't think I'm ready for that yet."

"Why not? I've heard so many things about you. They say you are exceptional." Nazir's tone took on a nasty tease. "You claimed to lead three other Novices past the centaurs and the Tigris yesterday. You claim you even took down a centaur. Why not show us that skill?"

Other Novices and Guardians noticed. A crowd was forming.

"Nazir, that's not appropriate." Ethan told him.

"Why not? It is only sparring. Why not give the pupils something to liven things up? They are both of equal skill. At least, she claims to be. Did you not boast your exceptional skill to Elder Heman?"

She wanted to hit Nazir. This guy did not think for one second she was exceptional. More than a few Novices and Guardians had the same look. Talk about a hostile crowd. Only Kleos, Nathaniel and Ethan were sympathetic, with a few in the crowd not particularly comfortable with the mob.

"What do you say, Novice Daniella?"

Some began whispering and grumbles sifted through the throng.

"Fine." She said. "Why not?"

Ethan tried to stop her. "Dani—!"

"She's made her choice." Nazir smiled. "Why not have an impartial judge? Kleos, you're a master of hand-to-hand. You should judge the roll."

"Roll?" Dani asked.

"The bout. The fight." Kleos told her. He glared at Nazir. There was more than casual hostility between them. "And I will."

"First one to submission." Nazir announced. His eyes shifted to Ethan. "Unless you have a problem with it, Stormthrower?"

Stormthrower?

"I guess not." Ethan told him, but looked worriedly at Dani. "To submission."

"Good. Then let us begin."

They created an informal circle. Those Novices not already engaged in some kind of training meandered over to watch. Even a few gifted passing by along the hills took notice. Dani and Michael stood in the center. She already regretted this decision. What was with people wanting to fight her, mock her or punish her all the time? Since she arrived, she hadn't caught a break. Now she was fighting someone?

Nazir spoke encouragingly to Michael on his side of the circle. At least, she hoped it was just encouragement. The way he looked sideways at her looked more hostile that a pep talk.

"Any advice?" she asked Ethan.

"You're stupid for doing this."

"Uh-huh. Tell me something I don't know. Advice?"

"Remember to strike through your opponent when you punch and keep your wrist straight, or you're going to snap it."

"Anything else?"

"You're an idiot for doing this."

"You said that already."

"It bears repeating. Remember how he said Kleos was a master?"

"Yeah."

"Nazir is a close second. His Novices are always good."

"It's only the first day."

"His Novices are always good on the first day."

Great. Michael stepped into the middle of the ring of Numen. Dani did too. They stood apart with Kleos at the center. He was equally unenthusiastic about this fight.

"Fighters ready?" he announced.

"Ready." Michael said, gritting his teeth.

"Ready." She answered, though truthfully she wasn't.

Kleos lowered his arm, glancing back and forth between the two. Michael itched to start. Kleos then raised his arm and jumped back.

Michael exploded at her. His fist came up and she barely avoided it. It was enough to make her jump back and enough to give him the confidence to attack again. He kept swinging, one fist and then the other. Michael was big. His reach was long. He wasn't the most agile boy, but he was big enough that it didn't matter.

She scooted back until she hit the ring of people. Kleos ordered him to step away and he followed. The people at her back shoved Dani forward. She caught Ethan's glare from the sidelines; hand in front of his mouth, watching.

"Come on girlie!" Michael jeered. "You know you want some!"

Who was this guy? A jock from a bad 80's teen movie? *Well, if he's going to set me up*, she thought.

"You ain't got nothing any girl wants, Tiny." She taunted.

Spectators laughed.

Michael's eyes flared. Before Kleos could part them, he jumped at her. This time there wasn't any skill. It didn't matter. He was fast and he was big. Despite Kleos trying to stop him, he swung hard. Dani brought her arm up to block. Success. She'd learned that much. He swung with his other fist. Not a success.

Stars burst through her vision and she hit the stones. She tasted blood. His fist connected squarely and she went down.

Michael went to kick, but Kleos tossed him back. The force of the throw sent him into his Guardian. "Stand down Novice Michael! You wait for me to declare the beginning of the bout!"

Michael heaved in anger. She could see that despite nearly getting knocked out. Dani slowly got to her feet. Ethan and Nathaniel were there.

"You alright?" Nathaniel asked.

"Do I look alright?"

He glanced at Michael. "Maybe don't piss him off again. He might take your head off."

"He'll have to get his hands on me first."

"He's going to." Ethan warned softly in her ear. He flicked his eyes over and Dani followed them. Nazir spoke to Michael; instructing. "I know how Nazir trains. He is telling him to take you to the ground and submit you. He'll even tell him to humiliate you for what you said, that little codpiece."

She shook her head, trying to clear the stars in her vision. "Your swearing up here is weird."

"Just focus. Remember: foot in the sternum and roll back."

"Why?"

"Because Michael is overconfident. He'll come at you hard." He patted her shoulder. "Try not to die."

"Thanks."

Dani returned to the center of the ring. This time, as Kleos lowered his arm, he warned Michael, "Wait for my signal."

He flexed his hands at his sides. Dani brought hers up to her temples again.

"Fighters ready?"

"Ready." Michael snarled.

"Ready."

Kleos brought his hand up. Sure enough, Michael barreled into her. Dani took a step back, brought up her foot just like Kleos showed her and grabbed onto him as she dropped back.

Unfortunately, she didn't roll. Instead, landed on her back with the big guy over her. His weight sunk her knee into her stomach. She groaned, him on top of her. His hands went for her throat. She blocked them, but could do little else.

"I'm gonna beat the tar out of you!" He seethed. "You're dead!"

She tried to push him off, but he was too heavy. She pushed him out with her leg, but only for a short time before he landed back on top of her. People egged him on. Nathaniel and Ethan yelled encouragement, but she could barely hear them over the drone.

She struggled with Michael, twisting left and right. She couldn't get him off. And the more energy she used, the less he had to. His bodyweight did all the work. She wouldn't fight him long.

She grabbed at his face. He seized her wrist, trying to pull it off. Dani struggled to hold on. She was exhausted.

"Take her down Michael!" Nazir crowed from the ring's edge. "Submit her!"

Her hand felt hot. She could see it redden, but it wasn't his grip on her wrist. It burned. It felt like her palm was molten lava. Michael hissed in pain as she grabbed for his face. She kept her palm flat against it, pushing. His grip loosened and he couldn't stay on her.

"UUUUUUURRRRRRRUUUUUUUUHHHHH!" he groaned. "Stop! Let go!"

The skin of her palm boiled. Michael lifted off. Her palm shifted up over his eye. Dani put all her strength into the shove.

Something like light burst from her fingertips. It wasn't bright, it wasn't a lot, but that close to Michael's open eye and he howled in pain. He tumbled back and grabbed the side of his face. Dani slithered back. Once far enough away, she raised her foot and kicked.

The first strike caught Michael in the mouth and snapped his head back. The next with her other foot came a millisecond after and popped him in the jaw. Two strikes and blood blossomed from his mouth. His eyes glazed; head lolling. Dani shifted sideways and leveraged her weight for a third kick across the bridge of his nose. Blood flew from his nostrils.

He dropped like a half-empty sack of flour.

The whole circle went silent. Dani caught her breath, slowly rising to her feet. Everyone stared at her. It was the same look she got from the guests at Ricky's party when she put her mom's boyfriend in the dirt. Shock. Fear. Disbelief.

She had to stop herself from going full Russell Crowe and asking if the audience was entertained.

Michael groaned, sputtering blood, lying on his side as red spittled out the side of his mouth. Nazir ran forward. "How dare she—?"

"Fight honestly?" Kleos finished, putting himself between her and him. "I don't know how she managed to keep her honor intact with such flagrant disrespect from an opponent! The question should be how dare Michael attack her unprovoked!"

"In battle, there are no rules." Nazir spat back.

"Exactly. She followed them and still won. Or do you not see _that coward_ lying on the ground?" he pointed to the Novice barely conscious next to him. "I think we can agree the fight was more than honest in terms of the victor. Does anyone contest?"

No one spoke up. Several Guardians attended to Michael.

That was how Elder Azariah found them when he came marching uphill, parting the gaggle of Guardians, Novices and random passerbys.

"What is the meaning of this?" The Elder demanded, and then spotted Michael on the ground. "What happened?"

168

"A roll." Kleos told him. "One Novice verses another."

Azariah stared at the bloodied Michael. "One Novice did that? In one round? Who?"

Everyone looked at Dani. Suddenly, she wished she could make herself invisible. When Azariah caught on, he could only look at her with disbelief. "Nazir, take your Novice to the healers. Ensure they give him enough panacea to heal his wounds properly. I'm assuming he will be in the Ward for some time."

Nazir helped Michael to his feet and draped one arm over his shoulder. He half-dragged, half-carried Michael off towards the Vale Bridge. Dani wasn't one to gloat, but there was something satisfying watching them leave.

"To the rest of you: our training is concluded for the day. Begin to your next session. Go!" The Novices departed. Before Dani could—and she kicked herself for not expecting it—Azariah called out. "Novice Daniella! To me!"

Cursing her luck, she marched herself over and stood in front of him. Bowing her head—more out of anger for the punishment or lecture she was undoubtedly about to receive than anything else—she asked through clenched teeth, "Yes Elder Azariah?"

His jaw clenched. She prepared for the worst.

Instead, "Very well done."

She blinked. "Excuse me?"

"To do such a thing to a much larger opponent takes a moderate amount of skill. Novice Michael is an aggressive foe. You came away practically unscathed."

As if on a broken record, she asked the second person in two days, "Do I say thank you?"

Azariah managed the smallest chuckle. "I would."

She didn't mind saying it this time. "Thank you, Elder."

"Do not become smug, Novice. Very few will underestimate you in the future. They will remember this bout. Take care you do not become careless. Dismissed." He bowed slightly, placing two fingers to his forehead.

She did the same, though unsure of what it meant. Then, she trotted off to meet up with Ethan.

"Is everything alright?" he asked.

"I guess. What does that mean? That bow you guys do?"

"It's called the reverence bow." He said. "It's our mark of respect."

The day was looking up.

Chapter Twenty

"Aer." Elder Caspar announced. "What is it?"

"What you breathe." Someone muttered. A few people giggled.

She managed to get to her next lesson in the Keep, in one of the strangest places she'd ever seen. Pedestals jutted from the walls in ascending spirals around a circular courtyard. Elder Caspar, a squat olive-skinned man with flowing robes, assembled them around himself.

"Yes." He frowned. "But it is also a weapon."

He turned and walked to a pile of small, smooth stones stacked in a pile at the center of the chamber. The Guardians circled around it.

"Aer is an unlimited element." Caspar told them. "It is all around you, unlike Fyre, Erthe or Water. The first angels used nature in their war. It is said they hurled mountains, caused floods and made volcanoes erupt. They struck with lightning and fire and turned the Heavens on one another. We may not able to do the same, but we can teach you to use the five *arche* against demonkind."

Caspar waved his hand. A breeze whipped down over the walls of the Keep and through the courtyard, ruffling their clothes.

"All Numen can control the elements to a degree." He told them. "Aer can bring a fallen sword to your hand when you have need of it, or even," he trailed off, the wind picking up around him and levitating him into the air, "mean the difference between escape or death."

He floated back down to his feet.

"As with all the elements, Aer will not listen to a weak will. You bend it to you. You may not be able to stop a mountain from falling on you, but a rock?"

The stone shot from his hand and hit the nearest Novice. He grunted, taking it to the stomach.

"That is what we are here to learn. Line the walls!"

The Guardians stayed in the center and the Novices fanned out. Dani and Nathaniel took spots next to one another. Ethan stood across from them.

"Why do I get the feeling this is a firing squad?" he mumbled none-too-enthusiastically.

"Think they'll let us have one last smoke?"

"I don't smoke."

"Me either."

"Novices!" Caspar announced. "Your task is to stop the stone from striking you! Do not move from your spots. Do not dodge. Instead, use your hands. Feel the wind in your fingertips. In your minds see a shield of air. Force it to your hand. Push the rocks away from you!"

Dani glanced at her hands. Shields? She extended one and tried to imagine it.

Then a rock the size of a grape smacked into her forehead.

"Ow!"

"Sorry." Ethan said, and then shot one at Nathaniel. He hit him in the neck.

"Mother sarding hellfires!" Nathaniel groaned, grabbing his throat. "What is this? Dodgeball?"

Ethan drew another stone in hand. "Focus." He told them. Then he hurled it at her.

Dani ducked and it struck off the wall.

"Do not move, Novice!" Caspar barked.

Groaning, she tried to think of shields around her hands. She held them up.

Ethan threw again. This time it hit her forearm. Pain stung down to her elbow.

"Better!"

"Fyre is the ultimate offensive weapon." Said Elder Atar, an elderly Elder if there ever was one. His skin was the color of good chocolate but creased with deep lines. He looked old; real old. He knelt before a pit, with a fire smoldering in embers.

She stood in a windowless, sweltering room with two other aeries—Ethereal and Pinnacle—while Atar instructed. It was ungodly hot, but at least he wasn't throwing crap at her.

"Fire is the most volatile element in existence, thus the arc of Fyre is the hardest to control. From the first fires of humanity to the nuclear bomb, fire is both helpful and destructive. Very few can combat the demonic with such an unstable weapon right away, but it should not be just a weapon. It can cauterize a wound, create a campfire when you are cut off in the wilderness; it could mean the difference between life and death."

"What is the one limitation of any *arche*?"

No one knew. So instead of waiting, Atar hovered his hand over the pit and the fire flared to life.

"It cannot be created. And fire, unlike other elements, is unpredictable and because of that, those who learn to use it are unpredictable. Your fires are almost out. Extend your hand. Stoke them."

171

The Novices all put their hands down towards the embers. Dani's was made of charred black-and-grey wood. Very little heat came off it.

"Call to the fire." Atar instructed. "Make your will supreme. Demand it's acquiesce."

Dani stared into the glow. Her palm was barely warm. She did as he asked, even whispering for it to move. Nothing happened.

"Look!" hissed someone. She glanced up. Flames sprouted in the pit of one Novice. He laughed in triumph. "It's working!"

"Very good, but do not lose focus." Atar told him.

"It's working! Look at it!"

Everyone watched. The flames grew brighter. He laughed out loud. "Yes! It's working! It's working!"

"Novice, be careful."

Too late. The boy pushed out his palms and the flames exploded in a mushroom flare. The fire hit him in the face and he howled in surprise. When he dropped back to his butt, his eyebrows were singed.

Dani nearly died laughing.

"How was Fyre training?" Ethan asked.

"Funny as hell."

On the way to Studies in the Anthenaeum, Ethan took Dani to Adare's market. She saw Shea and Roxelana, waving politely. Ethan paid for a loaf of bread, some kind of raw meat wrapped in cloth and various fruits with a pair of leather gloves in trade. He put what he bought into a bag and then they headed back to the Citadel.

"Do you need anything?" he asked. "Most Novices don't have much. Your Guardian is supposed to help you when you first start out in Empyrean, but with Mastema..."

Dani thought of her house from the centaurs. "I think I'm covered for food and the little girl Korë set me up with fresh water, but if you happen to have a Coke on hand, I'd take that."

"Can't say that I do." He handed her an apple. "Here. Eat. Trust me, you'll need it."

She accepted the fruit and bit into it. It was delicious. "Thanks. So, you treat all girls this nice?"

He laughed. "Not normally, but then again there aren't many girls here, are there?"

"There's the gifted."

He burned with embarrassment.

"I thought so. So, you and Airlea, huh?"

"Dani," he chided, "keep it down. And why all the interest? Jealous?"

"No." She switched subjects. "Well, then, can you tell me what the hell 'vespertide' is?"

Ethan tensed, gritting his teeth. "Nazir shouldn't have said anything."

"It wasn't just him. Some of the gifted mentioned it."

He shook his head. "Someone is going to get us in trouble one day."

"And will I know what it is that one day?"

He smirked. "Maybe."

They walked, eating their fruit until Dani was down to the core. When they were both done, they tossed them onto the grass. As she watched, the grass curled up around it and began to consume what was left.

"Nothing goes to waste." He told her. "Empyrean is more alive than you might imagine."

That was the truth. She wiped her hands and face. "So, how do I make money up here? If you don't have something to trade, do you just live on the bare necessities?"

Ethan shrugged. "Well, Novice Village is always stocked with food, but you don't live there. Some Numen do favors for the gifted and vice versa. There's no one way to get anything. You can look for plants or minerals to trade. Or," he shrugged, "there's always Earth stuff people might want."

"Earth stuff?"

"Things we aren't supposed to have up here. Judah runs a thriving black market. And that reminds me." He stopped and reached into his tunic. From beneath the folds, he withdrew a small chain and pendant. "I believe this is yours."

"My necklace!" she took it back. "Where did you get it?"

"I went back for the bag you left the night we met. You'll find it in your village."

She blushed gratefully. "Why?" And then, almost immediately, she hated how giddy she got. "Uh, thanks. I, um, appreciate it." She quickly switched subjects. "You mentioned Judah. Has he ever been here?"

"From time to time to see his pet."

"His pet?"

"Tigris."

She stared at him. "You're joking. That's his _pet_? What, they were all out of kittens at the store?"

He shrugged. "Some people on Earth keep ostriches."

"That's totally not the same thing!"

Ethan led her up the steps. Dani remarked, "You're not carrying your sword."

"Should I be?"

"I just thought you would. I don't know much about swords."

"You'll learn. Most Numen don't carry weapons around the city. There's no point. We might carry a knife or dagger, but here we don't need to protect ourselves constantly."

"Maybe you don't." Dani grumbled, thinking of some of the hostility she'd already encountered.

"The Gatekeepers are the only ones armed and armored. Most Guardians will carry a knife." He patted the one on his belt. "I'm sure Mastema has shown you his."

"He has." She could still feel the edge against her neck.

He led her to the Anthenaeum. The large library was filled with people. Dani looked for the Novices and spotted them a few stories up on a massive pedestal at the center of the chamber.

She cursed. "I hate climbing."

He put an arm around her. "May I?"

She blushed. Then she hated herself for blushing. Then she hated him for making her blush. "Fine."

"Don't sound so excited."

They lifted from the ground. Ethan flew her upwards, passing walkways and staring Numen as they rose, until they floated over the railing of the square lecture platform the aeries occupied. She got more than a few looks as they descended, her in his arms. The moment they touched down, she quickly separated herself.

"Thanks." She mumbled.

Elder Atid led the session from a lectern at the center. He bowed. Ethan returned the gesture. Atid was a dark-skinned Middle Eastern man with grey hair and spectacles. *I thought Numen didn't need glasses...* Nathaniel didn't anymore. It would suck to be nearly-immortal and nearly-blind at the same time.

She saw Lester's and Andreas' smirks when they spotted her with Ethan. Bouden was happy to see her. Dink less so. But what surprised her was the look Nathaniel gave her: upset.

"Novice Daniella," Elder Atid greeted, gesturing to a chair, "please join us. Guardian Ethan, thank you for bringing her."

"Of course, Elder. I apologize for her tardiness. It was my fault."

Dani couldn't sit fast enough across from Nathaniel, who softened enough to whisper, "Hey."

"Hey. Have I missed anything?"

"No." Bouden muttered next to him. "But apparently we missed a lot." He glanced at Ethan. Again, Nathaniel grimaced.

Dani squinted her best glare. "Shut it."

Atid introduced himself. He began explaining the history of the Anthenaeum and Empyrean. He talked about Gabriel the Archangel and about the duties of the Numen to protect humanity. Basically, he explained a lot that Dani didn't listen to. She tuned him out. She hadn't left Earth just to end up in another classroom.

She sat behind Dink, who didn't look at her. At least, not right away. As Atid spoke, she saw him glance back once or twice. When she caught him looking, he quickly turned around. She didn't say anything; she was too angry to deal with him right now.

After the third or fourth time, he steeled his courage and faced her. Dani had never seen someone so guilt stricken.

"Dani..." his voice was barely a whisper. "I—I'm sorry."

She purposefully ignored him.

"I can't imagine what you think of me."

"You're right. You can't."

His face was so pained it was hard to look at him, so she didn't.

"You're right to be angry." He told her. "What I did...I shouldn't have done."

"You're right again. You shouldn't."

Tears welled in his eyes. He shook his head, "I'm so sorry. If there's any way—."

"To make up for giving me to wolves for dinner?" she finally did look at him and let a lot of rage sit in that glare. "I'm pretty sure there isn't."

His mouth dipped around the edges. "I understand if you don't want to talk to me. I just wanted you to know how sorry I was. If I could take it back, if I could make it up to you, if I could somehow repay you, I would. I'd do it in a heartbeat. I want you to know that. I won't bother you again." He looked at Nathaniel and Bouden, who both dismissed him without looking back. He turned back around. "I'll leave you alone."

Dink visibly shook. Andreas gave him a derisive, disgusted snort. Then he looked at her and smirked, shaking his head.

"Wimp." He muttered.

That, she decided, she wouldn't tolerate. She could be angry at Dink all she wanted, but that—what word did Ethan use? Codpiece?—didn't get to pass judgment.

"Hey." She put a hand on Dink's shoulder, leaning forward and whispering into his ear. "I never said I didn't want to talk to you again."

Dink sniffed, turning towards her a fraction. "What?"

"I never said that." He assured him. "I'm angry, but I'll get over it."

"You will?"

"You were captured by five monsters who you thought wanted to eat you."

He sniffed again. "Six."

She chuckled a little, patting his shoulder. "Right. Six. All the more reason."

"You—you're not mad?"

"Oh I'm mad." She told him. "But I think I can get more joy out of messing with you from now on than leaving you in the doghouse."

He heard the humor in her voice and exhaled in relief. "Yeah?"

"Yeah." She patted his shoulder again. "And don't think for one second I'm going to be easy on you. I'm mean to people I mess with. Just ask Nate."

"Please stop calling me that." Nathaniel murmured.

"Deal?" Dani asked Dink.

He nodded gratefully. "Deal. Thanks Dani."

"Don't mention it," she sat back, "*Ailbe.*"

He laughed. Both Nathaniel and Bouden smiled. Andreas looked annoyed. Maybe he didn't like tearful reunions. Maybe he just didn't like Dink and Dani.

Maybe it didn't matter and he was a little codpiece for sure.

Studies were just that: studies. Atid taught the types of demons they'd face, spells and charms they could use, even history. Dani wasn't certain how a history lesson could save her life.

The next lesson was Erthe training in the Gardens under Elder Tertullian. It was more of the same: growing plants by thinking about it. Again, Dani felt useless. Then she went to a stream to learn Water.

This was getting ridiculous.

She was with Halcyon and Aether for water. She wasn't very hopeful about this session. In fact, the only interesting thing about it was Mastema, who appeared after an entire day of absence.

"Where the hell have you been?" she demanded.

He waited for her by the side of a stream flowing through the Garden. Everyone either avoided them or stared from afar. He didn't look concerned by it.

"I was away."

"Thank you for such a detailed excuse. You were supposed to be with me this morning!"

"I was not with you."

"Dear God, are you that dumb?"

His usual scowl deepened. "Do not insult me."

"Insult you? I—I—!" she couldn't even put it into words. She stamped her foot in the stream, splashing them. "You little sard nugget! And yes, I used that on purpose! The only good thing about this place is that I can cuss you out with different words!" Dani promised herself, *I am so learning every insult and cuss word up here for him.* "Where were you?"

"The Elder Council called me." He told her. "I could not refuse."

He stepped past her without an explanation. He was usually stone faced, but he looked bothered by his meeting with the Elders. What did they say to him?

The lesson, like the ones before it, wasn't very helpful. Dani did learn that water could be used to heal, which is what many healers used to treat wounds; manipulating the water in the bodies of others to heal them. But like before, Dani struggled with her new powers.

Dani and Mastema returned to the Keep for the final lesson and climbed the stairs to one of the highest rooms. Elder Harut was the final Elder to see for a power Dani was most interested in learning.

"Aether; the veil," Harut explained in a darkened tower room so packed everyone stood shoulder to shoulder. "It pervades this world and yet, we know so little about it."

Curtains drawn over the windows, enclosing them in gloom, Harut spoke with only soft lanterns to light the space.

"The veil is rumored to have existed since the beginning of time. Every supernatural creature—the centaurs, the cynocephali, even demons themselves—are hidden by its power. A mandanus will not see them, or see them as something else. We the Numen, however, can control it. But do not mistake me: you cannot make a demon or a mandanus do what you want, for free will exists, but they can be tricked. You can make someone not see you."

Harut disappeared. Every Novice backed away. Dani didn't. She'd seen this show a lot. A moment later, Harut appeared again, but then quickly so did a double of him.

The twin Haruts spoke simultaneously. "The veil is near limitless."

One Harut disappeared and the chamber around them transformed. Suddenly, instead of the cramped room, they were standing in a large, flowering field.

"When you make your enemy question their existence, you break them."

Dani reached out to where a wall had been moments earlier. Her fingers passed through air. Then the chamber reformed, but now much wider than it had been before.

"This is the room as it is," Harut chuckled playfully, "or is it? Your confusion is a testament to how quickly your minds can be manipulated. We will learn how to do this, but first you must learn to resist it. Form ranks."

The Novices got into two lines. Harut waved to the first two to come forward.

"What I will do is exert influence on you; manipulate the Aether and attempt to make you see what you most desire. You must resist. Focus. Remember who you are. Remember what you are. The veil is powerful because a lie is preferable. Do not give into such a lie."

The Novices stepped forward one at a time. Harut did nothing but stand in front of them. But as she watched, the first swayed a bit. He smiled. His eyes glazed, looking around him. It was clear that what he saw and what was there were two separate things.

The boy giggled, "Mommy?"

Harut slapped one hand across his face. He staggered and came to. The others laughed.

"Do not jeer." Harut told them. "To master oneself takes time."

The boy came to the back of the line. Everyone was snickering as he passed, repeating *mommy*, but Dani could see his face. If it were possible, he looked like someone who saw the greatest thing in his life and then had it snatched away. He was beyond devastated.

What did Dink say? Most Novices were orphans or runaways? She didn't laugh. It scared her someone could do that to a person.

The laugher died more and more as more Novices had their turn. Each one was slapped out of their vision by Harut. Each one returned to line a little shaken.

It came to Dani's turn. She stepped in front of Harut, hands at her sides, and waited.

Focus. Focus. Focus.

Then suddenly, she wasn't in the tower anymore. She was in Ricky's living room. Everything was the same; same dingy furniture, same pile of cigarettes in the ashtray on the coffee table, same usual drink in her mom's hand.

Her mother stood in front of her.

"Mama?" she couldn't believe it.

"Dani? Dani, what's wrong?"

Dani shook her head. She felt dizzy; like she drank cough syrup. But she had mind enough to say, "You're not real."

"What?" Her mom gave her a concerned look. "Dani, are you okay?"

"You're not real." Dani shook her head, closing her eyes. *It's not. It's not real.* But when she opened them, her mom was still there.

"Dani, it's me." Yvette put a hand on her daughter's shoulder. She felt it. It made Dani flinch. "Honey, please, you're scaring me."

"What's happening?"

"Honey, don't you remember? You went to the store to get us drinks. The eclipse party?" she sipped from her glass. "I swear, you're getting more forgetful by the day. Are you alright?"

"You're not real." Dani insisted.

"Honey, please, you just walked in. Is Nathaniel coming to the party?"

"Party?"

"The eclipse party. Don't you remember?"

The eclipse party. Dani did remember walking in. In fact, the longer she thought about it, the more she could remember. Walking up the steps to the house. Leaving the house earlier.

Leaving the house...

"There were people here." She shook her head slowly. "When I left, there were people. And I didn't go to the store. I went to the gym. Nathaniel was there..."

Wraiths. Running for her life. Ethan.

She glared at her mother. "You're not real."

A hand slapped her face. Hard. Dani blinked. Laughter. As if waking from a dream, she came to, standing in front of Harut surrounded by laughing Novices, except for Nathaniel.

179

"Silence!" Harut commanded. The crowd died down. "Very good, Novice. Most don't reject the vision the first time. Though it took you several seconds."

That earned her more than a few jealous, ugly stares when she turned around to rejoin the line. Andreas leaned against the wall, arms folded and snickering.

"You got something to say?"

He shrugged. "Depends. Do you miss your Mama?"

The entire day Dani felt the urge to hit someone. Now, she gave into that urge. She punched Andreas hard enough to send him down.

The chamber exploded in chaos. Andreas scrambled to his feet, but before he could hit her, Mastema appeared in the way.

"Get off me!" he shoved the larger man. Dani's Guardian didn't fight back. He waited until more people parted them.

"Enough!" Harut barked. "That is enough! We are here to learn to control the mind, not act like animals! Listen when I give you an order, Novice Daniella!"

"She will." Mastema promised.

"The lesson is concluded." Harut announced. "Our day is ending. Depart with your Guardians."

Andreas wasn't bleeding; Dani didn't hit him that hard. But he glared at her as he stalked off with Lester.

She noticed Mastema looking at her funny. "What? Are you going to lecture me?"

"Why did you hit him?"

"So he knew I could."

"Then no, I will not lecture." He followed the others out. No explanation needed.

Dani flexed her aching knuckles and followed too.

Chapter Twenty-One

A rhythm. It was what she needed and what she got.

The first day of training was nothing compared to the following month. Mastema's morning workouts remained brutal and his evening training sessions continued. In addition, he set up a modest tent next to her house. This meant he was around most of the time. He cooked over an open fire pit, but used other tools to make a better variety of food. Other than meals, though, they didn't talk much.

Combatives in the morning got easier. Some things came naturally. Ethan commented she was a natural striker. Unfortunately, she was smaller than most of the boys so wrestling—what they called grappling—was less easier to learn.

She hadn't won many admirers. Ever since her stunts with Andreas and Michael, she got more hostile looks from the others. Bouden, Dink and Nathaniel stuck by her, but she ruffled some feathers.

Aer, Fyre, Erthe and Water training continued to be difficult. And after a little under a month in the celestial city, the one training every Novice wanted to learn arrived.

"Flight." Caspar said. "The power over Aer to defy gravity. Flight can save you. Flight can give you an edge in battle."

They stood on the wall of the Keep above the Anthenaeum, overlooking the Vale. Caspar hovered before them.

"To learn this power takes one thing: courage." He told them. "Defy your fear. Use your emotions. Harness them."

"And if I don't want to plummet to my death?" Nathaniel asked from beside Dani.

"Then do not." Caspar said, as if that actually meant anything. "The power is within you. You must simply take it."

"And we do that how?" Dani asked.

"Jump."

She stared at him. Was he high? Every Novice looked at the drop with the exact same fear she did.

"Um," Nathaniel whispered, "does this guy just want us to excuse-me-while-I-kiss-the-sky?"

"I think so."

"Who is first?" Caspar asked. "Are there volunteers?"

Despite the eagerness to learn, no one spoke up.

"It is not about being fearless." The Elder said. "It is about facing your fear. Use it."

Still, none of the Novices spoke up.

The Elder sighed. "Very well. We will do this, as they say, the old fashioned way."

He waved his hand. Behind them, the air billowed hard and shoved them all forward. Everyone screamed and toppled over the side.

And then they were falling.

The Vale's treetops rushed up at them as she flailed her arms. She could do nothing but scream and wait for death. And unfortunately, they were so high up, waiting took a long time.

As they treetops neared, Dani and the others slowed. The air beneath them cushioned and they dropped slower and slower until just above the first branches, they stopped.

They hovered. Dani and Nathaniel exchanged looks. Did they stop themselves?

Nope. Caspar hovered down, hand held aloft and controlling all one hundred and forty-five Novices. "Not a bad start." He said with a grin. "Though blind panic won't help you."

"Totally cool." Nathaniel marveled.

A few of the others agreed.

"Yes." Caspar said. "Hopefully, one day, you will do this yourself. But until then—." He dropped his hand.

With a scream, every Novice dropped into the branches of the trees.

Dani spent a lot of her time in the market place. She found that her wooden cups, the ones the centaurs crafted for her, flavored any water she poured into them. There were about a dozen, more than she needed, so she traded them to Adare, making several shekels of Corinth and an Orich, which she used to purchase something she never thought she would: hot wax. Apparently, shaving cream and razors weren't a thing up here.

She also took to selling off some of the things in her returned bag. What Ethan said was true: Earth things like the spare music player and computer were better than gold up here. Shea was especially helpful in finding clients. All she had to do was avoid the Gatekeepers.

Usually, one or more of her friends tagged along with her when she went to the market. After shopping at a jinni vendor, Bouden asked, "Hey, Dani? Wanna see something cool?"

"If you take your pants off, I will hurt you."

He chuckled. "Nah. Still wanna see?"

"Sure."

He held his palm up to his mouth. He spoke softly into it. The air over his fingers quivered. And then, that same air disturbance floated off his palm, through the air and over Dani's face.

"*Dink is a loser.*"

Dink stood next to her, but didn't appear to hear it. He frowned. "What?"

Dani giggled. So did Bouden.

"How did you do that?" She asked.

"It's an aerwhisper." He explained. "It's how Numen communicate over long distances without messengers. You know the tower in the center of the Citadel? Messengers send and receive messages at the top. You can't say a whole lot or the whisper will fall apart, but you can send short messages."

"Oh, like magical Twitter?"

"Exactly!"

Adare was out at her market and smiled as Dani approached. "My dear, you look as lovely as ever."

"I get beat up on a daily basis and live in a shack. I look like hell, but thank you."

"Everything is half off today."

"Adare, there are no fixed prices."

"Oh, I know darling, but your friend there," she pointed to Bouden, "doesn't."

Dani saw Roxelana and waved, but her friend quickly dropped her hand when Airlea walked by. How was it that she was in a magical world and still suffering the problems she had in high school?

"Don't take it personally." Shea said, filling a basket with ears of corn. "Airlea is a bit of a pain when it comes to you. Roxelana doesn't want to get you in trouble."

"Why? What did I do to Airlea? I've barely spoken to her."

"True, but Ethan hasn't come to vespertide."

"You mean your super-secret club? What does that have to do with me?"

"He hasn't come since you arrived in Empyrean."

The implication hung in the air between them.

Dani was looking over some of the spices Adare sold. In the past month, she discovered that if she wanted anything flavorful, she needed to learn to cook. As she chose some in small canvas pouches, a commotion caught her attention.

Uphill, a crowd gathered. Numen Gatekeepers marched through the streets down towards the bridge. Dani and her friends stood to one side as they passed. Between them, purple-clothed Powers passed; some limping along with help, others on stretchers, and some covered by white cloths.

"What happened?" Dani wondered aloud.

"Demon attack." Shea answered behind her. "I just heard from some of the gifted. The Powers caught wind of a demon nest somewhere in the Midwest. They went to take it down."

"What happened?"

"Some type of unknown demon was waiting for them." He shook his head sadly."

"A trap?"

"Looks like it."

Dani watched the grizzly procession pass. It made her sick. Way too many of them were on cloth-covered stretchers. Way too many of them weren't moving.

"Swords are one of our most effective weapons. No two are alike."

Dani sat cross-legged across from Mastema. A set of swords lay between them.

"Most swords," he gestured, "are composed of adamantine-steel."

He picked up his sword; the long, hooked one from another era. "Every Numen favors a weapon of their choosing. Some will choose a spear, or a bow, even an axe, but the sword is unique. It isn't meant to be a primary weapon. Gatekeepers carry spears or bows for long range, but may carry a sword as an auxiliary. Naturals and alchemists favor knives, as they can be used for both defense and a tool. Most Guardians favor swords."

"Why?"

"What better tool in close quarters? Guardians are sent alone into the unknown. The sword is versatile." He held his higher. "My ancestors carried this weapon. It is called the khopesh." He slid his finger along the curved spine. "One deadly arc meant for cutting and a hook-tip to thrust in and pull," he tapped the backend barb along the point, "out the heart. It is an effective killing tool."

He put his sword aside. "Scimitars and sabers have a similar design; light and meant for hacking and slashing. Backswords like these," he held up a single-edged straight blade, "are for duels and armored opponents. The broadsword is double-edged, used for thrusting and blocking. All are single-handed weapons."

184

"Ethan carries a two-handed sword."

"A Montante longsword. It was used by his Italian ancestors, but none of that is your concern. You are too small to wield such a weapon."

"Hey! I'm not weak!"

"You misunderstand me. It is not that you cannot. It is that you *should* not. Those of small stature need to be quick and agile. Speed will be your ally."

They stood. "Everyone says relying on others keeps us safe against demons." She said. "It's practically a mantra around here. They should slap it on a coffee mug or something."

"And if others would rely on you," he told her, "we would speak of that, but no one will, so it is a moot point."

"I have friends."

Mastema went to the footlocker where he kept practice weapons, opening the lid. "I am aware of Ethan's and Kleos' charges."

"Speaking of them," she toed the hilt of one of the swords, "everyone keeps talking about you. Or actually, *not* talking about you. It's like no one wants to say what they're thinking."

For his part, Mastema didn't either. He dug around in the trunk without saying a word.

"Is there something I should know?"

Still nothing.

"Why don't people trust you? Judah says the Elders don't. Nazir called you a failure. And then you had to go before the Elder Council a month ago and—."

"I think that is enough." Mastema barked.

It took Dani aback. He glared at her for a second, his irises two burning black coals of anger, and then he softened and stood.

"We begin." He said calmly.

"With which weapon?" she asked, looking at them all.

"With none." He threw something to her, which she barely caught.

"Aw, come on! Sticks again?" this one was short, only about three feet long at most, with a hilt; a practice sword. "This is bull! When do I learn to fight with real weapons?"

"When you learn to fight with these." Mastema strode to the middle of the pavilion, his own baton in hand. He spread into a fighting stance, his weapon strangely pointed to the floor instead of up. "Come, Novice. Let us see what skill you possess."

Resigned to her fate, Dani got into her own stance. She kept her stick point-up, her hand out in protective position instead of tucked behind her back like Mastema.

"Attack!" he yelled.

She did, instantly regretting it.

Apparently, there was a reason he held his sword that way. If she attacked at his (supposedly) unprotected face he simply flipped his weapon up, knocked hers aside and hit her. If she went low, he stabbed down to block, knocked hers aside and hit her. If she tried to stab, he struck her hand, knocked hers aside and hit her.

It became a string of unending bruising.

He taught her to stand, to keep her free hand ready but protected against her side, to find the weak spot and attack. He instructed in strikes, counterblows, how to use both sides of the weapon: short (the edge facing her) and long (edge facing him) to strike. She did well enough to not get beaten silly, but it didn't stop the pain. Mastema was a Nazi.

They moved to two handed weapons, which were easier, but she realized very quickly why it didn't work for her. Though the distance the "sword" had was more and the two hands gave her more control, Mastema's reach was far greater than hers. She could move fast but she could get nowhere near him. Maybe with a hundred year's more practice, she could, but this time he wasn't pulling punches.

"Ow!" she screamed as he struck her shoulder. "That's like the elventy-billionth time!"

"That's not a number." He said.

Dani did her best Keanu Reeves impression, "Yet."

Mastema stared blankly at her.

"Keanu Reeves, Celebrity Jeopardy; don't you watch SNL?"

"What is SNL?"

Right. "Never mind."

"Which do you prefer? One-handed or two?" he asked.

"One handed." She dropped her practice sword to the ground. "What if I used two short swords? I could use one to fight and one to block."

"Why on Earth would you do that?"

She shrugged. "Double the weaponry, double the chance to hit someone?"

He shook his head. "That is a fantasy meant for children's books. No true swordsman would ever use two weapons at once, unless they were skilled well beyond on your years."

"Really?" She retrieved the two practice batons from the ground.

"The dexterity and coordination it would require takes patience." Mastema lectured. "Time. Practice."

"Uh-huh." She twirled the two sticks in her hands.

"And to learn to strike with one or both simultaneously would be too difficult to master. Most accomplish it only after years of study."

"You mean like this?"

Dani rotated her wrists, loosening them, and then swung. First left, then right, striking the air in front of her with each weapon, tumbling the blows into the same place, before spinning, striking and flowing into another stance. She used what combatives she knew to keep balance as she spun, flipping from one foot to another easily, then striking. She spun and cut, then did a quick round-off, landing on both feet in front of him and pressed the point to his chest with a grin.

Mastema didn't react, unimpressed. "I assume you've had some form of training?"

"Better." She grinned. "Baton twirling."

"Baton twirling?"

"You know: marching band, leotards, frilly little string coming out the end?" She grinned. "The only difference is that it's done by dumb blonde Valley girls and the object isn't to cut a person in half."

He shook his head. "It is more involved than that to strike with two weapons."

"Well, yeah, but what if I told you it I used the sticks to hit boys in the face when they mouthed off? Would that convince you?"

"No."

Mastema allowed Dani to practice using two weapons. It didn't go much better, but she was able to block some blows with the second short sword well enough to justify it to herself. She didn't escape unscathed, but at least she wasn't getting whacked in the ribs every five minutes.

Afterwards, she and Mastema feasted on some kind of beef, bread and asparagus. Dani used panacea bandages to heal her bruises so she'd be able to use her right arm in the morning. And with a house, they ate at a table like civilized people.

"In a week and half's time," he told her, "the Trials will begin. We must prepare you for them."

"What are the Trials?"

He paused, legitimately shocked for the first time she knew him. "You mock me?"

"You mean am I kidding? No. I have no idea what they are."

"Hellfires, did they not tell you of this?" He cursed again bitterly. "The Elders were to inform you. Every group of Novices undergoes the Trials. They are a test of your abilities. Each aerie is pitted against a series of three separate trials. Training is entirely devoted to these tests. Not knowing of them is certain to grant failure!"

"Why? What's the point of that?"

"How an aerie performs determines their worth in our society."

"What? Like standings in a bracket?"

"I do not know of what you speak."

She sighed heavily. "I mean, it's sort of like a competition?"

"In a manner of speaking, yes."

"What if you fail to win?"

"That has never occurred. Three attempts and never has an aerie failed all three. Should an aerie fail to garner at least one victory, either against another aerie or in completion of a Trial, the consequences would be dire. They would have no place amongst us."

"What are these Trials, exactly? Is it fighting another aerie?"

"It is fighting another flock as much as fighting yourself. The Trials are designed by Arbiters to be a foe unto themselves."

"You mean Heman and Azariah?"

"*Elder* Heman and *Elder* Azariah." He corrected. "And yes, amongst others. The Arbiters design them. Those in the city suitable for the task will be asked to lend their gifts to the Trials."

Great. Why hadn't she been told about the Olympic Games from Satan's backside? She knew the answer, but was just too incensed say it. Mastema was right. She should have been told.

"Those bloody Elders," Mastema muttered. "Any aerie not informed of the Trials would be hampered. You were to be studying for them since the beginning!"

How could people keep doing this to her? Heman had been unfair in the Vale. Asaph tried to have her executed upon arrival. Nazir set her up to get beaten. Andreas. Lester.

"Mastema, why is no one is helping me?" Dani demanded. "Why is everyone so hell bent on me failing?"

"You are an outsider." He told her. "Outsiders are not given the benefit of the doubt."

"But I'm not an outsider! I'm a Numen just like them!"

"You are a Numen not attested to in the Book of Metatron, a woman, and—in their eyes—a radical element. "

188

"So?"

"So, that is self-explanatory."

"No it's not!"

"It is for now." He finished his food and departed.

She called out, "Mastema? Please. If anyone would understand, it would be you. Why is it so important that I'm not in the Book?"

He paused, stopping at the edge of the pavilion. He glanced over his shoulder. Then, melting into shadows, he was gone.

Chapter Twenty-Two

"Do you have minute of free time?"

The following week, Dani's mood hadn't improved. At Combatives, they were into weapons, which she felt confident in until her first match. Despite two swords and Mastema's training, she lost the match to a Novice with a two-handed weapon. She needed to get faster, or learn to fight opponents who could put pounds behind their blows. Kleos tried to comfort her, pointing out Dink preferred a bow and arrow to straight fighting. Bouden, too. She could follow their lead. She, however, didn't.

It was Ethan pulling her out of Studies that changed the pace of the day. Elder Atid, using Aer, formed a figure out of smoke. She sat quietly with Nathaniel, Dink and Bouden, watching Atid move the grotesque monster while he lectured.

"I'm sorry, what?" she asked.

Ethan knelt next to her. "Can I borrow you for a little bit?"

She blushed. Ever since flying with him that day, she felt weird around the short, handsome Guardian. His cute curls looked cuter. His honey eyes were more honey-er. *Damn him.*

"I'm studying."

He glanced at the image. "Simple to remember: demonic imp. Common demon. They're similar to wraiths; low on the totem pole. Rotten skin. Decaying flesh. Take off the head or destroy the heart to kill them. Ready now?"

"Have you ever killed one?" Dink whispered excitedly.

"Yes. Dani? Time? You got it?" he looked anxious.

"Um, I think so. Do you guys mind?" she asked her friends.

All of them were okay with it. Mostly. Nathaniel looked bothered, but he said nothing.

"Give me a minute." Dani told Ethan.

He stepped away to wait.

She told them quietly. "Give me some time. I'll be back."

"I think he's wants to give you more than some time." Bouden joked.

Nathaniel slugged him.

"Ow! Hey!"

"Silence back there!" Atid called, then returned to his lecture.

"Thank you." She told him. "I'll be back as soon as I can. If Elder Atid is looking for me, tell him I went to the little girls' room."

"Do they have a little girls' room?" Dink wondered. "You are the only girl here after all."

190

She didn't want to think about that. Bathrooms in Empyrean were basically the same at Earth, though made of stone, but the last thing she wanted to think about was pee on the rim of the seat. She was very thankful the centaurs—who, she wondered, somehow knew how to make a human toilet—made for her a private commode at her house. Of course, how horse-people did the plumbing, she wasn't sure.

She joined Ethan. He held out his arm.

"Again?"

He nodded. Dani stepped into his arms, ignoring the jitters, and together they lifted off the ground. They flew up. Light cascaded down from the large dome skylight above them as they headed to the top.

The very top of the Anthenaeum was dominated by a large, circular platform directly underneath the skylight. A few dozen Chroniclers milled about the large pedestal. On a dais, a single Chronicler transcribed something onto scrolls and handed them to others.

Dani didn't need to ask. "The Book of Metatron I presume?"

"Yes. The Chronicler you see there is the Scribe of the Elder Council."

"You people really love your titles, don't you? Scribe, Consul, Arbiter, Novice. Don't you have anyone like a butcher, a baker, or a candlestick maker?"

Ethan ignored her joke. "He's the one who assigns Guardians to new charges. It's his responsibility until the Book is taken to a new celestial city."

"Why?"

"There's only one Book of Metatron, but seven cities." He told her. "Elysium, Beri'ah, Tartarus, Hyperuranion, Pleroma, Ayn Sof and Empyrean. They protect different parts of the world. They all need to know what names appear near them to retrieve the newest Numen. This solar eclipse was the responsibility of Empyrean. Our Novices came from this region of the world. The next solar eclipse will occur somewhere else and call one hundred and forty-four more Novices to a different city."

"Or one hundred and forty-five."

He got that serious expression he seemed to wear a lot lately. "That's what I wanted to talk to you about: you. Mastema told me that the Elders did not tell you about the Trials."

"Yeah. Why is that?"

He tensed. "I imagine because they don't want you to succeed."

"Well, I guessed that much, Sherlock. But why? What do they have against me?"

"I wondered that myself. In this case, I think it might have to do more with Mastema instead of you. Or both."

"To do with Mastema?"

"When he told me that you didn't know about the Trials, I assumed it has something to do with him going before the Council last month. You remember? Generally, Guardians are not taken away from their charges unless for special circumstances. That's when I got suspicious." He pulled her close, talking low so no one else could hear. "You have to understand something, Dani. You aren't the average Novice. I've tried to come up with a way of describing you without being insulting, but you're...well..."

"Abnormal?"

"A little." He sighed. "The Council has never been good with change, though I hoped they would be with you." His faced flushed for a second. "Some Elders outright dislike you."

"Dislike is the wrong word for it. Hate is better. They hate my guts."

Ethan nodded. "Others are suspicious of you. They speak on your behalf, but that doesn't mean that they trust you."

"You're talking about Elder Jeduthun?"

He couldn't hide the shock.

"Yeah. That first day? He and I had a not-so-nice chat."

He tried to be encouraging. "Elder Azariah speaks highly of you. Elder Castus believes in you, too. Some of the others—Caspar, Harut, Atar—they're sympathetic. They're your strongest advocates, but they are not completely on your side. I'm afraid that eventually, those on the Council who are on the fence might turn against you."

"You mean by Elder Asaph and Elder Heman."

"They have a lot of influence." He said. "The Gatekeepers are very loyal to Asaph. He's been their commander for over two hundred years. Heman has many allies on the Council and many supporters amongst the Powers. Many believe he will succeed Castus, should he pass."

"And how would that happen? Elders rarely leave the city, right? How could he die?"

"Yes, well, things still happen." He told her enigmatically. "My point is that everything is precarious for both you and Mastema. I think that's why they put you together." He held up his hand to stop her next question. "Don't misunderstand me: he is an excellent teacher. But to not tell you about the Trials makes me wary."

"Okay, someone needs to explain to me what is up with my Guardian." She folded her arms. "Why does everyone not like him? And don't give me any crap about not needing to know. I want to know. I need to know. And I know *you* know."

Ethan avoided her gaze. He wanted to lie. She could read it on his face.

"Ethan!"

"Fie, fie, fie!" he cursed, which Dani knew was Empyrean's version of the f-bomb. "I swear I thought he would tell you. But since he hasn't, then I guess you deserve to know. Do you remember what I said about a Guardian's job?"

"You guys go to Earth, look after future Numen, and then bring them here during the solar eclipse."

He nodded. "Yes, but its more than that. Guardian training is very specific. Combat and survival techniques are required along with all of the advanced knowledge, but it's more than that. Part of the process is mental. It's indoctrination. We are trained to die."

"Die?"

"To die for our charge. Our sole task is to get them to Empyrean. We accomplish it by any means necessary. Sometimes, we have to make a choice; a hard one."

She got it. "You sacrifice yourself if it comes down to you or us."

He nodded. "In our training, it is instilled in us as an absolute faith that our life is meaningless if our charge dies. We cannot let that happen. If they die, we die. Guardians throw themselves at overwhelming odds to give the men we protect a chance to escape. It becomes second nature. No one questions it."

"Did Mastema?"

"Mastema was the best of us. No other Guardian faced odds the way he did. He explained his name, right?"

She nodded.

"Trust me, he earned it. Most of us might get some kind of nickname or moniker from some trait or heroic event. Mastema didn't. He's just Mastema. Death incarnate. Demons fear him. But a few eclipses ago, something happened. We don't know exactly how, but he lost his charge. The Novice was killed, but Mastema didn't kill the demon that did it and he didn't die to protect him. When he returned to Empyrean, he returned in shame. Everyone knows the law. Mastema broke it."

"It doesn't sound like his fault."

"From what he said, it wasn't. He was the only witness, but ever since then the Chroniclers have never assigned him a name out of the Book. Then last month, he was brought before the Council. They warned him."

"About?"

"About you." He told her. "They decreed that should Mastema fail to train you properly, his position as Guardian would be forfeit."

"What's the worst they could do to him?"

Ethan expression was not a happy one.

"They'd kill him? They'd kill their own soldier?"

"Judah was right when he said the Council doesn't break tradition very easily. Mastema is a source of shame. There are laws which state that a Numen unable to perform their duties would not be welcome amongst us. Many interpret that as grounds for execution."

"So they didn't tell me about the Trials in hopes I'd lose and he would pay the punishment?"

"And should you fail, already under suspicion..."

He didn't have to finish that sentence. "I'd be next."

"That's my belief, yes."

She felt cold. "Did you tell him?"

"I have. He agrees with me."

She folded her arms, sniffing back anger. She pressed her hand to her mouth to stop herself from screaming. "This is so unfair."

"It is. I'm sorry."

"Sorry? I didn't ask for," she yanked back the sleeve on her left arm to show him her halo, "this! I didn't want it as much as they didn't want me here. I was supposed to be safe from demons in Empyrean, but it turns out I'm in just as much danger from the people I'm supposed to be a part of!"

Judah's last words hung in the back of her mind: *I'm afraid that your existence is going to make quite a stir in our community. I'd chance to say that by the end of the day, the very people who just saved you will probably put you to death.*

Well, that was true. It just took more than a day. His other warning should have told her that: *People fear what they do not understand.*

"What am I supposed to do?" she asked. "The Trials are soon."

"I know. Kleos, Mastema and I are working on that."

"Working on it?" she demanded. "What are you supposed to do? I'm pretty sure you can't help me cheat." Though she half hoped she was wrong.

"No, we can't. We would pay a heavy price if discovered and it would all be for naught." He placed both hands on her shoulders reassuringly. "But that doesn't mean we won't try. I'm not going to let something bad happen."

She couldn't look him in the eye. She just couldn't. It was unfair. It was worse than unfair. Dani's life hadn't been the best before coming here.

Ricky and her mom were their own kind of mess. But facing down death, all because she and her Guardian were outside the norm? How was that remotely better?

Chroniclers looked their way. Ethan quickly removed his hands, warm with embarrassment.

"I should go." She said, trying not to get red herself. "Uh...thanks."

"You are quite welcome." He bowed formally, probably more for all the Looky-Lous than anything else. "Should I escort you back to your studies?"

"I think I'll climb."

And quickly, she fled towards the nearest ladder to make her way back down. She didn't particularly like flying and she didn't like that she liked flying with him.

Chapter Twenty-Three

"Begin!" Caspar commanded.

She ran. A dozen Novices ran with her. They sprinted across the open courtyard towards the first pedestals. Dani was the first to make it, leaping onto the first, and then with a few quick steps, launched herself at the next in the spiral.

And missed.

She smacked hard into the side and landed with a pained grunt on the stone floor. Two other Novices did too. Others had more luck. They soared over the gap and made it to the next pedestal, their Aer arc lifting them. Others landed chest first and pulled themselves up; not failures, but not successes.

Bouden easily skipped from one to the next like a kung-fu movie master. Of course.

"A Numen's ability to overcome the obstacle of gravity is one that takes patience and a clear mind!" Caspar announced.

"Not focus? Amazing." She grumbled sarcastically, dusting off.

"And focus!"

There it is.

Dani rejoined the Novices at the center as the next group began. Her palms bled from scrapes and one elbow throbbed in pain.

"You okay?" Nathaniel asked, examining her.

"I'm fine."

"Dani," he touched her arm and she hissed in pain, "I think you broke your elbow."

"What?" She looked down at her arm. Sure enough, she couldn't bend it and she could barely lift it. "How did I not notice that?"

"You need panacea."

"I don't think so."

Dani had never gone to the Ward, the medical area of the Citadel behind the Keep. Usually, Mastema treated her wounds. Hell, he gave her most of the wounds to begin with. Pain shot down to her fingers.

"Maybe you're right. I think Mastema can patch me up at my house."

It was odd. A month and a half before coming to Empyrean, a broken elbow would have crippled her. She'd have bawled like a baby. Now, she looked at her broken limb like it was nothing.

"Elder Caspar!" Nathaniel called. "Novice Daniella needs panacea!"

Caspar frowned, coming to examine her. When he lifted her arm, she groaned between clenched teeth.

"Broken." He muttered, as if a shattered elbow meant nothing. "Very well. Novice Nathaniel, accompany her." A scream, collision and loud groan echoed off the walls behind them as another Novice fell. Without looking, Caspar sighed. "And take Novice Ailbe with you."

Caspar allowed them to go. Nathaniel helped her. Dink limped along after them. The trio crossed the Vale Bridge into the market. Roxelana met them as they came over.

"What happened?" She asked, then her eyes widened. "My God! Your arm!"

"It looks worse than it is."

"I doubt that."

Korë, playing nearby, skipped over. She waved and smiled at Dani, giving her a hug. Airlea, who stocked shelves in Adare's market, saw her with them.

"Airlea," Roxelana cradled Dani's arm, "can you go get healing herbs from the market?"

"What? Why?"

"Just do it."

Airlea glared and stormed off as they headed to Dani's house. Korë followed. Roxelana went inside as soon as they arrived, getting panacea and bandages for them. A few minutes later, she arrived with the herbs. They lay down in the pavilion and allowed her to play nurse.

"What is the meaning of this?" Mastema arrived, along with Ethan and Kleos. Dani couldn't help but notice how harried the trio looked.

"They're injured." Roxelana said, tending to Dani first. Airlea begrudgingly helped.

"We can take care of them." Her Guardian said, attempting to shoo her away. "You need to go."

"Why?"

"Because!"

The look on his face told Dani something was wrong. "Mastema, what is it?"

He ignored her, telling Roxelana. "You must leave."

Airlea was in complete agreement. "Roxelana—."

"She is my friend." She insisted, wrapping Dani's arm with the panacea-soaked bandages and held up an earthen cup steaming with some foul-smelling mixture inside. "Drink this."

She sniffed and gagged. "Do I have to?"

"It's a tincture; algaophotis and silphium."

"I'll pretend like I know what those are."

"Just drink."

She did. She doubted any magical healing would ever taste or smell good, but she drank it all the same and it took effect almost instantaneously. The pain subsided. She relaxed.

But Mastema was anything but relaxed. Ethan and Kleos looked similarly uneased.

"Can someone please tell me what is going on?" She asked. "Why do you want Roxelana to leave?"

Nathaniel similarly noticed the Guardians' mood. "Something has them spooked."

Dani turned her eyes on Ethan. Unlike her Guardian or Kleos, he wasn't as good at hiding things from her. "Ethan?"

He knelt, touching her arm. Dani pulled it away, even though it didn't hurt anymore.

"Tell me." She told him. "Don't lie."

"The gifted need to leave. Someone is coming."

"Someone?"

Dani was about to ask more but the sound of armored marching caught her attention. Ethan worriedly looked uphill. She stood painfully and stepped out of the pavilion, shielding Roxelana, Korë and Airlea.

Six Powers crested the hill. They wore full armor and armament, with Heman at the lead. The group descended and as soon as they reached her home, fanned out.

"Ethan?" She asked softly.

He muttered out of the corner of his mouth. "We wanted them out of here before they saw them."

"You look worried."

"He doesn't normally make house calls; especially not with an entourage of soldiers."

Heman frowned at her home, running his fingers through some of the vines and accidentally knocking off some fruits. Or maybe it wasn't an accident. Either way, he regarded them all coolly.

"Guardian Ethan, Guardian Kleos, I did not expect to see you here."

"We did not expect you here either, Elder Heman." Kleos answered, careful not to let any worry slip, though Dani noticed he, Ethan and Mastema all had sheathed weapons lying nearby. That wasn't by accident. What the hell was going on?

"What are you doing here?" Then, his eyes wandering over the pavilion, he noticed Roxelana. "And what are gifted doing here?"

"Treating them." Roxelana stepped into the open. "We lent our services."

"Not all of us happy to do it." Airlea added in her own defense.

"Silence!" Heman's dark tone quickly made the two gifted silent. "That is the duty of the healers of the Ward. You know the laws of Empyrean."

"They aided wounded Novices." Ethan clarified. "That should be commended."

"We'll see." Heman gave nothing away. "Novice Daniella, is this your home?"

"Yes. I couldn't be in the other aeries, so I made one for myself."

"You made it? Truly?" He brushed his fingers along the side where some healing moss grew. "Amaranthine wood? That is usually centaur design."

"I read some books." It was a bad lie.

But Heman ignored it. Instead, he let slip a gleeful, stupid grin. "Novice Daniella, it has come to my attention that we have been remiss in not informing you of an impending event. It is a tradition amongst our people. I apologize for the late hour notice. I am aware it will put you behind your fellow Novices in preparation."

She folded her arms, which hurt slightly. "Do you mean the Trials?"

She hoped to shock him, but sadly didn't. He only smiled wider. "No, no, I am sure you have been informed of them already; however, due to tradition, we were remiss in informing you of the Council's most recent decision: as per our laws, during the Trials you will compete alone as your own aerie."

All three Guardians were stone-faced, as if expecting the news. Only Dani could put it into words. "Alone? You mean me verse an entire other aerie?"

He had a grin worthy of the Cheshire Cat. "And that within a week's time, you will compete first."

"First?"

"I wished to tell you myself, as it would not...upset you." He said the last part as if he were savoring chocolate.

Ethan stepped forward. "The laws state that once she is informed of her trials, she also has a right to know her competitors. Who will she face for the first Trial?"

Heman grinned. "It will be Corona and Crux."

199

She felt Ethan stir at her side. "Corona _and_ Crux? Only two aeries should compete within one trial. It has never been three. We spoke with the Council of this."

"Yes. You were correct that one Novice against twelve would be unfair and we heeded your advice. She will face two."

"That is not what we meant. She will still be at a disadvantage. The two aeries competing with her will most likely ally against her."

Heman, for his part, simply shrugged, looking quite pleased with himself.

"This should have been brought up to us during our conference with the Elders." Ethan seethed.

"Are you suggesting that the will of the Council should be dependent upon the wants a single Guardian? Or two? I find it difficult to think that is within our laws."

Ethan didn't back down. "This cannot be your decision."

"It is. And Guardian, if I do not mistake myself, as an Elder of the Council and an Arbiter of the Trials, I would caution you against using such a tone."

"Why?"

Heman growled. "Do you forget yourself, Guardian?"

"I do not. Do you?"

For the first time, Dani noticed that Ethan's hand rested on the pillar, inches from the hilt of his sword. The Powers at Heman's back likewise had their own weapons at the ready.

"You pled your case before us." Heman told him sternly. "This is the will of the Council."

"The will of a few, you mean?"

The anger in Ethan's voice was easy to hear. She knew Ethan, like Mastema, never spoke this way to an Elder. Ever. She learned that law the hard way.

But before anything could happen, Mastema stepped between them. He guessed Heman's intention of bringing soldiers—intending to provoke her or him in a fight with a dozen bodyguards, no doubt—but didn't want her friends or his fellow Guardians sticking up for her like that.

"That is fine, Elder Heman." He said, bowing. "Thank you for informing us. Novice?"

Her eyes widened. Did he want her to follow his lead? But seeing everyone with swords at the ready, she didn't have much of a choice.

"Yes. Thank you Elder." She sounded very diplomatic. It left a bad taste in her mouth.

He sneered to Ethan. "Take a lesson from this Novice, Guardian. She knows her place."

She wanted to kick him in the nuts hard enough to knock them behind his eyeballs, but resisted the urge.

"Now," he turned his eyes on Roxelana, Airlea and Korë, "you, gifted. I expect to never find you near this or any Novice again. If I do, you may find yourself outside the safety of Empyrean's walls."

Roxelana bowed her head, afraid. Airlea just looked angry.

Heman turned and snapped his soldiers into formation. Taking the lead, they marched away. Only when they were out of sight did everyone let go the tense faux-nonchalance. Kleos sagged visibly. Mastema cursed something in Arabic.

Dani turned to Roxelana. "I'm sorry."

But Airlea stepped up, her arm around Korë. "I knew coming here was a bad idea."

"Airlea!" Roxelana protested.

"No! There is a reason we do not associate with Numen, Roxelana!" She scolded. "You just jeopardized our lives here. We need Empyrean and because you were friends with her," she leveled an angry gaze at Dani, "we almost lost it. You want to endanger your place here? Fine. But me? Korë? It's time you understood: that girl is trouble."

Indignantly, Dani was about to say something, but Roxelana nodded. She shamefully looked away from her. "You're right."

"Of course I am."

"Roxelana!"

"This isn't Earth." Airlea said coolly. "Do you not understand that everyone around you could have their lives ruined?"

Dani bit back her next words in shame. "I'm sorry."

"Come." Airlea took Korë's hand. "Roxelana?"

"I'm coming."

The three gifted departed. As she walked uphill, Roxelana turned back once with an apologetic expression, but then she left. Dani felt her heart sink.

"What the hell was that?" she demanded, spinning on them.

"We told you to get rid of the gifted." Mastema grunted.

"They're my friends. Or were! What did Heman want?"

"To upset you, clearly. I told you: allies are a weakness."

"They were friends, you—you sarding bloodhole! *Te odio!*"

"Dani!" Ethan scolded. "He came because he saw Elder Heman coming. He brought us to make sure nothing happened."

Dani fumed, but tried to calm down. "I hate Heman! He's got no brains and an ego the size of a Mack truck. He's—He's—!" She cut herself off. She couldn't bear looking at Ethan or any of the others.

"We knew he would try something."

"Yeah, and he did! I have to face a Trial on my own."

"He can't do this. He can't make you compete on your own."

"He can't?" she asked cynically. "Because I'm pretty sure he just did."

"We told the Council that the Trials would be unfair to complete in alone against another aerie. They agreed. We left under the assumption that the matter had been settled."

"Well, it looks like Heman and his friends unsettled it."

"*Elder* Heman." Mastema corrected from his place in the pavilion.

"Oh shut up!" She spat in his direction. "I don't give a multi-colored unicorn crap what rank or position he's in! Did you hear him? He knows pretty damn well what the other two aeries are going to do to me. He practically sang about it! And you did nothing to speak up in my defense."

"And what would you have me to say? I did what I did to keep you safe."

He aggravated her so much she stomped her foot into the ground, making a dent in the dirt. "You're my Guardian for God's sake! You didn't even try to stop him!"

Mastema frowned, not saying anything. He left to check his equipment.

"Codpiece!" she cursed. She turned to Ethan and Kleos. "What do I do?"

"Nothing." Kleos told her. "I doubt Elder Heman's presence here today was an accident. If he is telling you, he has an ulterior motive."

"Meaning?"

"Meaning that if he tells you about who is in the first Trial, then he must inform the other aeries. And unlike when the announcement is made next week, he can speak privately with them. Did you notice one of the aeries you're competing against?"

"Corona." She recalled, and then cursed. "That's Nazir's aerie. I'll be competing against Michael."

"And if Heman can speak with them privately, I wouldn't put it past them to make a plan against you."

"Zounds." She cursed under her breath.

"'Snails." Dink agreed.

She muttered, "So I'm screwed?"

None of the Guardians spoke. Nathaniel and Dink were silent.

"So," she paused, unable to look at any of them, "so I guess that's it, huh?" She felt like something sat on her chest. It was tight and hurt. She didn't want to cry in front of them.

"I think you should go." She told them. "I don't feel like returning to lessons. I'll see you tomorrow."

"We can stay." Ethan offered.

She shook her head and stepped inside her door. "No, I really wish you wouldn't." She slid it closed just as the first tear dropped. Thankfully, no one saw.

She ended up on the edge of her bed, stroking the feathers of the large white hawk. The bird didn't nip her fingers or do that air-explosion thing. It was as if it knew she needed something comforting and obliged her.

"A caladrius," Ethan remarked, sliding open the door. He grimaced. "Sorry. Everyone's gone except me."

"Even Mastema?"

He nodded. "He said you wouldn't want to train tonight."

"How did he come to that astounding conclusion?" She asked sarcastically. It irked her that Ethan ignored her request to leave, but she was too tired to fight him. "What kind of bird is this?"

"A caladrius." He repeated, stepping inside. "I didn't think one lived in Empyrean."

She glanced at the dove-white bird of prey. "I saw it once in L.A. before I became a Numen. What do you know about it?"

He leaned against the door frame. "The Greeks called them a dhalion, but Romans referred to them as a caladrius. They're a supernatural bird like a phoenix, but rarer and solitary. They're known as the 'bird of kings.'"

She knew something was different about her fowl friend. The pun made her smile. "Because the feathers look like a crown?"

He shook his head. "A caladrius was said to live in kings' homes because it could sense the greatness of certain individuals. To have one visit you was a great honor and a sign that you should rule." He extended his hand to the bird and it screeched, startling him. He jumped back. "But that's more ego than anything else on the kings' part. They called it the bird of kings because they assumed they were important. The name stuck."

Dani giggled. "I don't think she likes you."

"She?"

"I just assumed she was a girl. She felt like a girl."

"Felt like a girl?"

Dani shrugged. "I can't explain it. She just seems female to me."

He kept his hands raised. "Does she mind if I come into the room and sit down?"

Dani stroked the bird's feathers along the neck. "Maybe. Got something for her?" Dani took to feeding her. She assumed she ate whatever it wanted when she was gone, but she didn't mind the treats.

Ethan reached into a pouch on his belt and removed something, holding it out. "Keresh jerky?"

The bird dipped its head.

"That means yes." Dani translated.

He tossed the meat and the large bird snatched it out of the air, gobbling it down. As if still deciding about Ethan, she cocked her head to the side in thought while she chewed. When Dani nudged her gently, the bird made a very human gesture and flicked her beak to the bed.

"I think that means you can sit." Dani told him.

"You think?"

"Well, sit or don't. That's up to you."

Ethan warily stepped around the bird. It watched as he gave her a wide berth until he was finally around the foot of the bed and sitting on the mattress next to Dani.

"So it followed you here?" he asked.

"She." She corrected, petting her. "Maybe."

"It must sense something important about you."

"Is that a line?"

"A line?"

"I mean flirt—." She stopped herself again. Deciding against saying anymore, she asked, "I thought I told you to go home?"

"Fat chance." He said, and then grinned. "Sorry. Nathaniel is rubbing off on me."

"It's nice to hear people talk like they were born in this century."

"Hey, I was. Well," he grinned, "technically, I guess last century."

Dani flicked back some of her hair nervously. "Are you here to talk about Heman and the Elders?"

"I'm here to see if you're okay."

"That's Mastema's job, which he's doing terribly."

"If it makes it any better, he is concerned; just in his own way."

She couldn't stop the sarcasm. "Invisibly? Silently?"

"Cautiously." He told her. "He knows that if Heman put him in shackles, which he could have done today, then he wouldn't be able to help you. No one would."

"I wouldn't want that." She confessed, looking him in the eye for the first time. "I'd feel awful."

"Me too, I imagine."

That got her to laugh a little. It felt good. "Well, I'm fine. Honestly. There isn't anything I can do about the Council."

"Well, if anybody could survive the Trials alone, it'd be you."

"You're sweet. Thanks." Then she kicked herself. *You're sweet? Thanks? What am I, in middle school?* She quickly changed to anything remotely unromantic. "So, the Trials: what am I up against? You and Mastema told me that I have to compete against the other aeries. How does that work?"

"Well, it's not to the death." Ethan assured her. "That normally doesn't happen. It's more like to the...I don't know how you would describe it..."

"To the pain?" she smirked.

"Not exactly, but close. And good Princess Bride reference."

"You've seen the Princess Bride?"

"I became a Numen; not died. A few of us watch movies."

"How? Does it have to do with this 'vespertide' you all secretly talk about?"

"Maybe, but let's stay on track." He said. "To the pain would be pretty accurate. The Trials are run by the Arbiters. There's three: the Vale, the Training Grounds and Earth. The Arbiter's job is to judge them. What they choose to use and who assists is up to them. Numen warriors, gifted, maybe Hellions; it's different each time."

"Great. More cynocephali threatening to eat me."

"Well, you can at least be thankful they won't use the Tigris. I know it is hard to believe, but he's actually a big pussy cat."

"You're right. It is hard to believe. What's a Trial like?"

"There are some similarities. Vale is the first one. It's meant to test your ability to endure under harsh conditions. It's also pretty popular to watch."

"Watch?"

"The Trials are used as entertainment by the gifted. They watch, take bets; things like that."

"How very Hunger Games of them."

He smirked. "Except you won't die."

"Do I have to make it down the river again?"

"Any of the pair—or in your case, trio—who does passes the Trial."

"I didn't make it last time."

"But this time you know the object is to get downriver, not fight. Which means—."

"It's not about killing anything."

"It's the first lesson everyone learns: when to run and when to fight."

"Okay, so the second Trial: it's at the Training Grounds? What is it?"

"It's a duel. Again, its run by the Arbiters. And it's pretty popular to watch, as well. You'll use your combat training and abilities to face another opponent. The Arbiters will judge the bouts."

"So, like fencing?" Seemed simple enough. "And the last Trial?"

He licked his lips nervously. "That's where I have to stop. The final Trial is one that all Guardians are not allowed to speak about."

"Why?"

Ethan seemed genuinely pained to not tell her. "Some laws just can't be broken. It's why I was so upset when they told me you were fighting alone. I can tell you that the final Trial is the most difficult. It is also the one where you will use a real adamantine weapon."

That was enough to give her a cold chill down the back of her spine. A real weapon? There wasn't any situation she could think of where that was good. "Great."

"You'll do fine." He promised her. "I have faith in you."

She got through a training session with a broken arm and not cried like a baby. There was that. "Thanks, but I don't feel like I'm doing well."

"You are." he assured her. He didn't mean anything by it, but he put a hand on her arm. She flinched and he quickly snatched it back. "Sorry."

"No." She told him hurriedly. "I didn't mean—I didn't think—."

"I should go." He stood.

If she could, Dani would have smacked herself over the head. *Stupid, stupid, stupid.* It wasn't like she didn't like Ethan's touch, but she definitely didn't mean to insult him or stutter over herself like an idiot. Romance was the last thing on her mind. And yet? She got jitters every time he was around.

"I'm sorry too." She said before he got to the door. "It's just...this is all kind of strange for me."

"Strange how?"

Strange how? She was a celestial demon-hunter in a city that existed but didn't exist above the city in which she grew up. And she was attracted to a guy she didn't want to be attracted to since she spent most of her time fighting for her life, or reputation, or both.

And above everything else? Because men. Men were complicated. She had a hard time with complicated.

"Never mind." She said. There was no way she could explain.

Trying for some kind of normalcy, he said, "You know, if your friend," he gestured to her bird, "is going to stay here, you should give her a name."

She glanced at the caladrius. "It would be nice call her something other than 'bird.'" The hawk regarded her with steely, blank eyes. "What do I call her?"

He thought for a moment. "How about Caesar? If it's the bird of kings, why not name it for a great king?"

"Caesar is a boy's name."

"I don't recall you being a bird expert." He made it playful.

Equally playful, she asked, "And you are?"

He chuckled and disappeared out her door. Dani heard him take off from the ground and stepped out onto the porch to watch him go, his figure shrinking into the distance until he passed the hill. She sighed a little. As soon as he was gone, though, she realized she was staring like an idiot, leaning against one of the supports like a love sick puppy.

"Oh God!" She groaned. Had she really just done that?

She stalked back into her house and sat down on the edge of the mattress to untie her boots. She tried to put Ethan out of her mind. She acted like such a _buffoon!_ If he saw her standing there like Lois Lane watching Superman fly off, she would never have forgiven herself.

"I hate boys." She muttered.

"*You and me both, sister.*" Said a female voice behind her.

Her head snapped around. The room was empty, but she definitely heard a voice. The only other occupant was the bird.

"Hello?"

No one answered. She got up, looking out into the pavilion. A cold overcast rolled overhead, crackling with distant thunder, but the Arn was empty. She glanced down into the Vale, first at the area known as the Dalles, then down into the valley. She squinted. She could see the smoke trails of Hellion villages, but nothing nearby.

"Hello?" she called out. "Anyone here?"

Nobody.

She shook her head, returning to her room. "I'm hearing voices. Great. Living alone is making me crazy." She sat down on the bed again, one boot off. "Next thing you know, I'll be talking to my pet bird."

"*Who said that made you crazy?*"

Dani leapt off the bed with a scream. The voice was right next to her. She turned to face the white caladrius, which watched her with the usual blank stared. But then, as she watched, the bird's beak moved as if it were speaking. And it spoke clear as a bell.

"*A ton of people talk to their pets, honey, but I am not a pet. I choose to be here, thank you very much.*" The bird fluffed her feathers, her voice something deep and husky. "*Still, at least you don't call me an 'it.' Your boyfriend has no manners. That jerky was as disgusting as the way he talked about me.*"

She blinked. Once. Twice. Three times. She kept staring at the bird. The bird kept staring back. Then it made a low, screeching noise. It clipped its beak a few times, turning left and right the way birds did. The only difference now was its very un-bird-like way of communicating.

Dani managed to squeak out, "You—You talk?" The question seemed stupid given what the bird literally just did.

"*As your species says, OMG duh. Like, for reals or whatever. You know: the human garbage you all use to say yes.*" The caladrius responded, scooting a little closer on the footboard to her. "*Seriously, why is that? It's like every year, you two-footed ground-walkers find new ways to say the same thing! It's ridiculous to us. You are all a bunch of weirdos.*"

Dani's mouth dropped open on its own. A bird spoke to her! An actual, honest-to-God bird spoke to her like it was an everyday thing!

It cocked its—no, her—head to the other side. "*What? Tigris got your tongue?*"

"You're talking." Dani said.

"*Yes. I'm aware.*"

"You can talk."

"*Right again, girlie.*"

"You can talk to me."

"*Now you're just repeating yourself.*" The bird told her. "*Any more observations you would like to make?*"

Dani sat down on the edge of the bed. A fly could zip into her mouth and out and not get caught.

"*Please don't pass out.*" The caladrius said. "*I'm not good with beak-to-mouth resuscitation. There's a mechanics issue.*"

"How?" Dani was finally able to ask. "How can you talk to me? Why are you talking to me?"

"Well, there isn't anyone else to make sparkling conversation with around here. Besides, I don't know how. I've been talking to you for over a month. You just haven't heard me."

"I haven't heard you?"

"That is what I just said, isn't it?"

"When were you talking before? How can I understand you now?"

The bird did something that looked an awful lot like a shrug. *"No idea. You're the one who could suddenly speak my language."*

"Speak your language?"

"The language of birds, sister. Most humans can't understand us birds. I've gotten used to it. Then you just started understanding me and it freaked me out."

"I freaked you out? How do you think I feel?"

"No idea. Happy? I'm a pretty awesome chick; no pun intended. Well, that's not true." She sounded almost proud. *"I meant to make that pun."*

She was talking to a bird. Was she crazy? It wouldn't be the first time she considered it.

"I just...wow. This is sort of hard to wrap my head around."

"Right there with you, honey. You're my first human."

"Your first? What, like you own me or something? I'm not your pet."

The bird screeched. It actually sounded like a laugh. *"And you own me? Please. If humans knew half of what their pets were thinking, they wouldn't adopt them. Most animals feel like they own their owners. Cats are the worst. Cats are jerks."*

She shook her head. "This is unreal."

"Well, I guess that makes one of us a figment of the imagination, but I'm completely real. So..."

Dani liked this bird. It was hard not to.

"I know. My mind is, like, totally blown."

"What do I call you?"

"Names are a human thing. We don't really have our own. But I guess Caesar isn't bad, even if it is a little sexist of your boyfriend."

"He's not my boyfriend."

"His pheromones say otherwise. And his heartbeat goes all super-fast when he's around you."

She blushed.

Caesar chirped. *"Yeah! Like that!"*

"Shut up."

"*Trust me, now that we can talk, I'm SO not shutting up.*" She screeched excitedly.

Dani spent the rest of the day into the evening with Caesar. True to her word, she wanted to talk. The bird had lived in and around Empyrean for over a hundred years, with quote, "*those mean phoenixes and that overgrown house cat in the Vale.*"

"You never met your family?" Dani asked. She prepared food for dinner; vegetables sautéed in a skillet with some chicken and honeysuckle to nibble. She even had a Coke. Despite being in her bag for a month and warm, she didn't mind it. Caesar nibbled some of her food and drank from the fountain.

"*Nah. My mom kicked me out of the nest with my other brothers and sisters when I was young. Totally did a number on my psyche. I had to see a therapist and everything.*"

"Really?"

The bird gave her the equivalent of a 'you seriously fell for that?' look.

"Right. You're a bird. I forgot."

"*It's normal for my kind. I've been looking for a nice caladrius to settle down with ever since.*"

"You've been looking for love for over a hundred years? That's depressing."

"*And swooning over that hunky Guardians isn't?*" Dani burned with embarrassment. "*Besides, it's not my fault! You wouldn't believe how bad the dating world is out there. All kinds of creatures hit on me. Everyone thinks they're ready for this jelly. This one cow I knew? He was full of it. He tried to convince me he was so big he had to get strapped to the side of Noah's Ark to escape the Flood. Can you believe his ego?*"

"I guess not."

Dani stared out over the Vale again. Dusk settled. The skies streaked orange, purple and yellow over the peaks of the crater. Lights still burned in the valley, but torches moved downriver far from the centaur villages. Dani could only guess who they were.

"So are you going to stay?" Dani asked.

She looked up, beak dripping with water. "*Why wouldn't I?*"

She shrugged. "It's not like this is normal for either of us."

"*But its totes cool, right?*"

"Totes? No one says totes."

"*I say totes, toots.*"

Dani laughed.

"*I heard what you said, by the way.*" Caesar finished drinking. "*About the Trials.*"

Dani waved it off. "It's no big deal."

She sounded a lot more serious. "*Well that's a lie if I ever heard one. Birds are pretty good at reading emotions. You're worried about the them, aren't you?*"

Unable to lie, Dani went with sarcasm, "Ya' think?"

"*I wouldn't get all mockingbird with something that can knock you across a room.*"

She winced, remembering. "Yeah. Good point."

"*You don't need to be scared.*"

"I'm not scared."

"*Remember: I can hear heartbeats, see everything down to the bug crawling on your tunic,*" Dani wiped off a beetle, "*and I can literally smell emotions. You stink of fear. And it's okay to be scared.*"

Dani scowled.

"*You'll do fine.*" Caesar assured her. "*I fly around Empyrean when you're out. I watch everybody. I hear everything. Trust me, some of those old, wrinkling, sagging-butt Elders are more scared of you than you are of them.*"

"Thanks for the mental picture." Dani shuddered. "But they can also make my life hell."

She shrugged. "*Yeah. But then again, they're not that smart. Most of them are a bunch of misogynistic harpies with nothing better to do than pick on you. And trust me: for my kind, 'harpy' is about the worst insult you could use. The ones who give you grief can suck an egg. They fear you. Fear means you can beat them.*"

Dani felt better now that she could talk to Caesar. Friends were hard to come by here and—remembering Roxelana—hard to keep.

And ones that could listen in on people? That gave her an idea. "Let me ask you something: can you hear what people say or see what they do when no one is looking?"

"*I'm a bird of prey...so duh.*"

Dani leaned in close to her new friend. "So, would you want to do a girl a favor?"

Chapter Twenty-Four

She decided not to tell anyone about Caesar. She had an ace up her sleeve. No one knew she could spy on them. She hated to think about it that way. *Perusing.* That was what Caesar called it. She was going to <u>peruse</u> the city; not spy on it.

Caesar only demanded a few things in payment. First, a roost in Dani's cabin. She apparently hated sleeping at the end of the bed. Second, she wanted her feathers cleaned; something about how snow-white feathers were difficult to keep pristine.

And beef. She loved raw beef.

"Aren't you worried about your figure?" Dani joked.

"*Please, hon. A girl does not look this good at a hundred-plus by being lazy. The day I get fat is the day Hell freezes over.*"

The week ground by at a snail's pace. Try as she might, Heman's threat got under her skin. She tried not to show it.

The announcement of the Trails came the following week. Dani wasn't enthusiastic, but prepared to go. She couldn't hide. She was dressing when Mastema arrived early.

"You are not ready to go?" he demanded. "How can you be this late?"

"Don't you knock?"

"We've discussed this: no. Here." He shoved a new pair of raiments at her. "Put these on."

Dani's new clothes were more pristine the ones she had; custom fitted. They had the Arn symbol stitched into one shoulder.

"Why?" she asked.

"We have an important visitor arriving in Empyrean, for which," thunder sounded in the distance, "we are late. Come, we have to fly."

Mastema waited. Once changed, he led her out by the shoulder like some kind of impatient parent.

"What's the hurry?"

"We are late." He repeated.

"I understand th—AAAATTTT!"

Without warning, he wrapped his arms around her and took off. Dani shrieked as they shot off the ground and into the sky. Unlike Ethan, he was not a gentle aviator. "Mastema is My Co-Pilot" would never be her bumper sticker.

Mastema crossed and then descended towards the West Gate of Empyrean's Citadel. As they did, she peeked over the rim of the mountain.

The normally white clouds that surrounded the city were dark and thunderous. She could see something moving between them; distant, but coming towards the city. Lightning streaked, illuminating it in forks of light, but Dani couldn't make it out.

She was the last of the Novices to arrive. Dani spotted Nathaniel and Ethan near the front. Mastema came in hard.

"Ow!" she stumbled, nearly falling into Dink. She got her footing before completely knocking him over. She glared at Mastema. "Be gentler with the landing next time!"

"Learn to fly. Now follow the other Novices. Try not to be cheeky."

Dani spun on her heel, muttering under her breath, "I'll show you a cheek."

They descended the steps, forming their twelve columns by aerie with their Guardians. The twenty-four Elders assembled in front of them.

Dani stood on her own next to Aether. Andreas and Lester leered at her. She ignored them. Michael, two rows down with Corona, looked in her direction, too. He hadn't forgotten their first day. Revenge was a dish best served cold, but Michael seemed hot for it.

Through the large pearl-and-steel gates, the storm clouds gathered. A moment later, something burst through.

Six skeletal monsters—it took her a second to realize they were horses—shot from the thunderheads huffing flames from their nostrils. Bones of charcoal grey or tar-black, the beasts galloped on air towards Empyrean.

Then the coach appeared behind them. It wasn't golden or flaming like Hermes'. It was made from shadows, which dripped from the sides and dyed the clouds black. The wheels spun, seeding more black mist, obscuring the view of whoever traveled inside. The gates swung open.

A sense of dread made her shiver. Her heart sunk. What was something like that doing here? The horses neighed loudly. It reverberated off the walls. Those gifted allowed to come watched with mixtures of awe and horror.

Dani leaned over to Bouden. "You're the expert. What is that?"

"It's a chariot of the underworld." He told her. "A vehicle from Hell. They aren't supposed to exist in the upper worlds."

So it was demonic?

The carriage with its skeletal team soared through the opening. At the front, a cynocephali warrior wearing black armor pulled the reigns. The vehicle descended and touched down; a much better landing than with Hermes.

213

The coach stunk of rotten eggs. Dani remembered brimstone, rock sulfur, coated the surface of Hell. Anything from there stunk of sulfur. The coachmen trotted his carriage up to the Elders. He turned it so the door faced them. Elder Castus and Elder Jeduthun, the Co-Consuls, strode forward to greet their guest.

The door opened. Dani held her breath for whatever nightmare creature would disembark. But instead, a pale, feminine a hand extended to meet Castus's and slowly, the most beautiful creature emerged.

Not beast, nor demon, but an angel.

She stepped from the carriage and every man took a single breath. She was without a doubt the most beautiful woman Dani had ever seen. Her long brown hair cascaded down the sides of her face and around her shoulders in thick, luscious waves. Her bangs tied back and a simple golden circlet wove across her brow like a crown. As she stepped down, her dress flowed to her ankles; silk that glistened in the morning light. It was synched at both shoulders, exposing her smooth, unblemished arms. And when she stepped down, it was with the grace of a queen. Her face was one that belonged on a sculpture in a museum. She was gorgeous.

But the wings stole Dani's attention. They unfolded behind her as she stepped from her chariot; creamy vanilla colored, near-radiant in the sun. She stretched them outward, extending the width of the carriage and then folding back behind her.

She was fantastically ornate, but warrior-like in her beauty. A metal band, like a snake, wrapped around one of her upper arms. In her waistband carried a flail and sword. They seemed out of place on someone so lovely, but made her all the more striking. She was a war goddess incarnate.

Everyone whispered, even Dani. She leaned over to Ethan beside her. "I thought all angels were extinct?"

He shook his head. "She's not an angel. She's an Erinys."

"A what?"

"A Fury." Mastema spoke behind her. "And be quiet."

"You should, too." Ethan warned him. "They don't like being called Furies."

A Fury? Dani never heard of such a thing, but knew if something like her was invited to Empyrean, she wasn't a demon. Which, not being Numen or angel, made her a Hellion. An important one if everyone, including Mastema, showed up for her arrival.

"Who is she?" Dani asked. "Why is she here?"

Mastema made a noise somewhere between a scoff and a grunt of derision. Ethan was more kind. "That is Lady Alecto. She is the leader of the City of Dis and the Forces of Asphodel."

"Meaning?"

"Meaning she is the leader of every Hellion in existence. And as for why she's here," he licked his lips nervously, "she is here to preside over the Trials."

Dani never appreciated how many Numen lived in Empyrean until they all gathered in the Throne Room. The seats filled; brown-clad Novices, black Guardians, the purples, golds, reds, blues and greens of the other hosts. Over a thousand or more men attended, while more were still on duty throughout the city. The Elders, of course, took their places beneath the rainbow throne. The Elders, like all the Numen, arrived to venerate one person: Alecto. She commanded their attention.

Castus's voice boomed throughout the chamber, calling everyone to quiet. "Warriors of Empyrean, gifted citizens of our protection," what few gifted could gather in the doorway fought for a place up front to see, "I call this convocation to order! I present to you our esteemed and honored guest: Lady Alecto, Commander of the Forces of Asphodel and our closest ally."

Applause broke out as Alecto strode into the room. She was graceful as she was fearsome. But where she impressed Dani by the way she carried herself, more than a few Numen gave her looks of adoration that had nothing to do with respect. And why wouldn't they? Not only was she beautiful, but a warrior. She was the ultimate woman. More than a few of their stares were near-cartoonish. She imagined them dropping their jaws to the floor and rolling out their tongues.

Boys. She shook her head.

Alecto strode before the glass pool, torches and Elders to her back. The tips of her wings slid gently along the floor. When she spoke, her voice was like warm, smooth honey.

"Thank you, Elder Council. It is my privilege to be here." She smiled to the assembly. "And it is an honor to be before you. For so long, my kind has fought side by side with yours against the forces of Hell. So many of us, my sisters included, have pledged themselves to the great God of Light. It is a bond. And I am here to say that this bond is stronger than ever! The City of Dis, the Forces of Asphodel, stand with Empyrean!"

A round of applause. Alecto knew how to give a good speech.

"Thanks be to you." She calmed them. "But I am not here to only say this. I am here for two important reasons. The first," she turned to the Novices, "is to watch as our newest Earthborn display courage, cunning and skill, and join the ranks of the Numen warriors. I have no doubt that their place will be earned. To them I say: welcome and good fortune."

More applause. More than a few Novices stood, waving to her as if she were some kind of celebrity. Even Nathaniel was stupidly standing to get attention.

"But there is another reason I am here." Alecto continued. "In these times, the fires of Hell burn more brightly. My kind has always been on the front lines. We have always protected this realm and those below. But the demonic rise. We die at their hands. I have watched many brothers and sisters perish in battle. Our duty is to prevent their escape, but demons continue to creep into the world unnoticed. Numen and Hellion alike die at their hands. So many others suffer for nothing. So I have come here not just as a spectator, but as an emissary."

Her wings flared, causing many of the men to gasp. The drama was not lost on anyone.

"I come here, humbly, like so many times before, to beseech you not to forget your non-human brothers and sisters. For so long, Numen have protected the upper world. Hellions have protected the lower. Every day more of us die. I come to ask you to join with me. The demonic are rising. It is time we stop them together."

She turned on the Elders, holding out her hands. And then, she bowed to her knees. "I ask this great Council to remember us. We are losing. We need aid. As you call me here to preside over these upcoming Trials, I ask you once more to consider sending us assistance. It is with great respect and admiration I beg this of you."

Most, if not all, of the Numen broke into applause as she stood. Alecto was an amazing speaker. She inspired with words. Dani never met someone who could keep people's attention like that. The men on the Council enjoyed her speech, though with more smug and self-satisfied grins. They looked pleased by Alecto begging for help.

She turned and bowed once more to the room. When she turned to the Novices, the applause thundered. Her eyes penetrated through the crowd and as Dani watched, she searched the faces of each Numen.

Until her eyes met Dani's.

Their gazes locked. Dani flushed. Was she looking at her? Why? She looked away. She couldn't keep eye contact. After a few seconds, she looked back and Lady Alecto no longer stared her direction. The embarrassment lingered, though.

Castus called for silence again. The applause died. Alecto turned, standing patiently for their verdict.

"Lady Alecto, we thank you for reminding us that it is not just this city, or any city, that defends the world from darkness. It is all of us." He cleared his throat. "It is an honor for you to be here as witness to the next generation of Numen. And it is for that purpose that I announced the next Trials to commence!"

More applause. Dani awed at the near-blood lust from the other hosts; Numen eagerly shouting to watch the Novices fight for their place. The gifted were a little more constrained, but excited. And with Alecto standing before them, something else didn't escape her notice, either: the Council didn't say a word about what she requested.

"Do not be surprised." Mastema said behind her. "Lady Alecto has asked for aid for decades and received none."

"I'm surprised she still asks."

"When everyone you know dies," he murmured darkly, "there is no limit to what you will do."

Dani didn't doubt that.

Chapter Twenty-Five

In honor of Alecto, training was suspended. The Trials would begin in three days. Everyone released to their villages. As they left, she spotted Roxelana and Shea amongst the gifted audience. The two of them saw one another, but neither was eager to talk.

Nathaniel caught up to her at the bridge. "Congratulations on first spot in the Trials!"

"Aww, thanks Nate. I love it when people celebrate my impending death."

"You're not going to die. That hasn't happened in decades."

"Not comforting."

As they were about to cross, a small contingent of soldiers cut them off. At this point, Dani assumed every armed guard was for her.

She stopped. Sure enough, one of the four demanded, "Novice Daniella. Lady Alecto wishes to speak with you."

Nathaniel's eyes widened. "Really?"

Dani shook her head. "Pick your tongue up off the ground, Romeo. You're embarrassing." She sighed and said to the soldiers, "Sure. Lead the way."

She left Nathaniel and followed the group of escorts back into the Citadel, feigning disinterest. But secretly, she worried. *Why did she want to talk to me?* She spotted Ethan through the crowd; equally shocked by her new found fame. Lady Alecto, the darling of Empyrean, wished to speak to her. Oh goodie.

The four Gatekeepers marched in formation, leading Dani through the streets, past the Gardens and into the Fane. The sanctuary, lit by the many star-like lanterns, illuminated the beautiful Alecto in their glow. She waited at the feet of the Archangel; an angel herself in the gloom.

The Fury's beauty was startling up close. She turned and folded her wings back upon herself like a cloak around her shoulders, bowing to the soldiers. Dani saw them go all a-twitter with smiles and blushes. Did these guys spend any time with women?

"Thank you, kind sirs." She said to them, making more than one turn the same deep crimson of their armor. "You may leave her here with me."

"We can post outside if you wish, m'lady." The lead guard told her.

"That will not be necessary. Go with my thanks ere we speak again."

They fell all over themselves as they bowed and left. Dani tried not to make gagging noises.

As soon as they were gone, though, she couldn't find the words to speak, either. The leader of the Hellions was more intimidating than ever. It wasn't just her beauty, although Dani felt like an ugly toad next to her. No, it was her strength. She had a strength that could be felt. This woman was hands-down the most daunting person Dani met. No wonder everyone treated her like royalty.

She bowed, feeling like the redheaded step-child in the room. "My lady."

Alecto smiled softly. "My dear, you do not need to be so formal. It is a courtesy the Numen have extended to me for eons, but I do not wish it from you. You are free to be yourself."

"I am being myself." She lied.

Alecto gave her a playful look. "From what I hear, the very first week you not only challenged Elder Asaph, but Elder Heman and an entire contingent of cynocephali. Alpha Remus was quite troubled by your unceasing temperament. And I discovered you have already gone through many trials during your tenure here. You nearly blinded a man, as I understand it."

"He deserved it." She retorted.

"Indeed."

Dani blushed sheepishly. "I didn't mean to hurt him."

"He was—how do you say—being a jerk?"

Alecto knew a lot about Dani. Dani knew almost zero about her. "I really love your wings. I thought you were an angel when I first saw you."

She smiled even more gently, if that were possible. "Thank you. You are very kind Daniella, though as I am to believe, you go by Dani?"

"Yes, ma'am."

"Well, then we shall call you by what you wish. Yes, Dani, many have mistook me for an angel. My kind gave rise to the idea that angels have wings."

"They don't?"

"I am unsure. I have never met one."

"Well," she gushed, "it's easy to see why people think you're one. Are all Fur—er, Erinyes so pretty?" Mastema warned her not to call them Furies.

If Alecto noticed, she ignored it. "Yes, my sisters are of great beauty, though I would not be so boastful."

She felt like a silly fangirl standing next to this incredible woman, though Dani hated 'fangirl' as much as any things boys called her. But

Alecto had an almost disarming niceness. How was she the leader of an army of monsters?

"I'm actually not that kind." She admitted. "Most people think I'm rude."

"Well, they have not seen what kind of person you truly are, then. My kind—the Erinyes—have a way of judging the character of someone. " She turned, walking calmly with Dani around the statue's pool. The pacing was so soothing Dani just fell in step with her; mesmerized. "We can see faults as well as goodness. I see great goodness in you Dani."

"Thank you."

"Has it been difficult for you here?"

She shrugged. "A little."

"Do you have friends?"

"A few. A boy named Nathaniel I came up here with is a close friend."

"Is that so? Who else?"

"A few here and there have been friendly. A couple Guardians, some Novices. My Guardian is...well, he's okay."

"Mastema." She nodded. "I have heard great and terrible stories of him."

"Don't believe the hype. He's kind of a pain," then quickly added, "but a great teacher. Another Guardian helped out, too. Ethan. He's been really kind to me." She tried to keep the warmth out of her voice. "I, uh, don't know if you wanted to know all of that."

They moved around the backside of the statue, the horn pointed towards the sun-splashed doorway. Alecto regarded the archangel's likeness mildly, saying, "Dani, it is perfectly fine for you to do so. I have met many Numen. I have served with many. But when I heard of you, I knew I had to meet you."

"Why?"

She stopped, turning towards her. "There is great change in the world, Dani. It is in the air. The ways we have kept must change. My warning to the Elder Council was quite truthful. The fires of Hell burn brighter. I have seen them myself. Numen will need to face what is to come and I tell you truthfully: you are a part of that."

"Me?"

"I do not know how you were called. Nothing like it has ever happened before but," Alecto told her, "I, for one, am glad. You mark a change in the order of the universe. I believe you happened for a purpose. I came here to see that for myself."

Dani flustered. *Me? She came to see me?* Dani never felt special. Hell, she felt very un-special most of her life. Even amongst the Numen—even as the only girl—she was still that awkward girl who felt like she didn't belong.

"You are unique," Alecto told her, "but I see you as something more: an omen of things to come. I hope that you will remember this when the time comes for you to make your mark. Remember that you are not like the rest of your fellow Numen. You have a destiny to fulfill."

She didn't know what to say. For the first time, someone told her the complete opposite of what she was used to. She wasn't an outsider or a freak; she was important.

"I wish you luck in your Trials." Alecto told her. "I will be watching closely and with great interest. I am certain you will not disappoint."

With that, Dani was allowed to leave. As she walked away, she glanced back at the angelic lady looking up to Gabriel. Alecto was, for all intents and purposes, a fine lady; the first to say anything truly nice to her.

An omen of things to come. She didn't understand everything Alecto told her, but she liked what she heard. She could get used to someone believing in her.

———————————————————

Dani felt more confident than ever as she walked back across the Vale. She had the rest of the day and mused about what she might do with it. She would need to train and study eventually. But in the meantime she could—.

She stopped as she crested the hill. Below her, her house lay in ruins; boards ripped from the sides and plants cut apart. Someone took the torches out of their holdings used them to break in her window and smashed them on the ground. Food stores Dani put together over the past month—meats she bought, vegetables she picked—spilled across the stones. Someone lit the lamp oil and burned all of it in a huge pyre. They trashed her pavilion, broke her training equipment and left the house a broken shack.

Dani stared at what had once been her home. Her chest hurt. Something clawed up the back of her throat as she discovered the torn remnants of her bed.

Etched across the doorframe, carved into the wood, was a single word: WHORE.

She stood there, staring; for how long, she wasn't sure. The empty, lonely wind scattered her loose hair about her face. She stared at what was once her home; the one gift that made her feel human. Wanted.

She screamed.

Dani fell to her knees. Everything came out; every hurtful thing someone said to her, every insult, everything she held back until now. She screamed and screamed. She slammed her fist into the stones under her so hard her hand ached. She felt something break and pain radiated through her hand.

But she hit the rocks again and again, screaming through clenched teeth, ignoring the pain as her fist burned and turned red.

"Dani!" a voice called. "Dani! Oh my God! Dani! Stop!"

Footsteps. Arms around her. She heard other voices. She ignored them. She punched the rock until it cracked and bled. Or until her hand did.

"Dani! Stop! Stop it!"

She thrashed, screaming. Whoever held her cried out in pain. Her elbow hit something. New arms wrapped around her; stronger ones.

"Hold her!" A gruff voice commanded. "Hold her!"

She screamed again. "Let me go! Let me go!"

"Novice! Calm yourself!" the voice commanded. A face, darker than hers, floated into her vision. He smeared away tears. It was Mastema. "Get yourself under control, Novice!"

"Go away!" she screamed at him. "Get your hands off me!"

"I command you to calm down! Get ahold of yourself this instant!"

She clawed at him. She was just so angry. Everything she choked down for over a month raged to the surface. She struck at her Guardian. His hands were there. She heard words, a language she didn't understand.

Then darkness. Then nothing.

"I'm sorry."

She curled up on the rim of her broken fountain, a blanket wrapped around her shoulders. They wrapped her hand in a bandage. She broke it. It would take a few hours to heal under the care of panacea.

Ethan stood to one side, the concerned expression so deep it made lines in his forehead. "You don't have to be."

"She should be." Mastema said from his place against her ruined house. "Look at her hand. She is in no shape to train. Her Trials begin in three days. She needs every advantage—."

"Will you give it a rest?" Dani demanded harshly. She glared at her Guardian. "I am sick of you! For once can you just back off?"

He held a hand to her house, as if to remind her. "Because your enemies will 'back off' as you say?"

"You are so infuriating!"

"Mastema, please," Ethan begged.

Mastema frowned. "I am right, Stormthrower. We cannot delay. This is merely a ploy by the others to ensure she fails."

Dani sighed. "They're trying to psych me out, you mean?"

"I assume that means what I said, yes."

"He's right," Ethan conceded, "they are trying to keep you off kilter. I'll go to the Elders and tell them what happened."

"And blame whom?" Mastema challenged.

"I know who it was." Dani told them. "I didn't see them, but I can guess."

"And without proof, it would only be accusations. It would be your word against theirs."

How many times had that happened? This wasn't the first time it was someone's word against someone else. *Why fight?* they usually said. *If you know nothing will happen, why even bring it up?* She hated it.

"You must train. The Trial in the Vale will not be one of ease or comfort."

"Thanks. I wasn't aware." The sarcasm had extra bite this time.

Mastema strode off towards the house. She would deal with that later, but for right now she didn't care. It left her and Ethan alone.

"Are you sure you're alright?"

She shook her head. "Honestly? No. I'm tired. I'm tired of having to prove myself to everyone." She felt the same anger threatening to explode again, but tamped it down. "I know I don't talk about it, but endlessly fighting everyone wears on me. I couldn't take it anymore when I saw," she waved to her once-clean hovel, "all of this."

"You have us." He reminded her. "Kleos. Nathaniel. Dink. Bouden. Even Mastema, though he doesn't show it very well."

"I wish they didn't have to. Don't you get it? Every time one of you steps up for me, it makes it worse."

Ethan couldn't keep the hurt off his face. "You don't want us to defend you?"

Dani sighed. That was the problem: explaining how she didn't want to be alone, but at the same time explaining how not being alone made things worse. "It's not that, Ethan. I love that you want to help me," she bit back the warmth in those words, "but the people won't respect me when you do. They did this did it in spite of you sticking up for me. They think I can't protect myself."

"Can you?" he asked.

Could she? Physically, she might be able to take on one or two, but a lot of people destroyed her village.

The look on Ethan's face felt worse than any jeers or stuff Andreas and his ilk could do. It was pity. She didn't want pity. Unfortunately, she was starting to want other things and wasn't comfortable with that, either.

"I'll be fine." She assured him. "Really. They won't do anything worse than break my things."

"I'm pissed they think they can do this without punishment."

That made her smile a little. "And it's sweet—um, kind of you to say that." *Wow, smooth girl*, she kicked herself.

"What do you want to do about this? Do you want help cleaning up? Maybe Shea, or Roxelana could help—?" He stopped, realizing what already happened with her gifted friends.

"No. I'll be fine. Just leave it. Think of it as a new form of fung-shui. We'll call it Smash Deco. I'm sure it'll become all the rage around here soon." The humor hopefully covered up the hurt.

He smirked. "If you say so." He reached out for a second, as if to take her hand, but stopped himself and awkwardly dropped it to his side. He blushed. She blushed.

They were awkward, weren't they?

"Feel better." He said.

She flicked back some hair and tried not to look at him. "Thanks."

"Any time."

He walked off the pedestal and dropped off the end, soaring out over the valley. Dani watched him go, sighing to herself. Her and boys; they didn't mix.

Mastema was cleaning the pavilion when she arrived. Broken training swords and bowstaves, emptied crates and ripped up floorboards littered the space. Her intruders also took the tomes and scrolls Mastema brought her from the Anthenaeum and ripped up the pages, scattering the remains. He didn't try to fix them. A la Humpy Dumpty, it wasn't going to be put back together again.

"When you said they might put us in stocks in a dungeon if those got destroyed," she asked nervously, "were you serious?"

He gave her a very sarcastic look. She was rubbing off on him in more ways than one. "They will not revoke your library card, so you can make your best educated guess."

"Was that a joke?" she asked, half-hopeful for something human-like from him.

Unfortunately, that was all she got. "They do this to worry you."

"They do worry me."

"Then at least you are not a fool."

Dani was able to put some things back in place. A few earthen cups and dishes survived. She still had her campfire. And, after putting a few animal skin blankets over the tears, her mattress was more or less intact.

She was cleaning the pavilion when she heard rustling from the trees. She grabbed the nearest weapon she could find: a broken wooden baton. Held ready, she ran out into the square to confront her intruder.

Instead, she found Nessus. The centaur stood on the edge of the clearing, bow under his arm. He wore some kind of ceremonial tunic; silky, embroidered.

He bowed respectfully. "Dani."

"Nessus!" She dropped her baton. "What are you doing here?"

"Our commander, Lady Alecto, is in the city. She sent for an escort of centaurs." He looked past her. "What happened to your hovel?"

"My hovel?" she glanced over her shoulder. "Oh, the house. I'm sorry, Nessus, someone destroyed it."

"Why?"

"Because people are jerks."

He cantered over, touching the broken beams and places where they ripped plants out. As if sensing, he said, "Someone with great anger and jealousy did this."

"Tell me something I don't know."

He frowned, pressing his palm flat against the side. He closed his eyes and breathed deeply. As Dani watched, the vines moved. More of them grew from the broken ends, wrapping up along the boards and pulling them tightly into place. Holes filled in with moss or branches. New flowers and fruit grew to replace those destroyed. In a matter of seconds, most of the damage was undone.

"Wow."

"It is a temporary fix." He said, withdrawing his hand. "More extensive repairs will be necessary. But with the Trials to commence, we cannot venture far from the Vale. I'm sorry."

"It's fine. It's better than fine. Thank you."

"Cowards attacked you." He grunted, trotting around to her. "They should not have done such a thing. I worry for you, Dani the Novice."

"I can handle myself, Nessus the Centaur." She joked.

But Nessus wasn't in a humorous mood. "That does not mean you should endure what others will do." He stepped close, lowering a hand to her cheek tenderly. It wasn't sexual. If anything, it was strangely brotherly. "You show kindness others of your kind do not. You should be praised, not harmed, for such compassion. Do not lose this gift. It is a rarity in such times."

"I won't." she promised. "Thank you."

He withdrew his hand. "Until we meet again."

He turned and cantered off towards the Vale entrance.

A fluttering of wings and Caesar arrived. She swooped down, landing on the rim of the fountain.

"*Oh my God, hon! What happened?*"

"Boys." Dani grumbled.

If birds could glower, Caesar did. "*Which ones? Want me to do a fly over? I've got a full bladder.*"

Dani braved a smile. "Nah. Maybe later. Why are you back so early?"

The bird shifted on the edge of the fountain. "*I wanted to tell you what I learned.*"

"Learned?"

"*What did you think I was doing all day? Mating calls? No, I took a little tour of the Vale while all the excitement was happening in the main city.*"

After everything that happened, that made Dani nervous. "Caesar, if they found out what you were doing, you could get in trouble."

"*How?*"

"I don't know. But," she glanced at the house, "I don't want something bad to happen to you."

"*They don't know we talk. They don't know we can talk. If they did find out you knew something about the Trials, you could just say a little birdie told you. It wouldn't be a lie.*" If birds could smile, Caesar did.

"Funny." She had a point, though. "So, what did you find out?"

"*Oh, a few things. A bunch of Numen have been working in the Vale; Naturals and alchemists, I think.*"

226

Naturals and Alchemists; that meant plants and poisons. "What else?"

"Someone arrived today from Earth. I'm not exactly sure who he is. I've never seen him before."

"A Hellion?"

"Human, I think. Big guy. Thick beard. He had a bunch of people with him but they didn't look human. If I had to guess, I'd say they were—"

"Clay." She finished for her. "They're golems. And if I had to guess, the big guy is Judah. He makes them." She nodded to herself. "Okay, this is good to know. So poisons, plants and golems. Anything else?"

"Well, there's the centaurs. They're setting up along the top of the Vale. And if you had any idea how they were looking at me when I flew over—whew! It'd make a sailor blush."

"Caesar!" Dani groaned and giggled. "I really don't need to know stuff like that."

"Yeah, well girlie, sometimes a girl just has to share."

Dani shook her head.

Chapter Twenty-Six

The morning of the first Trial arrived. Dani hadn't slept much the past few days. The whole of Empyrean gathered at Vale entrance just after sunrise; Numen, gifted. Dressed in her eagle-standard Novice browns, Dani took her place with Crux and Corona amongst the pillars, ignoring Michael's sneer and other rude glimpses.

Aerie sigils decorated the Vale entrance archway: her eagle, Corona's circle and Crux's cross with a loop at the top—the ankh. Dani stood before her standard with Mastema. Some of the others came to see her off.

"Hope for the best." She told Mastema.

"False hope gives no hope." he quipped back.

Dani shook her head. "That's sweet. What is that? Poetry?"

Amongst the crowd, Dani looked for Roxelana. Even though they weren't speaking to one another, Dani hoped for some sign of her friend coming to see her off. There wasn't, unfortunately.

Nathaniel gave her a hug. When he did, he kissed her cheek. Dani didn't know how to react to that but didn't shy away from his affection. It wasn't the right time to have *that* conversation.

Ethan was last. No hug, but he ran his hand down her arm. "Good luck today. I'll be watching."

"How will you do that?"

"Same way as everyone else." He told her cryptically. "And I'll keep a close eye on you."

Dani tried to be funny. "Please tell me you won't be monitoring my frequency."

Ethan, who'd come to expect movie quotes and quips from her, shook his head. "I have no idea what that means."

"It's Star Trek."

"Oh." Again, awkwardness. It was a little better since he didn't get the joke. If he did it would make it super obvious she wasn't joking around.

"Um, thanks." She squeezed his hand affectionately.

Horns sounded. "It's time." Mastema told them. "Come."

Her friends joined the crowd. Dani stood on her own. The Elders positioned near the entrance, dressed as they had the first day with crowns and robes. Only eight stood apart. The Arbiters. Amongst them, Alecto smiled warmly in Dani's direction.

"Quiet please!" Castus's voice rang out loudly over the din of gathered Numen and gifted. His voice magically carried. "Thank you and welcome! Today marks the beginning of the three Novice Trials!"

The crowd clamored in excitement. Dani saw some of the gifted exchanging shekels. Bets?

Castus waved them silent. "As per tradition, each aerie must escape the Vale to succeed. As much as they face one another, they face the valley itself. They must make their way downriver past the bridge to the falls. There, they will find our river gate and a bell. Only by ringing it will they be declared victorious in their Trial. It matters not which aerie rings first, so long as one representative of each does. To accomplish this they have been given a loop of rope and a choice of weapons. They will have until noontide to achieve their goal. Aeries, are you ready?"

Dani had the cord looped over her torso and knife on her belt. She looked around glumly. The other aeries had twelve Novices to rely on; armed, ready, with better odds than her to succeed.

"Very well, then. Novices, let the Trial begin! Corona, descend first!"

The first twelve surged forward together. They had all assortment of weapons; swords, bows, axes. They looked confident.

After a moment, Castus called, "Crux, descend!"

Similarly, the next aerie descended.

Then it was Dani's turn. She felt almost silly, everyone silently watching her. She could feel people staring as she approached the archway.

"Arn! Descend!"

She withdrew her knife from its sheath and began downhill, feeling the near one-thousand pairs of eyes on her back. She waved over her shoulder for fun and hoped no one saw the fear in her eyes.

It didn't take long to see this wouldn't be like the last time. Last time, it was quiet and tranquil. It was still quiet, but not tranquil. Dani saw a Novice pinned to the tree only a hundred yards in; out cold, tied by centaur-arrow bindings.

She dashed through the underbrush, hiding when two equine warriors rode by. She kept to the rocks and boulders lining the cliffside. They wouldn't be able to follow her.

All around her, she heard sounds of battle. Two Novices soared past, using Aer to dart through the trees. She jealously watched them pass with ease, but then arrows lanced out of the underbrush, wrapping one Novice and pulling him down. The other landed in front of Dani.

She didn't know him. He drew his sword. She went for her knife, unsure of what he'd do. But one step and the rock beneath him shifted. It cracked open and swallowed him whole.

Holy...! Dani kept running.

She kept at a jog, getting her bearings quickly. Head downriver; it was easy enough to remember. She could hear the river rapids in the distance but instead of trying to trek the path that got her lost before, she kept the cliffs on her right and kept going.

It wasn't long until Dani heard screams again. She paused, kneeling down behind the nearest boulder. More screams. They were close. She knew better than to run towards the sounds of battle. Mastema taught her that much, at least. As Dani closed in, she could see it through the trees.

Three Novices stood back to back, adamantine weapons drawn. They were in the midst of a clearing, swinging their blades left and right. The wind whipped around them, moving the branches and trunks of the trees. She didn't see any opponents, but as she watched something exploded from the ground. In a shower of dirt and rock, it wrapped around one's wrist and yanked him forward.

"No!" he screeched, hacking with the broadsword.

"Braeden!" Another yelled. "Axe!"

Braeden, the third Novice, turned and heaved with a large axe. His blow came down on whatever it held the boy's wrist and sliced it off. But then behind him, something whipped out of the tree branches overhead, snaking around him and yanking him off his feet. Braeden let out a terrified scream before he disappeared.

It took Dani a second to realize it wasn't wind moving the trees. The tree moved on their own. They were attacking the Novices.

Naturals. Dani knew those who were gifted with Erthe could manipulate plants. But to attack?

Snatching up the fallen axe, the first boy spun on his knees and hacked apart another root that broke from the ground. The two remaining Novices defended themselves as best they could, adamantine weapons flashing the sunlight to cut down branches, vines and roots that backed them to the middle of the clearing. Even the grass rose up to bind their boots, forcing them to pull hard as they fought the losing battle.

"Run." Dani whispered. "Get out of there!"

But the boys kept fighting like idiots. She couldn't watch. They'd lose. You couldn't fight nature and win. She jogged away, getting as far from this place as she could before anyone spotted her.

But even as she climbed the rocks, she could hear them yelling. The one who snatched up the axe was pulled under. The ground opened up and swallowed him. The other boy slashed with his sword and jumped to the nearest rock face. The plants couldn't rise over the rocks. And that's when Dani knew how to save at least one of them.

"Hey!" she screamed loudly, waving her arms. "Hey! Over here!"

The boy turned towards her.

"Get to the rocks! They can't get you if you're on the rocks!"

The remaining blonde-haired Novice fled through an opening in the trees. The boulders Dani stood on extended down to the edge of the clearing and he leapt onto them, scaling deftly from one to another, slicing vines out of the way. The roots tried to grab him, but couldn't. He was free.

Dani joined him, both running uphill away from the hungry plants. The blonde was barely able kept up with her; exhausted. Only when they were out of sight of clearing did they stop.

"Thanks." He gasped, doubling over to catch his breath. "Zounds!"

"You're welcome." She sat down, catching her own. "I'm Dani."

"I know." He scowled, but she just saved him, so he extended his hand. "Chase."

"Nice to meet you." She shook it and he helped her up. "Where are the others in your aerie?"

Chase, whose blonde locks hung into his sky blue eyes, regarded her warily. He took a step back from her, his hand moving to the sword sheathed on his side.

Dani's own gripped the knife hilt. "Whoa there, tiger. I just helped you."

"And?"

"And I could have let you get eaten by trees like a demented game of Hungry Hungry Hippos. But I didn't. So settle down."

He warily looked her over, more so than she would have liked a guy to. Still, Chase didn't move an inch nearer his weapon. Then he relaxed. "Sorry. I wasn't expecting to make it out of there." Chase looked around. "So what now? My aerie got separated. The centaurs ambushed us five minutes into this blood hole of a valley. I'm not sure what to do now."

"Well, I suggest we keep moving. There are more things in this valley than centaurs and people-eating trees."

Chase agreed. Together, they scaled down the rocks on the other side, continuing downriver. She wasn't comfortable with him since they almost stabbed one another, but she didn't see a point in picking another fight. Besides, he wasn't half bad with the sword.

Chase was mostly silent next to her as they walked. He wasn't in that bad of shape; tall, built like a quarterback and had the All-American vibe. He kept looking around, expecting one plant or another to attack. He learned his lesson. Sparkling conversationalist or not, at least she wasn't going to have to babysit him.

"So what's it like?" he finally asked a few minutes later as they hiked over another set of boulders.

"Hm? What's what like?"

"Being the only girl."

She shook her head. "It's like a party twenty-four-seven, except there's no music, someone spit in the punch, and everyone's a jerk."

He laughed. "I heard you were sarcastic."

"That so? Glad I don't disappoint. What else have you heard?"

"You're tough. A lot of guys are scared of you."

"Really?" that wasn't exactly bad news.

"Yeah. But a lot of them are also pissed at you."

"Like who?"

"You know Michael?"

She smirked slightly. "I remember nearly putting his eye out."

"Well, he has it out for you."

They got to the forest floor again; no more rocks to keep them protected. They headed off overland. Chase kept behind her.

"So your aerie just left you to the centaurs?" she asked. "And then you ran into the trees?"

"Right."

"Not a great strategy."

He shrugged. Dani glanced over her shoulder. She hadn't really been looking at him. And for the first time, she saw something. It was almost the blink of an eye, but she saw it. His sideways glance, the nervous expression on his face, the fake nonchalance...

Trap.

She reached down towards her knife, feeling stupid for letting him stand behind her. Mastema taught her better. "Seems like a bad idea to split up."

"I guess."

She slowed her walk, trying to get him closer. She shuffled through what Mastema taught her about attacking behind herself. She knew knife verse sword was a bad fight any way you sliced it, but if she could get close, a knife was better than a sword.

"What aerie did you say you were from?" she asked.

Stupid, stupid, stupid. She focused too much on her surroundings. She didn't notice he wasn't walking anymore. She turned, knife about to draw, but he was out of reach. And with whoops and cheers, five Novices jumped from hiding.

At the lead, Michael beamed proudly and clapped Chase on the shoulder. "Good job."

She was surrounded.

"You're outnumbered." Michael chuckled, pointing the sword towards her. "Don't try to escape."

"Because you always need to outnumber me to take one little ol' me, don't you?" she sneered. "What is it Michael? Scared?"

His face tinged red, his sword grip tightening. "Keep talking. I'm going to take it out of you. Believe me."

She did believe him. For all the bravado, Dani was terrified. Six guys and only one of her.

"It was kind of a gamble," Michael joked. "We stayed back, hoping you'd show up. Of course, they got separated. But it all worked out."

"Chancing to fail your Trial so you could get at me? Are you insane?" Did he hate her that much?

"I say we have some fun." Michael joked to his friends. "Now, what can we do with one girl that will entertain six guys?"

"I got more than a few ideas." Chase chuckled.

"I'd stay back if I were you." Dani warned. "I'm not about to forget the kind of weasel you turned out to be."

Chase's smile slipped. "You think you scare me? I could have taken you back there."

"Yeah? Then why walk me into a trap?"

"Because it's more fun when you share."

He disgusted her. Andreas and Lester? They at least kept their hatred out in the open. But Chase was a whole new kind of low.

Michael licked his lips. "I'm going to enjoy this. Last time you took me off guard. Ain't no way that's happening now."

"Trust me, big boy, whatever you think is about to happen, isn't."

"Really? You're unarmed." He came within arm's reach. "You can't fly. There's no fire and you're not that good at Erthe. Face it: giving up will make this a lot easier."

Unarmed? She hadn't drawn her knife. He hadn't seen it; only Chase. And he hadn't said anything.

But she heard him. "Wait, Michael, she—!"

Too late. Mastema drilled it into her: *Take the advantage when you have it.* Her right fist shot out, tagging him hard in the side. He grunted, moving to block. She didn't care. That wasn't the point. Her left drew the knife and she brought her arm up, wrapping around him and pressing the edge of the blade against his throat, spinning the bigger man against her front.

The others moved in, but she barked, "Stop!" The froze. Dani pinned Michael by the blade. "Move another step and he's a dead man."

"She won't." Chase said, but didn't move. "She won't kill one of us."

"Really? Six guys verses one me and you think I won't? Are you delusional or just stupid?"

"You won't." Michael tried to pull down on her arm, but she dug the blade in a little; not breaking the skin, but letting him know not to try it. He eased up. "You wouldn't kill one of us. The Elders would sentence you to death."

That she didn't doubt. They could attack her and she could see the Elder Council dismissing it. She kills one of them and there'd be consequences. But she didn't let him go.

"You've got nowhere to go." Chase reminded her. "Think about it."

"Trust me, I am thinking."

"Let him go."

"Fat chance."

"What's your plan? Hold him the entire trip down river?"

She knew she couldn't. One way or another, this would end badly. She had no back up; no one help her. What was the plan?

And then: "*Hey sister.*"

A rush of relief washed through her. Dani heard the voice over her shoulder, as if she spoke directly into her ear.

"*Don't look up.*" The caladrius warned. " *Just whisper. Are you okay?*"

It was hard not to look for her friend. Instead she hissed softly so they couldn't hear. "I'm fine. Where are you? How can you hear me?"

"*I'm a hawk, sweet cheeks. We hear amazingly. I see you have some company. Want help?*"

"I'd like that."

"*I'm on it. I brought a friend.*"

"A friend?"

"*You might want to push that dirtbag away.*"

"When?"

"*Now.*"

Dani shoved Michael into them. As she did, Caesar broke through the canopy of the trees above them, her hawk cry deafening. Dani's ears rung. Her snow-white wings spread, breaking, and as they did a powerful

234

blast of air collided like a solid wall with Chase. Thrown off his feet, he launched through the air and struck the nearest tree.

The others closed in but someone burst out of the tree line. A horse and rider—no, a centaur—galloped into the open, swinging his massive longsword left and right. His blade batted aside weapons, knocked down two Novices and sliced open Michael's shoulder. No killing blows, but disabling them all in quick succession. He skidded to a stop, pommel of his weapon hammering Michael across the top of the head.

The remaining Corona Novice fled, but Caesar whipped past Dani and descended on his back. He screamed as her claws dug in and lifted him off the ground. He thrashed as she soared up into the trees and unceremoniously dropped him flailing through the air. The boy hit the ground with a grunt and didn't move.

Caesar made a sharp turn, plummeting downward to rest atop a fallen log. She chirped, flapping her wings victoriously. *"Take that ya' harpies!"*

Dani threw her arms around the large hawk. "Oh my God! Caesar! What are you doing here?"

"Think I was gonna let my girl go it alone? Sheesh. You have no faith in your friends."

"How'd you know where to find me?"

"Ask him." She nodded towards the centaur. *"He seems to know a lot about you."*

Dani rose to her feet and bowed, fingers to her forehead. "Nessus."

Her centaur friend smiled and bowed back. "M'lady. I came upon your friend while scouting for Novices. She is quite fond of you."

"You and Caesar can talk to one another?"

"Of course. Centaurs have always spoken the language of the avian races."

"Well, thank you for helping me, but why did you? You're supposed to stop me."

"True enough, but this exercise is about testing your abilities, not letting these heathens act in such a disrespectful manner." He quickly chained up the fallen Novices. "There is also honor amongst my people. You spared me when I was at your mercy. I am honored-bound to return it." He flashed a smile. "And I gladly return it."

Caesar leaned in and whispered to Dani, *"He is so hot."*

"Eww Caesar!" But she stroked the bird's feathers. "Thank you for coming. I don't know what they would have done."

"I do. And they got off better than they deserved."

235

Someone groaned. Next to the tree where Caesar threw him, Chase stirred. Her friend shifted to take off, but Dani waved her down. "I got this one." She hefted her knife and stalked towards him.

He was almost on his knees when he saw her. He went for his sword but Dani closed the distance and kicked. Her heel connected with his nose. He grunted, falling back in a small spray of nasal blood.

"Ugh! You broke my nose!"

Dani landed on him, pinning him against the ground, knife at his throat. "I'll do more than that you pathetic little worm!" she grabbed his collar, pulling his neck against the knife-tip. "Give me one good reason I shouldn't gut you like a fish!"

"Please!" he begged, coughing on his own blood. "It wasn't my idea!"

"And I care?" she pressed the blade in a little harder, breaking the skin.

"I swear to God! I didn't know what they were planning!"

"Even if I believed that, you went along with it."

"I'll do anything!" he begged. "Just don't kill me!"

She wanted to. She really did. She felt a murderous rage so intense she could visualize slitting his throat. But that wasn't her. Even as she thought it, she dismissed it. It wasn't her style to kill anyone, especially anyone at her mercy.

"Are there any more of you?" Dani asked.

"No! I swear!" Chase groveled earnestly.

She let him go and stood, sheathing her knife. She left him crying where he lay.

Nessus folded his arms across his broad chest. "I would have slew him."

"I'm not slewing anyone today." She wiped her hands. "I don't need that on my conscience."

"Want me to take him?"

"Yeah. He's not really any good to me." She looked up at him. "Talking to Caesar: you called it the language of birds. Is that something special?"

"Quite special. Very few human or Numen can speak to the avian races. It is quite an advantage over your peers."

She glanced at Caesar, who looked on approvingly. "*We make a great team, sister.*"

"We do. Thanks for coming to my rescue."

"*Anytime honey. So what's the plan?*"

236

"You should continue." Nessus advised. "The other centaurs will come to collect these heathens when I call."

"Any chance of getting by them without being seen?"

"They have secured land, air and water. The veil can help you, if you can, but a centaur's keen eye will not be tricked for long."

"Then how do I get by an entire herd of centaurs?"

Nessus glared at Chase, who still held his bloody nose. "I may have a way."

Chapter Twenty-Seven

Chase ran; blood streaming down his face, stumbling and falling. Behind him, Nessus pursued. Swinging his sword in wide arcs, he herded him into the open, the smile on Nessus's face visible even under his helm. He enjoyed himself.

Other centaurs joined in, riding after what they thought was their brother pursuing a Novice. Meanwhile, Caesar and Dani headed in the other direction; caladrius overhead as a scout, her on foot. She used the rocks for cover and pretty soon, the sound of Chase's frantic screams faded into the background.

She made pretty good time. The last few weeks conditioned her to run in exhaustion and her Numen side allowed her to go longer than regular human girls her age.

She didn't run into any other Novices. Halfway down the river she found a cut-over. It wasn't the same bridge as last time, but there were a few rocks that provided her a crossing when she used her Water arc to push aside the rapids. Caesar kept close watch overhead for anything coming after her.

The river flattened out further down. The same place she ran into the Tigris was empty, save for the occasional keresh or elemental. More than once she spotted what looked like a little man made of earth, with a large nose and big eyes, that ran when Dani came near. Gnomes.

As they entered the lower valley, it got warmer. The air smelled sweet. A fog rolled in.

From above, Caesar asked. "*How you doing down there, honey?*"

"Fine. How much further to the bridge?"

"*Not far.*"

"See anything?"

"*Nothing, but the fog is pretty thick.*"

It was. Dani came to a stop at a fallen log, taking a seat to catch a rest. She laid her head against another tree next to it. "Jeez. You'd think this Trial would be faster. I feel like I've been walking for hours."

Caesar circled overhead. "*You're almost to the bridge. Then it's the home stretch.*"

Dani yawned. "I'll just rest a bit, then keep going. Can you keep a lookout for me?"

"*Don't wait too long.*"

"Sure thing." She closed her eyes, inhaling the wonderful perfume of the valley. All she needed to do was rest up. A couple minutes tops and she'd be right as rain.

Her eyes were only closed a second before Caesar asked, "*You getting up any time soon?*"

"Hm?" she shook her head.

"*You need to get going.*"

She murmured. "Caesar, come on, give me a few."

"*You've been there fifteen minutes.*"

"No I haven't." she shifted comfortably against the tree. "It's been, like, two."

"*No, it's been fifteen.*"

"Well then give me fifteen more you stupid bird!" she barked irritably.

She could almost feel Caesar's hurt feelings. It was like a wave crashing on her. "*What did I do to you?*"

"Nothing. Leave me alone." She irked her. Why was she here anyway?

"*Dani, come on, you got to get up.*"

"What if I don't want to?" she just wanted to relax!

"*Dani,*" Caesar swooped down, coming to rest next to her, "*get up. We got to go.*"

"I said leave me alone!" She shoved the caladrius off the log. "Get lost!"

She flapped, scampering to another perch. The bird glowered. "*Don't be rude!*"

"Go away!" she closed her eyes again. "Leave me alone!"

"*What the hell...?*" her voice trailed off. Her head cocked to the side, pausing. "*Oh no! Fellbloom!*"

"Hm?" she couldn't have cared less.

"*Dani, we have to go! Now!*"

"You go. Leave me alone."

"*Oh no! Oh no!*" Caesar flapped over to her. "*We got to get you out of this fog!*" She landed on Dani's arm, flapping hard to pull her up. Dani tried to fight her off, but Caesar was strong. She pulled Dani to her feet even as she tried yank her arm free. "*It's not fog! Come on! Get out of it! Get to the water!*"

"What're you doing?" Dani shrieked. She tried to shove her off, but the bird kept pulling, dragging her on her heels. "Leave me alone!"

"*No! The more of this stuff you inhale, the less chance of you getting out!*"

"Get off!" she thrashed at the bird.

"*No! This isn't you talking! It's the fellbloom! Come on!*"

"Fellbloom? What the hell are you talking about?" Caesar dragged Dani towards the river's edge. "Let me go Caesar! You're not making sense!"

"*I am making sense, girl! And I know you only think I'm not because of the fog!*"

"Fog? You're crazy!" she was almost to the edge of the water.

"*You'll thank me for this later!*"

"Caesar! No—!"

Dani's feet slipped over the edge of the embankment and she dumped face first into the clear, crystal water. The cold was like a slap in the face. Instantly, Dani was awake. It was like coming out of a coma. She broke the surface, sputtering.

Caesar flapped around her to a branch over the water's edge. "*You okay?*"

Dani coughed, shaking her head. "What the hell? Wha—What was that?" She felt like she'd been sleeping for days. She treaded water, staring at the fog as it curled away from the river as if alive. "What's in the fog?"

"*I told you: fellbloom.*"

"Fellbloom?"

"*Lotus-blossoms.*" Caesar told her. "*Except this was in fog form. Stuff makes you sleepy and lazy and turns you into a slug. I smelled it in the fog.*"

Dani coughed. "Alchemists. They must have made some sort of airborne elixir." The fog moved as if under the power of Aer. The scent was sickly-sweet.

"*Lotus plants don't grow here in the Vale,*" Caesar said, "*I'm guessing you're right.*"

Dani burned with shame. She hit Caesar; called her names, yelled at her. "Thanks. You saved me again."

"*No problem. I knew it was the drug.*"

"Still," she treaded towards the river's edge, "I shouldn't have done that."

"*Well, the only way you get through the fog is on foot.*" Caesar said. "*And the moment you go back in there, it's going to happen all over again.*"

She reached the river's sharp embankment and climbed out, just to the edge of the fog. Already she felt slightly drowsy. "I'm screwed."

"Unless you can cause a little wind." Her friend suggested.

Dani shook her head. "Controlling Aer hasn't been a talent of mine."

"Try."

Dani extended her hand. Closing her eyes, she focused. Aer was like breathing and visualizing how you wanted it to happen. She visualized a tunnel in the mist. Stretching her fingers, she pushed outward with her mind.

Your passion can be your strength, Mastema told her once. *Do not let it control you. Control it.*

She opened her eyes. The fog curled backward. A tunnel formed through it.

Caesar beamed. *"I knew you could do it."*

She climbed out of the river, soaked. "Let's go."

"I'm so with you, sister." Caesar took off.

"You know I am not going to forget about you dumping me in a river." Dani called after her.

"Tell you what: you ever catch me and I'll let you pay me back!"

She started off through the fog again.

Dani kept going. She wasn't sure if any other Novices would make the same mistake of walking into that fog, but she didn't want to stick around to find out. No cynocephali waited by the supports and the moment she crossed under them, the fog slid back. She was free.

The river rushed through rapids below the bridge. Dani started at a jog again, sounds of a waterfall telling her she neared the bottom. The end was in sight.

"See anything?" Dani asked Caesar.

"Smooth sailing."

"How close are we?"

"Pretty close. I can see Empyrean's rim up ahead. The river rushes into a gate just ahead. Almost there, honey."

The rocks formed rapids. As she turned around another corner, she could see the eight-story gate. The river gushed through a large yawning, creating the falls down Empyrean's cliffs. A large bell hung from one side. And beyond that, blue sky and clouds.

"Almost to it, honey. And—" Caesar's voice cut off.

Dani looked up. Her friend was overhead one minute and the next, gone. "Caesar?" She couldn't see her anywhere. Fear coiled inside her rib cage. "Caesar!"

Caesar cried out. "*Dani run!*" and then her voice went silent again.

Before she could react, a hand broke from the mud and grabbed her ankle. She shrieked and drew the knife, stabbing down into it, but the fist holding her wasn't flesh. It was clay. A golem, a little smaller than the ones at the Hellfire Club, burst from the ground and pulled her off her feet.

Dani landed hard as the clay creature emerged. It wasn't as human-like as other golems. It resembled a man dripping with mud and dirt and rock. There were no eyes. A mouth, barely recognizable, opened and snarled.

Two more broke from the river's edge. Three of them blocked her path.

Dani kicked. Her heel snapped off a part of the cheek, but it kept rising. She pulled the knife from its hand and slashed the face, cutting away more earth, but to no avail.

She tried to pull free but the golem had a death-grip on her.

"Let go!"

She tried to summon Erthe, pushing the golem back under power over the ground. But unlike Aer, she wasn't doing well.

Free from the ground, the monster yanked her towards it. It balled up its other fist, morphing it into a large mallet of soil. It was going to beat her to death.

Dani focused. When it swung, she hunched like a sit-up and pulled herself in, then exploded upward at it. The blow missed and she landed face-first in the mud creature's chest, slashing off hunks with her knife. She scrambled up and the golem let her go as she toppled it over onto its back.

She leapt over onto the head, using both heels and her weight to tear away chunks. She kept stomping until finally, the head caved. Something fell clear and the body disintegrated into a pile of dirt.

Lying amidst the debris was a scroll, rolled up and wrapped with twine; no longer than her finger. Dani snatched it up. The parchment was warm with magic.

Golems weren't living creatures. Someone created them by a spell-scroll. The spell-maker, Judah, placed the scroll in its mouth to bring the creature to life. Taking the scroll out destroyed it.

Knife raised, she faced the remaining two. "Come on then."

They lumbered at her, footfalls shaking the ground as the two six-foot-tall creations charged Dani. She charged, too. She spotted a rock and placed one foot on it, leveraging herself up and onto the first one.

They collided, both pin-wheeling around. She stuck her hand into its mouth and with a yank, wrenched a scroll free. As they turned, they tumbled and the golem broke apart. A mountain of dirt toppled over her. She threw away the scroll as she landed.

Unfortunately, the weight of so much mud pinned her to the ground. The other golem leered over, big fists coming down and pinning her to the river's edge. Dani couldn't move.

"Ugh!" she angled her blade towards the last one's head and stabbed. The tip sliced in, but did no damage to the creature.

The weight was too much. She could barely breathe! Withdrawing the dagger from the mud, she angled it a little more down. As she felt the air pressed out of her lungs, she knew if she didn't do something soon it was going to kill her.

She stabbed again; this time, down through the side of the jaw into the throat. She felt the clay give way to something buried there. The golem's eyes widened. She didn't know if they understood death, but this one certainly felt when her knife connected with the scroll. Dani twisted and pulled the papyrus paper out with a clump of dirt.

The golem toppled over, lifeless.

The weight was enormous. Dani sucked in a lungful of air as she pushed to free herself. Without the golem pressing down, at least she could breathe. She pushed her way semi-free, digging to remove the rest.

She heard footsteps. Another Novice appeared at the top of the rapids. She didn't know him, but she recognized the Crux insignia he wore.

"Are you alright?" he asked.

"I'm fine." She said.

"Golems?"

"Yep." She shoveled more dirt off. "Mind helping me?"

The Novice sauntered forward but, before reaching her, stopped. He glanced around, and then instead of coming to her aid, knelt and retrieved the two fallen golem scrolls on the ground.

"I want to help. I do. But I'm the last one in my aerie." He scooped away some dirt with his hand. "I need to get to the end."

"And? You'll get to the end. It's right there."

"But I don't trust you—or need you, for that matter." He placed one scroll into a hole and pushed the dirt over it. He did the same with the second scroll.

"What are you doing?"

"You could stand to be a little nicer." He stood, wiping off his hands and walking around her.

"Hey! Help me!"

"Sorry." He said, though he sounded very un-sorry. "I won't."

Dani turned towards a noise and the two holes he dug began to form more earth around them. The piles quickly morphed into arms, then hands, then torsos. The golems began to re-form.

"Hey! I didn't do anything to you!" she yelled at his back.

"So?" he asked callously. She could even see him smile. He ran. In almost no time, he was at the wall. He uncoiled his rope.

Dani worriedly glanced back at the golems, now fully human and rising up off the ground. She dug at her legs to free them.

The Novice swung his rope up and through a hole in bell's large hammer. He looped the other end into a tie when it came back down, tightened it and then ringing it. The bell tolled. Once. Twice.

The golems reformed. One of her legs broke free and she scrambled out. But even as she did, a large mud hand grabbed her and pulled her back.

"No!" she grabbed for her knife, but another hand clamped down on her other arm, pinning it back. The second golem loomed over her.

It came down, folding over her lower body, crushing her underneath. The air exploded from her lungs. She groaned, unable to move. And the second monster fell over her face.

Blood rushed to her head. Air stopped coming. She reached with her only free hand for the last thing she had had: the vial of panacea. Praying it might help her, she unstoppered it and swallowed the contents.

The golem fell, covering her in darkness. The bell tolled again.

Chapter Twenty-Eight

Dani inhaled her first breath and nearly suffocated on air. She tried to sit up, but someone held her down, holding her to keep her from doubling over to vomit. Her head pounded with each heartbeat. She turned sideways, retching. Putrid water and mud vomited out into a bucket until she was allowed to lie back down, the headache subsiding enough to pass out again.

Someone spoke over her. She couldn't see them but could hear Mastema's voice.

"If she should die...I will return..."

She closed her eyes and disappeared into oblivion.

———————————————

She wasn't sure how long after she woke, but when she did a hand looped through hers. Through slits, she saw Nathaniel sleeping on a stool next to her bed and holding her hand. Large windows poured light down over stone slabs topped with mattresses. She was in the Ward, the infirmary nestled in a sheltered courtyard behind the Keep.

Healers moved amongst the beds, a fourth of which were occupied by Novices. As her vision cleared, she saw Michael two beds down; his arm and head wrapped in panacea bandages. Her anger woke her from her coma.

It woke Nathaniel too. He opened his eyes. "Dani!" He threw his arms around her.

"Hey, hey, I'm fine." She assured him, pulling him off. There was a pink scar over his left eye, bisecting his eyebrow. "What happened to you?"

He waved it off. "My own Trial didn't go so well. My aerie didn't make it to the bell."

"What time is it?"

"It's morning," he told her, "two days after your Trial."

"Two days?" *I was out two days?* She sat up. A dull ache throbbed in her chest. Her ribs felt like someone played them like a demented xylophone with sledgehammers.

"Careful. The golems broke three of your ribs and bruised a lung."

"How the hell did I survive that?"

"They had to use a lot of healing compounds on you." He paused, not wanting to tell her. "I thought you wouldn't make it."

"But I did."

"The Trials were awful. Crux won yours. One of their Novices rung the bell." He avoided her gaze as if afraid. "Dani, if you didn't take that panacea you might have died. The Elders weren't quick to come to you. The elixir kept you alive."

Dani didn't doubt it. "What about Corona? I had to deal with a few of them."

"Well, whatever you did," he glanced over his shoulder, "some of them are still here. One guy looks like you dropped him off the roof of a building."

She grinned.

"Michael's shoulder is sliced to the bone. They're keeping him under while he heals. Dani," he turned back, "there's been a lot of talk. Corona has the most people injured. They're blaming you."

"What else is new?" Wanting to change subjects, she asked, "How come you didn't win?"

He shook his head. "We got past the centaurs, but most of us hit that fog and couldn't go any farther."

"Fellbloom elixir."

He nodded. "The other aerie didn't get by it either. Crux, Coronach, Gylph and Aerial were the only ones. And," he bowed his head, "someone from my aerie died. A centaur arrow knocked him off a boulder and he fell into the river and drown."

"Oh God, who?" she felt her chest tighten, thinking about Dink or Bouden.

"His name was Damien. It upset a lot of people, me included."

"I'm sorry Nathaniel." She squeezed his hand. "So what happened?"

"The centaurs swear it wasn't them, but they're charging one of them: Nessus. Do you remember the centaur we met last time in the Vale?"

Dani couldn't believe it. *Nessus?* "I don't believe it. I know him."

"That's part of what people are saying: you know him."

"They're blaming me?"

"They don't believe it was an accident."

"I never met Damien! I don't know the sarding guy from Adam!" She saw his face flinch. "Sorry."

"Some accuse Nessus of playing favorites; intentionally going after us instead of Glyph. That's what Andreas is claiming, anyway."

"Andreas?"

Nathaniel shrugged. "He was there. He says Nessus ignored closer Glyph Novices and came after them, even though centaurs aren't supposed to endanger the lives of Novices." He shook his head. "I never thought the

Trials could actually be deadly. I joked about them." He sounded disgusted. "This is all messed up."

Dani's heart broke for Nathaniel. She stroked his cheek. "I'm so sorry."

He looked up at her and his eyes held not just sadness, but something else; something deeper. He squeezed her hand. "I'm just glad you're alive. I don't know what I'd do if something happened to you."

She felt afraid; not of Nathaniel, but of that statement. She saw the looks he gave her, especially when she was with Ethan. And now, his hand in hers, the other arm moving around to hold her, it was too much.

She withdrew her hand, patting him kindly. "You're a great friend."

His eyes flashed with hurt for a second, but they were interrupted. Elder Aleister, the Head Healer, appeared. He wore his usual white robes, with satchels of different medicines in leather holds, and deep-set frown. And he had a visitor with him.

"Dani," Judah's voice warmed with concern. The big man's rosy cheeks were blotchy from tears. He wore jeans and a flannel shirt, looking like the world's largest lumberjack. "I am beyond words with joy to see you alive and well."

"Hi Judah."

"Two months have certainly changed you." He came to her bedside, taking a seat opposite Nathaniel. "Both of you. You are much more warriors than when we last met."

"It's been two months?" *That would make it, what? October?* "It's good to see you too. You brought the golems?"

"Simple ones, yes." He nodded. "I'm more of an expert than the Numen; an independent contractor you could say." He chuckled softly, but it didn't have the strength of his usual laughter. "I cannot express how sorry I am for what happened. Once made, I cannot control my creatures to every minute detail. When I heard it was you they buried alive, I said to myself, 'Judah, if that young lady perishes because of you, I swear upon the life of my mother—a very gentle woman, I might add—that I shall rip you apart from the inside.' And I tell you, I took myself very seriously. I would even perchance to say—."

"Judah!" Dani startled him out of his rant. "You're rambling. It's fine. I'm fine. We're fine."

He blushed happily. "Thank you. You are a darling. If I were a poet, I'd immortalize you in song."

Dani shook her head. "You're strange."

"And that is why you are so fond of me."

She was. Judah was the most wonderful person she encountered yet. "Thank you for coming to see me."

He rose to his feet, dwarfing everyone in the room. "And I shall see you again at the end of these Trials, I'm sure. It is tradition."

"What does that mean?"

"Vespertide, m'lady." He said cryptically. "I am sure you've heard of it."

"Of course."

"Until we meet again, then. I need to check on my creatures and I perchance may be able to see Tigey."

"Tigey? You mean the Tigris?"

"He is my little schnookums."

Nathaniel pointed out, as if it were not obvious, "It's a twenty-foot tall lion, Judah."

"And he loves it when I scratch behind his ears."

And with that, the sorcerer-bar owner left, whistling a tune.

Nathaniel shook his head. "He is all kinds of bonkers."

Elder Aleister cleared his throat. "It is good to see you awake Novice Daniella. And you, Novice Nathaniel. I believe you've been here every day since her admittance."

She squirmed uncomfortably. *Every day?*

"Well, you were wise to take the panacea before the golems buried you." Aleister told her. "It gave us the critical time to get to you."

"Thanks for coming so quickly." She tried not to be sarcastic. "Has anyone else come to visit me while I was out?"

"Quite a few, actually; Elders, a few gifted admirers—one in particular, a Shea I believe—and a number of Novices from the Aether aerie. One of its Guardians did, too. Ethan."

She brightened a little but tried to keep it out of her voice. "Really?"

"Yes. Why does that surprise you?"

She noticed Nathaniel's scowl. "No reason. What about my Guardian? Mastema?"

Aleister flustered a little. "I have not seen him since the first day."

"Great. My own Guardian didn't visit."

"He's probably busy." Nathaniel assured her.

"Doing what? His only job is to help me." She crossed her arms.

"I'm sure Mastema cares." Nathaniel said. "He's probably very concerned."

"I was not concerned." Mastema told her. "I did not feel the need to see you."

Dani stared at him, so angry she wanted to chuck him over the side of the cliff. When Vespers came, she was released and Nathaniel walked her back to the Arn. She still ached, but the elixir healed her ribs and lungs. Mastema waited for her. He even had the guts to be angry it took her so long.

"I almost died you *pinche idiota!*" she screamed.

"But you did not."

"And that makes it better *how*?"

He closed his eyes, sitting cross-legged in the pavilion. Dani groaned, stomping her foot and nearly shattering the plank under her. "Could you at least pretend to care?"

"By spending valuable time with you when there was nothing I could do?" he didn't open his eyes from meditation. "The healers were caring for you. There was nothing to be gained by my presence."

"That is not why friends visit people in the hospital!"

"We are not friends."

"I get that now!"

Silence. She wanted to smack him across the face, but she'd never get the chance. She would get about two steps before he stopped her.

She grumbled. "You're aggravating."

"And you are acting like a child." He finally opened his eyes and he looked bored doing it. "You failed the first Trial."

"I was so close! And, in case you forgot, I was alone!"

"I saw. And yet, you did not reach the bell." He stood. "The next Trial is soon. We must prepare for the duels."

"I just got out of the Ward! I nearly collapsed a lung!"

"Yes. Do you not remember that you must achieve one Trial victory?"

She gave him a dirty look. "Yeah, I do. I also remember that if I don't win, I'm not the only one who gets the ax. Literally."

If the revelation shocked Mastema, he didn't show it. "You face incredible odds. Training will prepare you. And in this Trial, your friend the caladrius will not be able to aid you."

"Excuse me?"

Mastema gave her a knowing look and then glanced into her house. On a perch, Caesar waited.

"Do not take me for a simpleton. I saw you call on her."

"How'd you see that?"

"The Trials are heavily monitored; not to mention, a favorite entertainment of the gifted." Mastema said. "You manifested a very unique gift. You were wise to keep it to yourself."

"Thank you."

"You were also a fool. You cannot allow others to fight your battles."

She steamed. "Did you miss the part where I was on my own? Or the part where that coward Chase led me into a trap? Would you have rather watched what they had planned? *Would that have been entertaining?!* Yeah, Caesar and Nessus helped. So what?"

"I do not approve of weakness."

Her fists balled. "No matter what you say, having friends is not a weakness."

"It is if they fight your battles for you. Eventually, they will not."

"Screw you!" she screamed. "What is wrong with you? Did your mother not love you or something? Ethan and Kleos keep telling me what a good teacher you are, but I don't see it!"

"You did not notice you survived most of the Vale thanks to my teachings?"

"Look you pompous," she searched for the word, "culus! You might be good at telling me how to fight, but you suck when it comes to the other part of being a teacher."

"Such as?"

"Giving a crap! Not being a complete bloodhole when it comes to helping me! At least Caesar and Nessus did! I'm doing the best I can!"

"One of those is a bird." He said, her rant having no effect. "The other is charged with favoritism."

"So?"

"So why do you think the Elders are sending him into Hell as punishment?"

The question made her go silent for a moment. She stared at him. "Excuse me?"

"Nessus is a great warrior. You think you are the only Numen to ever befriend a centaur? I have known him for many centuries." Mastema's face was a blank slate. "He is an excellent commander, a fierce warrior and a proud centaur. He has never once showed favoritism to any Novice or Numen. He gives no quarter. But now the Elders question him. What changed?"

Dani's eyes widened. "Do they know—?"

"Of course they know. This house, your alliance in the Vale; they know all. Now a Novice is dead at his hands. It is the excuse they need to punish him. They will send him to the frontlines of Hell in a matter of months." His eyes narrowed. "But they do it not because of him, or the Novice he killed. By now the entire city knows Nessus's punishment. The Elders need not tell them. The blonde haired Novice he ran down most likely spread rumors of it already."

"Chase? He led me into a trap where they... where Michael wanted to..." She still couldn't say it. Even now, her stomach tightened at the thought of their leering eyes.

"It matters not. The gifted, the centaurs, other Novices; the message is sent. You will have allies no longer."

Help me and there are consequences. Help me and there are punishments. The message was pretty clear. "That's unfair."

"What have you learned of fairness?"

Dani groaned loudly and spun on her heel.

"Where are you going?"

"Anywhere but here!"

She left her house and marched across the stones. She didn't care what he did or didn't do. She nearly died in the Vale and he didn't trouble himself to be concerned. So now, neither did she.

Mastema appeared, blocking her path.

"Consarn it!" she cursed. "Leave me alone!"

"It is not my duty to leave you alone." He said emotionlessly.

"Back off!" Couldn't he see she was upset?

"You are my charge. I will not send you into another Trial unprepared."

"Unprepared?" she demanded. "I went in there prepared! Look what it got me!"

"Do not act like a child."

She slapped him. Hard. Her hand connected squarely with the side of his face. When he turned back to face her, he glared. "Finished?"

"Get out of my face." And she pushed past him.

He could have stopped her. He chose not to.

She left the Arn.

Dani didn't know where she was going. She just walked. The sun set, casting shadows across Empyrean's crater. The lights of Sanctuary Hills bloomed in the darkness. Gifted gathered at their houses; warm, cozy, at home. She saw families. Children. They were safe.

She crested the hill near Novice Village; another community she'd never be a part of. Dink was practicing his archery. She could see Nathaniel and Bouden sitting by the fountain, talking.

She felt like they were miles away.

"Looky, looky," Andreas sneered, appearing downhill. "A murderer taking a stroll." Lantern in one hand, basket in the other, he came up with Lester and Michael. *Of course they're friends*, she didn't say. They had baskets full of fruit and vegetables, foraging the hills for dinner. "Aren't you a little far from your village?"

"Buzz off." She noticed Michael's shoulder was still bandaged where Nessus sliced it open. "How's the arm?"

He snarled. "Better than you'll be if I ever go sword to sword with you."

"I doubt you'll get that chance during the Trials."

"Who said anything about Trials?"

A threat. It was sad she expected them now.

"She's baiting you." Andreas told him. He jutted his chin toward Dani. "See, unlike you, you baseborn coward, Michael fights his own battles. You get murderous centaurs to do your bidding."

"I didn't kill Damien."

"Don't say his name." Lester warned. "You don't get to."

What else was new: unfair blame. But instead of fighting, she wearily left them behind. She had enough fighting for one day.

"Don't think for one second we don't see what you're doing!" Andreas called after her. "We all know how get those Guardians to help you! There's only one thing they'd want from you and we're pretty sure you're giving it to them!"

She froze. Halfway down the slope her feet slammed into the ground. Her anger burned in the pit of her stomach. They said all this stuff to her. They accused her of all these things that weren't her fault. And now he says something like that?

"Everybody knows." Andreas crowed. "They can't get it on the regular from the gifted. You know, rules and all. Is that how you got the centaur? I wouldn't put it past you. Everybody knows you've used that path plenty of times. Why not a centaur?" The guys at his back chuckled in agreement. "What is it now, boys? There's Kleos, the bearded guy. Though to be honest, I didn't think girls were his thing. Then there's her Guardian, obviously."

Her fists clenched at her sides. Painfully. When she looked back, the boys had big, fat grins on their faces; ones she wanted to wipe off.

"Don't forget the Novices she's putting out for." Michael pointed out. "Especially Nathaniel. He's got it bad. You done him yet?"

Her hands shook. She tried her best to keep them at her sides.

Lester smirked. "And then there's Ethan. Everybody knows they've been doing it since she got here."

She snapped. Her mind went blank. Dani heard herself scream. She barely remembered charging uphill. It was a stupid move. She was outnumbered. They had size and weight on her, not to mention she was hurt.

She was also pissed.

She didn't attack smart. She didn't think about it. If she had, she wouldn't take a blind swing at Andreas. He jumped back from her sloppy attack, laughing, but his own confidence made him stupid. She spun and delivered a swift kick to the groin. He dropped.

Michael hit her first. His basket dropped and he connected with her jaw, knocking her to the dirt. She rolled, recovered, and swung for a kick. Her heel connected with his ribs, then she rose and put her fist through his jaw.

Lester seized her around the waist. "You little—!" he pulled her back, but she grabbed at his face, lashing with her fingernails. He screamed.

It didn't last long. Another pair of arms pulled Lester off. Andreas and Michael came at her, but Guardians suddenly swarmed down on them; Aether, Corona, every person in Novice Village hearing the fight.

One pulled Dani to her feet. She nearly hit him.

"Dani! Whoa! Calm down!" Ethan cautioned, pinning one arm behind her to stop her. "Dani! Stop!" He pushed her to her knees.

"Get off of me!" she screamed ferally.

A crowd gathered to watch. They had an audience.

She heard Andreas, "She attacked us!"

Kleos restrained him. She least got some satisfaction watching him cradle his junk in pain.

"I did not!"

"She did!" Lester insisted. "That bloody quim went crazy!"

"Call me that again!" she dared, spittle flying angrily down her chin she was so furious. "Call me that again! I dare you!"

"Qui—"

"What is the meaning of this?"

Everyone went silent. Standing at the edge of the crowd was Mastema. Her Guardian's presence made everyone back away. He strode forward, lanterns splashing orange and yellow patterns across his obsidian skin. He was terrifying; partially because of his expression.

"I demand to know what transpired. Answer me!" he glared at Ethan. "Release my Novice."

Ethan did without question. Dani stood. "They insulted me. They said I—"

"Quiet." Mastema didn't bother to look at her. "Return to the Arn."

"You let her go?" Michael demanded. "She attacked us!"

"Unprovoked?"

"Yeah! She came out of nowhere!"

There were a few murmurs of agreement, but Mastema's eyes narrowed in suspicion. He stalked over to Michael, who cowered in his presence. "It is my experience, one does not attack unprovoked unless they are demonic. Is she a demon?"

"No."

"Then I'll ask again: was it unprovoked?"

He scowled, looking away.

"Look when I am speaking to you."

"Why?"

"Because those who are guilty cannot meet the eyes of their accuser."

Michael shifted his gaze, getting that look Dani saw a hundred times. He jutted out his chin defiantly, staring Mastema down. The Novices next to him, even a few Guardians, stepped away like he would spontaneously catch fire.

"I'm looking at you," Michael grunted, "so?"

"I'm not your accuser. She is." He pointed to Dani. "You look at her and tell me it was unprovoked."

He couldn't. The moment Michael did, he avoided her gaze.

"That is what I thought."

If Mastema was even a fraction nicer, Dani would've felt grateful. But when he looked at her, the scorn was just as strong.

"Do not let me see you near my Novice again." He told Michael. "Do you understand me?"

He nodded.

"Leave."

He turned and walked off, close to pissing his trousers. He was terrified. Any person in their right mind would be. But even as her Guardian turned away, he snarled silently in Dani's direction. Everyone was brave when no one was looking.

"Everyone back to your quarters!" Ethan announced. "That goes double for Aether! If I see even one of my Novices out of the village, you'll be scrubbing the latrine!"

Dani spotted the boys—Nathaniel, Dink and Bouden—standing off to one side. Nathaniel mouthed silently to her, *Are you okay?* Dani shook him off and said nothing.

Ethan touched her arm, like he had before her Trial. Dani shrunk back from it. Mastema interrupted them.

"Novice, what were you thinking?"

"Excuse me?"

"That was unwise."

"Unwise? _Unwise?_ Are you sarding kidding right now? Do you know what they just accused me of?"

"It matters not."

"It matters quite a damn bit!" she shrieked. "I am sick and tired of this! I'm tired of every person I meet telling me they think I'm evil or a danger or a whore! What? Am I just supposed to take it?"

Ethan spoke up on her behalf. "She has a point."

"And what will it change?" he asked him. "The Elder Council already believes she is not worthy. Her fellow Novices turn more and more against her. What will coddling do?"

"Well I'd like at least one person to finally stand up for me! Isn't that your job?"

"My job is to help you stay alive, which is difficult to do when you act imprudently!"

"You're the one that's difficult!" she just wanted to hit him so badly it physically hurt to stop herself. She got up in his face, which was hard to do since he was several inches taller. "Every day—EVERY DAY—people say stuff to me! Every day I hear them talk about me behind my back! What am I supposed to do? What Mastema? Am I just supposed to be a good little girl and keep my mouth shut? Because I sure as hell am not going to do that!" She had it up to here. *No more*, she thought. *No more*. "I can't take this! You want me to pass a Trial? I can't do that if everyone is stacking the deck against me!"

Her Guardian was silent. He made no expression. Ethan's face was equally blank, though she could see the sympathetic pain in his eyes.

After a few seconds, Mastema asked calmly, "Do you feel better?"

Her nails dug into the palms of her hands. "No."

"Precisely. Nothing changes. You attacked them and nothing changed. You vented your frustrations and nothing changed. But you still failed your Trial. You must still complete in two others. So no matter how unfair you feel your situation is, nothing changes."

She wanted to throw up. On him. In his face. Her anger was like a furnace.

"Forget you." She stalked past him. "You don't care."

At her back, Ethan called out to her. "Dani—!"

"Let her be." Mastema told her. "She must learn for herself."

And she planned on doing just that. Without him.

Chapter Twenty-Nine

The following week, Mastema was a no-show. It gave her time to cool off. She didn't do much during that time; she went to lessons, she went to Studies, and she went back to the Arn. No friends, no Roxelana, no Ethan, no one. Korë once stopped her in the market to cheer her up with another grass doll, but Dani kept on walking. It hurt to see the disappointment on the little girl's face, but she didn't want to be around people.

Caesar was there. Her friend insisted on hunting for her food. She brought back dead squirrels, rabbits, even a turkey-like bird. Dani cooked them on the fire, but even roadkill didn't cheer her up.

She did spend time practicing with swords. She envisioned gutting Lester, Andreas and Michael, then skewering their heads on spikes. It was very Vlad the Impaler, but sometimes anger brought out the worst in her.

Nathaniel, Bouden, and Dink tried visiting, but she didn't come out of her house. None of them were bold enough or stupid enough to try to come in. Ethan was the only one she couldn't avoid for long.

It was a week after when she came out during Vespers. The sun was setting. No one was there. Or so she thought.

"So, sulking?"

She glanced up. Ethan perched on her roof, legs dangling over the side. He tossed her a small sack with honeybread baked in cinnamon, paired with strawberries.

"Bought these for you."

"From Adare's. They're my favorite."

Ethan shrugged off the ledge and floated down like a graceful angel. "I'd ask if you were okay, but I'm not stupid."

"Smart man." She put the fruit into the bread and took a bite. "Thanks."

"I find food helps."

"I've lost weight up here. There's no junk food." She chewed. "You know what I could go for? A fish taco. Fish tacos always hit the spot when I was pissed off."

Ethan's eyes widened a little. "Fish tacos?"

"They're my favorite. Did they have fast food back in the day?"

He smirked. "What do you mean 'back in the day?' I had a burger a few weeks ago when I went to Earth. It's a perk of being a Guardian."

"Vespertide, you mean?" She was guessing. She handed him breaded-fruit. "Do you think you could take me next time?"

257

Ethan regarded it in his hand solemnly. "Trust me. The first trip down won't be pleasant." He took a bite. "Anyway, that's not why I'm here."

Dani sulked towards the fountain. "Let me guess: you're here to tell me I'm being stupid to mope around?"

"To tell you that you're wrong about Mastema."

She sat. So did he. "How am I wrong?"

"He cares."

"He has a funny way of showing it."

"He's not like you, Dani. He's not even like me."

"Yeah. He's a Pod-Person. Did the Wizard forget to give him a heart or something?"

"I think he was born without it, but that's not what I mean." Ethan told her. "Mastema has never been warm and cuddly, but that doesn't mean he doesn't care. He's trying to help."

"By doing what?"

"By training you. He knows what I know: no one is going to give you a break. He knows the Council has it out for him since his failure and they want to use you to hurt you both. He knows the other Novices aren't going to accept you. More than a few of them are dangerous. Instead of trying to make you feel better, he's trying to toughen you up."

"I don't want to toughen up. I want to just be me: Dani."

"Well, that's not always possible." Ethan shook his head. "None of us go through training and come out the other side the same. Do you really think you're the same girl that came up here two months ago?"

That was true. Dani already broke her elbow and didn't bat an eye.

"Training is meant to turn you into something different. The Trials are just an intense version of it. For you, your whole time in Empyrean is going to be a trial. Mastema is trying to get you ready."

"You mean by being the most awful person in existence?"

"I mean by giving you what you need when no one else will." He said. "That first day in the Vale? Every Guardian purposely helped their Novices fail. I sent Nathaniel down with a weapon I knew he couldn't use. Mastema sent you with his own knife. He entrusted you with it without ever meeting you." He held up a finger. "He sent you with something you could protect yourself with. And since then? He's trained you to be on your own. He knows others won't treat you fairly. You'll never be part of a group, so he didn't train you to fight in one."

"He could at least show some interest in me."

Ethan pursed his lips. "What do you remember about the Ward after your Trial?"

"When I was out cold? Nothing. I was practically comatose. I remember something he said; partly, anyway."

Ethan laughed softly, shaking his head. "Yeah, I remember. I don't remember the exact quote but I think it was," his stifled his laughter, lowering his voice to imitate Mastema, "'If she should die, Elder Aleister, I will not be kept at bay. I will return and hold you and your healers personally responsible for her by the point of my sword. You will not fail in keeping her alive. I will return.' Or something like that. Elder Aleister looked like he was going to piss his pants and that's hard to do to an Elder. Mastema can be plenty terrifying."

He did that? He threatened an Elder? If anyone but Ethan told her that, she wouldn't believe them.

"He's still a jerk."

"I wouldn't argue with you." He said. "Mastema is a taskmaster, but that doesn't make him uncaring."

"He doesn't tell me anything." Dani pointed out. "Most of the time I have no idea what he's doing! He doesn't come to half my lessons and when he does, all he does is yell. How am I supposed to know he cares?"

"You won't. That's not the point. He just wants you to succeed."

"He's got a funny way of showing it."

"He does. But trust me, when you need him, he will be there."

She doubted that but didn't say anything. She had enough dysfunctional people in her life, her mother included in that. She did not need a teacher-figure with an anger problem.

"Just trust him."

She grumbled, "Fine. But don't ask me to buy him a gift on Father's Day. Or Christmas. Or Arbor Day."

Ethan chuckled. "Agreed." He put an arm around her shoulders and hugged her. "You'll be fine."

"Thanks."

Ethan left, walking this time. Dani sighed heavily and finished her bread.

From the roof, she heard Caesar jeer, *"Dani and Ethan, sittin' in a tree. K–I–S–S–S–I–N–G."*

"It's only two S's." Dani grumbled, chucking bread at her. "And shut up."

———————————————

She curled up in her bed as Vespers sounded that evening.

"*So, when are you and Ethan setting a date for the wedding?*" Caesar asked from the foot of the bed. "*Can I be a bridesmaid? I look stunning in a dress.*"

"I will Kentucky-fry you." Dani warned.

"*Oh come on. I have to live vicariously through you. I got, like, zero prospects.*"

"How does a bird get prospects?"

"*You know all those bird calls you hear on Earth?*"

"Yeah."

"*Well, we don't call them 'cat-calls' because of ...you know...the cat thing, but they're basically the same thing. Male birds are all 'I've got the most plumage' or 'look how many nuts I gathered' or 'I caught the biggest worm.' Men. Sheesh. They all think they got the biggest worm.*"

"That is <u>waaaaay</u> too much information, Caesar."

"*It's hard out there in the bird world. You've got more of a chance than I do.*"

Dani blushed. "I'm not trying to date Ethan. I don't even know if it's allowed."

"*Considering they're all a bunch of dudes, probably not. But there shouldn't be a rule against it since there's never been a female Numen, right?*"

"Right. Probably not."

"*So that loophole is WIDE open.*"

Dani laughed. Having Caesar around felt good and though she hated to admit it, she liked being around Ethan. He was sweet in a way a lot of the guys weren't. Kleos was kind, but that was more professional than anything else. The rest of the boys were similar. The only one that worried her was Nathaniel. He liked her more than just a friend and it was difficult to ignore.

"He doesn't like me." She said.

Caesar was a bird, so she couldn't give any kind of sassy eyebrow raise or you-kidding-me look, but she might as well have. "*His pheromones say different.*"

"Eww."

"*I'm just saying, honey. The vibes he gives off are not platonic. They are super UN-platonic.*"

"Thanks."

Caesar's head snapped up, turning sideways.

"Anyway, even if I wanted to do anything about that, it's definitely not the right—"

"*Shh!*" the caladrius hushed.

Dani sat up. "What is it?"

"*I heard something.*"

The tone of Caesar's voice said it all. Dani went still, listening. She heard nothing, but that didn't mean anything, either. Caesar tilted her head left and right.

"What is it?"

"*I hear someone.*" She whispered back. "*I hear...many someones.*"

Many? Dani dropped to the floor and made her was stealthily to the door. Caesar remained where she was, listening for the intruders. Dani sidled up next to the door and inched it open.

Outside the torches still burned silently. It was fully dark and she didn't see anyone—

Movement. Dani's heart leapt into her throat. Something, or someone, moved at just out of the light. Then, just as quickly as they appeared, they were gone.

"Someone's here." She hissed to Caesar. "But I can't see them."

Caesar glanced up. "*They're everywhere.*"

"On the roof?"

She nodded.

"How many?"

"*I don't know.*"

Heart thudding in her chest, Dani looked for a weapon. She didn't know who was here or why, but she had a suspicion it wasn't a social call.

"*What do we do?*"

Dani shook her head. She had no weapons and no ideas. The roof above her creaked with footfalls. Now she could hear voices.

"They're only two entrances." Dani told her. "We'll make a break for it."

"*How?*"

"Can you fly me?" she wished she didn't have to ask. She hadn't mastered any kind of flight.

"*Not far.*"

"We'll have to try."

Dani glanced through the door across the square; the pedestal against the edge of the cliff. Those who lived in the Arn before—the feathertongues—used it to commune with visiting birds. Now they could use it to jump. Of course, it meant Dani need to practically leap to her death.

Creaks. Footsteps. Someone came to the edge of the roof.

"We run for the pedestal." Dani told her.

"*That's nuts.*"

"Do you have a better idea?"

Obviously, she didn't. Hiding or fighting wouldn't work. Anyone that snuck down here wouldn't just give up. They might be the ones who trashed her village last time. Now they were here when they knew she would be, too.

"We've got to try." Dani told her as she heard footsteps approaching. "Are you with me?"

"*Totes, sister.*"

"Get ready."

Dani moved away from the door to the square and chose the pavilion. She heard creaks on the floorboards outside. They blocked both exits, but the pavilion was the best bet.

Both doors ripped outward from their frames. Four figures loomed in the torchlight; two at each door.

Dani jumped, grabbing the top of the doorframe and kicking with both feet, knocking them back. She landed, ducked and Caesar flew over, wings extended. A loud concussion of air exploded outwards. The gust hurled both of them backwards into two supports, pin-wheeling them off hard to the ground.

The other two came in behind her from the other door. Dani bolted out into the pavilion, seizing one of the wooden staves. From her left, a man leapt down from the roof. He was armed with the knife, wearing red raiments and a mask over his face. A Gatekeeper. Dani spun and launched the pole around, striking him across the face. He went down.

She shot from the pavilion and sprinted across the square. Caesar darted out behind her. There were about five or six of them; all of them in masks. Some wore Novice brown. Two wore Guardian black.

Above her, a familiar voice screamed. "Get her!"

Caesar turned, screeching and dive bombing the advancing intruders, who all shrunk back from her swiping talons. That gave Dani time to sprint to towards the cliffside.

One caught up to her.

"I got you now you—UUUURRRRRRGGGHHHH!"

His arms wrapped around her, lifting her. With practiced skill, she wrapped one leg with both of his and he stumbled. His grip loosened. Dani broke his hold, grabbed his wrist and twisted him down painfully as she spun.

She delivered a swift, nose-breaking kick to his face.

"She's getting away!"

Four were on the roof. The one who gave the orders was a Guardian. As she watched, they took off into the air after her.

"*Dani! Go!*" Caesar swung high, attacking the lead Numen with her talons. He screamed and tumbled out of the sky, but he took the caladrius with him. "*Go!*"

"Caesar!"

"*Fly on your own! You can do it!*"

Dani sprinted, covering the distance to the pedestal. But as she approached the edge, she skidded to a stop before going over. There was no way she could fly on her own!

"*Dani!*" Caesar cartwheeled off the soldier, who dropped to the roof of Dani's home, thudding down and rolling off. She turned toward her. "*I'm coming!*"

Something shot out of the dark, silver and shining in the orange torch fire. Adamantine chains wrapped around Caesar and she dropped from the sky into the arms of a Guardian, who caught her and wrangled her to the ground.

"No!" Dani turned back, but the intruders formed a semi-circle around, pinning her to the cliffside.

Everything came to a stop.

"Leave her alone!" Dani screamed. "Let her go!"

"The bird?" The lead Guardian touched down, mask and hood obscuring his face. "Why? Chicken sounds delicious."

"Screw you!" she balled her fists. They burned. There was no way she could take on a dozen, but she wouldn't let them kill her friend.

"My, my; all bravado now. It's not as easy when the odds are stacked against you."

"You mean when you bring twelve men to take on one girl? You think that makes you men?"

The Guardian stepped forward. "You were warned before. You should have learned when we broke your house."

"And what now?" she asked. "You're going to kill me?"

"No. The law prevents us from killing you." He shook his head. "But your pet? Not so much. And there's no law against a beating." He raised his hand to the others. "Two of you help me grab her."

She searched the faces of her attackers. She knew some of their voices. If she had to guess, the Guardian leading them was Nazir. Any number of the people she pissed off lately could be among the others.

Dani spat at their feet in disgust. "Come try me, lap-pinkie."

"You think you can defeat us?"

"I'll make you wish you killed me." She swallowed her fear and raised her fists.

The masked Guardian drew a knife from his belt, holding it like he knew what he was doing. "You don't belong here. You should have left the first time we came here."

"I thought you said you weren't going to kill me?" she asked, staring at the knife.

"I didn't say we wouldn't cut you a little bit. And if you struggle, accidents happen." He gestured to the others. "Kill the bird. Burn the house."

"No!"

The Novice holding a struggling Caesar seized her by the neck. She screeched. With her wings pinned, she couldn't free herself. She was at his mercy.

But the man's head, not Caesar's, snapped sideways with a dull *thunk!* As if he were a marionette doll with strings cut, he dropped Caesar and dropped to the ground.

Materializing from the veil, Mastema stood with the unconscious attacker at his feet. He carried two wooden swords. His eyes fell on Dani, then on the Guardian leader. The two stared one another down.

The masked man visibly swallowed in fear.

Mastema leapt over the fallen body, swinging one wooden stick at the nearest attacker. He blocked, but the other sword came up and struck him in the neck right below the jaw. The Novice dropped. When he did, Mastema's other weapon cracked down on his spine.

"Stop him!" the leader ordered.

The group turned on Mastema. Even he couldn't fight them all. But before they could attack, something dropped out of the sky in a flurry of wings; not a bird, but a woman. Alecto landed between them.

Something shot out of the darkness and quickly wrapped around one man's legs, stumbling him into the ground. Kleos dropped from the roof of Dani's house, bowstaff horizontal, onto the back of a Novice and sent him face first into the stone.

Despite still being outnumbered, the two Guardians and the Fury backed all of the remaining attackers away.

"Remove your masks." Alecto ordered. From behind her, the sound of horse hooves thundered close. "In seconds, my centaurs will outnumber you."

The masked Numen pulled their wounded and nearly unconscious comrades back towards them. They stood between the three and Dani.

"Do it now." Mastema threatened. He stared down the lead Guardian. "Quarter will be shone unless you do not surrender my Novice."

The leader glanced over his shoulder at Dani. Even under the mask, she could see a smirk cross his face.

"Or..."

He leapt backwards under the power of Aer and kicked her backwards. She landed, rolled and pitched over the side of the pedestal.

"Dani!" she heard Alecto scream.

The world fell away. Dani tumbled, her hands scrambling for a hold. As she fell, she caught the lip of the pedestal and stopped herself from plummeting to her death.

She swung a little, lost her grip and caught herself again. Below, the Vale was a dark pit. She screamed, death-grip on the ledge slipping again. She kicked, trying to leverage herself up, but her boots only scraped the side.

Numen shot over the side and flew off into the dark. A moment later, Alecto appeared. She carried an adamantine blade, swinging at the retreating intruders. When she saw Dani, she sheathed it.

"She is here!"

Alecto grabbed Dani's arm. Mastema and Kleos both took her other and tunic, pulling her to safety on solid ground and into Alecto's arms.

"Are you okay?" she cradled her face. "Dani, are you alright?"

"It's fine." She pushed away her hands. "It's fine."

But she already felt herself falling apart. She kept repeating herself. "It's fine, it's fine, it's fine."

It's fine, it's fine, it's fine. Her mom's favorite lie.

Tears welled up in her eyes. Alecto's comforting wings floated around her. The world dissolved behind crystal cascades of tears.

Chapter Thirty

"This is a disturbing accusation, Lady Alecto." Elder Castus said from his throne. "Do you have any evidence?"

The twenty-four white robe Elders looked indifferent despite what she told them happened the night before. Maybe it was knowing before she even arrived, but to Dani they seemed frailer than before. Incompetent. Out-dated.

At her side, Alecto frowned. "You heard the witnesses."

"Yes, yes," Elder Berith spoke, "Guardians Mastema and Kleos have testified. But you are not certain the identities? Yet you wish us to arrest several members on your word?"

"Is my word not enough?"

"We, of course, respect your word, Lady Alecto. You are the fairest of ladies. But even if what you say is true, we must understand all the facts. For example, what did Novice Daniella do to provoke such an attack?"

"I didn't provoke anything." Dani stepped forward. "They attacked me."

"And without proof," Elder Heman spoke up, "we have no evidence with which to bring charges for the crime. It is all hear-say."

"The evidence of intruders in her village does speak for itself." Jeduthun said from his place in the middle, but it was a far-cry from actual support.

Another Elder jumped on that. "That is still not grounds to accuse soldiers who have performed admirably for this city! We are at war. The demons have stirred unlike anything in centuries. Their monstrous leader just killed a patrol of Naturals healing a curse in Arizona. Sacred land has been marred." He turned back to Dani. "I will not support any kind of investigation that questions the loyalty and service of men who seek to defend us."

Even though she knew this would happen, Dani still couldn't believe it. "They almost killed me."

Heman stood and declared to the assembled group. "This still is only baseless story; not supported by evidence and spoken by a Novice who has a history of dishonesty and defiance. It is my belief that even if these stories are true, they are not the whole story. No one attacks unprovoked. I demand to know, Novice Daniella: what did you do to warrant such an attack?"

Her mouth dropped open. Her near-death experience was _her fault_?!

The accusation was enough for Castus to intervene. "Elder Heman, you are out of line."

"How am I?" he demanded. "I am seeking the truth."

Castus, just like Dani, could see many approving nods amongst the other Elders. Even Jeduthun looked worried. Clearly, there'd been a change of heart about her. She didn't have the benefit of the doubt anymore.

Alecto tried one last time, "My lords—."

"The point is taken." Castus brought the debate to an end. "Elder Heman, I will remind you that if the Co-Consuls have not allowed you to speak, then you do not have the right. Sit down." It was technicality, but it was all Castus had. Heman sat, but with very self-satisfied smile. "Lady Alecto, your support is admirable, but she is a Novice. It is beyond your capacity to speak for her."

Alecto looked insulted, but bowed respectfully and, with apologetic smile to Dani, stepped back.

"Novice Daniella," Castus began, "I cannot speak for everyone on the Council, but I do not doubt the events as you tell them, but without cause we cannot charge those you suspect of this crime."

"So you just do nothing?" she demanded.

"We will make inquiries."

"What the hell does that mean?"

Castus frowned at her tone. "Elder Asaph will look into the matter and his Gatekeepers will stay vigilant around the Novice quarters. They will keep you safe."

"Keep me safe?" she asked. "Keep me _safe?_ You mean keep me safe from people you won't even question!" She couldn't keep the indignation out of her voice. "You're assigning an Elder who hates me to look into people who hate me."

From his side, Asaph started, "How dare you—!"

"And you're assigning Gatekeepers to protect me? Two of the men who attacked me were Gatekeepers!"

Elder Asaph looked like he could crush a stone in his fist.

"How am I supposed to stay safe? How am I supposed to live here if this is what happens? That can't be your decision!"

"That is enough!" Castus roared. Immediately, the chamber fell silent. Even Dani balked at his anger. "Our ways have not changed for millennia and cannot be curtailed for one individual. You became a part of this city; subject to its laws equally. Those laws govern this Council and govern you. You will abide by them or you will suffer the consequences. One of those laws is not questioning this Council or its decrees. The ruling about this matter is final. Do I make myself clear?"

She could do nothing else, so she said nothing else.

With a slow breath, Castus reminded her, "Your second trial begins in two days. Duels begin at Morning Lauds. All Novices report to the Training Grounds."

Mastema spoke for the first time. He hadn't been much help here. "When will she know which Novice she faces?"

Heman spoke up. "As an Arbiter, I must ask what you mean?"

Mastema glanced sideways at Dani. Something was wrong. "Normally, the aeries match up their Novices, one against the other in single combat. She is one Novice. She will face one opponent. Which opponent?"

Elder Heman looked pleased as he leaned forward. "The law states that one entire aerie faces another entire aerie. Novice Daniella is, true, one Novice, but she represents the Arn. In the past, if one aerie should not have the full twelve, some Novices fought more than one. It is the law. And the law requires she faces all twelve opponents."

"Twelve?" she asked. "I'm fighting twelve people?"

"Of course. The law is clear. And, by lottery, you have been chosen to fight Corona."

"Corona? The ones from the Vale? I already fought them!"

"Yes, you did." His smile widened a fraction.

Mastema had the presence of mind to ask, "The law also states that the aerie with the most undefeated Novices is declared the victor of the Trial. Should she lose one duel—"

"She will fail her Trial."

Dani was done. She wasn't going to stand there and watch Heman get any kind of pleasure telling her how unfairly he stacked the deck against her. She stormed out.

"Novice Daniella!" Castus called. "You were not dismissed!"

But she continued going and no one was stupid enough to stop her.

"What are you doing?" Nathaniel asked when he found Dani in her house with a satchel filled of all belongings she could fit: money, food, leather canteens of water and an extra set of clothes. It wasn't much, but it was enough. And like the day she became a Numen, she was running away.

"I'm leaving." She said, wiping tears from her cheeks. "I'm getting out of here."

"Where are you going to go? You can't leave Empyrean." She stormed past him, satchel in hand. Nathaniel followed her out. "Dani! Wait!"

"Leave me alone Nate!"

"Don't try to play me off like that! Stop! You're not making sense! I know somebody tried to trash your place but—!"

"You think that's all this is?" she screamed loud enough to make him back up. "You think that's all?"

"What is it, then?"

She screamed through clenched teeth. "My God! Boys! I swear!" she shook her head furiously. "What do you think the other night was? Just a bunch of good ol' boys on a panty raid? They nearly killed me! They almost killed Caesar! Almost every day I've been here it's been punishment." All her pent up rage spilled out. "I'm sick of it!"

Nathaniel was taken aback.

"Everyone here keeps on pretending this isn't a big deal, but it is! I can't stay here and wait until they're allowed to do something worse to me!" Nathaniel tried to touch her, but she smacked his hand away. "Leave me alone!"

"Dani, you're my friend. I can't let you just leave!"

"Oh God Nathaniel, will you give it up!" she cried. "I can't take it anymore. I can't take the way you look at me, or the way you want to be around me, or the way you care about me. I'm not in love with you! Will you stop trying!"

The look on his face nearly broke her heart. She never saw him look so betrayed.

She pushed past him. "I have to go. Don't follow me."

He didn't. She left the Arn. She had no idea where she was going. She couldn't leave Empyrean. It wasn't like she could call a cab, but just like at Ricky's house, she wasn't staying either. She didn't bother to go into Sanctuary Hills. She hadn't spoken to Roxelana or Shea in some time. Instead, she walked away along the Vale cliff, hoping to put some distance between her and the rest of the supposed paradise.

As soon as her house disappeared into the afternoon-bathed hills of green, Ethan appeared. He descended from the sky at a run, landing to catch up with her. "Dani!"

"I'm tired of telling people to leave me alone, Ethan. Don't make me repeat myself."

"Just stop!" he caught up to her, falling in step. He knew better than to get in her way. "What are you doing? Did you really walk out on the Council?"

"I don't care what those weasels say. I'm not listening to them insult me!"

"Dani, they're the Council."

"And that means what? You don't understand. You weren't there last night."

"Did you want me to be?"

"I don't need anyone to save me." She growled.

He didn't have a reply. "Where are you going?"

"I don't know." She walked ahead of him.

"Are you going to take the second Trial?"

"No."

"The Council won't let you quit."

This was from a new voice. She stifled the urge to scream a ton of insults at the world and turned around. Standing next to Ethan was Mastema, the last person she wanted to see.

Folding her arms, she asked, "What are you doing here?"

"I came to see the unwise decision you made."

"Mastema, you're not helping." Ethan chided.

"Do not tell me what will help her." He shot back, and then glared with his dark eyes at his charge. "You are foolishly impudent."

"I don't even know what that means."

"It means you are being insolent and—"

"Oh for the love of God, I know what it *means* means!" she shouted. "I meant I don't know what you expect of me! I've done everything I can to fit in, but I'm not like the others and they all know it! They remind me of it every day. Well, congrats, they got what they want."

"And you simply give in?"

"Are you serious?" she stormed up to him, getting in his face. "Explain to me how doing *everything* I've done is giving in? You think I'm going to stay after all this crap? I'd rather be demon food."

She stalked away from him. Mastema was all demands. She didn't care what Ethan told her about him; about how he showed his concern. She didn't care. Not anymore.

"You are making the wrong choice."

His words froze her. She wheeled on him again, hands balled into burning fists. "Excuse me?"

Her Guardian stood stone-faced. "You are making the wrong choice. If you leave, they will be truly victorious over you."

Even Ethan was horrified. "Mastema—!"

"Victorious?" She shrieked. "Victorious? You think I care about anything from those malignant, misogynistic monsters? You think I want to be a Numen anymore?"

"You were born to be one, whether you want it or not." Mastema told her. "It is your destiny."

"Screw destiny!"

"Then live in exile." He told her harshly. "No civilization, even a celestial one, can thrive without change. No change comes without a price, usually to those who wish to change it. I thought you would change it. I believed you stronger."

"Screw you!"

"Exile yourself to the Vale. Run to the Dalles. No Earthborn will follow you there. You will be safe in your cowardice until what you run from comes for you." He leveled his steely gaze on her. "You run because you are afraid, but by running you guarantee your fate."

Then her Guardian vanished.

He left Ethan and Dani alone. She couldn't believe he said that to her, or the hole that it left in her chest.

"Dani..." Ethan's voice was soft. He didn't know what to say. "I'm sorry."

Tears stung her eyes. She shook her head. "Leave me alone, Ethan."

"I'm not leaving you alone."

"Why?" she asked, streaks of pain running down her cheeks. "Why do you care so much?"

He opened his mouth to speak, but nothing came out. She could see he wanted to say something. She didn't know why he couldn't, but she knew what it was. She knew for a while, but couldn't bring herself to say anything either.

"Please," she begged, "I can't do this with you."

"Do what?" he faked like he didn't know. "Dani, please, don't leave."

"I can't do this." She repeated and fled.

Tears ran down her cheeks. Mastema's words echoed in her mind. *Run to the Dalles. No Earthborn will follow you there.* She crested the hill. The entrance to the Vale lay below.

As if knowing what she wanted, the switchbacks appeared. Dani ran downhill and without a second thought, descended into the most dangerous place in Empyrean. Even that was better than the supposed paradise of the Numen.

Dani kept running until she was under the canopy of trees and muggy confines of the Vale. She ran until the only sounds were bird calls and the patter of creatures in the underbrush. Only then did she stop to take a breath.

She cried her heart to pieces. The fear, the anger; she sobbed against a tree. She ran away and knew why, but it didn't make it any easier. She was leaving everything and everyone. Again.

It was running from Ricky's all over again: a world of unknown before her and a world she knew behind her.

Dani trudged on, hiking towards the river until she reached the water's edge. She couldn't cross it, but didn't want to, either. There wasn't anything across the river she needed to reach, or downriver for that matter. So she went up.

Ethan told her no one went to the source of the Crystalline River. Numen couldn't fly in the mist for some reason. If anyone came looking for her, it would be the best place to hide.

The hike was initially easy. The constant conditioning made the going better, but the slopes got steeper and steeper as she ascended. The rushing river turned to intense rapids, even more voracious than the ones downstream. Then the rapids turned to falls. Difficult now, she found a path and made her way up slowly.

The falls formed the mist that hung thickly in the air around Dani as she climbed over jagged rocks and slippery stone, obscuring her vision. It matted her hair to her head and soaked through her clothes. Light spilled through in rainbows, creating beautiful illusions around her. She almost tumbled over the side of the rock-face. Footing was nearly impossible.

And then she broke from the mist, climbing to the top. She pulled herself up and when she could see, she barely believed her eyes.

A sheer-cliff valley bowled into the rock. A column of water gushed over a falls, so wide the spray sent clouds across the rim of the Empyrean's crater. But the water didn't descend from the cliffs. It descended from the sky. Water appeared in mid-air and washed down onto the rocks as if born out of nothing. The spray obscured the magical spring from below.

It was the source of Crystalline River, but how was that possible?

Dani sat on the lip of the gorge, marveling at one of the most stunning things she'd ever seen. It was peaceful. For once, she felt safe. All it took was fleeing paradise to find it.

It wasn't until the sun dipped low that she realized she needed a place to sleep. She brought blankets, but nothing to create a shelter. She spotted a small cave through the falls. It was reachable.

It took some time to climb down to it, but she found a way down that wasn't fear-inducing. She reached the mouth of the cave as the sun cast the gorge in shadow. Deep into the crater of Empyrean's mountain, the falls perfectly covered the entrance. If anyone came for her, they might miss it.

Darkness set in over the Dalles. What little light there was glimmering off the water backlit the cave in a water-splashed eerie glow. She brought a torch, which she assembled and lit.

Satisfied with her new shelter, she found a place for her things away from the water. She lay the torch to one side, along with the extra oil and rags. She made bedding out of folded blankets and kept her food high to keep dry. She had enough for a couple of days, but eventually she'd need more. That was for another day.

Darkness fell. In the distance she heard the blare of Vespers; the end of the day in Empyrean. The sound was so distant. She was safe for now.

She ate a loaf of honeybread, drank from a canteen of water and ate a slice of beef she'd saved from rations. Elder Azariah taught some survival training, since even in the modern world they might get cut off from civilization. Dani was glad for it.

With nothing better to do, she lay down to sleep. The torch was a comforting night light but the bed of blankets was hard. As she lay there, thinking how stupid she was to run—yet not regretting the decision—she wondered how long before someone came for her. Would she even survive until then? She tried to put it out of her mind, listening to the sounds of the crashing water on rocks. She let her eyes slip closed.

But then they opened. She sat up. The sounds of the waterfall tried to lull her to sleep, but she knew she heard something. And as she listened, she heard it again.

Someone was at the mouth of the cave.

Chapter Thirty-One

Dani stood slowly. She couldn't see anything beyond the torchlight, but she heard someone. She quietly slipped out of her sleeping spot and slunk into the darkness. No way would she stand in the open.

She didn't call out. She wasn't stupid. She kept her hands loose and ready for anything that might come at her. As she moved away from the light, her vision adjusted to the gloom.

As she stepped gingerly down towards the mouth of the cave, all she could see were the luminescent, frothing falls in the moonlight. The roar of the water deafened her, but she listened for the sounds again.

After a minute, she relaxed. She must have been paranoid.

Then something collided with her.

Dani screamed, lifted off her feet and thrown across the cave. She threw her arm out, not down, and avoided snapping her wrist to break her landing. She hit the ground and rolled, coming up, but whoever her invisible attacker was, he was fast. Someone struck her in the face.

Dani fell, pain searing across her jaw. Immediately his weight sank down on her, but she was ready. As she felt him sink down, she rolled and threw him off. She heard a grunt of pain; a man's voice.

She stood, hands out in defensive posture, ready for another attack. Her mind scrolled through moves she'd learned, but they didn't immediately come to mind. She didn't need to *think*. She needed to *do*. Real fighting, Kleos told her, wasn't about thinking of the moves. It was about making them as natural as breathing.

When he came at her again, she could see his outline. He was taller, with a wide reach. She knew he was strong by his hold. She wouldn't overpower him. He shoved her back against the cave wall. She struck out with her heel, connecting with his leg, but he didn't let go.

She was losing. Even as she raked his shins with her boots, even as she fought back with elbow-strikes at close range, she knew she was losing. He was too tall, too strong, and too experienced. She felt a foot strike at her ankle and he threw her sideways. Dani landed hard and tumbled down the slope to the falls.

"No!" She tried to stop her slide.

No luck. The throw tumbled her down into the falls. Water gushed around her and carried her the rest of the way.

She swept out into darkness.

Dani opened her mouth to scream but the torrents of water forced down her throat. She landed in the gushing rapids. Enveloped, pulled under, she flailed helplessly. The ice-like cold stole the warmth from her body.

Dani tumbled, swam, tried to rise only to be thrown under again. The river sunk and then she went over another falls, bouncing off the surface of boulders down into oblivion. Cold dark waters came up to grab her.

Her vision darkened. She had no air. She couldn't kick anymore. Even as the waves smoothed out and she rose to the surface, she couldn't fight anymore. The river swept her from the Dalles. Slowly, she slipped into the darkness.

The last sensation she felt was a hand closing over her arm, pulling her towards the light.

———————————————

"She's alive." Said a voice. "Retrieve the Numen. Inform them their companion lives."

"She is not well. She will be disoriented when she wakes." Said another, more familiar voice. "I should stay with her."

"Your affection for this human is the cause of our misfortunes, Nessus." The first voice was harsh and biting. "You should not continue such an association."

The second speaker ignored the comment. "You retrieve the Numen. I will stay by her side."

With a hard clap of many footfalls, someone departed.

She slowly came to. Dani winced as she opened her eyes to the harsh light of day. White clouds dotted the sky beyond the spread of branches. She blinked. *Where the hell am I?*

A face moved into view; out of focus at first, but slowly sharpening into Nessus.

"Are you alright?" he asked.

"Where am I?" she groaned, her lungs painfully taking a breath. Her right arm ached. Her ankle felt worse.

"My home."

"Your home?"

She sat up, which was excruciating all on its own. She lay in the middle of what constituted the centaur's home. It was a tent or something to that effect; animal hides stitched together over wooden posts to form walls, with a flap for an entrance and a wide space the size of a tiny corral. Off to one side were folded sheets and cushions for sleeping and a table for eating, with a small garden full of vegetables and a fire for cooking. No chairs, obviously.

Vines grew from the amaranthine posts, holding plates and cookware like natural hangers. The tent had a flap pulled back at the top, allowing the warm glow of the sun to pour through.

The only clothing Dani wore was the blanket. She quickly yanked it up to cover herself.

"Breathe easy, Dani." Nessus cautioned. "You were attended to by the female healers of my village. Your honor is intact."

"Um, so no one saw my...you know...?"

"No." He extended her folded raiments to her, dried. "My kind believes in a code of honor. We would not disgrace you by laying you bare without consent."

"Does anyone consent to that in your village?" she managed the smallest of smiles.

The centaur turned his back and allowed Dani to redress. Her raiments smelt fresh and flowery. Did centaurs have laundry detergent? She doubted it, but hey, they forged chain-throwing arrows, so what could stop them from inventing modern conveniences?

"I'm done." She announced, once redressed. Nessus turned back. "How long was I out?"

"A day." He offered her a bowl of water. "Drink. You must be thirsty."

"No, thanks, I've had enough water."

He didn't smile at her joke. He was more serious; not that he was ever jovial, but he seemed tense. Scared.

"Nessus," she hesitated, "I heard you got in trouble because of me. I'm sorry."

He bristled. "You are not the reason."

"Yes I am. You saved me and they punished you. They told me they're sending you to Hell to fight. Is that true?"

He frowned, ignoring her question. "Please drink. The water is flavored with special berries from the Vale. It'll provide you some strength for your return journey."

"My return journey?"

The flap entrance pushed aside and the centaur Dani knew as Buer cantered through. Unlike Nessus, who wore a simple tunic top, Buer wore full armor and carried his sword. Nessus backed away from him.

"The Numen have arrived." Buer told them.

Dani perked up. "Numen?"

From behind him, Ethan and Kleos stepped through. Both were unarmed, but Buer gave them a wide berth.

Buer spoke to them in grunts of disgust, "As you can see, she is alive. Our fisherman pulled her from the river half dead. It would be of great kindness that you take her from our lands, ne're to return."

Dani didn't like his tone. "What's your problem?"

Buer regarded her coldly. "I take no issue with you."

"It sounds like you do."

"In truth? Aye. Due to you, the Council selected our village for deployment to the Fiery Underworld. Do you know what you have done, stupid girl?"

"Buer!" Nessus scolded, but one look from the armed centaur cowed his protest.

"You Numen dictate and you do as you please with no regard for any of us. Even ones as low as you in your society cause havoc wherever you go."

"Hey! I'm not the one sending you to Hell!"

"No, but your relationship with Nessus caused it to happen. There has always been a divide on this mountain; we do not enter your Citadel and unless for the Trials, you do not enter our Vale. Our societies stay separate, but you hold the power. Now our men must leave our mates behind. For Nessus," he shot her friend a cold look, "this is of little consequence. With no family and only that caladrius for comfort, he leaves little behind."

Nessus flinched with shame, not looking Buer in the eye.

"For those of us with family, they lose much. You take no blame Daniella of Empyrean? If you cannot see your fault," he leaned down, "then curses be upon you and your kind!"

She couldn't look him in the eye.

"Drink and be gone. We do not appreciate intruders."

She wanted to explain herself. She wanted Buer to know it wasn't her fault. But even as she formed her snide comeback, she realized it was pointless. Who was to blame? The Council? Sure, but what good would that do? Nessus? She wasn't throwing her friend under the bus.

Instead she drank her flavored water. It made her feel better. Dani handed the bowl back to Nessus. "I'm so sorry."

He only nodded, accepting it. Ashamed, she followed Ethan and Kleos out under the watchful gaze of Buer.

Nessus called out to her as she departed. "Dani?"

She paused at the entrance. "Yes?"

"Tell Caesar good-bye for me?"

Her heart ripped in two. "I will."

Buer saw them out. Outside, the open clearing next to the river dotted with similar hovels to Nessus's. Each one housed a centaur family; each decorated differently with diverse skins and ornaments. They all resembled large yurts with walls, some larger than others and covered with various helpful plants.

When they emerged, a small herd of children with upper bodies of pre-teens and lower bodies of Shetland ponies galloped by. It was startling. She'd only seen the warriors before. Women tended to fires, hung clothes on clothes lines, and galloped down to the river to bathe or catch fish. One centaur spoke to a wolfling-cynocephali, haggling over a trade. A group of hunters with bows and spears returned with a keresh carcass hanging on a spit between them.

More than one centaur shot her an ugly look as Ethan and Kleos led her away from Nessus's hovel. Centaur soldiers glared from under helms as they trotted by in formation, the cadence caller keeping time while also managing to grunt a nasty-sound in her direction.

"When are they leaving?" Dani asked Ethan.

"Soon."

"I thought they wouldn't leave until Spring."

"When Alecto departs, so will they." He told her. "Her interference with the attack on your home caused concern about her favoritism towards you. When she leaves, so do they."

"All because of me." She muttered miserably.

He tried to cheer her up. "Their families will remain safely here in Empyrean. We'll protect them. They have that."

"But with everyone they love being sent to literally the worst place in existence, I doubt that does much." She shook her head. "How did you find me?"

Ethan gritted his teeth. "I scouted the Vale for you. I needed help, so I called on Kleos. We were flying over when the centaurs hailed us."

"I didn't want you to look for me." She scowled.

"I had to."

"No, you didn't Ethan."

They headed downhill towards the river's edge. As they walked, it was his turn to scowl. He angrily stomped ahead.

"He was worried." Kleos confessed.

"Yeah, well, I didn't ask him to be."

"It is my experience that being worried about someone isn't usually by permission."

The centaur village and Nessus disappeared behind them. They were silent. Unfortunately for Dani, walking in silence gave her time to think and gave her time to feel more guilty. She hated overthinking things and this was why!

"He'll come around." Kleos tried to cheer her up.

"Yeah, well, I'm used to him pretending I don't exist."

Kleos shrugged. "At least you know it's pretend. That makes the cold shoulder easier."

"No, it doesn't."

"So, can I ask how you ended up the in the river?"

Ugh. Dani almost forgot about that. "I found a place to live and then got evicted."

"Evicted?"

"I found a cave up there." She pointed back upstream to the Dalles. "Someone was already using it."

"Someone? Dani, no one has ever been up there."

"Well, someone was; a Numen or gifted or someone. All I know is he really didn't want visitors."

"So you've seen the source of the river? What is it?"

She glanced sidelong at him. "It's kind of hard to explain. It comes out of the sky." She tried to put it into words. "It's like...it's like it just appears."

Kleos smiled. At least, she thought he was smiling. It was hard to tell.

"Why is that funny?"

"It's not." He told her. "It's nice. It's water from Heaven."

"What's so great about that?"

"Dani, our whole existence is because of a celestial war that split Heaven in half and an impossible mission to stop demons. It's nice to know something pure still exists; not ugly or disgusting or broken. It's nice to think that when they die," he looked up into the sky, "our loved ones aren't gone."

She doubted that, or at least doubted the source of the river meant anything like that. Heaven didn't seem real. How could something so pure exist with so much crap down here? It was an odd thought for someone like her.

Dani asked, "So what's the plan? Are you guys taking me back?"

"Ethan wants to drag you back to the Arn, since he figures you won't go quietly."

"He figures right. Why would I? For the second Trial?"

"The second Trial is over. After that stunt in front of the Council? Hopefully you didn't expect something else." Kleos rarely sounded snarky. This was one of those rare moments. "The Council declared you a failure in the second Trial, but I think that was more for show. You are the first person to refuse to participate. Hellfires! You're the first person to ever run away, as far as I know."

"So no one else is missing?"

"No. Why?"

Then who attacked me last night?

They reached the river. Ethan extended a bag to her. "Here."

Dani hesitated, accepting it. Inside was some cooked and dried meat, freshly picked vegetables and bottles of elixirs. "What's this?"

"I already figured out you weren't coming back."

He was definitely angry, but it was more than anger; worry, probably a little annoyance. She rarely *didn't* annoy someone.

"Are you?" he asked. "Are you going to stay out here?"

She nodded bitterly. "I can't go back."

"We can protect you."

"If you believe that, you haven't learned anything." She braided and tied back her hair like Roxelana showed her. "It's not safe for me there. Breaking into my home, setting me up to fail; it's only a matter of time before someone succeeds."

"Dani, you could have died out here."

"Would anyone care if I did?"

"I would!" He said it and blushed with embarrassment.

But she shook her head. "I can't go back."

"If you fail all three Trials, the Elders will come after you. Or, at least, they won't stop anyone who does."

"No one needs me around."

"I do."

Dani felt her heart summersault into her throat. "Ethan..."

"If it will get you to come back, I'll say anything. Dani, please, don't do this."

She shook her head again. "No."

"Then what are you going to do?"

"I'm going to stay here until I know what to do next."

"That's insane."

She folded her arms, all the warm and fuzzy gone. Ethan was a warrior, but he was stupid when it came to women. "I'm not going to change my mind."

"Why are you being so hard-headed?"

"Why are you being such a jerk?" she shot back.

Silence. Neither of them was backing down.

Dani was the one to walk away. "Both of you go." she said, taking her fresh clothes. "And don't come back! I mean it this time!"

"Don't do this Dani!" Ethan called after her.

She ignored him. It hurt her to do that.

She was sick of being weak. She was sick of being an outcast. But more than anything else, she hated living in the woods like animal. She was pissed. She wanted to take it out on someone and she had an idea who.

She climbed back up the mountain into the mist, scaled above the spray and walked to the mythical falls that Kleos believed were a sign from God, or Heaven, or whatever. The sun dipped behind the Dalles again. She scouted the cave for signs of life and the mysterious intruder. She had no weapon, but she wasn't leaving. Her things were inside. If she was going to last out here, she needed them.

Whoever he was, the mystery man either meant to kill or scare her off. Either way, he wasn't friendly. Dani waited for over an hour for him to appear. The sun set completely, but he didn't. Finally, unable to wait any longer, Dani climbed down. She couldn't wait forever.

She crept to the cave, careful to avoid slipping on the rocks. As she passed under the falls, the light sifted around in brilliant spectral colors. She could see inside as she came around the bend. Her clothes, her torch, all her belongings lay at the back.

And between her and them was the man.

He squatted inside, waiting. Their eyes met. When he stood, he looked maybe a little older than her; eighteen, maybe nineteen? And she wasn't sure if 'he' was the right word, anyway. His face was thin, but beautiful. There was a blush to his cheeks and softness to his eyes. The length to his eyelashes didn't strike her as manly. He had an ethereal beauty that made her think *girl*. His hair curled; black and highlighted with blondes and browns. And his eyes were the color of the sky; clear as summer morning.

He wore only trousers, leaving his wiry chest and large feet naked. He saw her, making no expression as he stepped into the open. His arms were incredibly long like a swimmer's. Toned. He was like a child in a man's body.

Dani held up her hands. "Whoa! Hey! Look, if this is your cave, you can have it. I don't want it. All I want is my stuff and I will go."

The boy, or man, or whatever, said nothing.

"Okay, Strong-and-Silent. Look-it, I know a Guardian you should meet. You two can have an epic staring contest, but in the meantime, all I want is my things."

Again, nothing. He made no move towards her but no move away, either.

She took a step in. "Look, just—." She stopped when he also took a step towards her. "Hey, all I want is what is mine! Back off!"

She took another step. He took another step.

"I don't want to fight."

One step for her. One step for him. He moved gracefully.

She took a step to the right and he mirrored her.

"Are you a Numen? Gifted? Did you leave the city, too?"

He didn't answer. There was something sad about his eyes. The way he looked at her wasn't predatory. But their previous encounter didn't make her feel any safer with him. He was Tarzan with the scrawniness of Jane.

"Just back off." She warned him. "I get my things and we both go on our merry way. How does that sound?"

She took one more step to the right and again, he moved right. Nope. There was not going to be any merriment.

After all she endured, after all the things she went through, after all the crap, she was tired. She spent months fighting for her life and reputation. She wasn't going to keep up with it. So when he stepped in front of her, now both of them only feet apart, she knew the expression on her face was one of pure irritation.

Forget this, she thought.

Then she ran at him.

Chapter Thirty-Two

He was strong and he was quick. So Dani had to use the one advantage she had left: surprise.

The strangely beautiful man came downhill at her. The moment before they collided, Dani stopped and planted her feet. When he attacked, she spun her hip into him; a body throw. Mastema taught it to her to use against people larger than her, which was almost everyone. The turn allowed her to wrap him with one arm and throw him around, tumbling him down toward the mouth of the cave. It worked, but he rolled quickly to his feet again.

Dani kicked. He blocked and struck to her mid-section. His hands were like bricks. He picked her up and hurled her backwards farther into the hollow. She landed hard, unable to roll and took the brunt across her shoulder.

She scrambled to her feet, now able to get to her clothes and equipment. Unfortunately, she still had him. The two paused, gauging one another. Neither would rush into this fight again.

She seized the long-stemmed torch. It wasn't lit, but she could still bash him with it. "Back off."

He didn't. His feet clattered almost soundlessly on the rocks as he charged uphill. It was like slow motion; legs pumping, arms swinging, face serenely calm. Dani arched back with the torch and swung. He rolled his shoulders under, each muscle snapping out of the way of the blow. He came up and struck to her face, forcing her to drop it.

He seized Dani around the back of the neck with both hands, pulling her down into a knee-strike. Dani brought her hands down, blocking the blow. She shoved into him, pushing him back and brought her heel up. She connected with his chest and knocked him backwards.

Running on exhaustion, she jumped and struck to the knee, trying to collapse it. Her attacker, however, was one step ahead and jumped back out of reach. He swiped with his forward hand, backing her away, keeping her at a distance. Dani kept her hands up, taking the blows across her protective forearms. Round and round they went.

Dani anticipated as much as she delivered. She fought smart. When he gave her an opening, she took it, but she didn't go overboard. The entire fight, his face remained calm; no anger. He fought as if he were watching himself, not actually participating.

He swung wide and she came to it, stepping into his strike and blocking hard with one arm, delivering a counter blow to the nose. When she hit him, his skin felt like smooth stone. It hurt to hit him. He pushed back, striking across her face and nearly knocking her down. But as much advantage as that gave him, he didn't seize the opportunity. He stepped back, waiting for her to come again.

It kept going. There were five of these little bouts. Each time they circled one another. Each time she struggled, fought, kicked and punched until she was forced away. She was beyond exhausted. When they parted, she caught her breath before going again.

Circling, Dani spotted a loose stone between them. She didn't look at it. You never looked where you attacked. It gave your opponent too much of an advantage. Instead, she shook herself loose, appearing to ready for another go.

Dani charged, but instead of going directly at him, she sidestepped. She hooked the stone with her foot and kicked, willing the Aer to shoot the stone at him. He dodged it. A second later she leapt up and struck him across the jaw in flying punch. It was a stupid, desperate move. She knew it was. She even suspected he knew. And he did what she wanted.

His hand, large enough to palm her entire face, wrapped around her neck and caught her. He spun her into a wall. She landed hard against the side of the cave. Her vision exploded with stars. But she had the presence of mind to seize his wrist and elbow, bending them in opposite directions and twisting his joints.

He grunted in pain. His grip loosed. Dani kicked to the inside of his leg and her throat was freed. She spun him down, bending his arm out straight and shoving into the joint to force him to his knees. He screamed. Then the arm flowed up until his wrist trapped behind him between his shoulder blades.

Dani's free arm flew around his neck, pinning them together painfully.

"Who are you?" she demanded. "Just who the hell are you?"

The moment her battle ended, fatigue set in. She sat, the man kneeling before her, still bound by her arm around his neck and wrist on his back. He continued to struggle, attempting to free himself from something she knew was nearly impossible. Their weight kept him against her. The longer it took, the more his joint locked up.

Minutes turned into hours. Hours turned into eternity. She demanded the same thing over and over:

"Who are you?"

"Who are you?"

"Who are you?"

He didn't answer. Strong-and-Silent wasn't speaking.

"Fight all you want," she said, "but you won't get out. What do you want from me? Did the Council send you?"

Through the cascades, the light of the water became brighter. Was it already morning? Light poured in through the opening, illuminating the cave. Had she spent all night fighting with this guy?

"I will ask you one more time." She warned. "Who are you?"

And then, just as she thought it would be another useless question, he spoke. He turned to look at her in the light of dawn.

"Why is it that you ask my name?" His voice was soft, almost child-like.

She blinked away sleep. "Wha...why did you attack me? Why did I have to wrestle you to the ground?"

His startling blue eyes were so unnaturally bright it was hard to look at them. It was like they reflected daylight. They were so calm, so peaceful, she could lose herself in them; not romantic, but dazzling.

"Who are you?" she asked again.

He reached up with his free hand. It wasn't threatening. He extended his fingers to the arm pinning his throat and touched it.

And then Dani screamed.

Her shoulder separated, pulling from its joint with a thick, painful wrench. She dropped his wrist and collapsed onto the ground, holding her shoulder. The pain was excruciating. She couldn't think. She wanted to vomit. Her right arm hung uselessly next to her.

Her attacker slowly rose to his feet. As he stood, the rising sun burst through the cascade of waves as it crested the mountains. It folded around him like a halo and the man transformed.

Sunlight hovered to his shoulders. As if molding from the dawn's rays, the light spread outwards until it formed into a pair of unimaginably bright wings. They stretched out, glimmers becoming crystalline feathers of sun, touching the sides of the cave. The brilliance made it difficult to see.

The pain rolled over her. She backed away as the winged man walked towards her.

―――――――――――――――――

Fire crackled. Whatever Dani expected to happen, didn't. Instead of killing her, the man with glowing wings made a fire and food. She sat up against a rock, the dull aching pain in her right shoulder mind-numbing. It was so bad she wished for the salty, disgusting elixir of panacea. Anything to take away the pain.

Her attacker was silent. He knelt on the opposite side of the fire, watching her with the same calm expression. But unlike before, he wasn't just a man. The sparkling, gossamer-like twin suns hung across his back, translucent as if made of glass. They glowed in the dark, radiating light and warmth. When he moved, they moved.

"Do not be afraid." It was the first words he spoke in some time.

She swallowed hard. "That'll be kind of difficult."

Again she couldn't get over his very un-masculine beauty. His size, his stature, his muscles all said male, but his face was something like a beautiful painting. It belonged in an art museum.

"I will not harm you." He told her. He extended bread to her, along with fried vegetables and a piece of meat. The smell was intoxicatingly wonderful. She was starving, but she didn't take it.

"It is not poisoned." He promised. "You need to eat. No one can struggle for a night and not be hungry."

He spoke like her; not the mixtures of old slang and unused expressions like the older Numen. He spoke like an everyday person, but the crystal wings told her he was anything but.

"You eat first." She said. "Prove it."

"I do not eat."

"Really? Why is that?"

"Angels do not eat."

Angel? "You can't be an angel. They're all dead or gone."

"I am neither, yet I am."

He kept the food out to her. After a minute, she took it. "You have wings."

They flared, a mixture of fiery daylight and crystal. They were beautiful, but terrifying. He pulled them around himself, illuminating him like a cloak of sunshine.

"Who are you?" she asked.

He looked away towards the dawn. "It is of no importance."

"Trust me when I say, it is to me."

He went silent a moment. Then, very softly, he breathed, "You may call me Gabriel."

She stared. She couldn't help it. The food was completely forgotten. "Gabriel? As in Gabriel the Archangel?"

"It is the title I once held." He acknowledged bitterly.

"You're the Archangel Gabriel?" She stood, painfully holding her shoulder. "The founder of Empyrean?"

"Yes."

"If you are who you say you are, then why are you here? No one has seen you in...well, forever. Why are you in a cave in the Dalles and not in Empyrean?"

"I cannot go there."

"Why not?"

"Because I cannot."

It was the strangest conversation; too unreal. He looked like any other person, minus the radiant wings. This was an angel? She expected something else; something more.

"Your shoulder must be reset." He told her. He extended his hand. "Please."

He touched her. It was just a brush of the fingers. She grunted in pain. Her shoulder shifted into place. She dropped to her knee, groaning.

"I am sorry." He apologized. "It was not my intention to hurt you further."

She glared up at him standing in front of her. "Then why the hell did you attack me in the first place?"

"All I encounter must be tested. That is law."

"Law? What law? What in God's name is going on?"

Gabriel stood up straighter. His wings flared, fanning outward. He levitated from his feet above the floor. His eyes swirled with the same daylight of his wings. Suddenly, the timid boy was now an angel; a true angel.

He spoke with a deep, serious authority. "If one be worthy, one must be tested. And you, Daniella, have passed the test. So to must you now begin your sacred journey."

"Sacred journey?"

"Will you, given the holiest of missions, accept and take this mission upon yourself? The Archangel Gabriel, messenger of The Most High, demands it. Will you accept?"

Dani's spine tingled. Her skin broke out into goosebumps. She slowly rose to her feet. The weight what he said, no matter if she could understand or not, sunk in. A holy mission. Gabriel's words made her stomach twist. An archangel just asked her a very important question.

And there was only one answer.

"Hell no. What do you think I am? Nuts?"

Chapter Thirty-Three

Gabriel's angelic glory faded. He dropped to his feet. His wings disappeared. "Pardon?"

"Are you insane?" she asked. "You pulled my arm out of its socket, you nearly drowned me in the river and you expect me to join some holy mission? No. Hell no. However you say 'hell no,' use that."

Gabriel stared at her, confused. It was an odd look for him. "You must not understand. I am—."

"The Archangel Gabriel. Yeah, we covered that."

"I am the Angel of Truth, Messenger of the Lord God. I am the founder of Empyrean."

"Uh-huh. We covered that, too." Apparently, angels weren't good with cynicism.

"But you passed the test!" His voice sounded like a toddler, not a messenger of God; and one who didn't get his way. "You stood your ground with me in combat."

"Which was so much fun." She said wryly.

"But you earned the right. The law is clear. You are the one I have waited for; the one whose sign I have sought to—."

"Sucks to be you."

Sucks to be you? Did she really just say that one of the most powerful things in existence?

"You do not understand."

"I do not need to." She imitated. "You attacked me. I don't care why." She grabbed her knapsack from the ground.

Gabriel, now less Archangel and more self-obsessed child, tried to stop her. He stepped in her way. "But—But you cannot do this!"

"Why's that?"

He didn't answer. Had no one told him no before? Probably not. He looked helpless. To Dani, that was the odd part. Weren't angels all-powerful? Greatest creations of God?

Dani flung her knapsack over her shoulder and stepped around him. She could barely believe she was doing it. Angels. The one thing she wanted to know the most about and she walked away from one.

Before she reached the mouth of the cave, he called out behind her. "Wait!"

She stopped. Something in his voice made her pause. Gabriel stood with his hand out, his face all grief and pain. If Dani didn't know any better, she would have thought he was on the verge of tears.

"Give me a reason." She told him.

And he did; the last thing she expected him to say, "Please."

Something like shining, liquid glass leaked from the edges of his eyes, glittering brilliantly in the darkness of the cave. Crystal-like tears streamed down his cheeks.

"Please." He begged. "I need your help."

"To do what?"

"To save my city. To save my brothers and sisters. To—To—," he sobbed, "To save the world from our mistake."

_____

She stayed. After Gabriel's begging, even the coldest, most savage person would have. But she wanted something first.

"I need to know why you attacked me." Dani insisted, sitting cross-legged in front of him. She wasn't above giving demands, even to an Archangel.

And Gabriel's proud demeanor, his fierceness; all of it was gone.

"Why?" she demanded again. "Why attack me?"

"To test you."

"Test me? What for? How am I supposed to save anything?"

"Only the strongest have ever had the will to survive. Only they can save others. Only you can do what must be done."

"I'm supposed to be some kind of savior?"

He nodded. "Even at their weakest, the strongest will rise. I had to see if you were as strong as I believed you to be."

"For Freaks' and Geeks' sake, what was the point of that?"

"Our existence," he explained, "from insects to humanity, is defined by suffering. Everything suffers. Not one creature from birth to death is ever truly handed anything."

"Tell that to politicians' and corporate CEOs' kids."

Gabriel's expression, if only for a moment, softened. "Suffering is universal. It speaks to the very heart of the human soul. When someone suffers, it reveals who they are."

"And what does that have to do with me?"

"There is that part of the human soul that some cannot tap into fully." He straightened a little, becoming more of the angel she met. "It resides in all humanity, but it is not something all humanity can use; an implacable power. The unconquerable spirit. Whoever was chosen would need it."

289

"You do not see it Daniella del Lucio," he continued, "but you have the unconquered spirit. Your spirit—your will to overcome—is strong. I saw it when we fought. You would not give in, no matter how many times we struggled. That makes you chosen."

"Chosen? Jeez, what is it with you people and destiny?" It was partly a joke, but partly not. "Why are you up here hiding in the Dalles? You're the Archangel of this city."

He bowed his head. "I am unfit to walk its streets. Just as with you, something drove me here: failure."

"Failure?"

"You have read it, have you not? The Song of Sacrifice? Our last lament to the world?"

She nodded. "It's the story of how you fell. Lucifer attacked and you fought him. You lost almost everyone."

He frowned. "You do not understand fully, then."

She was getting tired of the word games. "Then enlighten me."

"And how should I do that? How do I tell you about the loss of my entire species? How do I tell you what it means to watch your civilization perish by your own hand?" He took a calming breath. "I must show you."

"Show me?"

He held out his hands. "Let me show you what happened to my people; allow you to feel what true failure led to."

She hesitated. "What? Like we Vulcan mind-meld?"

Gabriel's expression was dark. "It is the only way."

She sighed. "Fine."

"I will warn you, the images will be overwhelming."

"Sure." She joked. "That's what all the boys say."

But the moment Dani took Gabriel's hands, the world took on a whole new meaning. Sarcasm turned to dust. Her body disappeared. Gabriel's life exploded through her eyes.

"We were once God's crowning glory." His voice was distant. The world around Dani melted away. Images of brilliance and light, and yet more chaotic and dark before light existed, formed in flashes of unimaginable intensity. "The universe was formless. What existed before my Father's arrival was nothing more than void and disorder. We called it the waters of creation. Chaos. Darkness."

"Then God spoke being into the world. We were created. The universe was made." Dani could see everything. Literally. Indescribably, she saw atoms form; not out of nothing, for it was already there, and yet it was not there. Subatomic particles and the beginnings of Creation exploded into existence. It was more than sight or understanding. It was everything. "We, His angels, took Creation and made it in His image."

Beings of pure sun rays moved through the universe; traversing from one side to the next in seconds. Their eyelashes were like fire and their voices were like thunder. She knew every one by name, because Gabriel knew them. She could not see God, but she knew He was there. It was a closeness she couldn't understand, but did at the same time.

"We were at peace. But as you know, one among us was not. He was Lucifer." A bright spot, brighter than all the others, bloomed before her eyes. "He was my eldest kin; my brother, our strongest in the face of the Darkness. None other shone as brilliant as he."

Dani snapped back into herself. She was crying. It was if he showed her the most beautiful thing in existence, and then forced her to live in a dark closet for the rest of her life.

Gabriel bowed his head. "I am sorry. It is difficult for someone to see and then return."

She wiped away tears, trying to get her breathing under control. "Why did you stop?"

"Because you do not wish to see what happens next. To show you what followed could destroy your will to live, as it did my kind. Lucifer rebelled. Heaven devolved into war."

"And?"

"War had never been. Our existence was a paradise. Music and soul were one and the same. Creation sang and with it, we added to the chorus."

Dani remembered in the Song of Sacrifice that angels sang everything into existence, down to pure emotions.

"But when the sound of war came, it ravaged us. Brother and sister slaughtered one another. Whole aspects of Creation were wiped from existence. Emotions never felt by humanity, sensations never experienced, parts of the cosmos untouched and beings never known; all of it was destroyed."

"Why?" Dani asked, blinking away tears.

"Humanity." Gabriel told her.

"Lucifer rebelled because of us?"

"God created you in His image to be His new crowning glory. Humanity had a piece of Him: a soul. You were not to be bowed to, as some believe, but an example to follow. This world, this Earth, was the very end of Creation." He shook his head. "Have you never wondered why this world is the only one of its kind? Why the rest of the many galaxies and planets are empty? We destroyed them. We emptied the universe of life. We created the seven celestial cities—these fortresses—to protect what God made and Lucifer wanted to destroy."

Dani shook her head. To think that all she saw was gone because of one angel?

"Lucifer was defeated and was cast into Hell, along with his creations: the demons." Gabriel told her. "The first demons, the first dark creatures born and bred for war, he made. We do not know how he made them, but they were cast down with him; bound to the place of torment by my brother Michael. They were never to be let loose again."

"I think the ones I've seen beg to differ."

"Their offspring thrive." Gabriel corrected. "All creation begets creation. From the sharing of electrons that form elements, to the continuation of the species; everything wants to carry on their existence. The original demons begot more demons. It is those you face today."

"And then you left." Dani reminded him. "You left us to fend for ourselves."

"We were failures." He said. "We decimated Creation. We did nothing but destroy like impudent toddlers."

"You make it sound like you were children."

"We were children." The statement took Dani by surprise. "We are not human. We were not born. We were created. We came into existence exactly as we remained; finished, never to grow older or wiser. Humans mature and learn. Angels do not."

"Wait, wait, wait, you're telling me you were just kids? That you broke the universe...by *accident*? You slaughtered each other."

"And we did not understand that slaughter." Gabriel told her. "We killed without remorse for we did not know remorse. We did not understand, the way a child cannot understand. My brothers and sisters perished and we cared not."

Dani imagined angels as fierce warriors; all-powerful and wise. But children? Angels were literally the children of God? The image of kids killing one another was so awful it made her sick.

"God saw us blindly laying waste and His anger was fierce. He devised the ultimate punishment." Gabriel's squeezed his eyes shut. "He made us understand."

"He made you understand?" She didn't get it.

"Every horrible thing—every depraved act of murder, every life taken—God opened our eyes to it and forced us to witness what we did."

Dani put together what he meant. "God made you grow up?"

"Can you imagine what it is like to take billions upon billions of lives and destroy everything and everyone you know, only to see every face and hear every scream for the first time—all at once? In one instant, He made us realize. Every weapon across Creation fell from our hands in horror."

Ethan's words that night at the Hypogeum came back. *We know that something happened to them; to the angels. I've heard some call it PTSD, or some kind of Heavenly shell shock...*

"So that's why you left?"

"We fled." Gabriel corrected. "We could not bear to look at this one world untouched by our War. So ashamed of what we lost, many of us fled; seeking out another form of existence. I know not where. Some of us stayed, forcing ourselves to watch what humanity would become and what we failed to be. Even flawed," a tear flowed from one eye, "you are more than we could ever be. I escaped here, to a fortress I built against the Devil; my own brother."

"Then you left the Song of Sacrifice," Dani finished, "as a memorial."

"And as a warning to not follow in our footsteps." He nodded. "Then the Numen appeared. They protected the gifted and other species left orphaned by our battle, but they took up our war and ignored our warning."

"Then angels didn't create the Numen?" She asked.

"No. We had no part in that."

Dani frowned. "Then why stay in Empyrean?"

"It is my home." The Archangel told her. "It is where my heart, my truth, still lies. Within its walls lies something special to me; a symbol of who I was." He shook his head. "And I stayed to watch you: humanity. Your capacity for love is more than your capacity for evil."

"Tell that to the hundreds of wars, rampant racism and greed during our entire existence as a species."

"But there are the millions upon millions of good works humanity has done during that same time." Gabriel said. "Those acts are countless. Selfless sacrifice. Kind words. Leaders who took people from slavery to freedom and those who took up the cause of love afterwards. Those give me hope."

He went quiet. Tears like sapphire flowed down his cheeks. He wiped them away.

"I think we're more failures." Dani admitted softly.

"I knew a human once; a failure. He sent his wife and children to face his punishment. And for that, I punished him. I hurt him as I hurt you. And then he understood what was meant of him. He changed. He became more."

293

"And I'm the same?"

"The greatest of humanity were not those who were born great, but became great. A lowly born can be more king than those who wear a crown."

She knew she had to ask now. "What do you want from me? What am I supposed to stop?"

He took her hands, but this time no images flashed through her mind. "You know things in the world are not safe, but it is more dangerous now than ever. You know of what I speak."

The Numen that died the night she came, Alecto's talk of the fires of Hell burning brighter; she knew, but shook her head. "It doesn't have anything to do with me."

"It does. Only you have a strength inside you different from the rest. You have within you the ability to stop this. You are not a failure, Daniella del Lucio. All your failure brought you here. You were chosen."

She pulled her hands back and stood. "I don't want to be chosen."

"We cannot escape our fate." The angel said from his seated position. "If God wills it, God wills it."

"Then God can shove it!" All her anger, all that drove her here, came out. Dani glared at the Archangel. "Where was God when my mom started drinking? When people tried to kill me? This is why no one likes God. He's a jerk, or He's a kid with a magnifying glass only playing God. And me? I'm just me."

"That is why only you can succeed." Gabriel seemed to expect her anger. For an angel, he wasn't trying to be impressive anymore. Then he did something she didn't expect. "Then I beg you." He rose to his knees in front of her. "If all others demand, I only ask: I need you. I speak of darkness in the world, but it is not just in this world. It is here. It is in this city."

"What are you talking about?"

"I am not omnipotent, but I feel that darkness has come to Empyrean. It threatens all life here. I cannot stop it, but I can help those who would. So I give you this warning: the enemy is in your midst. Those you care for are in danger. I have seen those I care for die in front of me. Do not allow it to happen to you."

Faces flashed through her mind: Nathaniel, Roxelana, Dink, Shea, Bouden, even Caesar. Mastema. Judah.

Ethan.

"Destiny is a path no one can force you down." Gabriel told her. "Like it or not, you must go under your own free will."

"If destiny is a path, it's a sucky one." She hesitated before asking, "What's my mission, then?"

"I do not know."

"Sounds like a crappy mission."

"I cannot explain what I do not know, but I feel the darkness coming. I know it is within the city. I cannot go there." His eyes drifted to her. "Only you have the strength to face what is to come. Return to the city. Be among the Numen. Trust that I know this much: when the final battle comes, you will decide the fate of everyone."

It wasn't a mission. It was barely a direction.

"When dawn comes, it will be the third day. You must make your decision by then. It will not be fair, but destiny is not a road. It is a choice of paths, Daniella." Gabriel bowed his head. "Which do you choose?"

As much as she hated it, the choice was pretty clear. She cursed under her breath.

Part III
Lightbringer

Chapter Thirty-Four

Dani set out the following morning as dawn came, hiking down from the cave. She departed with a good-bye to Gabriel, but even before she was gone, she felt him leave. He disappeared with nothing but a whisper of wind.

She hiked back down the Dalles into the forest, moving faster than when she came up here. She made her way through the forest, downriver and up the cliffs. A crowd gathered on the Hill's side of the Vale Bridge; waiting for word just like the first and second Trials. As she passed near the bridge, she spotted Roxelana, Shea and Airlea in the crowd. The shock on their faces was easy to recognize. Dani kept going.

Empyrean's Citadel was empty. The streets were vacant and eerily quiet.

Until…"*Dani?! Dani, is that you?*"

"Caesar?"

Her friend swooped from the sky, pin wheeling down in an excited rush. She banked hard, her head plume extended brightly in a crown of feathers as she landed on Dani's shoulder.

"*Oh thank God!*"

"Caesar!" she nuzzled the bird. "I missed you."

"*I missed you too! You don't call! You don't write! Where have you been?*"

"It's a long story." She said, stroking the bird's neck. "Where is everyone?"

"*They're in the Throne Room. The last Trial is about to be announced.*" But Caesar wasn't one to be distracted. "*Why didn't you tell me you were leaving? I was worried sick!*" The bird nipped her ear a little.

"Ow! What was that for?"

"*Not telling your best friend you were leaving!*"

"Okay, okay! Jeez! I'm sorry."

She huffed, flapping from her shoulder and sailing down to the ledge of a nearby well. She glared pointedly. "*Well next time tell me when you're about to sneak off. You gave me a heart attack! You nearly killed an endangered species!*"

Dani grinned stupidly. "I missed you Caesar."

"*I missed you too, jerk.*"

Together, the two of them made their way to the Keep. Caesar glided overhead, flapping from one roof to another.

"How much trouble am I in?" Dani asked.

"Your exit was somewhat nasty. The word 'traitor' was thrown around a lot."

Great. I can add that to list of ugly things people say about me. It was a long list.

They came to the steps of the Keep and Caesar returned to her shoulder. "So arriving late to this meeting is probably not going to go well, huh?"

"Understatement of the epoch, my friend."

She approached the closed, double-doors doors. Twin Gatekeepers moved to block her path.

"What are you doing here?" one asked.

Dani recognized the voice, but not the face. Where did she know that voice from?

"I'm here to see the Elders."

"The Elder Council called the assembly to order." The Gatekeeper said. "You may not disturb the proceedings."

"I'm not here to disturb, jack. I'm here because I'm supposed to be here."

"According to whom?"

"According to me." She put her hands on her hips. Caesar's feathers stood on end threateningly.

He balked at the sight of the bird. Then it hit Dani: the man standing in front of her was one of the men that attacked her. That's how she knew him and that's how he knew to fear Caesar. He was there.

"You're going to stop me?" she threatened. "How did that work out for you last time?" she stepped in, nearly nose to nose with him. "That's right. I know it was you. I know you're one of them. You're scared. You're scared because you know exactly what my bird can do."

Caesar nipped at him with her beak. He winced.

"So if you don't want a beating, I suggest you step aside." He looked genuinely scared; shaking under his armor. "Or I can tell the Elder Council."

"They would never believe you."

"How about my Guardian, Mastema, then?" His name struck a nerve. "How about I tell him? How about at night, when you lay down to sleep and dream little rapey dreams, he comes to visit you? What do you think? Will your death be quick or slow? I'm betting on slow."

The Gatekeeper took a step back. "Let her through." He told the other guard.

"The Council has already—."

"I said let her through!"

The other guard nodded. Dani stared the man down as she walked past him. As she did, she whispered, "I won't forget this. Don't think I'm done with you."

And she left him there.

Caesar adjusted on Dani's shoulder. "*Nice threat.*"

"It wasn't a threat." She steeled herself for what came next. "Now here's hoping I can sneak in without anyone noticing."

Both guards slammed their spear-butts down. The large double doors groaned with the sounds of locks and chains, slowly grinding open loud enough for all of creation to hear.

The Throne Room filled with light as it spilled through behind her. Hundreds of Numen turned. The Elder Council all stood, Dani framed by the morning light in front of them. To one side, every Novice and Guardian inhaled a collective gasp. She could even see Mastema, Ethan and Kleos among them. To the other side stood Lady Alecto who looked on, pleased to see Dani.

Caesar leaned down and whispered. "*I think they noticed you.*"

"How dare you show your face here?" Elder Heman was quick to speak first. "How dare you disrupt the sacred traditions of this city?"

The Throne Room emptied, save for the presence of her Guardian, Ethan and Nathaniel. Lady Alecto also elected to stay, but the powerful Fury made no effort to join the conversation.

Dani said nothing either.

"You make a mockery of all we are!" the Elder shouted. "You dare not face your second Trial and then you arrive as if that is somehow excused? Why do we not place her shackles now?"

"Because she has done nothing wrong." Elder Jeduthun said. "There is nothing in our laws demanding she participate in the Trials. It is simply unwise not to do so."

"Then she should not be allowed to participate in the third!"

"Why?" This came from Elder Azariah. "If she wishes to attempt the third Trial, she should be allowed."

"The gifted rely upon us for protection. She makes us look like fools before them!"

"Are you saying that one Novice can make us, the ruling body of this city, fools?" of course Elder Jeduthun came up with that quippy retort. "What strength does it show if we punish her, other than we are petty?"

Heman began to speak, but then immediately stopped. He had nothing and dropped back into his seat.

Dani smirked slightly. *That's right: sit down.*

Mastema stepped forward. "Elders, my charge may very well have made an unwise choice in her Trials, but it is neither punishable nor unreasonable. She perceived a threat. She avoided that threat. She has returned to attempt her remaining chance to join our ranks."

"And again I demand to know why she should be allowed?" Heman was not letting it go.

Castus cleared his throat. "It is my understanding that the law does not speak to avoiding a Trial, but it does speak to allowing a Novice to attempt all three. Elder Atid, you are our Chief Chronicler. Am I speaking within the law?"

Empyrean's head librarian nodded. "That is the law."

"Then is the matter settled?"

Clearly, it wasn't for Heman. Dani telepathically told him to eat vomit.

Castus faced Dani now. "You understand that by not appearing for your second Trial, you forfeit any chance at victory for it. You were declared a failure."

"I understand."

"And you understand that failure in this Trial will mean punishment under the law?"

"I do."

He nodded, satisfied. "Novice Daniella, this has been a trying time for you, but you will be held to the same standard as all Novices and all Numen. No privilege will be awarded."

"At this point I don't expect it." The biting comment made more than one Elder shift uncomfortably in their seats.

"May I ask where you were? All Empyrean was searched, as was the Vale."

"I went to the Dalles." She said.

"The Dalles? Traversing the source of the Crystalline River is nearly impossible." The Elder's eyes narrowed. "And what did you see?"

She saw the Archangel Gabriel. She saw her power frighten a being of Heaven. She was warned that something was coming and it involved her. She saw the founder of Empyrean look afraid as he spoke of the sins of the angels returning on their children. And whatever was about to happen, whatever they were about to face, was coming from within. *Evil is already in your midst.* Dani was the only one that knew.

And she was going to keep it that way.

"The Crystalline River falls from Heaven." She told them. "It was the most amazing thing I've ever seen." She tried to keep her voice as sincere as possible.

She glanced sideways as Mastema and Ethan. Both of them frowned. They could tell she was lying, but said nothing.

"Then you are to be left to your lessons." Castus declared. "We welcome you home."

"Thanks. It's good to be back in the good ol' C of E."

Castus frowned farther. The Council broke and left. She suspected many of them did not wish to be in the room with her.

Lady Alecto approached. "Daniella, it is good to see you once more. When they told me you fled, I believed the worst. You renew my faith."

"Thank you...m'lady? Madam? I'm sorry, how do I address you?"

"Anything is fine."

"Then thank you," she said, blushing, "for before...at my house. You saved me."

"You were worth saving. I hope you remember that for the times to come." Dani could hear a dark edge to her voice, but it quickly faded when the Fury smiled. "Your travels are such a whirlwind. You must tell me all about them."

"Sure." Dani joked. "We'll get coffee and talk all about it."

The Fury smiled politely at her joke. "Yes, well then, I must be off. There is a third Trial to oversee." Lady Alecto bowed and turned, wings sweeping behind her as she left.

That left her alone with the three people she upset the most. "So, I'm guessing you're pissed."

Mastema, Ethan and Nathaniel were equally stone-faced. She hated that. Why did guys do that?

"I'm sorry. You have to understand—."

"We do understand." Ethan interrupted. "Dani, of course we understand. We always have."

"It was you they worried for." Her Guardian said stiffly.

"Just them? Not you?"

He didn't give an inch. "My concerns are only for those who I feel are in need of my concern. You were not of my concern."

"That's a lot of 'concerns' Mastema. You weren't worried about little ol' me?"

"No."

Was that his way of saying he wasn't worried or didn't care? She didn't know. She never knew with him.

"So, are you angry with me?" She knew they had the right to be. Two of them she romantically turned down. The other she just yelled at. Worry or not, that was an awkward thing to come back to.

Nathaniel was the first to say, "I'm not."

"You're not?"

"No." The single word spoke volumes. The tone told her he wasn't exactly okay, but he wasn't angry. "It's good to see you again, Dani."

"Thanks. You too."

"Mind not running off again?"

"Deal." She looked at Ethan painfully. "And you?"

Ethan still hadn't said anything about what happened between them. It was there, like a gigantic neon elephant in the room, but he didn't acknowledge it. "I'm glad you're safe. That's all that matters."

It was the best she was going to get and she knew it. "Thanks. So where does that leave us?"

"Your third Trial." Mastema said. "We must prepare."

"And what is my third Trial?"

Her Guardian's expression darkened. "To do what every Numen is born to do: you must kill a demon."

Chapter Thirty-Five

"Kill a demon? I have to kill a *freaking demon?*"

Empyrean was different. After the announcement of the third Trial, lessons suspended. Three weeks and the Novices would leave Empyrean for Earth to hunt. Dani took a week to resettle. She had to get used the idea that she would fight for real. The first two Trials were training. The Third was the actual thing.

After the break-in at her house, she decided to meet in a better spot. So the following week, she, Mastema, Ethan and Nathaniel met at the West Gate. The battlements were a nice, quiet place. Plus, they overlooked Los Angeles.

Dani did the math. It was late November, maybe December now. Below, she could see Christmas lights all over the city when she looked through the clouds. Time passed normally below, but things remained the spring up here.

"You do realize," she said, "this Trial is bat-crap crazy."

"It is the final rite of passage." Mastema told her. "In order to truly understand what it means to be Numen, you must destroy the thing we are sworn to destroy: the demonic."

"It's not as daunting as it sounds." Ethan assured them.

"I remember the wraiths you killed in L.A." Dani told him. "Trust me, it's pretty damn daunting."

"I remember those things every time I shut my eyes." Nathaniel grumbled. "They're like demonic pitbulls."

Mastema chuckled. It was a strange, creepy sound. "There are such things, you know."

"*What?!*"

"Well, they are not pitbulls, to be precise. Hellhounds, actually. But they are—."

"Mastema, we're trying to inform them, not terrify them." Ethan scolded. "Ignore him. I haven't seen a demon outside a wraith in years. And despite what some describe," he glared sideways at the other Guardian, "it's not terrifying."

"You expect us to believe that?"

"What I mean is that you're not sent alone. Every Guardian helps their charge track and kill the demon. Also, the Powers go as well to ensure you're never outnumbered. And two Elders oversee each aerie."

"Oh goodie."

Mastema frowned at her sarcasm. "Every aerie works in concert to destroy specific nests of demons. The forces we bring are immense. There is little danger."

"Demons naturally gather together, wraiths especially. They will hold up in warehouses or abandoned buildings; any place that is empty. Since their primary hunting grounds are the streets and poor neighborhoods, that is where we will hunt, as well."

"Demons prey on the poor?"

"That surprises you?"

No, it didn't. She didn't imagine demons stalking people in upscale neighborhoods.

"Every so often, demons will kill an affluent individual," he said, "but more than most attack the homeless or the disadvantaged. Large cities, at least when it comes to the wraiths, are their preferred areas."

"Why?" Nathaniel asked. "What do demons want?"

"Wraiths are pack animals." The hatred was easy to hear in his voice. "They are the feral beasts of demonkind, but as with most demons, they prey on weakness and vice: lust, greed, anger, fear. They feed on it in the blood and flesh of their victims."

Ethan translated. "It's not about the kill. They feed on all the negative emotion in our blood. The homeless and the poor are usually the most prone to be the victims of them. They have no one to help them and because of that, they have problems with drug addiction, violence, theft; things people shouldn't have to endure. And that doesn't include what drove them into homelessness in the first place: alcoholism, abuse, mental illness. They're a psychological meal for demons. It's," he shook his head, "terrible. People shouldn't have to live like that."

Dani agreed. She met more than a few homeless in her lifetime. To think they were prey for demonic animals...

"So they eat them? And no one notices?"

"The deaths of those society cares nothing about generally go unnoticed or unreported." Mastema grunted in disgust.

Ethan added, "In America and other modern countries, dozens die per year. Demon killings don't always look like demon killings. The veil protects them. And they feed on Numen and gifted as well, so sometimes they don't need to snack on the disadvantaged." He was bitter as he said that. "In countries that are less technologically capable, there's really no telling how many are demon-killings. It could be more. Demons are born out of darkness, disease and depravity. It's getting worse year to year."

"So how does it work?" Nathaniel asked. "How do you hunt a demon?"

"Well, as I said, an aerie usually goes on a hunt with two Elders overseeing the Trial, but since Dani is in an aerie by herself," he glanced at her, "we don't know."

"Yes, we do." She said. "I had to face the first Trial on my own and I would have faced the second the same way. I doubt they'll change it for the third."

"But this is different." Ethan reminded her. "The others were safe in comparison. They won't send you to slaughter."

"Don't be so sure."

"The Council has decreed," Castus told them, "that as it is tradition for a single aerie go on a single hunt, that Novice Daniella must complete the task without the aid of other Novices."

Dani and Mastema stood before the assembled Council of Elders. Some looked displeased, such as Elder Jeduthun and Elder Azariah. Even Elder Aleister looked like he wanted to speak up. Others, like Elder Castus, seemed as if it were the only option. Elders like Heman, however, looked so pleased he was doing a happy dance under his robes.

Dani didn't argue. There was no point. She had a near-litany of things she could say, some of them so good she begged for a reason to use them, but she didn't. Partially, it was Mastema next to her. It was clear her Guardian was ready to crap a brick he was so furious. Yet, he held his tongue. She might as well do the same.

Look how much more mature I am, she thought cynically while trying not to imagine slapping the spit out of Heman.

Mastema bowed. "I am to assume that as her Guardian, only I will accompany her?"

"It is the law, yes."

"Then I pledge my life to see her succeed."

Dani felt something for her Guardian she never thought she could: appreciation. She knew what that statement meant. If she failed the Trial, he would be put to death. If things went badly during the hunt, it would amount to the same. He would give his life for her. She didn't doubt it.

Mastema was not cuddly in any sense of the word, but for the first time she knew that when it came down to it, he was committed to her.

A clearing of the throat brought everyone's attention to Alecto, who stepped forward. "It is my understanding that the Trials are not completely following the rules set forth by the first Numen." She flicked her eyes to Dani and flashed a small smile. "Elder Heman, you will oversee her Trial, correct? Only one Elder will oversee Aether in your place?"

Heman shifted uncomfortably. "That is correct. I volunteered."

Of course you did, pendejo.

"Then I would like to offer my services as a second judge."

Every Elder stared. None spoke up, except Jeduthun who—Dani suspected—wasn't happy with Heman's choice. "Very well."

Heman protested. "Lady Alecto, though an admirable judge of character, is not a Numen. She—!"

"Is a warrior of highest degree and will offer a fair assessment of the Novice." Castus finished for him. "Unless you wish to challenge her experience?" Heman didn't. He said nothing. Castus turned back to them. "Then, it is settled. Lady Alecto will serve as a second judge. Are there any questions you have for this Council, Guardian Mastema? Anything you wish to add?"

"Nothing this Council will wish to hear me say."

Dani barely avoided giving him a sideways glance. Was that a little sass he threw their way? *Damn, I'm gone three days and Mastema grows a pair.*

"Then we are adjourned. Novice Daniella's Trial will commence. Novice, take the next two weeks to prepare yourself."

She spoke up. "Where am I going for my Trial? Every aerie is sent somewhere different, right? Where am I?"

"You are to return to your place of origin: Los Angeles." Jeduthun told her. "You are going home."

With the Council dismissed, Jeduthun came down to the main floor to speak to them. Alecto departed with Dani thanking her silently.

"I'm afraid that my interventions amongst the Council have not been very effective." Jeduthun said. "A demon hunt is by itself dangerous. To be hampered in such a way, I fear for you both."

"Well, I'd like to say I'm surprised, but I'm not." Dani grumbled.

He pursed his lips, biting back his next statement—which she assumed was along the same lines—and instead agreed, "My dear, I wish I could tell you something different, but the mood of the Council is not easily swayed."

"Yeah," she smirked cynically, "there's more than a few of them I'd do more to than sway. Like sway them off a cliff."

Mastema nudged her.

Jeduthun was a member of that Elder Council, but he smiled. "A biting commentary, but a valid one. Very well. I assume you have heard the tradition of the third Trial?"

"I haven't."

Jeduthun smiled wider. "Excellent. I adore surprises."

"What surprise?"

The Elder glanced at her Guardian. Dani looked at him. Mastema's face was an impassive mask, but when she looked closely, she saw something tug at the corner of his mouth.

A smile. He was actually smiling. *Holy crap.*

"It is tradition," he said, "for the Novice before their third Trial to choose a weapon."

Now it was Dani's turn, but her smile was a big, foolish grin. "Is that right?"

Jeduthun led them down to the lowest level of the Keep to the Forge. Dani hadn't been here since the first day.

The massive, adamantine-braced doors opened and the heat of the fires boiled out in thick, acrid-metallic wafts. Hammer strikes sung through the air like music as Dani followed inside; each strike on steel a melody and each hiss of metal in water the chorus. Sylphs and salamander elementals watched as they passed. The deep orange glow of liquefied adamant flowed through the forges. Jeduthun led them down past the large mass of celestial iron in the middle to the other side.

The vault door Jeduthun and Mastema lead her to was the one she saw gifted take finished weapons through that first day. Sunlight poured through the open doors. The heat dissipated as they left the Forge and a short hallway led to a room full of pure daylight.

Jeduthun stopped at the threshold. "Welcome to the Armory."

It wasn't a room. At least, it wasn't a *just* a room. The chamber was circular, wide enough to fit three houses across, but once she looked up, she saw it wasn't a chamber at all.

It was the base of a massively tall tower that extended upwards at least a hundred feet. It took Dani a full minute to realize that she was standing inside the large tower that dominated the view over Empyrean and where messengers sent and received communications from other cities. The inside walls dotted with large, circular pedestals underneath octagonal windows. Like the Anthenaeum the platforms were gathering places, but instead of tomes or scrolls, each one was covered in arms and armor.

Swords. Spears. Shields. Helmets. Bows. Chainmail. Breastplates. Each platform was dedicated to a particular type of weaponry or armor. The nearest platforms on the ground level contained bracers and greaves. The next level up she could see a circular rack of different spears. Even the walls were covered.

Dani once visited the Washington Monument when she was little; a school field trip she begged her mom to go on. Her mother gave her hell for how much money it was, but eventually let her go. Seeing the Monument from the inside was breath-taking. The sheer size of it! She felt that way staring at the Armory. She could barely see the top.

"Empyrean's adamant mines are the largest in the world." Jeduthun said. "When warriors fall, their weapons are lost. We must replace them. Some of the other cities rely on us to rearm."

"Amazing."

"I couldn't agree more." Nathaniel and Ethan walked in behind her. Her friend stared, too. "I mean, I knew this place existed but...wow."

"As per tradition," Jeduthun said with mild sarcasm, "which the Council is so worried about lately, every Novice is given a chance to choose the weapon and armor they see fit. Each weapon is an extension of oneself. Choice is important."

"My own was chosen here." Mastema told her. "I knew it the moment it was within my hand. Ethan chose his centuries later. I was present when he picked up Stormthrower."

Dani raised an eyebrow at him. "Stormthrower? That name people keep calling you? It's because of your sword?"

Ethan grimaced. "I told you: sometimes we get names and sometimes it's from our weapons."

"You have to explain it to me."

"Some other time."

"Yes." Jeduthun said. "For now it is important you choose a weapon and armor. It should suit your needs. Who you are as a person and as a warrior are shown in your choice. Only you will know when you put your hand on one if it is right for you. So choose wisely."

The old Elder bowed, backing out of the room and leaving Dani and Nathaniel with their Guardians. It was a lot to take in. She didn't even know where to start.

She was still staring up when Ethan leaned over her shoulder and whispered into her ear. "Start on the first floor and work your way up."

She gave him a mean glare.

"Just a friendly suggestion." He grinned.

They started with spears that lined every inch of the wall on the ground floor. Dani was not a spear person.

"Adamantine spear point." Mastema told her, following her from weapon to weapon. "Tridents, diamonds, armor-piercing, halberdier. Most use fraxinus for the spearshaft."

"Use what?"

"Ash tree. The wood repulses the demons."

She lifted one off the rack. Spears were heavy. She knew that before, but she never appreciated it until she thought of carrying one into battle.

"Nope. And I'm pretty sure axes are out of the question, too."

"Swords then." Mastema said, holding out his arm. "They are several echelons above."

The pair ascended. As Dani soared past the first few levels, she could see dozens of tables with axes, spears, maces and morningstars; all manner of weaponry used to stab or bludgeon. Other Novices and Guardians scattered about the tower, working to find their own weapons.

Five floors up and the swords began. Mastema settled on an outcropping, which had a rounded rack of shorter blades.

He reached out and retrieved the nearest one. "You have shown remarkable adeptness with short swords as opposed to long swords, though I leave it to you, Novice. The question is: which type? We have the xiphos like this," he held out the double-edged straightsword to her grip first, "which is an excellent personal weapon of the Greeks."

She lifted the blade. It felt comfortable, but wasn't right. She handed the weapon back.

"Falcata or kopis." He handed both over. They were of similar design; slightly curved with a single edge, meant for slashing. Both were heavy. Too heavy. She handed them back. "Very well. There are others."

Mastema took her to dozens of platforms. There were some two-handed weapons she didn't mind, but swinging them felt awkward. She'd never been good with double-handed blades. She looked at the gladius and spathe, one-handed Roman swords which felt right but were meant for either thrusting or from striking from a horse. They didn't feel comfortable to her in a ground fight.

She favored the scimitars on the next pedestal; light, quick, and meant for someone of smaller build. She could move better with them. Still, she wasn't convinced any of them were her weapon.

There were more modern ones: cavalry sabers, intricate straightswords designed to be tactical, even a Chinese Jian meant for graceful strikes. None of them fit, either.

Mastema didn't disapprove of her pickiness. In fact, he looked like a proud parent helping her pick her first car. He explained each weapon's design and purpose. And the more she tried and the more she disliked, the happier he became. Who knew someone so demanding and picky would approve of her being picky as well.

Well, not picky, she told herself. *I'm selective. Selective sounds better.*

They were about halfway up, floating to a higher platform, when Dani spotted something off to the left.

"Wait!" she said. "There! What are those?"

Mastema paused in the air. The platform she pointed to was small, with swords facing tip-in into the middle of a circular table. Unlike the other platforms, this one didn't have dozens of blades; only a few.

Mastema floated near. "You do not want those blades."

"Why?"

They drifted down to their feet and Dani walked over. There were only about six or seven. The weapons were thinner and more elegant than the others. Most of the blades were single-edged, with flowing saber-like curves. They were meant to be single-handedly wielded, with small guards and hilts; used for slashing and hacking.

But most amazing about them: they glowed. Each blade had a luminescent quality to it. She touched the warm metal. The blades radiated their own light, mixing with the sun's. They were breathtakingly beautiful.

She withdrew a sword. The light faded once she picked it up.

"This doesn't look like adamantine steel." She said, looking down the spine of the blade. The metal was a lighter shade of silver.

"Empyreal steel." Mastema said, picking up another sword. "It is a pure form of adamantine called light-steel."

"Light-steel?"

"The blades glow." He told her, putting the sword down. "They radiate their own energy. Those who wield them are said to ignite them in divine fire, but I have never seen such a thing."

"Totally cool." She gushed.

He snorted. "The blades give away your position when they kindle, making them impractical. The metal is also soft. They are weak and flimsy."

"They do feel lighter." She raised the sword. It felt half the weight of a normal adamantine weapon. "So why make them?"

"Most often they are accidentally forged and the metalsmith does not wish to waste the steel, but empyreal steel is good for those Numen who can channel their power."

"Channel?"

"Just as a Numen can use the *arche*, they can channel their power into a blade. Adamantine is resistant to influence. It is why our armor and weaponry are made of it. Empyreal steel is the opposite. It absorbs it. It makes it stronger than a normal weapon with half the weight."

"Totally cool." She repeated, touching her finger to the tip.

"And useless if you cannot channel your power into them. Which I remind you, you have not mastered."

She glowered at him. "Way to rain on my parade."

"I only speaketh the truth."

"Speaketh to mine rear end." She liked the swords. She liked how light they felt in her hand. She tried out a few, going down the row until she came upon one in particular. The sword wasn't wide, no more than two-thirds her hand-width. The blade curved forward in a single, flowing arch. She picked it up, feeling it in her hand. She practiced, slicing back and forth. She could move with it. It felt better to her than any weapon she held today.

And the best part was it came with a small dagger of similar design. She picked it up, saying half-sarcastically giddy, "*Oooooo*, it comes with accessories!"

Okay, more than half-sarcastically, but was it girlie if she got excited about an instrument of death?

Mastema frowned. "Only fools fight with two weapons."

"Haven't you called me a fool multiple times?"

"You cannot be in earnest want of these blades."

"You mean am I serious? As serious as the Tigris with the case of the munchies. I want them."

"Very few wield empyreal steel. Many deride them as glow sticks."

"Well," she said playfully with a twirl of her new blades, "where do I sign up? Because I'm ready to party."

Chapter Thirty-Six

She chose a scabbard for the sword to go on her right side where her left hand could reach it; belted on with a single leather strap and buckle to move tightly with her. Mastema refused to get her a bandolier to carry it on her back. Some things, apparently, he wouldn't allow her to do because it would, as he said, make her look "brainless." In laymen's terms: stupid.

She got a sheath for the dagger to go at the small of her back within easy reach of her right hand.

"Do not think for one second you will use both at once." He told her. "I will not have my Novice acting as if she were in some fantasy pulp fiction comic."

"How do you know what a comic is?"

"Empyrean is above California. I have seen conventions in my travels."

Mastema at Comic-Con. She could picture it, odd as it was.

She chose armor, too. Since she was on her own for the foreseeable future, she couldn't be burdened by thick, heavy armor. Dani was too small for thick plate armor and it wouldn't allow her to move quickly or run if needed. She chose a pair of bracers and greaves similar to Mastema and Ethan; simple adamantine covers for her forearms and shins, with protrusions that went out over her elbows and knees for added protection. Gauntlets strapped across backs of her hands in order to further protect her, the straps sliding over her palms. And with a few Corinths to a gifted engraver, Dani made one last addition: twin symbols of Arn eagles etched into the metal.

Mastema approved.

They returned to training. Her Trial was days away. She would return to Los Angeles. She would hunt demons. She needed to know how to fight. And now that she wielded real swords, she realized just how little she knew.

"Again!"

Dani's hand flew to the grip of her weapon, the other to her scabbard, and drew her blade. In one sweep, the sword shot out and sliced upward.

"No! Again!" Mastema ordered. It was the umpteenth time in as many days. "You are too slow on the draw and you do not use both hands. Your sheath is weighted to support pulling forth your weapon into a strike without holding it. That is the function of a scabbard!"

"Quit yelling."

"I am not yelling!" he yelled.

She re-sheathed the sword. At least she could do that without looking. It'd taken about a hundred attempts and a cut hand, but it pleased her Guardian enough to tone it down a few decibels.

Still... "Again!"

She grabbed the scabbard and stopped, cussing.

"Wrong! Again!"

"Why the hell are we even doing this?" she asked. "I already know how to use a sword."

"No, you know how to duel with a sword, and poorly at that." He stalked over in front of her. "But when a demon attacks, you have seconds to defend yourself. No opportunity should be wasted. Your first strike should be from the draw. Surprise your enemy. Take the advantage!" he stepped in front of her. "Again!"

"You're standing in my way."

"I'm aware." He said. "Do not worry. You will not hit me. You are terrible in combat."

Dani bared her teeth and grabbed the grip to draw. Mastema's hand shot out, palming the pommel and shoving the blade back in. He stumbled Dani backwards and before she could react, struck her hard in the nose.

She saw stars and dropped to the floor.

"Ugh!" she grabbed her mouth and nose. She could taste blood. "You broke my nose!"

"Panacea will heal it." He said callously. "Again!"

She glared at him from the ground. "Screw off!"

"Insults later. Again!"

Dani shot to her feet, blood dripping down her chin. She was farther away now, so it wasn't as easy for him to get to her. She tensed. His hands remained at his sides.

She moved. The sword sung out of the scabbard. It whipped in an arc at his neck. She was going to take his head off.

Except she didn't. Mastema stepped in, blocking her wrist. His other fist came up and even with the close-quarters strike, he sent a shock of nausea through her gut and up into her chest with a hard blow. She doubled over, dropping her sword.

"Better. Again!"

"Get knotted!" she croaked from the fetal position on the floor.

"Again."

She heaved in anger, glowering at him. She wanted to kill him with a stare.

"I said again!"

"I don't care what you said!"

He kicked her hard in the shoulder, sending her sideways onto her back, then stepped away several paces. "The enemy is a demon. Pure evil. It is murderous in nature and will give no quarter, so do not quiver like a child. You are better than that. Rise and fight. Again!"

Her arm hurt. Her sword lay between them, hilt to her.

"Rise! Again!"

She grabbed the blade. Mastema moved towards her at the same time. In a split second she chose not to stand. Instead, she rolled. She rolled over her own weapon, using her motion as she came over her shoulder to bring the sword up. The momentum swung the blade right at his midsection. Mastema saw it and jumped over the strike. He sailed past her, rolled and came to his feet.

But by the time he was up, so was she. She charged.

Dani sliced. He ducked under. She came around, striking low. He spun to avoid it, nearly taking the edge of the blade across his back. He spun, striking out with his foot but Dani back-stepped, sword coming up and for the first time thrusting down with the point. Mastema leapt backwards deftly.

When Dani came up for the fourth strike, he was ready. He seized the back of her wrist, stopping the blade's path. He twisted, yanking her hand and sword up and around, bending her back. She lost her balance.

But her other hand held the dagger. She drew it from her back and brought it up to his neck. The point pushed against his jugular.

They froze.

Dani breathed hard, dripping blood. So did Mastema, at least as far as breathing. They stared at one another over Dani's weapons. His face was the usual detached, cold stare she came to expect, but this close—this time—something was different. It was in his eyes. She almost missed it.

Surprise. She surprised him!

"I should kill you for that." She snarled.

"Good. You are learning."

"Thanks."

"You are learning a little, at least."

His hand shot up, batting her dagger away. He in-stepped and knocked her footing out with his heel, releasing her wrist and dropping her to the floor.

"Very well done, Novice." He said, leaning down and tapping her forehead. "You utilized your resources without thinking. You acted. Your instincts are your true weapons. The sword is useless without them." He turned and walked off.

"You ass!" she cursed, but smiled with stained-red teeth.

"Wench." He gave away nothing, but she could tell he was being as playful as Mastema got.

"Culus!"

"Harlot."

"Asswipe!"

"How very modern of you." He retrieved his own sword, the khopesh, from where he laid it. "Now we must see if you can channel enough of that defiance to use your swords."

She got to her feet, returning the dagger to its sheath but keeping her blade handy. "What does that mean?"

"Your power comes from your aura," he said, holding his sword with both hands, "just as the power of Aer, Fyre, Erthe, Water and Aether do. An empyreal blade gives its wielder unparalleled strength in combat. I do not doubt it, but I doubt your ability to use it. In the heat of battle, we are not focused on ourselves. We are only focused on our enemy. That could mean your blades are useless."

"So how do I use them?"

"It is pure emotion. Have you ever done something you normally could not? As when a mother lifts a car off of her child, have you called on a power within yourself?"

She remembered her hands; burning hot, nearly blinding Michael. "Yes."

"How?"

"I was pissed off. Or scared."

He nodded. "Rage. Fear. They are forms of passion. In and of themselves they are useless and distracting, but channeled they are power." He raised his sword. "Are you ready?"

"To do what?"

"Defend yourself."

He swung. Dani raised her sword but the blow from Mastema was so powerful it tumbled from her hand.

"What are you doing?" she shrieked.

"Pick up your blade. Do not un-learn your lesson." He warned. "I will attack again."

"Aren't you going to teach me first?" she snatched up her sword, backing away.

"I am teaching you." He told her. "I will strike at your head. Are you prepared?"

"No."

He swung. Dani ducked and brought her sword up. The blades sung off one another.

"Stand your ground. Move with the battle. I will strike the other side of your chest. Are you prepared?" He didn't wait for an answer and swung.

Dani blocked again, barely. She nearly fell over from the sheer force of the strike.

"Overhead." He raised his sword high in both hands. "Move with it this time."

He came down. Dani blocked and swung his sword away to one side, then slashed with her own. Mastema dodged, batting her blade with the flat of his own. Then he sliced long ways. She dodged this time, striking at his legs. She forced him to back-step, parting them.

He paused. "Very good."

"Not bad, huh?"

"How did you feel?"

She shrugged. "Scared. Angry you're being a douche-nugget."

He made no show of emotion. "Use it. Channel that fear and anger and...douche-nuggetry...into your blades. Feel it within them. Make them a part of you. Focus. To your mid-section. Are you prepared?"

"Maybe."

He stabbed up with the point. Dani swept it away.

"Again."

He stabbed again. Again, she blocked. Nothing happened with her swords.

"I said focus."

"I am!"

He stabbed. She barely blocked it.

"I thought you were going to warn me!" That one got close.

He stabbed a fourth time. She felt the tip snag her tunic and she cut with her sword. "Cut that out you freak!"

He stabbed up and the edge of his blade ran along her outer bicep, slicing it open. White hot pain opened her arm. Blood spilled out. She howled, knowing from experience it was only going to hurt worse the more blood that flowed to the wound.

Mastema drew back. "Fight, damnation, fight!"

He swung, full-arc baseball swing, around to cut her in half. Dani didn't have time to think. Fear spiked up her spine. She angled her sword down and around, bringing their blades edge to edge and blocked.

Mastema yanked back, the hook of his khopesh yanking her sword to stumble her. He brought his high and down to cut her in half. Dani's sword came up. Her other hand drew the long dagger. Her feeble-thin blades met his in an X.

And they stopped his sword.

They drew down together, staring at one another over their weapons. She panted in anger and fear. He cut her arm open! He nearly killed her! But then she saw her swords. Both blades glowed. Light shimmered through the metal.

"Very well done, Daniella. Your mind is focused, your instincts sharp. The best honed weapon is here." He tapped her forehead. "Never forget that. Fight with your all."

She looked back at him speechless. It took her a second to realize that was first time he ever said her name.

He unhitched his sword from hers, stepping back. He cautiously paced, raising his weapon. There was a glint in his eye as he brought his blade into both hands.

"Are you prepared?"

She nodded.

Mastema attacked, hacking with his blade. She blocked, swept it aside and struck. He brought his weapon up and sparks flew as they collided. He parried, spun and swung, but she dodged back, cutting once with her sword and then leaping forward, attacking with the dagger. He barely avoided it.

They fought across the pavilion; blades colliding, parrying one blow and delivering another. She didn't think. She moved. She went with what felt natural. Everything she needed to do came to her. Muscle memory took over. Any anger fueled into her fire. Any fear she pushed down into her swords. She used it. She embraced it.

She battled with both blades, something he swore she could never do, but as fast as Mastema was, his weapon was slower.

He caught her sword with his, throwing it aside and flipping it into a strike to her neck. But even as his blade came to her throat, her knife came to his. They stopped, edges inches from taking each other's life.

And the fight was over.

He regarded her seriously; not his usual dismissive expression. He was not spiteful. If anything, he was proud. He withdrew his weapon.

"I thought you once a fool and a waste of time." He said. "I doubted you as others did. I took you to be weak. In my eyes, you were a failure. For that, I am sorry. I was the failure."

And then he did something she didn't expect. He touched his fingers to his forehead and bowed the Numen sign of respect.

"You fight in spite of your setbacks and what others believe of you. You succeed where others doubt. I have not seen that until now."

He placed his sword on the floor and stepped around it to her. Taking her wrists, he crossed her weapons over her in a formal pose, hands on her shoulders.

"To each Numen, these words are spoken. They are our creed and embody all we are. Hear them. Know they are earned:

Let no man, woman or creature take your life from you.
Let no other stay your blade but you.
Give no quarter unless earned.
Give no mercy unless needed.
Let your heart and your mind guide you and keep you.
Let the light shine upon you.
Live selflessly so others may live by your example.
Die so others might take up your cause.
Welcome death and in death, conquer it.
And should you die, and they find your body in the streets come morning, may the blood of your enemies be upon the palm of your hand,
And your last words be:
I am Numen.
I am Earthborn.
I am the light in the darkness.

He stepped away. Dani uncrossed.

"By taking up this creed you commit yourself to protecting this city, this world and this vow. And by doing so, you become a true Earthborn. Do you accept?"

"I do." She said without hesitation.

"Then I do swear, here and now, to stay by your side, protect you and guide you. And should it come, it will be my honor to die beside you."

He stepped back and again, bowed in respect. And for the first time, Dani returned it.

And she felt for once someone earned it.

Chapter Thirty-Seven

Dani slept easy the night before her Trial.

When she woke the following morning, she dressed in her Novice battle raiments; thick Arachne-weave, belted sword and dagger, and her greaves and gauntlets. She tightened her gauntlets and braided her hair back into the intricate, tight weave Roxelana showed her.

And, to her surprise, her friend waited for her outside.

"Hi." Dani couldn't believe it. "What are you doing here?"

"I'm here to apologize," Roxelana blushed, "for what happened before. Dani, I'm so sorry."

"You don't have to be."

"I am." She said. "Dani, I let Airlea get to me."

Dani smiled in thanks. "Honey, it's not your fault. If anything, you got in trouble because of me."

"You're leaving and," she paused, "and I don't know if you'll come back. The Trials weren't serious until now. I don't want to think of you leaving and I didn't apologize and—."

Dani hugged her. Screw the rules. "Roxelana, I'm not going to die."

"How do you know?"

"Because I'm too stubborn." She smiled at her friend. "I'll come back. I promise."

Roxelana smiled gratefully. "I'm not in the business of losing friends."

Friends. That made Dani's heart warm. "Good. Then I'm not alone. I'll be back. We'll celebrate."

She smiled tearfully. "Okay."

As Dani departed, she caught sight of her reflection in the pool. Judah said she looked different after her first Trial. The Dani looking back from the reflection in the water was that: different. Same face, but in her eyes she saw something new.

Caesar perched on the fountain. "*Good luck.*"

"Will you be nearby?"

"*I got your back, sister. Where you go, I go. You know that.*"

The caladrius took off. Roxelana departed. As Dani prepared to trek to the Citadel to meet Mastema, she paused. Caesar soared away into the distance. Free. Unencumbered. No fear. She wished she could do the same.

And then... "Screw it."

She marched, armor clinking, over to the pedestal in cliff's edge. When she got there, the sheer vertigo almost pitched her over the side. The drop off the cliff was a *looooong* way down. She almost couldn't look.

This is totally nuts.

But she was here. She made it this far. She wasn't about to turn away now. Swallowing hard, she prayed aloud, "If they find my dumb ass at the bottom of this cliff, please, please, please don't let them laugh too hard."

Dani looked one more time at the death-drop she was about to go over. She wanted to puke. Then she took another step and plummeted over.

She screamed. She screamed like a little girl. She pitched forward in a swan dive and dropped. Her stomach fell up into her throat. Her arms went out. She screamed some more, mostly swearing at herself for being so stupid. And down she went.

The ledge fell away. The ground shot up at her like a cannon. Dani tumbled into the valley with nothing holding her up.

As she fell, her screams kept coming. She picked up speed. Farther and farther. Faster and faster. The distant ground became less distant. She was stupid! She was a freaking moron! And she was about to die.

But when her fear kicked in, so did her brain. *I can do this*, she told herself, falling faster. She steeled herself and gripped down. She flung her arms to her side, her legs together, and she willed Aer to push her up. She demanded she fly. She focused, visualizing a tunnel of air around her; lifting her up. She pushed against the ground with it and refused to plummet to her death.

The air wavered, but the ground kept coming. She fell faster, nearing the tree line.

"No!" she cried.

The earth angled away. An invisible hand of Aer pressed on her chest and arched her up. Picking up speed, the treetops slanted to her chin, and then the ground paralleled with her body. The wind whipped nosily past her ears. She shot away from the cliff and hurtled outward into blue sky overhead as her insides flew back towards her ass.

Then she screamed in joy and shot up into the sky.

"WHOOOOOOOOOOOOO HOOOOOOOOOOOO!"

She climbed; higher and higher, the sun radiating around her. Dani lifted from the valley skyward. The ground dropped away. She looked back, her home already far below her. She spotted Roxelana watching from the ground. She could still see her smile.

The wind roared joyously in her ears. She turned her shoulders and willed herself sideways, arching up and around. Her teeth dried out as she smiled.

And she laughed. She laughed like she hadn't in years.

She was flying!

But ten she passed over the Crystalline River. She closed her eyes joyously to the sun's rays while the hand that kept her up drop out. She dropped too, screaming like an idiot. Numen couldn't fly over large bodies of water.

Dani dropped like a sack of rocks from a hundred feet in the air.

"Oh son of a—!"

She banked hard, flailing and angling herself away from the water's edge. Her power returned and she jumped forward, shooting towards the bridge. Steadying herself and feeling like a dolt, she shot down—controlled this time—over the gifted homes and towards the Citadel.

The faces and forms of the Numen below came into view. She recognized Kleos as she came down three body lengths over them.

"HEY!" she screamed.

Kleos ducked and looked up. Even through his beard, she saw him smile.

Ahead of her, walking together, were Nathaniel, Bouden and Dink. Armed, armored, Dink and Bouden carried their bows with modified raiments; leather protective gear and gloves. Nathaniel carried his boarding axe in his belt, and what looked like a buckler on the other.

Dani sped up a little, willing herself faster. "INCOMING!"

They jumped out of the way as she shot past, nearly clipping Nathaniel as she lowered her feet. Unfortunately, flying didn't have a learning curve. She brought her feet down, but came in a little too hot. The moment her heels touched, she stumbled and fell over. She rolled end over end and like an idiot, fell face first like breaking hard off a skateboard. She scorpioned over, feet practically kicking her in the back of her own head.

Some things just weren't glamorous.

She came to a stop and groaned in pain. Mastema's training hurt, but that felt like a cakewalk after that. She hurt. She hurt bad. And she burned in embarrassment.

The rush of footsteps and suddenly, her three friends pulled her up. And they were gushing in excitement.

"Did you see that!" Dink yelled. "Freaking awesome!"

Bouden raved. "Hell yeah! Totally epic!"

"Are you okay? Jesus Dani!" Nathaniel was the only one worried.

Through her friends, she spotted two familiar figures at the other end of the bridge. Ethan and Mastema both folded their arms and watched on. When the others saw, they instantly shut up. Dani blushed with embarrassment.

Ethan smirked a bit.

Her Guardian scowled. "I hate it when they learn to fly."

―――――――――――――――

Numen, gifted and even centaur gathered at the West Gate to see the Novices off. Mastema's armor shined. He was armed head to toe: khopesh, knife and a third blade protruding from his right boot.

All Novices departed, leaving Dani alone with one last well-wisher.

"Dani," Alecto bowed, "I am honored to oversee your Trial."

"Thank you. Any advice for a first time demon-slayer?"

She made only the smallest of smiles. "Do not miss."

"It sounds like good advice."

"I will meet you in the mortal realm." With that, Alecto departed.

Hermes, dressed with his winged hat, bowed in respect as they arrived. She returned the gesture. He stood next to his fiery chariot, the horses' hooves clapping the ground and sparking embers.

"My lady, it is once more a privilege to accompany you."

"Don't be snarky." She said playfully. "You don't talk like everybody else up here. It's just weird when you do it."

His elfin smile was mischievous. "Four months has changed you."

"How do I look?" she mockingly curtseyed.

"You look great. Have you gained a few pounds?"

"Hey!" She pointed good-naturedly. "I'll make you eat those wings."

"'Snails, how I missed your wit!"

Dani curtseyed cutely. "Thank you. Now let's go."

She climbed into the chariot and Mastema followed. They sat opposite one another as Hermes climbed aboard the front, turning the horses towards the gate.

"It has been some time since I went to Earth." Mastema mentioned, resting comfortably.

"Really? How long?"

"Decades."

"Oh. So have you ever ridden with Hermes?"

"No. Why?"

She braced herself. "You'll see."

322

The carriage took off. Her Guardian nearly tumbled into her lap. The fire horses accelerated, pulling them fiercely behind. Cinders and smoke bloomed around them as they lurched off the ground into the sky.

Dani cheered. "That's why!"

Their chariot steered through the open Gates of Pearl. The Gatekeepers saluted as they passed. Up ahead, Hermes cheered as well.

And then the chariot turned and plummeted down.

"Better than a roller coaster!" Dani laughed.

Mastema did not share in her enjoyment.

Empyrean fell away into the Heavens. Dani watched from the window as the team of horses picked up speed. Their hooves hit nothing but air, but sparks flew past. Then they hit clouds and everything disappeared.

She sat back, sighing. Mastema sat across from her, scowling. That had not been fun for him.

"What's it like to go back?" she asked.

"To Earth?"

"No. To Disneyland."

"I do not know of what you speak," he shifted uncomfortably, "but it is strange the first time you return."

"How?"

"Things have changed since you left."

"With L.A.?"

"With you."

A few seconds later the carriage rumbled. Both Dani and Mastema braced themselves as they descended from the clouds. Below, a sea of black filled with the artificial stars of the L.A. skyline. Dani leaned against the window. Even from up here she could smell the city; dirt, asphalt, car exhaust, and takeout food. She never noticed it before.

"You will notice a lot of new sensations." Mastema told her. "You have been in a place untouched by modern humanity. You will be more aware of many things."

It felt like a lifetime since she was here. The air was cooler, the Christmas lights and festive decorations were visible; staring at L.A., she felt like a stranger.

She thought of her mom. How was she? What was she doing? Did she miss her? Suddenly, her mom kicking her out of the house didn't matter. Dani missed her.

Hermes cut over the top of L.A. and angled toward the warehouse district. They descended onto an empty side street. The horses and carriage touched-down hard and came to a stop.

Hermes opened the door. As Dani stepped out onto the street, something was wrong with her eyes. She blinked. There wasn't much light but the world looked wrong. It was like everything was in High-Def. She blinked hard. Dani didn't just see the street; she saw <u>down</u> <u>the</u> <u>block</u>.

Mastema stepped down behind her. "You dwelt in Empyrean. Your eyes have adjusted to see much more than before."

All her senses kicked into overdrive. The smell of the city was much stronger now, too. She could smell hotdogs a few blocks away. She knew there was a street nearby; not just from the distant sound of cars, but the smell of exhaust and the distinct clap of feet on the sidewalk.

She inhaled deeper, enjoying it, but then she sensed something else. She felt something on her skin; something wrong. Her smile faded. She listened. Something tugged at the edges of her senses.

"Sulfur." She recognized the scent. "Brimstone."

Mastema nodded. "Demons are nearby."

"How close?"

"Close." Said a voice. From the shadows, Alecto and Heman appeared, backed by a small group of armed-and-armored Powers. Alecto looked like the warrior she was: a mix of black and silver armor—adamantine and another metal—with her sword and flail. Heman likewise dressed for battle. He wore his armor over his white raiments.

"Guardian Mastema. Novice." Heman curtly pointed down the street. "The demon nest is located within an abandoned warehouse. There are as many as five, but we do not know precise numbers."

"How do you not know?" Dani demanded. "Aren't you supposed to scout it first?"

Mastema nudged her to be quiet.

"There is a rooftop door we suggest you take." Alecto told her kindly. "Our Powers will keep a perimeter around the building to slay any that escape."

Dani wanted to say something but didn't. Mastema asked, "If we should need of your assistance?"

"The mighty Mastema in need of assistance?" It didn't sound like praise from Heman. It sounded condescending. "Should you be in of need, send a Fyre signal. We will come."

Five demons? Ethan took on five wraiths. Mastema was a good fighter; even better than Ethan. But he had the element of surprise and he didn't have to go with Dani into the thick of it.

"We shall report to you when it is done. Come." Mastema started walking. Dani followed.

324

The light was dim. Dani kept her hand on the grip of her sword, ready to draw. As they approached the warehouse, the stench of sulfur thickened. It was chokingly awful. She gagged.

"You get used to it." He told her.

They stopped one building over. The warehouse was small and squat with only two stories and loading docks facing the street. A faded sign for a laundry company took up one wall. The usual litter of the city twirled around in the soft wind. Dani spotted a ladder up the side. They could use that to access the roof.

Or...

Mastema launched from the ground, soaring up to the roof of the building behind them. Dani sighed, summoning the Aer and sprang herself up after him. She vaulted the edge of the building and landed beside him.

She smiled. Demon hunt or not, that would never get old.

"There are more than five." Mastema murmured softly, observing from the ledge.

"How do you know?"

He pointed. Down, opposite from them, was a homeless man sitting against the loading dock. Dani hadn't noticed him, something felt wrong. He wasn't right. And then she heard him snarl; like an animal. A wraith's growl.

"You learn to sense them." Mastema told her. "Smell, sound, even taste; there are at least three near those large doors into the building." He pointed again. "There is another on the roof."

Sure enough there was. "A look out?"

"I would normally say nay," he said, "but, aye. There is something strange in their behavior."

"How?"

"There are too many of them, for one. Wraiths like small packs to hunt better and share less food. There is more than one pack here."

"How many total?"

"I would guess more than fifteen."

"And that's unusual?"

"Wraiths are animals. They do not have 'lookouts' as you so eloquently put it."

"So they're organized."

"Two things that never bode well: demons that are prepared and numerous. I would normally suggest a contingent of Numen to take on such a group."

"And we're not getting one because...?"

325

"If we leave before you attempt to kill a demon," he told her, "then you fail your Trial."

"Mastema, this is not worth our lives."

"Yes, it is." He said fiercely. "This is what our lives are made for. Do not give into fear now. I know there is more courage in you than that."

If Dani hadn't been facing a baker's dozen of demonic wraiths, she would have been warmed by that statement. As it stood, however…?

"Okay." She nodded.

"You must slay one wraith." He told her. "That is all that is required. Heman and his Powers can be brought in to slay the rest. We will signal them once you kill the demon on the roof."

"I'll follow your lead, then."

But before either of them could do anything, someone screamed; not demonic, but human. A girl not much older than Dani ran into the street light. She wore jeans, a band T-shirt and long blonde hair. Two wraiths chased her. The ones on street level howled like laughter and leapt forward. The girl skidded to a stop. She flailed her arms and screamed louder, but the wraiths were on her. They seized her arms and legs, pulling her down.

Dani moved to jump down, but Mastema stopped her.

"What are you doing?" she demanded. "They'll kill her!"

"We are outnumbered."

"But they'll kill her!"

The girl's screams echoed in the night under the hungry howls. The demons dragged her towards the building.

"They will take their time. That gives us the advantage to finish your Trial and rescue her."

"You're worried about my Trial? Seriously?"

"The plan has not changed." When he noticed her look of disbelief, he sighed heavily. "As soon as you slay one demon, I will signal Heman. He will arrive with reinforcements. We cannot take them alone."

She bit back an angry insult. "Fine. Let's get this over with." They hadn't even started and already the plan went sideways.

He stepped back from the ledge and then launched across to the next roof. Dani was right behind him.

As they descended, the demon on the roof spotted them. He looked homeless. His skin was dark brown like hers, but the veil quickly pulled back, revealing the monster underneath. His face became sickly pale. His eyes turned puss-white. His teeth slid out daggers and he rose onto all fours, snarling.

They landed. Mastema raised his sword. Dani drew hers.

"Down foul beast." Mastema warned.

It snapped its jaws like a feral dog.

"Now Daniella."

Dani steeled herself and approached, lowering her blade to the side and back. She was calm. Controlled.

The wraith attacked.

On all fours, it lumbered towards her, howling. Its nails scrapped the rooftop, spraying gravel and stone. She lined up her strike.

The wraith lunged. She struck.

Unfortunately, she didn't judge right. As her sword came up, the demon jumped over her blade. Skin separated from her cheek as the demon clawed her under her eye.

She fell and rolled, turning towards it. The demon landed on a vent and vaulted backwards, legs and hands extended, long claws protruding from its fingers.

This time her sword found its mark.

The radiant sword went point first through its chest, doubling them both backward. The moment the empyreal sunk through its chest, the creature dissolved with a scream. Dani dropped hard, a cloud of foul chalk billowing around her.

Dani coughed, trying not to swallow. She shook herself off as she came to her feet. Resisting the urge to vomit demon-dust and her breakfast, she stood. She was bleeding, but alive.

She won.

Mastema approached. "You did well."

"Not well enough." She touched her cheek. "Was that it?"

"What did you expect?"

"A real fight." She grinned. She couldn't help it. "You were tougher."

In his own version of cynicism, he said, "Truth is spoken. Come, before the others hear us."

Dani and Mastema turned to leave, but before they could, nearly a dozen wraiths crawled over the ledges; same sickly pale faces, same teeth, same white eyes. The demons hissed as they clambered onto the rooftop. At the lead was a big, vicious looking monster with rotten-colored skin around his mouth. His lips pulled back into a razor-filled smile.

Dani and Mastema both drew their swords, standing back-to-back.

"Oh look," she murmured, swallowing her fear, "just what I wanted: a real fight."

Chapter Thirty-Eight

Nine wraiths made a ring around Dani and Mastema.

"We can fly." She whispered.

Mastema murmured back. "They will strike before we are able."

"Signal Heman?"

"I have no fire to send up a flare."

"You didn't bring a flare gun?"

"Why would I bring a flare gun?"

"You know, in case we get surrounded." Facing down demons, surrounded, and she decided on humor. She'd make the funniest corpse.

"We fight our way out together." Mastema told her softly. "Get to the verge of the roof and fly to the horizon, not up."

"Why?"

"Put distance between you and them."

Dani nodded. But then she remembered. "What about the girl?"

"Consarn it!"

The wraiths stalked closer, eager to start snacking. Their putrid, snapping jaws frothed. One, a female with greasy black hair, hissed teasingly. Her claws slid out like Edward Scissorhands hands, except less Tim Burton-y and more Nightmare on Elm Street. She clipped them together enticingly. Dani leveled her glowing blade at her.

And then she got an idea.

"You can use the veil, right? Go all Hollow Man?"

"I do not understand."

Irritated, she asked, "Can you become invisible?" she was getting this man a TV if they survived this.

Mastema turned his blade from one demon to another. "Yes."

"Good." Dani drew her knife. "Get ready."

"For what?"

"For an insane plan that might not work."

Fear. Dani had it in spades. But fear, as Mastema told her, was something to be channeled. She held out her empyreal-steel blades and channeled that fear into them. *Let's see how bright I can make these.*

Two mini suns flared to life. Even Dani looked away. The wraiths ducked from the sudden sunbursts. It was all the time Mastema needed.

He disappeared from Dani's back. A second later, he materialized in front of one and decapitated the creature. He spun and took down another.

Dani took the offensive, too. The glow from her weapons created a nimbus effect, and Dani swung. The dark-haired demon didn't have time to stop her. Both sword and knife dug in, dousing the glowing blades inside her. Light exploded out her throat, nose and eyes as she disintegrated. Dani pulled the blades apart, throwing demon dust in every direction.

The surprise worked. A third of the monsters were gone. Unfortunately, two thirds still remained.

A wraith attacked, hurtling through the air toward Dani. She summoned Aer and blasted it back. She turned, the next monster in front of her. She came to a knee and slashed out. It's leg disappeared below the knee. Dani shoved her sword into his belly.

Another landed on her back. Pain shot up her leg as the creature slashed its claws into her thigh. The Arachne-weave took most of the brunt, but she screamed and shoved her knife backward, dipping the molten-yellow blade into the top of its skull.

Mastema slashed through the wraiths. Mastema: destruction and anger. He was aptly named. He separated one's arm at the shoulder, then bisected the creature with a single blow. He stabbed one through the chest and pulled its heart free with the hook of his blade. Even as more climbed over the ledge, he held his ground.

"Go!" he screamed. "Save the girl!"

"No! Mastema—!"

"I said go!"

Dani was up. He lead the demons away and the roof access was in sight. She just had to be quick.

She dashed across the roof, sheathing her knife and throwing open the door. Stairs. She jumped down the first flight, the sounds of battle fading behind her. Only her sword lit the way.

The stairs led to a single doorway stripped off its hinges. Dani shot through onto a gangplank above the loading bay. Two or three trucks could fit inside, but it was empty. Instead, the demons nested here; something—or many somethings rather—created little sleeping areas out of disgusting refuge. And three waited inside.

They surrounded the blonde girl in the middle of the dock area. They saw and snarled at Dani like dogs with a fresh kill. In front of them sat a small table with lit candles. What the hell was that? Mood lighting for Sunday dinner?

"You want something to eat? Try something with teeth!" she raised her weapon.

One of them vaulted from the ground onto the railing next to her. Dani slashed with her sword, but it ducked back, flipping onto the gangplank. It sprang at her, claws extended. Dani, instead of standing her ground, rolled forward with sword raised. Her blade sliced along his body from sternum to belly as he descended. By the time she reached anything he might need in the future, he was ash.

She jumped the railing and levitated down to the floor. Her feet landed hard and she drew her knife, ready to take on the last two.

"Now, now, boys," her weapons flared a little brighter as she poured her anger and fear into them, "there's plenty to go around. Come and get it."

The beasts shambled at her, howling for blood. She couldn't fight them together, so she rolled between them. They slashed at her with their claws, but missed. She landed in front of the girl and the table with candles, coming up to put herself between the animals and their victim.

"Okay, maybe we try this again." Dani warned. "Leave now and you don't die. The girl means nothing to you. Leave and you live."

The creatures sauntered forward, keeping low on hands and feet, jaws snapping.

"What is with you guys? Is she worth dying for?"

"Yes." Hissed a voice behind her. "I am."

Something snapped around Dani's throat, yanking her head back. Her wide eyes came face to face with the girl she came to save. Unfortunately, she wasn't a girl.

Her hair was a sallow, pale yellow, but her face was the truly horrible thing. The skin was rotten. Open, oozing wounds bled all kinds of foul fluid as her cracked lips peeled back in a twisted smile. She stank of rotten eggs, tightening a cord around Dani's throat.

"Yes, Numen, I am that important. I am their messenger; their prophet. I come with glad tidings. And I bring blood."

Then she opened her mouth and bit down on Dani's neck. She screamed.

She kept screaming. The demon, whatever it was, chewed into the flesh near the base of her neck. Blood spurted out. She could hear deep gulps as it slurped up her fresh blood. Dani's whole right side went numb.

She was going to die.

And then, like a jolt, Dani snapped out of it. Everything Mastema taught her kicked in. The muscles in her shoulder tore on its teeth as she stabbed up and back, burying her knife into the creature's neck. It wasn't a killing blow, but the thing released her, lurching back and taking her dagger with it.

"Kill her!"

The wraiths surged forward. Dani staggered to her feet. She could barely move one arm, but she sure as hell was not going to die without a fight.

She sliced the air in front of the first wraith, missing it. She turned, moving foot to foot, striking as the two monsters danced around her. She couldn't land a blow. She was too slow. She lost too much blood.

One slashed open her left thigh again. Dani staggered. Another slice of claws and her beautiful glowing sword dropped from her hand.

Dani collapsed onto a disgusting trash heap. She was weaponless. The wraiths drooled hungrily as they closed in for the kill.

"Kill her!" the blonde demon repeated, yanking the blade from her throat. Murky blood oozed from the wound. "Kill the little Numen wench!"

As death closed in, Dani felt one last surge of power. She had no weapon. The fear of death rushed down her arms. As if guiding it, guiding her resolve to live, she willed it into her hands. They burned. And this time, Dani knew where to send it.

Her hands exploded in light; pure, white. It shot from the palms of her hand in two brilliant beams. The light struck the wraiths. Their eyes widened and mouths opened in a scream. But they couldn't. As the energy struck, their skin, flesh and bone crumbled and collapsed.

The two demons writhed in pain. Dani screamed for them. It hurt so badly, but she poured that energy into them. The light burst through the creatures' backs, burning a hole through them. As if burning them up from inside, the light reduced them to dust.

Staggering to her feet, she closed her hands and the light dissipated. What remained of the two wraiths was a little more than smoking ember piles.

She couldn't believe what she'd just done. And she wasn't the only one.

"How...?" the blonde demon stared at her, dropping the empyreal-steel dagger to the floor. "That—that's impossible!"

Dani's hands ached. Bleeding, fists clenched, she turned on the remaining demons as it backed away.

"No!" She raised her putrid hands. "You—You—Don't! Please!"

Dani raised her hand. Whatever she did, she didn't know if she could do it again. But the warmth returned. She bared her teeth.

"Please!"

Light erupted from Dani's hand, lifting the thing off her feet and flailing into the opposite wall, where she exploded into ash and dust.

The only remnant of the demon was a scorch mark on the wall.

331

Chapter Thirty-Nine

She hurt. Badly. Dani didn't know what she did, but she retrieved her swords and unsteadily stumble-climbed the stairs. Her head spun. She felt sick. Was it blood loss? Was it whatever she did to the demons? She wasn't sure. But Mastema was on the roof. She wouldn't leave him to die.

When she pushed through the door, he was on his back on the ground. She could smell the blood on him. His sword clattered away and a demon reared up over him.

Dani threw out her hands and blasted the thing with light. She didn't care what this was. Fueled by rage, she shattered the demon apart. The attack was so sudden that the other four leapt back in alarm.

Dani cast out blasts of light like a goddamn superhero.

Again and again, light after light tore through them. One tumbled over the side as her arm reduced to ash. Another lost his head. The remaining two tried to flee. Dani burnt them to ash as they fell over the edge of the building.

She felt something at her back; a sixth wraith. Its jaws opened to strike. But before he could, something white whipped by and snatched it off his feet. Caesar shrieked, lifting the demon into the sky, turning and throwing it hard over the side into the darkness. Dani heard it wetly land on the pavement below.

Caesar whipped around and soared back down, fluttering to a perch on the nearest power line. "*I got ya back, honey!*"

Dani staggered, smiling. "Thanks Caesar."

"*Is your Guardian okay?*"

"Mastema!" Dani slid down next to him. Bloody gashes crisscrossed his face, neck and arms. The wounds were deep. "Mastema!"

She touched him and he groaned in pain. He was alive.

"It's okay!" Relief washed through her. "I'm here!"

"Demons..." he moaned.

"They're dead."

"Need...panacea..."

"I'll get it." She stood, but her vision swam. She lurched to one side. "*Dani?*"

"Caesar...go get...help..." she held up her hands. The skin was raw and blackened, peeling away bloody in places. She nearly vomited. "Get...Alecto..."

Then darkness rolled over her.

The first thing she heard was Heman's voice and the tone wasn't kind. "It is impossible that the two of you alone destroyed a nest of this size."

Mastema's voice was equally unkind. "And if you were not here, then who aided us?"

"I will not believe that a single Novice and her Guardian completed such a task."

"You call me dishonest, Elder?"

"I call the situation impossible. Two Numen could not accomplish such a feat."

Another voice: Alecto's. "We found them nearly dead."

Silence. Dani's eyes drifted open, staring into the starless night sky. Standing over her, Mastema, Alecto and Heman argued with one another.

"Yes," Heman said, gripping his sheathed sword, "but with so many demons—"

"Demons of which you failed to inform us." Mastema interrupted harshly. She was surprised to hear him raising his voice. "We walked into an army and barely survived. I will not stand by while the one responsible questions our account of the events."

"How dare you!"

"The truth is," Alecto stepped in, "that there are many questions we cannot answer. The Trial cannot be declared a success," Heman tensed and she consoled, "or a failure without the facts."

"What facts?" Dani murmured.

Both Mastema and Alecto dropped to their knees and helped her sit up. He held a vial to her mouth and poured it in. Dani choked on the panacea. "Ugh!"

"Drink." He ordered.

She did, finishing the vial. Warmth rushed through her body as the elixir did its work. It still tasted like the underside of someone's shoe, though. "You really need to flavor that stuff."

"You are lucky to be alive." Alecto said. "You fell unconscious."

"And I really wish this was the first time." She grumbled. It happened a lot recently.

A bandage covered the side of her neck where the demon bit her and two more covered her thigh and arm. But her hands were the worst. Bound in gauze-like bandages, she could feel the painful burns with each movement.

"We must know how the two of you killed so many." Heman told her. "Even a well-armed contingent of Powers would be hard-tasked to destroy this number."

Dani tried to think of a way to explain. She could shoot laser beams out of her hands. How do you even start that conversation?

A hawk screech brought everyone's attention skyward. Caesar swooped down to rest beside Dani. The bird nuzzled her.

"*Hey girl.*" She said. "*Sorry it took so long to get them here. I didn't want to leave you.*"

Alecto nodded to the bird. "The caladrius came to me. It saved your life."

"It's a she." Dani told him. "And her name is Caesar."

"You know this bird?"

"Novice Daniella can speak the avian tongue." Mastema told her. He eyed Heman. "Do you still believe she is *just* a Novice?"

Heman didn't look impressed. "It still does not explain your success."

"We fought." Dani was annoyed with him. "I almost died. Are you seriously suggesting we cheated? Because if there is a way to cheat in demon-slaying, I'd love to know it."

The Elder frowned. Mastema spoke up in her defense. "She makes a valid argument, as I have repeatedly tried: unless you suggest collusion with demons, it was Novice Daniella and I who decimated this nest."

Heman tried to refute the argument, but he had nothing.

"Then you will declare this Trial a success?"

He didn't like it, but he nodded. "I have never seen a Novice perform such in battle, Novice Daniella. You have...skill." The last word sounded like it hurt to say.

"Or something like it."

"I must see to our perimeter in case of another attack, but we cannot depart until we attend to other matters. We will see to them when I return." He bowed and left.

Alecto rose. "I too must do my part. Very well done, Novice Daniella."

"It's just Dani to my friends."

Alecto smiled warmly. "Very well done, Dani." She departed.

Mastema helped her up to her feet. His tunic was torn and he had bandages across his chest and arms. "You fought bravely."

"Yeah, well, not as well as you. You took on, like, six by yourself."

"I have more experience."

"That wasn't it." She said seriously. "Mastema, you almost died for me."

He adjusted the bandage on her arm. "It is my duty."

"Mastema." She stopped his hand. "Thank you."

Her Guardian was many things; stern, uncompromising; at best a cold fish. But he avoided her gaze now. "It is my duty."

She hugged him. She didn't care if it wasn't what Novices were supposed to do. She hugged him.

It took a minute for him to peel her off and recompose himself as the manly, unemotional warrior he paraded around. "I lost consciousness during the battle. How were you able to come to my aid?"

She shrugged. "Adrenaline, I guess."

"You guess?" he didn't believe her.

"I mean, Caesar helped. It's all kind of foggy."

"The fog of battle? I would think of a better story."

"What is that supposed to mean?"

Her Guardian wasn't an idiot. Vague answers didn't satisfy him. But before either of them could say anything else, Heman and Alecto returned.

"My scouts report no new sightings. For the time being we are secure, but I do not wish to test our fortune." His eyes shifted to Dani. "Mastema tells me the wraiths were organized. Being so numerous, it raises questions."

"Such as?"

"Such as what we found on the main floor."

A dozen purple-clothed Powers waited on the warehouse floor, examining something amongst the trash. She ignored the two scorched piles of ash and black-mark where she burnt the demons to cinders. Instead the focus of fascination was the table the female demon knocked over; something the Powers handed to Heman.

It was a statue, one unlike anything Dani had ever seen: the head of a monstrous creature, carved completely out of stone with a wide mouth and horns protruding from the forehead. Inside the mouth, several writhing humanoid figurines made the teeth. Formed from the rock behind them, the unmistakable depictions of fire poured from the "throat" to torture the humans in frozen agony.

Mastema stiffened at her side.

"What is it?" she reached to take it, but he stopped her hand. "What?"

"It is a graven image."

"A what?"

335

"Demon idol." Alecto explained.

"A demon idol? As in, to worship? I didn't think demons were particularly religious."

"They are not. At least, not wraiths. Wraiths are animals. We have never found idols amongst their kind."

Mastema continued her line of thought. "And with the other strange activity amongst these demons, something is amiss." He looked to Dani. "Was there anything strange about the demons? Where is the girl?"

"The girl? You mean the blonde? She was a demon, but...I don't know."

"You do not know what?"

"She didn't look like a wraith." Dani told them. "She could talk; like some kind of rotting person. It was a trap to lure us in. Do you think they knew we were watching?"

Her question went unanswered. All three stared at her in disbelief.

"What?"

"Dani," Alecto said, "what you are describing is not a wraith. It is an imp."

"Imp?" she knew the name. But from where? She tried to think and all she could come up with was Ethan. *Why?* Then another memory came to the front of her mind: studying in the library with Dink, Bouden, and Nathaniel. They were researching demons when Ethan came to talk to her about the Trials. *Simple to remember*, he said. *Demonic imp. They're similar to wraiths; low on the totem pole. Rotten skin. Decaying flesh. Take off the head or destroy the heart to kill them.*

"Imps are similar to wraiths, right?"

"Similar, but one would never associate itself with wraiths."

Heman added. "I have never seen this idol before. What were they worshiping here?"

"Something powerful." Dani said.

"Why do you say that?"

"Different types of demons in large numbers, worshipping an object? I'm not an expert on demons but if it's that unusual, there's something special about that statue. Do we take it with us?"

Mastema snarled in disgust. "No."

Heman dropped it to the floor and her Guardian drew his khopesh, bringing it down on the idol. The statue exploded into rock dust.

"Such hellish things do not belong in Empyrean."

He and Dani left the warehouse without another word. Mastema was eager to be far away from the broken remains.

"What's wrong?" she asked. She and Mastema walked back to Hermes alone. Her Guardian was more silent than usual, if that were possible. "Is it the demon stuff back there?"

"No. It is you."

Seriously? "Me? What did I do?"

"I am not angry, Daniella." He assured her. "What I meant was I have trained many Novices. It took me centuries to master the ability to fight so many at once. Years have passed since I have seen anyone with skill to match my own." He met her eyes. "Tonight you slew multiple demons unaided. How?"

Dani wanted to tell him. She owed him that. But she couldn't. She didn't know why. Maybe it was Gabriel's warning, but she couldn't bring herself to tell him. Her mysterious ability was just that: a mystery. She didn't understand it and felt like she should keep it to herself until she did.

So instead of answering, she lied. "You trained me well. And I had Caesar."

Overhead, her friend cawed happily.

"Daniella, I know when you avoid the truth."

"I'm not lying."

"I am not saying you are. I am saying there is half-truth in your words." Her Guardian wasn't stupid. "You are different since you returned from the Dalles. Something happened there, but you will not speak of it."

"Shouldn't that tell you something?"

"Why will you tell no one?"

"Because no one needs to know. At least, not yet. And why are you suddenly so concerned for me?"

"I have always been concerned for you." He said. "From the moment you became my charge, I was concerned."

"You told me you weren't."

"Then you are not the only liar."

She shook her head. "Is it because of your oath as a Guardian? I know all of you have to give your lives for us. I know that's why you took on all those monsters back there. But you don't have to worry about me."

"Yes, I do, but that is not why."

"Then what?"

"Because I see something purely good in you. That is why I, for once in over a century, feel a sense of joy." Dani expected him to feel a lot of things. Joy wasn't one of them. "It is why I am thankful I chose you."

"Chose me? You were assigned to me."

"I volunteered."

The out-of-character softness in his voice startled her. His usual blank expression etched faintly with something else; something she never saw before.

"You...you chose to be my Guardian? Why?"

"There are always Guardians who do not have charges; not many, but a few. They serve other duties for the Council. When they informed us of you, a female Novice, many wished not to take you. They saw you as a potential failure."

"You thought I wouldn't fail?"

"No, I believed you would." He said. "I knew the Council would seek to destroy you. Any Guardian would likewise be deemed a failure. Should you fail, the harshest punishment awaited them. So I took you on."

"Because you thought I would fail? Why?" Then it dawned on her. The sound of his voice wasn't sorrow. It was pain. The callousness, the emotional distancing, wasn't an act. She heard people who were suicidal distanced themselves from others before killing themselves. "You hoped I'd fail and then the Council would execute you."

"I could never take my own life. I am not brave enough." Mastema shook his head. "I wanted to prepare you; give you the best chance. But I also knew it wouldn't be enough for the schemes of your enemies in Empyrean. I would die. I know what others think of me. I am not deaf to their chides. They believe me a failure. They believe I do not care. But I do. I care for one individual: you." His gaze was like that of a proud parent. "I saw in you something I have not seen, even in myself. Strength. My intent to die led me to you and to realize there is more I can still live for. You wish not to tell me of your time in the Dalles? I accept that. You saved my life more than on that rooftop tonight. I died the day I lost my charge. I gained it back the moment I stepped into battle with you."

Dani never met her father. She never knew what it was like to have a proud parent. Her mom tried, but failed. Mastema didn't.

"You never talk about the demon that killed your charge." She remarked. "Why? What was it?"

"I do not know. I never encountered such a demon before and have not since."

"Then I'll make you this promise: if you help me, then we will find that thing and kill it. Together. Deal?"

"Why would you help me?"

"Because it turns out I'd be dead if it weren't for you; same way you'd be dead if it weren't for me. I think it's pretty fitting, don't you?"

She only saw it once before. It was rare. But she saw him do something rumors said never happened.

She saw him smile.

Chapter Forty

Trumpets blared as the one hundred and forty-four Novices marched into the Throne Room triumphant. The Numen, gifted and other creatures of Empyrean cheered them on like Olympic champions before they assembled around the glass pool. The Elders stood before their thrones. Every demon nest was destroyed; every demon either dead or on the run. And everyone thankfully alive. Lady Alecto stood on the floor, praising them as they passed. She caught Dani's eye and gave a slight nod of approval. Dani never felt so exhilarated. Even amongst people who despised her, she felt the warmth of pride burn on her cheeks.

The applause died. Some gifted gathered at the entrance. Dani spotted Roxelana, who beamed with pride. The Elders returned to their seats, save for Castus who spoke over them all.

"Novices! Elders! Earthborn all!" he declared. "Today we stand triumphant! Today, demonkind was driven from their dark dwellings. The darkness sought to prevail and prevail it did not! And all because our newest warriors had the courage and the strength to take up arms against it!"

More applause. Alecto beamed in admiration.

"From the demons of Spanish Harlem who sought to kill the innocent, there was the aerie Gylph!" Cheers went up. "From those in El Salvador and Brazil, to Ontario, monsters sought blood, but Corona, Meridian and Pinnacle stood tall!" Cheers again. "And in Virginia, in the city of Richmond, they feared the aerie Ethereal!" Banging of hands and feet accompanied a new round of ovation. "But demonkind could not run far, for Crux and Jubilee were there to cleanse the midlands of America. And Halycon stood against the fires of hell in Minnesota!"

Even Dani's heart beat faster under the roars.

"The demons sought shelter in the skies above Chicago, but Aerial was there to meet them! And when they dug deep into the depths of New Orleans, Nexus rooted them out!"

Dani clapped with the others.

"And Coronach spoke for the dead in Peru. They brought justice to a town beset by the beings of Hell! And Hell fled!"

An eruption of cries surrounded them.

"And finally, when demonkind wished to enter the city of angels— when they came to our very borders, Aether was here to greet them with sword, and spear, and bow!"

More cheers. Nathaniel blushed. He threw his buckler up, which expanded outward mechanically, bringing a new round of cheers with its black-stained surface.

Castus and the others went silent. Only one aerie wasn't spoken for yet. More than a few looked to Dani; Alecto among them. The expressions were the same. She and Castus locked eyes. His winter blue irises shone and for a moment, she believed she would go unnoticed.

But then, "And when demons gathered to worship a graven image, to put to slaughter sacrifices to their dark gods, a single Novice stood against them: Arn, the eagle, the army of one! She was there!" Applause built. "And there she defeated them mind, and body and spirit!"

Shocked, the crowd began to applause. Dani broke into a wide smile. Some Elders clapped for show, but many more rose to applaud her. Hands clapped her on the back.

"It is now we recognize our newest number," Castus announced, "as full warriors of the Earthborn of Empyrean. One and all, they are welcome amongst us!"

The Novices basked in praise. After a few moments, Castus called for quiet again.

"As per our tradition," he said, "if any one of our Elders calls for special recognition of these Earthborn, let them speak! Many deeds have transpired. Let them be known!"

Almost immediately, Heman shot to his feet. In loud, self-important boom he announced, "Novice Michael! Come forth with your Guardian!"

Michael and Nazir strode forward, both kneeling at the feet of the Elders.

"For your bravery in the face of overwhelming odds, I hereby recognize you for your courage in leading the attack in New York." He bowed, fingertips to forehead, in salute. "Henceforth, stand and be honored as Michael the Courageous! Nazir the Brave!"

The hall echoed as one. "Michael the Courageous! Nazir the Brave!"

Dani murmured to Nathaniel, "We don't have to call him that, right?"

He shrugged.

Elder Azariah stood next. "Novice Bouden! Come forth with your Guardian!"

Bouden's eyes widened. He barely was able to walk he was so nervous. Lorcan practically had to drag him. Both knelt.

"In battle," Azariah said formally, "it takes great skill to combat an enemy, but the mind is the greatest weapon of all. Had it not been for your

341

knowledge of the demonic to surmised the location of the demon nest in the Port of Los Angeles, our forces may not have eradicated the demon menace. For that, may you be recognized in our chronicles with the greatest honor and as most blessed of seers. Stand and be recognized!"

This time, Dani did applaud.

Others came forward. Two were made leaders of their aeries. Another would be inducted into the ranks of the Powers upon ascension from Novice. Two more were given titles like Michael.

A female voice spoke above the rest. "I call forth Novice Daniella and her Guardian Mastema!"

The summons broke the revelry. Lady Alecto stood before the Elders, all eyes falling to her before turning to Dani and Mastema. Silently, everyone stepped back. She felt a bump on her shoulder. It took her a second to realize Mastema nudged her forward. Even then it took another to take her first step.

Dani and Mastema came forward and knelt before Alecto. Behind her, some of the Elders looked displeased.

"Novice Daniella," she began, and then corrected, "Dani. It is rare amongst your kind to show such bravery in the face of overwhelming odds. The wisdom to send you into such a battle alone is one I will never understand."

Dani smirked slightly at the jab to the Council.

"But you prevailed where few could. For your deeds, as an overseer of these Trials, I formally announce that henceforth you will be recorded in the chronicles of Empyrean as an example to others. And by the power bestowed in me by your Elder Council, I call you to rise, draw your weapons and name them before this court."

A murmur flowed through the crowd. Dani had no idea what that meant.

Alecto waved to her encouragingly. "Rise, Dani."

She glanced at Mastema. He nodded. She stood, drawing the dagger and sword, holding them out to Alecto.

"Empyreal steel." She noted. "A rare weapon."

Dani hissed softly so only Alecto could hear her. "I don't know what's going on."

Alecto smiled widely. "It is a great honor amongst your kind to have named weapons. Only the greatest of Numen earn such a privilege. The names should reflect who you are." She leaned in. "That is why most of the Elders look angry and your fellow Novices look envious."

Dani grinned. She didn't dare look; only fantasized.

"Now," Alecto straightened up, speaking louder for the whole Throne Room, "name these blades, Novice Dani. Name your swords so henceforth all seven cities may know them and demonkind fear to speak their names."

Dani stared down at her swords. They didn't look like much. In comparison to Ethan's or Mastema's, they were puny. What was she supposed to call them? A million names buzzed through her head. She needed to call them something important; something grand. But what?

The names should reflect who you are, Alecto advised. *Yeah, well, I'm nothing but a sarcastic outcast. What the hell reflects that?* She glanced down at her small swords, nothing more than...

A smile curled her lips. She raised the sword, "From now on, this sword will be known as," she suppressed a laugh, "Pointyend. And this dagger will be called Pigsticker!"

The room went silent. If Alecto expected her to be serious, she was sorely mistaken. One hand flew to her mouth, choking down a laugh.

The rest of the room was quiet as a tomb. Stunned faces of hardened warriors and proud Elders waited, expecting her to get serious and change the names. But she liked them. They suited her.

Mastema looked on the verge of a stroke.

"I, uh," Alecto managed to keep a straight face, "I then, by the power of the City of Dis, the forces of Asphodel, and in the name of Empyrean," she lay her fingertips to the blades, "name these weapons Pointyend and," she could barely say it, "Pigsticker. May demons fear to speak of them for ages to come."

People applauded; awkwardly, but applauded. Shea and Roxelana were dying of laughter out of earshot in the corner. Dani resheathed her weapons and returned to the Novices with a wide grin.

Her Guardian murmured, "I will never let you speak in public again."

"Fat chance of that happening."

Castus stood. "With no more honors, let us welcome our newest members and let us celebrate tonight a great victory!"

The Novices departed, first through the ranks of congratulatory Numen, and then into the gifted outside. Shea and Roxelana joined her, both of them hugging her fiercely. More gifted came forward, having heard what she did. Nathaniel and the other boys inserted themselves between Dani and her sudden throng of admirers.

"Alright, alright, back up! Back up!" Dink yelled at them. "No autographs! No flash photography! You'll all get your commemorative Dani is a Total Badass T-shirts in the mail!"

She rolled her eyes and giggled happily. Life was good. Life was finally, freaking good.

"And that's pretty much it." Dani told them, passing the plate of food across to Bouden as she finished her story. "We survived."

"Survived?" Dink grinned widely. "You ruled!"

"*Ay de mi!* I'm so famous! Hopefully it won't go to my head!"

The boys laughed.

They decided to eat at Dani's place. Her food, her cups that flavored water; it was all better than Novice Village. Caesar roosted above them on the roof, nibbling her own meal. She was among friends and felt happily accepted.

"I can't believe you took down over a dozen demons." Bouden raised a cup in toast.

She raised hers too, joking. "To Pointyend and Pigsticker! Maybe people pee themselves laughing when they see it in history books!"

"To Pointyend and Pigsticker!" the whole lot of them dissolved into cackles.

"Thanks." She swigged down the sweet water. "So, the Port of Los Angeles? What happened?"

"We hunted down a nest where wraiths stored people in a container for food." Bouden said. "They were mostly homeless runaways; kids, not much older than us."

Nathaniel shivered. "Horrible. And what's weird: it wasn't just wraiths. Those things—imps or whatever—were working with them. And they had weapons of their own."

"Really?"

"Yeah." Dink looked like he wanted to gag. "Disgusting things. I swear I'm never going to get the stink off. They're like the world's worst Port-a-John, if it had been clogged up and—."

"Dude, I am eating." Nathaniel reminded him.

More laughter.

"You know," Dani said, finishing a piece of bread, "I'm surprised there were more than just wraiths on our hunts."

344

Bouden shrugged. "There've always been other types of demons. They're rarer than wraiths, but they're still around. Besides, it was just a couple imps. Nothing to write home about."

"Didn't Aerial fight some kind of demonic birds?"

"Strixes." Nathaniel nodded. "A flock of them. And Pinnacle fought off some type of water demons."

"Tannin. A type of sea demon from a...I don't know...some old country or other."

"Canaan." Bouden reminded him.

"So what's with all the variety all of a sudden?" Dani asked.

Bouden chewed thoughtfully, "What are you getting at?"

"I just got this strange feeling on my hunt. Those demons worked together, which they never do. And they had that idol."

"You think something is up?"

She was warned by an Archangel that something was. And the stories Numen told only added to it. "Can I tell you all something? Something I didn't tell anyone else?"

But before she could, she felt the familiar change in the air. Ethan and Kleos appeared from the sky.

"Are you all ready?" Ethan asked, landing.

"Ready for...?"

He smirked. "Vespertide."

"You're finally going to tell us what that is?"

"Better. We're going to show you." Ethan smirked. "Come on. Unless you don't want to go."

They left their food and followed the Guardians to the ledge. "Where are we going?"

He pointed to the river gate. "Follow us."

Ethan shot into the sky with Kleos, turning towards the end of the river. The boys followed. Dani was right behind.

Empyrean, the Vale and Sanctuary Hills dotted with fires; a mirror to the stars above. They aimed for the river gate. Ethan was in the lead, followed by Kleos, then the others. Just below, dozens assembled before the gate.

"Hey! I see Shea and Roxelana!" she called.

Below, in the dark along the bank, she spotted the two familiar shapes who waved to her. The river gate opened ahead of them. The spillway increased as the river gushed outward.

Dani put on speed, catching up with Ethan. "What are we doing?"

He grinned ear to ear. "It's a back door into Empyrean! The ladder is another way down to Earth!"

"What ladder?"

"Just watch!"

Ahead, one of the Numen on the bank of the river stirred the air with magic; casting a charm on the water. The raging, gushing waters frothed and rose off the ground. The falls churned up and formed bands of liquid crystal. Beams of water laced together into a pattern of interlocking rungs. The rungs formed a square-like ladder that shot downward. The river coursed through them, adding more to the lattice until not a falls but a single tube extended into the clouds below.

Numen and gifted jumped through the middle and dropped out of sight.

"Hang on!" Ethan yelled, dropping lower. "The ride gets bumpy!"

They shot over the heads of the crowd and then just as they were about to splatter on the river wall, Ethan and Dani and the rest shot left and through. Light burst around them as the moonlight hit the water, making a kaleidoscope of silvery luminescence. Dani and the others shot out of Empyrean. Dani's stomach dropped.

She screamed.

They fell. The water beams turned to clouds. Her vision blurred. And then she hit the ground.

Dani's boots touched down and she fell right into a pair of legs, nearly knocking someone over.

"Hey! Watch it!" growled a voice. "You made me spill my drink!"

Dani looked up and came face to face with a wolf-cynocephali dressed in jeans and a T-shirt, talking to a jinn.

Dani looked past him. If she hadn't seen lions the size of houses, waterfalls appearing from the sky and angels, then the single column of cloud depositing Numen and gifted into the parking lot would have looked weird. Instead, it was the new normal. People fell from it, landing more gracefully than she did and walking away as if it were an everyday occurrence. It was night. The world was in sepia again. She was on Earth.

Dani got up amongst the grumble of party-goers and turned to see the neon sign of the Hellfire Club blazing over the building's back lot. The familiar sounds of L.A. filled her ears; cars, music, and the yelling of a golem bouncer as he tossed a drunk dogman from the bar.

"Hard landing?" Ethan asked. "The first time is always hard."

She glanced at the sky. "A ladder? Seriously?"

"It's a portal to the city. We use it when we come for recreation."

"Recreation?"

"You seriously think a city of men just hangs out up there all the time? By the Lady of Dawn, no. Judah allows us to use the ladder to come to the club."

"Why?"

"To have fun; socialize with the gifted here and in Empyrean without the Elders knowing. Let's go. I'll buy you a drink."

The Hellfire Club's back entrance led them to the main floor. Golem bartenders served up drinks to the newly arrived Earthborn and gifted. It was easy to see what attracted Numen here. The club thrummed with the sound of that medieval-like house music and they quickly found female company to occupy them.

Shea and Roxelana wandered around the bar, dressed exotically; their clothes a mixture of medieval fantasy and modern chic. She gleefully hugged her friend.

"I'm so proud of you!" she gushed. "Dani, you did it!"

"Thanks!"

"I love the hair, by the way." She touched Dani's braids.

"Oh, you know, I got them styled by a friend."

The two girls hugged again.

"Judah!" Ethan exclaimed, shaking hands with the bar owner as he approached, dressed in a dazzling white suit. He looked like the State-Puff Marshmallow Man, if the Marshmallow Man could lift a truck.

"Merry vespertide my friend!" Judah exclaimed, extending his hand to Dani to take and kiss the back of. "My lady, it is so wonderful to see you. I told you this was tradition."

"Tradition?"

"After the Trials, the new Novices participate in vespertide for the first time." Ethan told her. "Some of us come down here almost every month."

"That explains Airlea." She gave him a look.

He blushed. "Yeah. But that's been over for a while."

"Hmm." She blushed, liking that.

"Our boy here was quite enamored with the idea of bringing you along." Judah told her.

Ethan blushed this time.

"Let me show you to your table." The big man led Ethan, Dani and her friends to a booth. "Drinks are on the house for newcomers. Stay away from the galenicals for your first time. The belladonna is quite deadly. Might I suggest the Cantillation? It is a wonderful drink. You will not regret it. And Ethan ordered you something special from our dinner menu. Now, I must excuse myself. The rowdiness of your fellow Numen can get out of hand." The big man bowed and left, yelling across the bar. "Rudolf! God's blood, get those two jinn out of my club! I don't want to see their fiery faces here again!"

The drink he suggested arrived. It came in a martini glass, swirling with beautiful oranges, reds and yellows like a sunset in a glass.

"Is it alcoholic?" she asked.

"No." Roxelana assured her. "Hellfire doesn't serve alcohol. It makes drinks from different elixirs to cause sensations."

"Sensations?"

"Try it."

Dani sipped. When she did, she heard the most beautiful music. A chorus of voices, the strumming of the instruments, and the full ensemble of drums and flutes mixed mesmerizingly with an explosion of flavors.

"*Vaya!*" She savored the taste and softening music.

"Judah is incredible with elixirs." Ethan said, arm across the seat behind her. "He makes healing potions, compounds and charms to sell, but most of his elixirs are for fun."

A golem arrived with a plate loaded with fish tacos. The smell was intoxicating. Dani smiled at Ethan. "You ordered this?"

"You said you missed them."

Roxelana and Shea gave her knowing looks over their glasses.

They ate, drank and talked. It was the most relaxed she'd been in months. Across the table, Dink threw his best moves at Roxelana; which meant he was awkward and she teased him. Shea split off, hanging out near the bar with Kleos. On the floor, some Numen started a floor show. Using Fyre, Aer, Water and Erthe they danced and manipulated the elements to the beat of the music. The crowd cheered them on like a supernatural dance circle.

Dani enjoyed her drink and food happily. "So?" she asked, taking a sip of her drink to another soft chorus. "Stormthrower? Am I to assume that's your sword, or is that just what all the ladies call you in bed?"

Ethan blushed deeply. "It's a gift of mine."

"What kind of gift?"

"You'll see one of these days. So, do you feel any different?"

She ran her fingertip around the rim of the glass. "A little. I don't feel at home here anymore," she took a bite of fish taco and smiled, "but it's still familiar. Does that make sense?"

"You've been in Empyrean for a while. It's your new home, but you grew up here. It's natural."

"It's more than that, though."

"What is it?" Ethan asked.

She bit her lower lip, taking a sip from her glass. The music sounded sad; beautiful, but sad. "Can I see my mom?"

Ethan didn't seem surprised. "Is that what you want?"

"Kind of. The last time I saw her, she kicked me out of the house, but it feels like something I need to do."

"There's rules against it," he admitted, "especially since we aren't supposed to reveal ourselves to mundani. But we aren't supposed to be here, either. If we went, you couldn't allow her to see you. If you're okay with that, why don't we go?"

"We? Are you coming with me?"

"Just because we killed a bunch of wraiths, doesn't mean there are more out there. Staying away from our former lives protects anyone we might have left behind as much as ourselves. And, yes, I'd feel better if I went with you." He quickly held up a hand. "I'm not trying to be sexist. I would just feel better if I went, too."

Dani didn't find it insulting. It was sort of sweet...and also incredibly sexist, but she could let that go for now. "You would do that?"

"Of course." His hand was still on the back of her palm. He laced his fingers into hers.

Dink and Roxelana went to dance. Nathaniel and Bouden were left to their own devices. Together, holding hands, Dani and Ethan left the booth. He spoke briefly to Kleos to tell them where they were going. He grinned at Dani with a very knowing smile, nodding to whatever Ethan said and then jokingly pushed him back in Dani's direction.

"He says we need to be back within the next two hours."

She gave him a look. "Is that all he said?"

"No. He also told me not to try anything."

"Is Kleos going to stand up for my honor?"

"No, he said if I tried anything you might kick my ass."

Dani grinned. Following him, they left Hellfire and headed out into the city.

They took a bus. The fight with demons took a toll on them. Flight was difficult. Using the Five, they headed up north into Sun Valley and got off at her old stop. Stepping off, the once-familiar streets seemed oddly unnerving. Together they headed down her street.

Ricky's house was dark except for the glow of a TV through the window. Dani stood just outside the gate, paralyzed by the idea of being here again. They hid behind the veil and she knew no one could see her, but she still felt exposed. The familiar panic surged back. She even faltered a little, feeling the veil slip. Ethan took her hand. The comfort took the edge off.

"Are you alright?" he asked.

She nodded.

The front door opened and out stepped her mother. Dani couldn't believe she could see her again. Her eyes were sunken and dark. She looked like she hadn't slept in days. The perfume of cigarettes hung thickly around her, which she added to when she lit up.

Dani's mother didn't look good.

She stood only feet from her, but Dani felt like there should have been miles. Her mom kicked her out of her life. She left her only child out on the streets. But right now, that didn't matter. Right now, all she wanted to do was hug her and tell her she was alive.

Which she couldn't. And she didn't.

Yvette sucked down a lungful of acrid smoke, taking out her cell phone and dialing a number.

Dani whispered softly. "Can she hear us?"

"Not unless you want her to."

She didn't. Dani hesitantly stepped away from him, letting go of his hand. The comforting warmth still clung to her palm, but she was fine. The ringing on the other end of her mom's cell phone continued in the dark.

The other person didn't pick up. The voicemail kicked in.

"Hey," her mother said, voice shaky, "it's me. Call me back please."

Is she calling Ricky? Dani wondered.

"I," her mom hesitated, "I miss you. I try calling every day. I don't know if you still have this phone or if you got my messages. I'm worried. Please call me back."

Who is she talking to?

"I'm sorry about what happened." Yvette's hand went to her mouth. The cigarette shook. "I'm so sorry Daniella. God, you don't know how sorry I am." The first few tears streamed down her cheeks. "I messed up. I was drunk. I just need you to call me. Just let me know you're okay. I need to hear your voice." She wept. "Please *cariño*."

The automated message clicked on to tell her she talked too long. Her mother cried, dropping her phone and sagging against the door.

Dani's chest tightened. She literally stood in front of her. All she had to do was drop the veil and tell her she was alright. Then she wouldn't torture her mother. The things her mom did, the times she hooked up with the wrong guy, even what happened with Ricky; it didn't matter anymore. Watching her mother cry broke her heart.

But she couldn't do it. She couldn't let her know. There were rules, but it was more than that. As much as her new world was dangerous, Dani fit better into it now; not this one.

Ethan placed a hand on her shoulder. "Are you alright?"

"I don't know." She shook her head. "She'll always be my mom and I'll always want to see her but," she bit back tears, "I'm not ready to let everything go. I love her, but I just can't be around her. I'm not ready to talk to her again." She looked up at him. "Does that make me bad person?"

"It makes you human."

"But I'm not human, am I? I'm not a mundanus. I'm a Numen."

"I think most of us are a little more mundane than we admit. Maybe one day, you'll be ready."

"But I can't tell her I'm alive anyway. Ready or not, it won't matter."

"No, but letting go of the anger might be a good thing."

Ricky opened the door, bag of trash in hand. Dani's blood boiled. Yvette jumped up. "Ricky!"

"What the hell are you doing out here?" he snapped.

"Nothing." She wiped her tears away. "Nothing."

"Like usual. I shouldn't have to take the trash out in my own house. Jesus, Yvette! I put a roof over your head and all you do is bum around here uselessly. You're as ungrateful as you daughter."

"Sure, honey. I'm sorry."

"Don't be sorry. Just earn your keep. Your kid ain't coming back. Stop trying to call." He shoved the trash into her hands. "Throw this out."

Anguished, Yvette took the trash down to the curb and Dani watched her mother follow his every despicable order. It hurt to watch. Ricky reduced her to little more than a maid. She shrunk past him.

"Get inside. Clean the place up." He told her. Yvette disappeared indoors. "Worthless."

Ethan apologetically touched Dani's shoulder. "We should leave. You don't need to see this."

351

"I know. But can I do something first?"

"Sure. What?"

Still hidden, Dani strode up the walkway as Ricky threw open the screen door. He shouted inside. "Yvette, I swear to God, if a cold one isn't open when I—!"

He didn't finish. Dani grabbed him by the back of his head and slammed him into the doorframe. She heard a thick crack and Ricky bounced off onto the walkway. Blood exploded from his nostrils; his second broken nose from her.

He groaned in pain. Dani left him there like a pile of trash.

Chapter Forty-One

They arrived back at the Hellfire Club just after eleven. Breaking Ricky's nose was cathartic.

Roxelana spotted them first, next to the bar with Shea and Kleos. "Holding hands now, are we?"

Dani and Ethan jumped apart. He kept his hand entwined with hers ever since they left Ricky's.

"Where's my charge?" Ethan asked, trying to smooth things over.

"He went out back to wait for you." Kleos told him. "I'm about to collect everyone before the ladder descends. If we leave any of them behind again..." he didn't finish the sentence.

Ethan nodded. "Yeah. I remember last time. Zounds that was close."

"Help me with them?"

"Aye. Dani, wait with Nathaniel out back?"

"Sure."

"We'll get the gifted." Roxelana promised, but still smiled knowingly at her friend.

Dani left, walking away in embarrassment. How the hell did she forget she was holding his hand? It was funny that something so innocent was such a scandal amongst her new people. It wasn't the worst thing she'd done with a boy; not that she went far with any guy. Hand-holding was about as PG as it got, but for Numen, it was R-rated. Weird.

She found Nathaniel out back in the parking lot, sitting against the side of the building. Rudolf, the golem bouncer, was the only other company.

"Hey." He greeted.

"Hey."

Like Kleos, his expression changed the instant he looked at her. Unlike Kleos, though, Nathaniel didn't need to see her with Ethan to know. "So, Ethan huh?"

"How'd you...?" but the answer was pretty obvious. She brushed back some loose hair and folded her arms uncomfortably. "Yeah. Ethan."

"Does he feel the same way about you?"

"I don't even know how I feel, Nathaniel."

"Yeah you do." He stood up. "I mean, he's smart, attractive and can handle a sword."

"You're smart, attractive and can handle a sword."

"Thanks, but he's had decades of practice."

353

Trying to lighten the mood, she asked, "Nate, please tell me when you say 'handle a sword' you're talking about an actual sword."

He laughed; not fake, purely real. Purely her friend. "Yes."

She bit her lower lip nervously. "Are you mad?"

"Mad? No." He shifted uncomfortably. "Disappointed? A little. You know I care about you, Dani."

"I do. And I'm sorry. Nathaniel, you're a great guy but—."

"Please don't give me the great guy speech." He said, cutting her off. "I hate that."

She winced. "I'm still sorry."

"You don't have to be sorry." He told her. There was a familiarity to Nathaniel; a way that made her feel comfortable. "Dani, you're a person, not some toy to be owned. I like you because you are who you are. It sucks you don't like me, but I guess that's the way it is. I thought..." he trailed off. "I thought when we both became Numen, it was destiny. I thought we were meant to be."

"I've heard a lot about destiny lately." She said. "I find it overrated. You'll find someone."

"You remember Numen don't marry, right?"

"But there could be something. Roxelana is cute."

"I think Dink is into her."

She joked. "You think Dink has a chance? We call him Dink, for God's sake."

He laughed in agreement. "'Snails, that's true."

She winced apologetically. "I should have been up front with you. He's your Guardian."

"Yeah, well, if you want to make it all weird you can point that out."

She smiled and punched him in the shoulder. "Thanks Nate."

"You can stop calling me Nate at any time, too."

"Never going to happen, Nate."

They stood together, listening to the sounds of L.A. It was nice to think that they could visit. The sights. The sounds. The smells. It wasn't lost to them.

But in all the revelry, something made her pause. She glanced at Nathaniel, who also stood frozen. Together, they inhaled. *It can't be.* Under the usual smells of L.A., there was something else:

Sulfur.

She met his eyes. "Do you...?"

"I do."

They tensed, backing out of the parking lot. The hairs on the back of Dani's neck stood up. Her hands came away from her sides instinctively. She knew the smell of Hell very well now.

Movement at her back. Dani turned but before she could, something swept out her feet, flipping her through the air onto her back. Stars exploded through her vision.

Nathaniel got thrown across the parking lot, smashing into a parked car. The crunch of his body collapsing into metal was sickening.

Dani spun over and kicked, striking at her attacker. But just as quickly as it came, the thing fled back into the gloom. She caught sight of a pair of red eyes as it took off into the air.

She rolled her to her feet. She was weaponless. Frantically, she search for Nathaniel and spotted him across the lot. His body caved in the back window of a sedan.

Rudolf ran her way. "Are you okay?"

"Get help!" she yelled. "It's a demon!"

Something black melted from the shadows above the street light, landing on top of the golem. The big clay man was massive, but when it struck, it bashed him into the asphalt. Rudolf grunted as a clawed hand slashed through the back of his skull and ripped the animation scroll to shreds. His clay body dissolved into a pile of earthen grey mud and clothes.

Dani spun to face the creature, putting herself between it and Nathaniel. It rose onto its feet. The street light overhead cast its hooded face in shadow.

"Stay back." She warned. "I've already killed a few of you tonight, so unless you want to add your name to the list, stay away."

The demon hissed. When it took a step, she heard scraping claws. Whatever kind of monster this was, it had enough sharp edges to slice her apart.

Dani raised her fists defensively and prayed the others came soon.

Two talon-adorn hands folded from its cloak and threw back the hood. The skin of the creature was soot-black. As the cloak came back, the light revealed a scorched tunic the color of burnt ash. Its eyes were blood red; no irises; just black dots for pupils. With hardly any hair, what remained was nothing more than a patchwork of seared scalp. Its cracked lips pulled back, bearing sharpened teeth. It was a smile; a nasty, devilish smile.

"What," she swallowed her fear, "what do you want?"

The thing took a step. Dani backed up. It took another. This time she held her ground.

"I won't let you hurt him."

She tried to think. She could summon that power to her hands again. The panacea healed them, but the pain was still fresh. But when she tried, she couldn't feel the warmth come like before.

Dani double-stepped back, keeping her hands up. She wanted to be as close to Nathaniel as she could get. The creature lolled its head left and right, playfully taunting her. It hissed laughter.

"Come on then, freak!" If she had to fight this thing, she wanted it over with.

The cloak ripped. A pair of massive, bat-like wings exploded from its back. They stretched in the streetlight like leather. The demon shrieked and leapt into the air. It launched across the parking lot and smashed both talon-like feet into her chest. Dani's tunic tore. Her skin ripped. Her lungs collapsed. She flew back.

She smashed into the chain-link fence next to the cars hard enough the wires ripped and collapsed around her. Her head spun. Her vision blackened around the edges. As she landed, the monster stalked towards her. Beneath the cloak, it carried a blackened-steel sword, a flail, and a cup. Snatching the cup, it forgot Dani and clambered onto the car next to Nathaniel.

"What're you...what're you doing?" she groaned, lifting herself up painfully. "Stop...! don't...!"

The demon grabbed Nathaniel's shoulder, digging its claws into his flesh to pull him free of the glass. Hovering over him, it raised a goblet of dark metal that shined sinisterly in the lamplight. A dark liquid filled the basin.

The creature raised the goblet to Nathaniel's mouth and dug its claws in deeper. He screamed in agony and the demon tipped the chalice over. Putrid, green-black liquid poured down his throat. He gargled, choked, and swallowed.

"Stop!" Dani climbed to her feet. "Stop it! What you are doing to him?"

The demon poured. Nathaniel tried to turn his head away, but it seized him by the back of the head and emptied the cup into his mouth. His body went limp.

"I said STOP!"

Light coalesced across her fingers. She threw them out. Brilliant, white light exploded from her palms and struck the creature. The blast knocked the chalice free and the demon flew clear. With a flap of wings, it leapt into the night.

The light extinguished. Dani collapsed onto her knees. She felt dizzy, stumbling towards Nathaniel. He tumbled off the car just as Dani got to him, catching him. His lips were stained inky green and his face was pale.

"Nathaniel?" she cradled his face. "Nathaniel!"

The door opened, laughter and music wafting out. Kleos, Ethan and the gifted stepped into the dark.

"Somebody help me!" she screamed.

Their smiles vanished and they ran to Nathaniel's side.

"What happened?" Ethan asked, kneeling beside him. "What did this?"

"I don't know!" she cried, shaking. "It was some kind of demon. It killed Rudolf." Tears streaked her face. Kleos tried to take her place, but she shoved him off. "I'm not leaving him!"

"I'm trying to help him." He cautioned. "Please. Let me."

She stepped back. Kleos took her place. "Are you hurt, Dani?"

But Dani wasn't listening. "It came after Nathaniel. Why didn't it come after me?"

Kleos repeated. "Dani, are you hurt?"

"What? No. I'm fine."

Kleos went to work, checking his vitals. "His pulse is weak. His skin is clammy. What did the demon do to him, exactly?"

"It had a cup. Some kind of cup. I think it dropped it."

Kleos looked around. He spotted the goblet lying a few feet away and retrieved it. As he did, Judah appeared. "What happened?"

"Nathaniel's been attacked." Ethan told him. "Call Hermes. Tell him to get down here immediately."

"Right away." He disappeared inside.

"Kleos, get everyone back to Empyrean."

"What about you?"

"I'm staying with my charge. Go. Take Dani."

"I'm not leaving." Dani insisted.

"You are. Now go!" He turned back to Nathaniel. He closed his eyes, placing his hands on his cheeks. He bowed his head and began to chant. The words were strange. They resonated in the air. She could feel her skin prickle with magic.

"What is he doing?" Dani asked.

"Healing spell. He will try to stabilize him." Kleos took her by the arm. "We have to go."

"Can he save him?"

"Ethan is skilled. He can keep him alive until helps comes."

"I want to stay."

"Dani," Kleos gripped her shoulder, "we are not allowed to be here. Vespertide is strictly forbidden. If they find you, you will be punished."

"What about Ethan?"

"He knows the consequences. It's his duty."

Guardians were sworn to protect their charges. He couldn't leave Nathaniel no matter the cost. She looked back, watching him chant the spell to keep him alive. Overhead, dark clouds swirled. A column descended from the sky and the ladder sucked them up.

———————————

The portal dumped her and the rest on the shores of the Crystalline River. She took off towards the Citadel, while Shea, Roxelana and the others returned to Sanctuary Hills. As she arched into the sky, she spotted a bright light breaking from the clouds below; Hermes' fiery chariot coming fast. He had Ethan and Nathaniel.

She landed before the Keep at a dead run. A crowd gathered, lining the street as healers carried Nathaniel in. They were already ahead of her as she ascended the steps two at a time and ran towards the Ward.

When she arrived, Ethan was out front. Elder Jeduthun, Elder Castus and Elder Asaph were with him.

"He's already inside with Elder Aleister." Ethan told her.

"How is he?"

Asaph interrupted them. "Guardian Ethan, explain to me how you and Novice Nathaniel were out of the city. The Gates are sealed for the night. No one is allowed to leave."

"Elder Asaph, please, not right now."

"Yes right now!" The Head Gatekeeper scowled. "You breached our borders. I want to know how!"

"Guardian Ethan is right." Jeduthun broke in. "Now is not the time. We have an ill Novice and no means of knowing what poisoned him."

"It was this." Ethan pulled the goblet Kleos found from his belt. "A demon carried it."

Castus took it, almost fearfully, and held it up to the others.

"What is that?" Dani asked, pretending she'd never seen it before.

"It is a dark grail." Jeduthun mused. "A cup of poison or instrument of Hell."

"How does that help Nathaniel?"

"For now, it does not. We have never seen such a thing." Castus told her. "The goblet appears to be made of stygian."

358

"Sti-what?"

"A dark element similar to adamant found in Hell. It is a cursed object."

She was getting impatient. "So can you save Nathaniel?"

"We will try our best." He handed the grail to Asaph. "Inform Elder Aleister that we do not know the specific ailment with which the Novice was cursed, but his healers should immediately begin purification. Purge the poison and destroy that cup. I do not want such damned things in the city."

"Yes Elder Castus." Asaph left in a hurry.

The two Consuls turned back to Ethan. "Describe this demon."

"I didn't get a good look at it." He admitted.

Jeduthun frowned and looked to Dani. "Perhaps, then, we should ask the person who was really there."

"Dani wasn't—."

Jeduthun wasn't listening. "Novice Dani?"

She didn't bother lying. He knew and Nathaniel's life was at stake. "It had wings and black skin. Its eyes were red and it had claws and teeth like nothing I've ever seen." Yet, even as she said those words, she could have sworn the demon looked familiar.

"Did it carry other weaponry?"

"A flail and a black sword."

"Stygian-steel." He and Castus exchanged looks. "It is no doubt the demon our men have encountered many times."

Dani remembered Kleos' warning on the first day; the vision in the flames. "What kind of demon is it?"

"We do not know. It is in none of our chronicles or tomes."

"Why did it attack us?" Dani demanded.

"That is a good question. You should return to your home. There is no more to be done until the healers can remove the poison."

"I don't want to leave Nathaniel."

"I understand that, Novice, but you are not needed here."

"Screw not being needed!" She jutted out her chin. "Like hell I'm going home."

The Elder knew he wouldn't win. "Very well. You may stay but you may not enter the Ward until the healers allow visitors. And you will return to your home afterwards. The events of tonight have caused concerns about our borders. The city will be put into lockdown."

Both Elders departed.

Ethan pulled Dani aside. "Are you alright?"

"I'm fine. I just want to be here when Nathaniel wakes up."

"Sure. I'll let the others know you are okay and come back when I'm done."

She squeezed his arm gratefully. "Thank you."

Ethan left. It felt like forever while waiting. She paced to get her mind off things, which of course meant it was all she could think about. How could this happen? What were the chances of *that* demon finding them in *that* parking lot? What the hell was it doing there?

The door to the Ward opened. Elder Aleister appeared. Dani practically bowled him over. "How is he?"

"Resting." He wiped his hands. "We were able to coax the toxins from his system."

"Toxins? I thought it was some kind of a curse."

"In our world, they are one and the same." Aleister frowned. "He is not cured. I have never encountered such a poison. Whatever this is, it is very powerful."

"Will he die?"

"It is contingent upon what the poison was meant to do and how well we fight it. The next few hours are critical."

Her heart sank. "Can I see him?"

He nodded. "It would be good for him to have company. He comes and goes from consciousness, so be wary."

Dani went inside. The Ward was empty save for the healers. Nathaniel was their only patient. He lay on his back, his skin the same sickly pale color; sallow, almost jaundiced. She took a stool to his bedside.

"Nathaniel?" she took his hand. "Nathaniel?"

No response. His eyes stayed closed, but moved under the eyelids.

She sat with him for a while. His sweat stained the sheets yellow-green; his body trying to get the poison out. Dani kept her hand on his, praying silently for a miracle. She lost herself in thought. Time slipped away.

A hand on her shoulder woke her from her trance. Ethan stood over her. She sighed heavily and rubbed her eyes. "How long has it been?"

"An hour. You should go. I can stay."

"I want to be here when he wakes up."

He pulled over another stool. "What were you thinking about?"

She shook her head. "Why was that thing there, Ethan? Why was it at the Hellfire Club? Do demons normally swing by?" Her sarcasm was bitter.

"No. Judah may not be Numen, but he doesn't serve demons. His club is protected."

"Then how? Why were we the unlucky ones it attacked?"

"Dumb luck." He told her. "It happens to all of us. We end up in the wrong place at the wrong time. That thing killed Titus. He was one of the greatest Guardians and it got him, too."

"But a demon that kills Numen just so happens to come when a large crowd of us show up at the club? It's too much of a coincidence, isn't it?"

"What are you suggesting? Like I said, demons can't get into Hellfire. Judah's spells keep them out."

"Maybe it got by the spells. Maybe it did it before."

"Not possible."

But she knew. It bugged her why the demon looked so familiar. She'd seen it before and it came to her then. "That's not true."

Ethan raised an eyebrow. "What?"

"The first night—the first time at the Hellfire Club—the demon was there. I ran into it." She'd been weaving through the crowd looking for Ethan when she bumped into it. She remembered the blood red eyes and teeth. "It's been inside Hellfire."

"But Judah—."

"It was there Ethan." Dani insisted. "I saw it."

A moan interrupted them. Nathaniel opened his eyes. The whites of his eyes were inflamed and yellow. His teeth were stained sickly green-black and he moaned in agony.

"Nathaniel!" she hugged him fiercely. "You're okay!"

"What happened...?" he croaked, his voice hoarse. "I don't...remember..."

"Rest." Ethan told him, leaning over Dani. "You've been poisoned. Can you recall anything about your attack?"

His eyes moved from Dani to Ethan. His grip on her hand tightened. "You're...together..." he murmured painfully. "You...and him..."

Dani blushed ashamedly. "Nathaniel, that's what we were talking about when that thing attacked us."

"Attacked us?"

"You don't remember? Try." She encouraged, joking a little to lighten the mood, "What do you remember, Nate?"

His eyes changed. One second he was Nathaniel, and then he wasn't. His jaw tightened. His hand gripped like a vice. The look on his face suddenly became very un-Nathaniel-like. Feral.

His other hand seized Dani by the throat. His grip was like iron. He pulled her towards him, inches from his face.

"My name is not Nate!"

Chapter Forty-Two

Nathaniel shot up off the bed with a hand around her throat, choking her. Crisscrossing his skin were dark, black veins. They throbbed angrily underneath his ashen skin. They bled into his face; pulsing. His sallow eyes looked about to bleed. He choked the air out of her, shoving her into a pillar next to his bed.

Ethan grabbed him around the body. "Nathaniel! Stop!"

Nathaniel flung his head back and struck Ethan in the teeth. With one arm, he threw him into the wall. Ethan sunk to his feet, stunned, but rushed into him again. He collided with his charge, trying to take him, but Nathaniel seized Ethan by the throat, unable to go down.

"You want to hurt me?" Nathaniel accused cruelly. "You chose _him_ over me?"

She coughed. "Nathaniel...!"

He looked demonic.

Ethan drew a knife from his belt and slashed his arm. The cut opened, but didn't bleed. Still, it hurt enough to make him drop Dani.

Ethan moved to stand between him and her. "Nathaniel, I'm warning you. Back down."

The expression on her friend's face wasn't his. A sinister smile played across his lips. The black veins pulsed darker. "Why? So you can take her from me again?"

"She's not yours to take."

"Nathaniel, this isn't you!" She insisted. "Please, you're my friend!"

"He can't hear you." Ethan warned. "Whatever that demon did bewitched him."

"We can't kill him!"

"I'm trying not to." He glanced back to Nathaniel. "Novice, I am your Guardian. I am instructing you not to attack."

Nathaniel's voice was dark. "Why?"

"Because I don't want to kill you." Two healers watched on in shock. "Go. Get help. You too, Dani."

"I won't!"

"Don't tell her what to do!" Nathaniel growled. "She's mine!"

Nathaniel attacked. Dani backpedaled. Ethan swung the knife, but clearly he didn't want to hurt Nathaniel any more than Dani did. His strike was slow. Nathaniel smashed his fist into Ethan's temple, driving him to his knees. He kept hitting, drawing blood.

"Nathaniel! Stop it!" she cried.

363

He hit Ethan a fourth time. The knife dropped, clattering on the stone. Her friend glared up at her, black teeth bared. Grabbing Ethan by the hair, he flung him hard into the stone floor. He lay there, unmoving as Nathaniel stepped over him and came for Dani.

She had two choices: fight or run. She didn't want to hurt him and she needed to get him away from Ethan.

So she ran.

She burst from the Ward into the courtyard. Nathaniel leapt out behind her, arms wrapping around her. He flung her sideways. Dani landed hard on her hands, rolling across the stone. Pain shot up her arms and shoulders. She rolled over, but before she could get up, he was over her and pinning her wrists back onto the ground.

"Where do you think you're going?" his breath stank of brimstone. She gagged. "You think you can get away from me? After everything I've done for you?"

She heard shouts and voices. "Please, Nathaniel, I'm trying to help you!"

"Help me? I don't need your help!"

Footsteps. Someone was coming.

"I own you!"

Then Nathaniel shot off her. Mastema wrapped his arms around under Nathaniel's shoulders, looping up around his neck and pinning his arms back. Her Guardians wrestled him away. Mastema groaned with effort, trying to hold him, but Nathaniel was strong. He began to break his hold.

Dani felt her hands begin to burn. She held them up, the palms coursing with light. "Nathaniel! Please stop!"

"Get off me!" he screamed ferally, swiping at Dani like an animal. "She's mine!"

Ethan appeared in the doorway; bloody, limping, holding the knife and hobbling towards them. He wouldn't reach Mastema in time.

One arm pulled free. Nathaniel clawed at her Guardian. "Let me go!"

Tears stung her eyes. Dani held out her hands. "Nathaniel! Please! I'm begging you!"

"I'll kill you!" he screamed. "I'll kill you!"

The look in his eyes said it all. He writhed his way towards her like a rabid dog. Mastema drew his dagger. He wouldn't let him hurt her. She had no choice. She wouldn't let someone kill her best friend. She couldn't.

The energy surged to her hands. She had to do it.

"I'm sorry."

Then she hit him with a blast of light.

The brilliant energy struck Nathaniel, stopping him dead in his tracks. It wasn't anger this time. It was love. She cared for Nathaniel. It hurt her to do this to him.

His arms shot out. His eyes widened. The explosion knocked Mastema off. Through the luminescent rays of light, Nathaniel stared at her. His body shook violently. The anger seethed across his face, but then went slack. He screamed.

Dani screamed too and poured her soul into it.

Ethan covered Mastema as the lucent nimbus of energy exploded over them. The air shook. The beam pulsated through Nathaniel's chest and in a violent eruption, shot him backwards. Tears blurred her vision and she squeezed them shut.

Nathaniel landed on his back, blank eyes to the starry sky. Dani pulled back her power, screaming in pain. She squeezed her hands closed and the light vanished as he collapsed to her knees.

Sudden darkness swept around them. Her hands sizzling. Nathaniel lay with arms splayed, unmoving; a red burn seared across his naked chest.

Dani began to cry.

Nathaniel was dead.

A rush of armor and the sounds of weapons drawn, Gatekeepers arrived. They fanned out into a line, but stopped when they saw them.

Mastema and Ethan stood slowly. Ethan staggered over to her. "Are you okay?"

She sobbed. She couldn't stop it.

He wrapped her in his arms. "It's okay."

She cried harder. Everyone else looked on. No one said a word.

Then, with a lurch and painful groan, Nathaniel shot awake. Mastema, Ethan and Dani all jumped back. The soldiers' swords came up.

"Nathaniel?" Dani scrambled over. "Nathaniel!"

He groaned. His skin was no longer sickly-yellow, but rosy, pink and flush. The black veins slowly melted away. When he opened his eyes, they were normal.

"Wha—What happened?"

Dani cried tears of joy and hugged him. "You're okay!"

"Dani...what's going on?"

She sniffed back tears. "You're okay."

"Where am I?"

"You don't remember?" She couldn't believe it. "You're at the Ward in Empyrean. You were poisoned."

"Poisoned?" he shook his head.

"It's fine! It's fine!" she gushed, and for the first time, it really was. "You're safe now." She'd never been happier to hug him, even if her hands hurt so badly to do it. "I thought I lost you."

He exhaled painfully. Ethan and Mastema helped him stand. "Yeah. Me too. I feel like I've been hit with a truck."

She was about to explain but caught the eye of Mastema and Ethan. Their expressions told her easily enough: *say nothing.* The look was nothing but fear. What Dani did scared them.

"It's not important." Ethan told him. "What's important is you're alive."

Armor and swords clinked as Asaph burst through the wall of soldiers. "What is the meaning of this? I demand to know what is going on!" He drew his scimitar, pointing it at Nathaniel. "Get away from him!"

"All is well!" Mastema said, raising his hands. "The danger is passed!"

"We were told he attacked my healers." Aleister said. "He was crazed."

"He's fine." Ethan told them. "It was the poison."

"Poison?"

"The poison from the grail affected him; made him mad with rage. We were forced to stop him."

Asaph's scimitar lowered.

"I'm fine." Nathaniel said sheepishly. "I'm okay now."

"How do we know if this is true?" Asaph asked, weapon still in hand. "We do not know what that demon did to him. He may still be possessed."

But Aleister held out his hand. "No. Look at him. He is not in any way affected. How did you cure him?"

Dani was about to answer, but Ethan interrupted her. "The blow to the head dispelled the curse."

It was a terrible lie, even by Dani's standards, but Elder Aleister didn't argue. He only nodded in shock. Ethan's eyes flicked to Dani. Again, nothing but fear there.

Asaph huffed. "Elder Aleister? There is no danger?"

"Nothing is certain," Aleister said, "but the spell seems to have passed. We should get him back to the Ward. My healers can tell us more."

The Head Gatekeeper put up his sword. "Away with your weapons!"

Immediately, every soldier withdrew their swords and spears.

"Take him inside." Aleister ordered. "Come. We must attend to this curse."

The healers took Nathaniel. Aleister was relieved. So was Dani. Mastema and Ethan seemed less enthusiastic.

Asaph growled at them. "This commotion threw the entire city into a panic. You disrupted our patrols. My Gatekeepers pulled out of the Sanctuary Hills! You should exercise more caution." He turned and stalked off.

"Are you hurt?" Ethan asked.

"Just a few scrapes and bruises. I'll be fine. My Guardian trained me how to take a fall."

Mastema's mouth twitched slightly. "That was an amazing feat, Novice Daniella."

"I know. I'm sorry I didn't tell you about it. I think I acquired another gift. It's how I saved you at the warehouse. I wasn't sure exactly what it was but—."

"Please, refrain from speaking." He said quickly, holding up a hand. "We should not talk of this. Not yet."

"What? Why? What did I do wrong?"

"Nothing."

"Then why are you acting like I did?"

Both Guardians hesitated. They exchanged furtive looks; ones that made Dani nervous.

"It's not the right time." Ethan cautioned. "We need to get you back across the Vale."

"What about Nathaniel?"

"He will be fine. Right now, I'll feel better if you were home."

Dani left with them. They walked from the Ward through the Keep. Her hands hurt, but weren't burnt like before; no need for panacea.

"I still don't understand." She shook her head, crossing the Vale Bridge with them. "What did I do? Is it some kind of healing power? But that wouldn't explain how I destroyed a demon with it."

Both Guardians were silent, but their looks said it all.

"What is it?" She demanded, jumping ahead and stopping them. "Stop walking, both of you! Whatever is going on, you'd better start talking. What is this thing because it's freaking you out."

"Dani, not right now." Ethan said.

"No! No! No!" she stuck a finger in both their faces. "I'm tired of people telling me when is and when isn't the best time for something! My friend almost died and I saved him. I want to know how!"

Both of them were silent.

"Fine. Then I'll ask the Elders." She tried to step by them. Mastema grabbed her arm. "Let go of me."

"No."

"Why not?"

"Because if you tell the Elders, they will kill you."

The statement caught her off guard. "Kill me? What do you mean? You know what it is?"

"I suspect what it might be. And it is not something you want them to know. Daniella, if the Elders discover your power, you will be a threat to them."

Ethan agreed. "He's right. Please, Dani, don't tell anyone until we know for sure. Just trust us—trust me. Keep it to yourself."

She did trust him. That was the problem.

"We should return to the Arn." Mastema advised. "The city is chaotic and this night disturbs me."

Dani rolled her eyes. "You're so cheery. You should entertain at kids' parties."

Her Guardian ignored her.

The bright full moon overhead lit the way. Gatekeepers had pulled out of Sanctuary Hills, but the celebration of the end of the Trials continued. Gifted were out; singing, dancing, celebrating, a hillside of festivities.

But Dani didn't feel like celebrating. As they crossed, something still bothered her. Even as they got to the other side and walked towards her home, she couldn't get it off her mind.

"Why poison Nathaniel?" she wondered aloud.

"Hm?" Ethan cocked an eyebrow.

"It's the thing that keeps bothering me. Why not just kill him? The demon easily could have. Why didn't it?"

Ethan shrugged. "Torture you? Turn him on you?"

Mastema shook his head. "I know at least a dozen other cursed elixirs that cause more torture, not to mention numerous spells. The demonic have crafted many effective methods of inflicting suffering. She makes a valid point."

They got to her house and took a seat in the pavilion. Dani was exhausted, but her mind wouldn't shut up. "My point exactly. What did the demon want? Did it want us to kill Nathaniel? But that doesn't make sense, either."

Ethan shrugged again. "Maybe it wanted Nathaniel to kill some of us."

"If that were the case," Mastema frowned, dipping his hand into the fountain and cupping water for a drink, "it would have poisoned both you *and Nathaniel*. One cursed Novice could not kill that many. Asaph and his Gatekeepers would slay them before they could do much harm. There would be little reward for something so complicated."

"He still caused a ruckus." Ethan pointed out.

"Exactly." Dani said. "So other than to piss off Asaph, I don't see the point. And why attack us at the Hellfire Club? It's super dangerous for demons and there's nothing for them to get. All that's there are golems, Judah and—."

She froze. The moment she thought of it, she knew it was true. She knew exactly why the demon was there. She couldn't believe she hadn't thought of it before.

"Dani? What is it?"

"All that's there at The Hellfire Club are golems, Judah and," she kicked herself, "the ladder."

Dani leapt to her feet and ran into the house.

"The ladder? The portal to the club, you mean?"

"You said it yourself: it's a back way in Empyrean." A cold chill ran down her spine. She grabbed her swords and armor. "It's a way around the defenses! This whole city is on lockdown. No one in or out, but," she came back out into the pavilion, "the ladder bypasses all of that. Does Asaph know about it?"

The revelation dawned on Ethan. "No, he doesn't. Other than the centaurs and the gifted, no one knows about it. But Asaph's patrols would spot anything wrong as long as they're..." he trailed off. Fear creeped into his eyes. "...as long as they aren't pulled off duty by anything."

Mastema's expression darkened. "Which happened when Nathaniel's attack called Asaph and his men to the Ward. The Hills are defenseless. It was a distraction."

"And allows anyone coming through the ladder to go unnoticed." Dani finished, strapping on her gauntlets. "That demon poisoned Nathaniel, and then he freaked and all the Gatekeepers came running. Then it could—."

"Sneak in." Ethan shook his head. "But the ladder can only be opened from the inside. It shut when we came back. No one would leave it open. We're safe."

But they weren't. *The enemy is in your midst*, Gabriel warned her. "No, we're not."

"What? Why?" Ethan asked.

But Mastema didn't argue. He retrieved his khopesh.

"I think the demon has a way of opening the ladder." She said, belting her blades. "Don't ask how, but I know it does. It's the only thing that makes sense. That thing did this to get inside."

"How?"

"You told me to trust you, so I'm asking you to trust me. It wants the ladder."

Mastema checked his bracers. "What could it want here?"

"Not sure. All I know is that we need to alert everyone before something happens."

And then they heard it. It carried along on the wind through the dark, night air: a blood-curdling, frantic, life-begging scream. Dani turned in the direction of the voice. It came from uphill.

Then more voices joined it. A chorus of screams formed an unholy song across the hills.

Chapter Forty-Three

They found a dead gifted halfway uphill. Dani swallowed her horror and continued up, her feet flying across the ground as she cut through the knee-high grass; springing several feet in each stride. She moved like a stone skipping on water.

Gifted ran as howls tore through the night. A home was on fire. Dani headed towards Novice Village.

An explosion bloomed in the darkness, shattering the pavilion to pieces. The sounds of battle urged her on. Novices and Guardians poured from their barracks. And in the gloom, Dani saw the demons.

A wraith in a disgusting molted suit pinned Dink to the ground, shark-like jaws open to strike. Mastema launched himself through the air and swung the khopesh like a deadly pendulum, guillotining the creature. The head separated and the wraith exploded in ash.

Dani drew Pointyend, the blade flaring to life as she leapt over Dink. Bodies lay strewn around the square. They were mostly Guardians, killed defending their charges.

A body lay bloody and broken in the fountain, a wraith gnawing on it. It raised its wet face from the open neck, long feminine locks of hair matted to its face. It hissed at Dani and slashed with its claws, but Dani dodged and struck with her sword. Its arm vaporized in a cloud of dust and black blood. Dani cut it down with the second stroke.

She felt another coming and spun, drawing her knife and slashing open its shoulder. She kept moving, slicing and cutting it down.

A third wraith flung itself from the roof of the nearest barracks and landed on her. Dani rolled, shaking it off but the demon bit down on her calf. She kicked, forcing it off, but both her weapons fell out of her hands. The glow dissipated. She crawled away and the demon scrambled towards her.

The shaft of an arrow exploded from its neck. Dink, bow in hand, strode towards them and notched a second arrow. He hit the demon in the heart and it collapsed, dissolving to ash.

He ran to Dani's side. "Are you okay?"

"I'm fine!"

"They're all over the Hills." He told her, notching and firing. "How the hell are they here?"

"I'll tell you later!"

Smoke and flames billowed into the sky. Ethan and Mastema rallied around the remaining Guardians and Novices, helping to drive back the monsters. Andreas, axe in hand, beheaded one. Bouden summoned Aer and blasted one across the square.

Ethan, Montante sword flashing in the fiery light, leapt into the middle of the square. The humungous blade wove around him with expert precision. It sliced through the air, never slowing its deadly arcs as he cut down two, dispatching them with single strokes. His blade flew over his head in three quick loops, hacking the head off a wraith with each swing and then coming up and under to take a fourth.

But more flowed downhill towards them; too many to fight alone.

"Mastema!" someone screamed. "Fall back!"

Her Guardian stepped from the fight, facing mass of demons. He sheathed his khopesh. "

"Mastema!" she screamed. "What are you doing?"

Her Guardian held out his hands, closing his eyes. Around him, the fires that engulfed Novice Village swarmed. Burning brighter, billowing up off the charred remains, he summoned them towards himself with Fyre. Flames licked past her and coursed over his hands. The demons charged right towards him, jaws open.

With a slap of both palms together, flames exploded outward.

The fire cut right through the front lines and disintegrated them. The ones behind tried to stop before the inferno took them, too. Only the back dozen had a chance to flee.

Just like that, nearly two dozen demons were gone. Dani stared at her Guardian.

"What is it, Daniella?" he asked in a bored tone.

"Seriously? You have to ask?"

"I am named for a monster of destruction." He turned around. "Did you think that was a coincidence?"

Was that a joke? She didn't ask.

"They are headed to the Vale Bridge!" Someone warned.

"Oh God! The gifted! Roxelana! Shea!"

He called to the others. "Any who can fight, follow!"

They took off into the sky. Behind her, a dozen Guardians and Novices followed.

Dani soared down the Hills. Fires burned across the countryside; not the comforting family flames, but households ablaze. She could see people running but pushed that aside. She angled down towards the market, where other darker forms ran towards.

Demons filled the market square. When she landed, she stabbed down into an unsuspecting wraith, killing it.

"Dani!"

Shea stood his ground, using a rake to fend off a white-eyed monster. Kleos landed beside her and threw an adamantine dagger into it. The demon staggered. Kleos threw again and again, launching one weapon after another, spinning off his feet and firing a dagger through its eye. The creature fell dead.

"Shea!" Dani ran to his side. "Where is everyone? Adare? Roxelana?"

"Most of the gifted fled across the Vale to the Citadel, but Adare and Roxelana went back for Korë! She was at the house!"

Her blood ran cold. "She's still there?"

"These things came too fast!"

"Get across the bridge." She stepped past him. "I'll get them."

Dani ran uphill toward the gifted homes. Demons retreated from the market as more Numen arrived. One leapt at her from a vendor's tent, but she dodged and stabbed it through the back, continuing on.

She arrived at the house. "Roxelana!"

"Dani!"

Adare, Roxelana and Airlea knelt in the garden in front of the home. Dani flew up the steps. "We have to go!"

"Dani! It's Korë!"

She felt her heart sink. Nestled between the three gifted, the young girl lay prone on her back. In the dark, what she thought were just shadows were in fact dark, red stains. Blood. Deep gashes cut through her dress. Dani sheathed her blades, running to their side.

"She's hurt!" Tears streamed down Roxelana's cheeks. She cradled the young, blonde girl's head. "Dani, she's hurt!"

"It'll be fine!" But when she knelt, she stared in horror at the wounds across the young girl's body. There were many along her torso. "She'll—She'll be fine."

Dani touched her hand. It was cold and clammy. The terrified little girl stared up with her sapphire eyes; pleadingly, shaking in fear.

"You'll be okay. We just have to get you out of here."

Adare tried to move her into her arms. She whimpered painfully.

"We can't move her." Airlea said. "She's too injured."

"But we have to!" Roxelana pleaded.

Snarls and crashes poured from inside the darkened gifted house. Dani shifted in front of them.

"They're still here." Dani said, hand on the hilt of her sword.

More snarls. Dani was about to draw her blade when a small hand stopped her. Looking down, Korë's hand was over hers. Dani took it.

"I won't let them hurt you." She promised.

She shook her head, pleadingly. Red speckles framed her young, innocent face. She held out her other hand.

"What is it?"

Korë pulled her close. Dani leaned down. The little fingers laced around the back of her neck. Her other squeezed her arm. Her smile quivered. As much as she could, she hugged Dani.

And then, as Dani watched, the light faded from her sapphire eyes. In seconds, the little girl was gone.

"No!" Roxelana moaned. "No! Korë!"

Adare cried. Airlea put a hand over her mouth, sobbing silently. Dani knelt, frozen; her arms still around her in her last hug.

Small tears fell from her eyes onto the little girl's frozen face.

More snarls from inside; more sounds of breaking furniture. Turning, she dropped Korë's hands and folded them over her. She stood, drawing her blades. They glowed to life.

Roxelana called out to her. "Dani—!"

"Go." She said, walking towards the house. "Get out of here."

"But Dani—!"

"Take Korë with you." She kicked the ajar door back wide with one foot and stepped inside. "I'm right behind you."

The inside was a large, darkened living room. Her blades illuminated the gloom. Stepping into the center, she saw the eye-shine and heard growls just out of the light. Demons, at least four, surrounded her. They crept forward.

Dani kicked the door closed and swung with her shining blades.

———————————

The remaining gifted fled across the Vale Bridge; some on their own, others carrying their wounded or dying with them. Shea took the wrapped body of Korë in his arms, fleeing with Roxelana, Adare and Airlea. Dani remained on the other side, her swords caked in blood.

Not a single wraith left that house alive. Her hands shook in rage. But they didn't burn... *Why didn't they burn?*

Numen scrambled to put out fires. Others tended to the wounded. She knelt next to Lester as Bouden did his best to heal him.

"He's bad." Bouden said, a cloth pressed against the wound in his side. "He's going to need a healer."

Lester groaned in agony. His chest shuddered in a way Dani knew wasn't good. His breathing was ragged like something was wrong with his lungs.

A Gatekeeper dropped from the sky, landing next to Ethan and Mastema. "Demons are all over the Hills."

Mastema spoke calmly, wiping ash and black blood from his khopesh, "What number of foes?"

"Dozens. Wraiths, imps; coming from the Vale! They ascend the cliffs as we speak. We do not know how they bypassed our defenses."

Ethan and Dani exchanged a look.

"A demon leads them." The Gatekeeper reported. "A monster with coal black skin."

"Red eyes?" Dani asked.

He nodded.

She got to her feet. "We have to kill it."

"They will attempt to take the Bridge." Ethan said, sheathing his sword "We need to defend it while the Citadel organizes their forces. Otherwise, they'll cross. We have too many gifted and wounded to allow them to do that." He announced to the assembled Numen. "Anyone who is not wounded or tending to wounded should stay here. We'll make a stand as best we can. Those of you unable to fight, get across the bridge."

Everyone started moving. Dink and Bouden began gathering arrows while Dani went to join Ethan.

"I need your help." He said.

"With what?"

"I need you to go into the Vale."

Her eyes flared threateningly. "You are not asking me to sit this out."

"That's not what I meant."

"Really? Because it sounds like you're about to send me away from the fighting while everyone I care about stays here."

Ethan winced. "Okay, I am—BUT," he stopped her next tirade before it began, "it's not what you think. I need you to get the centaurs. We need their help. They can spread the word to the other centaur villages and come to our aid."

She scowled. "Why not send someone else?"

"Because in the event of an attack, they'll protect their villages. They won't leave. I need you to convince them to come help us."

"And why would they listen to me? I'm not sure if you remember, but I'm not their favorite person."

"Then find a way to convince them. Nessus respects you. He'll listen."

"And the others who won't?"

"I have faith in you."

She glared. "Don't play like that."

"I'm not."

She wanted to say no. She desperately did. Her friends, her Guardian, even that cocky idiot Andreas were about to stand and fight a battle they couldn't win for long while she ran in the opposite direction.

"So I'm supposed to get them, then what?"

"There is access to the Vale on the other side of the river, remember? Order the centaurs to close the ladder and stop these things from getting through. They'll know the spell. Then bring them to the Citadel and we'll meet you at the bridge." He put his hands on her shoulders. "Dani, please, this is important."

"Be honest: are you asking me to do this to keep me out of harm's way?"

"Would you be angry if I said yes?"

"Hell yes."

"I am," he told her truthfully, "but we need them. Convince Nessus and convince the others. Please, Dani."

She hated it, but nodded. "Fine."

A bloom of fire erupted through the night sky. Ethan stepped away. "I'll see you soon."

"Promise?"

"I can't." He drew his sword.

Another inferno danced into the air. The Numen gathered towards the bridge, Ethan among them; ready to make a stand.

Dani didn't think about it. She just did it. She stepped in front of him, put an arm around his neck and pulled him down. When his lips met hers, she savored the taste of his kiss. She didn't care it was tacky. She didn't care it was stupid, or girlie, or not the right time. To hell with that.

Ethan's arms closed around her. She inhaled the scent of his skin and the taste of his lips. When she pulled back, he stared, dumbfounded.

"I *will* see you soon." She promised, then turned and leapt onto the Bridge's railing. She looked back one last time. "And, uh, don't read too much into that."

He slowly nodded. "Right."

"Because this isn't the right time and it's sort of complicated and—." She stopped herself from rambling. "Um, yeah, we'll talk later."

"Right."

She swan dived off the Bridge under the power of Aer and shot upriver.

I'm about to walk into a hot mess. Demons are attacking the city, she thought. *Screw it. Why the hell not? I may not live until tomorrow to regret it.*

Chapter Forty-Four

"*Dani! What's happening?*" Caesar swooped overhead. "*This place is crawling with hellspawn! How the hell did they get inside?*"

"I need to find Nessus and the centaurs! Can you point me towards their village?" It only occurred to her now she had no idea where it was in the dark.

"*Sure. Why?*"

"Just get me to them!"

"*Follow me!*" Caesar pulled up, spreading her wings as she and Dani danced over the treetops. Caesar flapped, rising and banking right. "*This way!*"

The Vale was pitch-black below; a sea of shadows dotted only by the vague shapes of the trees.

"*There it is! It's straight ahead!*" Caesar called. "*Other side of the river!*"

Just below on the opposite embankment, the familiar centaur village burned brightly. A majority of them gathered around a huge bonfire. The warriors galloped around it, dressed in full battle armor with adamantine steel gleaming in firelight. Families with little centaur foals and weanlings ringed the warriors, chanting. It was some sort rally; cheering on their warriors before leaving for Hell.

"*Follow me!*" Caesar shot down.

Dani dropped with her, both of them coming down towards the gathering. Some of the warriors spotted them as they came towards the light. Startled, bows and arrows raised in their direction. Apparently, they weren't prepared for visitors.

"Whoa!"

An arrow whizzed by her head. She descended, dodging follow-up shots. The centaurs notched other arrows and re-aimed. Dani jolted upwards and with a scream, flew into the midst of the centaur gathering. Dani landed and rolled to a stop—

—to a stop in front of a wall of spears, arrows and swords.

Centaurs formed a solid phalanx in front of her. Even as she came to stand, more galloped behind her, surrounding her in a ring of weapons.

Dani threw up her hands. "Wait! Wait! I'm a friend! Don't kill me!"

"She is armed!" one screamed.

The centaurs advanced. Dani quickly backpedaled, only to nearly impale herself on the weapons behind her.

"Now, now, wait a minute!" She cautioned, hands away from her swords. "Let's all just calm down. I'm not here to hurt anybody."

Caesar swooped down from overhead and landed on her shoulder. The centaurs did the opposite of calm down. Weapons rose higher.

"Kill the intruder!"

"I'm not an intruder!" Dani argued.

"To arms!"

"No! Wait!"

Caesar's crown plumage rose threatening. This was getting out of control.

But before any centaurs attacked, one broke through the front lines and galloped in between Dani, Caesar and the rest.

"Hold!" Nessus cast off his helmet. "Stay thy blades, brothers! They are allies!"

Another centaur cantered forward. "Allies they are not," Buer growled, his own sword drawn threateningly. "That Numen girl was warned to stay far outside our borders, yet she returns to wreak more havoc! It is because of she that we are being banished!"

That didn't go over well. Angry centaurs glared in her direction. More than one stepped forward, but Nessus cantered around Dani and Caesar threateningly. They quickly backed away.

"It is not the fault of any man here, nor she that stands behind me!"

Buer raised his sword. "You would defend her after everything that happened?"

"I would seek to defend the innocent!"

"Innocent, she is not!"

"Stop it! Both of you!" Dani stepped between them. Buer's sword turned to her. "That's enough! I'm not here for some sort of equine pissing contest! I'm here for your help."

"Our help? Are you daft? Have you no notion of what pain you caused this village? To hell with you!"

"Sorry. Hell is already here." She turned away from him, not caring he pointed a sword at her back. To the rest of the village, she warned. "Demons have entered Empyrean. We are under attack. They've killed dozens already and now they're planning to attack the Citadel. I'm here to ask for your help."

Whispers flew through the assembled soldiers. Swords lowered, but no one moved.

"Where is your proof?" Buer demanded.

"Are you insane? Why do you think I'm here?"

"We do not have permission to be in the Citadel by decree of the Elders." He shot back. "The whole reason we depart for Hell is because of your interference. If we anger them further, our village could pay harsher penalties."

"And if you don't come with me, a lot of people may die. And if they die, who's here to protect your families when you leave?"

"You would lead us to ruin. I have heard vile tales of thee!"

"Oh my God, will people please stop blaming me for crap that's not my fault!" she threw up her hands. "Are you stupid or do you really believe half the crap you hear? Because if you're stupid, at least I can forgive that. If you really believe I'm some kind of monster, then you're still stupid, but also gullible." she was almost three feet shorter than the centaur, but she scared him with her anger. "Get it together! Why the hell would I tell you we're under attack if we're not under attack? What would I get out of that?"

Buer had no retort. Next to her, Caesar said to Nessus, *"Darling, she's telling the truth. They're here. We need your help."*

Nessus glanced first to Caesar, then to Dani, then to his fellow centaurs. He raised his sword. "To arms. Prepare for battle."

"You do not have the authority to give such an order!" Buer growled, moving in front of him.

Nessus moved quick; too quick for Buer. His sword came to the other's centaur's neck.

"Will you listen to this girl once more?" Buer demanded. "You are exiled because of her."

"I am my own man." Nessus shot back. "And I said to arms. An enemy comes to our gates and you do nothing? You will not stop that which threatens your home?" he looked to the other centaurs. "Will you, brothers? Will you allow demons to come for your children and beloved because you mistrust one who asks for aid?"

The other centaurs were silent, but Dani recognized the looks of shame.

"If it be my error that we are sent into the depths of the Underworld, then I take such fault, but I will not allow shame to keep me from my duty. An enemy entered our lands. I mean to kill them! Who is with me?"

Swords drew. Several centaurs stepped forward, bowing, placing their swords to their brows. After a moment, even more did the same.

Buer scowled, but he reached back and removed his helmet from a saddlebag, placing it onto his head. "Form ranks! Numen, where be these demons?"

"The river gate."

"To the gates!" Buer ordered. As he galloped off, the other centaurs rode out behind him, flowing downhill.

Caesar landed on Nessus's shoulder. Her voice was all honey. *"Darling, you are definitely your own man. You're my kind of man, too."*

He smirked. Dani almost gagged.

They stormed downriver; centaurs galloping ahead full speed, Dani and Caesar above them. They passed under the bridge and headed for the river gate.

Ahead, she could see same lattice of water columns as before. The portal. And from it, a dozen demons emerged. She recognized the familiar human shapes of the wraiths mixed with the ranks of putrid, rotting imps. Their skin looked sickly brown or green. Their lips rotted back from thick gums and teeth. If they had a nose, it turned up into the air, smelling oncoming meat. They would have looked almost cartoonish had they not carried an assortment of armor and weapons made from black steel. What had Castus called it? Stygian?

The centaurs fired a volley of arrows as they descended the stones, leaping from one boulder to another deftly. The arrows struck down the first few demons pretty easily, either washing them into the river to be swept back down the ladder or killed by a shot to the head.

The demons collided with the oncoming centaurs. They trampled most, but a few took down some of the Hellion defenders. Nessus stumbled, falling over a long-shafted spear.

Caesar screamed. *"Nessus!"*

She rocketed downward, talons spread. Her claws snatched the creature up by the eye sockets and launched it over the ladder. It screamed as it fell out of sight down the mountain.

Nessus rose, swinging his longsword wide and decapitating a wraith. Dani landed beside him, empyreal sword flaring to life. More demons leapt from the ladder onto the bank. They had to close it.

"Nessus! Portal!" Dani's sword collided with a heavy two-handed blade of an imp. Only her own power fueling the brilliantly-lit blade made her strong enough to stop it. "Close it!"

He cut down his opponent and raised his hand, palm out. He spoke in the magical language; the one Ethan used to cast a spell keeping Nathaniel alive. The angelic language. The interlocking pillars of water dissolved.

Dani parried another blow with her sword and drew Pigsticker. She shoved the white-hot dagger into the demon's side under the arm. It screamed and burst into a cloud of stinking ash, demonic armor all that was left.

More demons rushed towards the entrance of the ladder, but before they could reach it, it collapsed. They screamed as the river washed them back out and they tumbled into the clouds below, gone forever.

The centaurs dispatched the remaining demons.

Caesar dove down, landing on a rock beside Nessus. *"Are you hurt, baby?"*

"I am fine." He sheathed his sword and announced to his fellows. "We drove them back!"

The centaurs cheered.

"We have to keep going." Dani told him. "More will cross the bridge. There's an entrance on this side somewhere. Do you know it?"

"Yes. Go. We will follow." Nessus called out to the others. "Brothers! We have slain the enemy, but more still come! My sword is not yet bloody enough! Who is with me?"

Cheers. The centaurs ascended the boulders upstream. Apparently, flat ground really wasn't required. These guys weren't just half-man, half-horse. They were more like half-man, half-Billy-goat. They climbed quickly.

"Come on Caesar." Dani launched into the sky.

Beside her, her friend cooed, *"Mmmhmmm... Can my man fight or what?"*

Dani landed on the cobblestones of the Citadel streets. Her muscles ached from near-exhaustion, but she took off at a run, Caesar above her. She had to get back to the others.

The dark was afire in an orange radiance. From the Keep, Fyreballs lanced outward across the Vale from defenders. Arrows, ballistae, and other projectiles followed. The acrid smell of smoke and brimstone filled her nostrils as she descended the slope to a line of defenders. Among them, Asaph shouted orders.

"Novice!" he yelled. "What are you doing here?"

"Elder Asaph, the centaurs are coming. I ran ahead to see what I can do."

"Do?" he shouted. "The enemy is within our walls. And don't think for one second that you and your companions have escaped my suspicion for this. First Novices, now demons circumvent our defenses. Mark my words this is not the end."

Fine, whatever, she thought. They had bigger problems. "In the meantime, what do we do to stop them?"

"Our defensive line is here. We are within range of the Keep. We must hold them here to secure the time necessary to bolster the defenses of the Keep."

"Where are the others?"

"Others?"

She looked around. Ethan, Dink, Bouden; none of them were there. "Where is everyone from across the Vale?"

Asaph looked to the bridge. There were dozens of Numen and demons fighting along the walkway. Dani's horror dawned on her.

"We need to help them." She said.

"And if we do, we give the advantage to the demons. Here we are strongest where they cannot bring their numbers to bear."

"Those are my friends! We have to help them!"

"And we'll die if do."

"Well screw this then!" Dani stormed off.

"Novice Daniella! Get back here!"

But she wasn't listening. Sword drawn, she hurried across. Dozens of bodies and piles of ash littered the ground. Mangled corpses, half-dead defenders; the bridge was thick with bodies, mostly Powers and Gatekeepers unlucky enough to be here when the fighting started. As Dani moved towards the thick of it, the bodies of black-clad Guardians and brown-clothed Novices began to appear. She tried not to see if it was anyone she knew.

As she ran, she looked out over the Vale. A large group of demons scaled the cliffs from the dark valley below. Above them, something dark flapping large bat wings led them over the rim. As she watched, by twos and threes, a large contingent of demons poured into the Citadel far from the Keep.

She couldn't deal with that now. The main fight was here. Wraiths and imps poured onto the Bridge, the last of the invaders. If she could, she tried to stop them before they could fully climb over, kicking some off the side to fall to their deaths below or cutting them down with her sword. In other spots, she attempted to help wounded escape or overpower demons who outmatched the defenders, trying to turn the tide in the Numen's favor.

She wasn't paying attention, battling an imp back over the side, and didn't see one behind her. It raised its dark mace, but an arrow shot by Dani's ear and struck it through the neck, forcing it off and into the abyss.

Dink notched another arrow and screamed, "Dani! Duck!"

She did and he fired, striking an second demon in the chest behind her. Dani stabbed back into its heart, killing it. She ran for where Dink and Bouden knelt.

"You guys okay?" she asked, the three of them hunkering to one side. "Where are Mastema and Ethan?"

"Farther back!" Bouden pointed. "They told us to make for the Citadel."

"Good idea. Go! I'll get them!"

They reluctantly left, fighting through the ash and soot that clogged the air, creating a haze across the Bridge.

Next, Dani found a single Gatekeeper, armed with a spear, fending off two wraiths prowling around him like wolves on the hunt. His back was to the edge. Dani recognized him; the same Gatekeeper who attacked her in her house. She wanted to leave him to get eaten.

Wanted to, but couldn't.

With the wraiths distracted, Dani ran in. Sword swung in a wide arch, she sliced open the back of the nearest wraith and spilled black blood from its torn skin. It howled, turning to swipe at her with claws. She dodged back, striking down hard and cutting into its shoulder. Dani kept hacking until it went down.

Unfortunately, the other decided she was a better target than the Gatekeeper and tackled Dani, biting into her shoulder. Her Arachne-weave held up, but pain shot up her arm. Pointyend dropped from her hand and the blade faded.

An adamantine speartip lanced through its shoulder and yanked up. The demon screamed. Behind it, the Gatekeeper skewered the creature sideways, using the tip to pull it off.

With a snap, the spear broke. The wraith turned on the Earthborn and attacked, gnawing into his neck and throwing them back against the ledge of the bridge. Dani watched in horror as thick red blood splattered from the neck of the screaming man.

She grabbed for her dagger, but her left arm wasn't working very well. She could barely stand. Her eyes locked with the Gatekeeper as she feebly tried to rise, but her knees gave way. She couldn't help him.

As if he knew, the man wrapped his arms around the creature. With no weapon and no way to fight it off, he pulled back with all his might and screamed one last time. Together, he and the beast pitched over the side of the bridge and out of sight. He was gone.

In pain, bleeding slightly under her armor, Dani stumbled to the edge. A wave of nausea hit her, crippling her to her knees again. She grabbed for her sword but couldn't lift it.

An imp howled, seeing her and stalking towards her with a stygian axe. He rose to strike, but the demon only got that far. A single stroke hacked it in half through the back of the head and it dissolved. Behind it, Mastema landed. He flicked his blade to clean ash and blood off.

"Rise, Daniella. Death is not something to wait for, but rush towards."

"You sound," she swallowed hard, "like a demented fortune cookie."

"You have said that before. It was not funny then. It is not funny now." He offered a hand and helped her up. "By the by, I believe you wanted my sayings on bumper stickers and T-shirts."

"Is that a joke?"

"Battle is the only appropriate venue for humor."

Ethan appeared, large sword in hand. "We're pulling back. Most of them are on the Bridge. We need to go." He saw Dani and ran to her side. "You're hurt!"

A sound turned them back across the bridge. A wave of demons, like the sea over the beach, churned over the remaining Numen defenders.

"Go!" Ethan told them. "Get her and anyone you can to safety! I'll be right behind you."

Mastema pulled her against him. "Come, we must away!"

The two of them launched towards the Citadel. Around them, the remaining defenders fell under the demons. There was nothing they could do and Dani turned her head away. She didn't want to see.

But something she did see. Ethan raised his sword in both hands, pressing the blade flat against his forehead in meditation. Overhead, thick black clouds rumbled and crackled with thunder. The wind picked up. In a blinding flash, a streak of lightning snapped from the heavens. Ethan extended his sword, taking it across the blade and slicing outward. The fork of energy exploded towards the advancing wall of monsters. The electricity lanced through them, destroying the first ones and halting their advance.

Anyone behind Ethan who could run, did. When the flash dissipated, Ethan himself took off. Nothing more could be done.

Stormthrower. Dani understood now.

They landed before Asaph, who marshalled the remaining defenders. They were the last line before the Citadel.

"Elder," Ethan bowed, "we are the last across."

He nodded stiffly. "Understood, Guardian. You fought well. Take your people to the Keep. It is secure."

"Wait!" Dani yelled weakly. "The demon…" she was fading fast. "They're inside. They climbed the cliffs. They used the attack to get into the Citadel."

The Elder scowled. Already, his last stand was compromised. He drew his scimitar. "We must warn the Keep."

"Let me guess," Dani paled, trying not to vomit, "you volunteer?"

"No. My place is here. I will not abandon my post or my men. I would die first." And he meant it. Dani could see it in his eyes. At least that she could respect. "You must go. Take the wounded into the Keep, bar the doors and warn the rest of the Council."

"What about you?" she asked. "They could be coming up behind you."

"Fortune will either smile upon us or bless us with death." Asaph told her. "Either way, we come to meet it. Get to the Keep. Warn the Elder Council. Find the demon and destroy it."

She could hear the howls of the demons approaching across the Vale. By the sound of it, there were many.

"You'll need help here." She said.

"Your duty here is done, Novice. Follow my orders."

"I've never been good at following orders."

"That has not gone unnoticed." Then Asaph placed two fingers to his forehead and bowed towards her. "But there is little else you can do. Follow these orders as I give them for once: go to the Citadel, warn the Council and slay the creature."

Dani could barely believe his gesture of respect, but she returned it, knowing what it meant. If Asaph died, this would be their last encounter. If he lived, she would never get that kind of respect again.

So she left. She followed orders for once.

Chapter Forty-Five

The Keep's doors were shutting when the last wave of refugee Novices and wounded arrived. The Gatekeepers ushered them into the Throne Room, which was filled with similar refugees.

Rows upon rows of wounded laid about the Throne Room like a field hospital from Hell. Healers tended to the injured, while gifted aided as volunteers. Dani laid next to the mirror pool, her reflection looking far worse than she expected; pale and sickly, and covered in dead-demon ash. Mastema retrieved panacea, pouring it onto her wound and forcing her to drink it.

Elder Jeduthun arrived. "What happened? How did these demonic insurgents get in?"

Ethan sighed. "Elder, please, if we thought for one minute this would happen—."

"Then obviously, you thought wrong." He raged furiously. "By what avenue did they enter?"

"The river, sir." Dani spoke up, feeling better with the panacea coursing through her. "There's a portal—a ladder—leading to the Hellfire Club. We didn't think any demons could get through." She burned with shame. "We thought wrong."

The look of contempt on Jeduthun's face was enough to make her avoid his gaze. Looking at herself in the pool, she felt more like she deserved what had happened to her. It was partly her fault. They didn't tell anyone. Now people were dying.

"I see." Jeduthun scowled. "This is not the first ladder. Numen of many generations have used such things. But after this attack, I'm sure you're aware of the gravity of not informing us."

But it wasn't just anger on his face. It was his own shame. He skipped over talking about it when Nathaniel was poisoned. She noticed the frowning at the edges of his mouth. It took her a second to notice the guilt.

He knew Judah. He knew what kind of place Judah ran. It wasn't far-fetched to think he knew of a way to the Hellfire Club. Which meant the guilt was his. He let this happen, too.

"We must continue to help the wounded." He said bitterly.

"Elder, there is more." Ethan spoke up. "The demon that leads them, the one who attacked Nathaniel and killed Titus, is here in the Citadel. It got past our defenses."

Jeduthun cursed. Dani asked, "Is everyone accounted for?"

"There are dozens missing. There is no way to tell. That doesn't even include the centaur Hellions or Lady Alecto."

"The centaurs have been called." Dani reassured him. "But I haven't seen Lady Alecto. Is she staying in the Keep?"

"Her quarters are nearby in the Citadel. I will dispatch someone to her. In the meantime, we must deal with this threat. There are many likely places it could attack. I'll send soldiers to the most probable sites, but any force will be substantially small."

"We can help." Ethan said. "There are a few of us unhurt. We can help."

"I cannot ask that of you."

"You are not asking."

Jeduthun didn't waste time arguing. "We do not have anyone protecting the Fane."

"Why the Fane?" Dani asked.

"It is the center of our reverence." Jeduthun told her. "If the enemy wishes to strike a moral blow, it could be there. There is a side exit from the Keep. Daniella's Guardian, Mastema, should know the way."

"I'll take as many as I can." Ethan promised.

"Thank you. I will inform the other Elders. We need to secure this Keep." Jeduthun left.

"I'm coming." Dani stood shakily.

"No, you are still weak." Mastema told her. "The panacea is working, but you are not ready to fight."

"Oh screw you!" Dani shot back. "I'm not letting my friends die while I sit around and wait. Let me help."

They didn't want her to go, but like smart boys, they knew better than to argue. "Fine. But you protect yourself. No more heroics."

"How about heroine-ics?"

"Don't get snippy."

"Well, if she's going, then I am." Dink said.

Bouden chimed in. "Me too."

"Me three."

Nathaniel appeared, newly dressed in his raiments and carrying his axe. He looked much better than when Dani last saw him, but like her, he wasn't one hundred percent yet.

Mastema shook his head. "We should attempt to recruit more than the sick and the wounded. I do not plan on dying this evening."

They took three Powers and two Gatekeepers out the side entrance with them. Dink armed up with more arrows and Mastema forced Dani to take another dose of panacea. The alchemists worried about taking too much, as there would be side effects, but considering where she was going, she didn't. Sneezing, running nose, watery eyes; who had time to worry about that now?

The Fane wasn't far. They moved through the empty Gardens; no sign of demons here yet. The elementals that usually dwelled here were missing. The sounds of battle in the distance weren't encouraging, either. They slipped inside the Fane. The many lanterns cast an eerie glow similar to the fires outside stoked by the demonic. Dani didn't like that kind of foreboding.

"Stagger out!" Ethan ordered, taking charge. "Dink, Bouden and the archers take position up top near the shrine. Dani, Nathaniel, I want you both nearby to protect them. And don't question." He pointed specifically at Dani. He was keeping her back and she knew it. "Everyone else form a semi-circle near the door. Engage as necessary. We hold here until they come or until the Keep signals the all clear."

Everyone moved to their assigned positions. Nathaniel smiled genially. "You look like hell."

"Speak for yourself. What the hell are you doing here?"

"I'm not staying inside when everyone I care about is outside."

"Me neither."

"Glad we feel the same way." Dani blushed and he added. "Not that you feel the same way. I know you don't. That's not what I meant. What I meant was that we feel the same way about other people. People other than us, I mean. Friends, really. I—" he paused, embarrassed. After all the things that had happened, it was still high-school-crush awkward. "How long before this isn't weird anymore?"

"Well, if we survive this, we have a really long lifespan. So, conservatively? Let's call it a century."

"Awesome."

"Shut up, Nate."

He smiled.

They stationed on the ramp to the shrine, facing towards the entrance. The Gardens were quiet and dark. Moonlight filtered down, casting the whole orchard in eerie blues, blacks and greys. Dani tensed, her shoulder aching. Behind her, the three archers readied their bows. Ethan stood alone, he and the other soldiers fanning out at the bottom.

She smelled them first. Brimstone was easily recognizable now. Just at the edge of earshot, she heard them. Rustling bushes, low growls. She drew her sword, allowing it to glow to life with her fear and determination. Nathaniel's adamantine buckler expanded into a full, round shield. Ethan drew his longsword. He placed the tip down onto the floor of the Fane, the grip and hilt a T in front of him.

It landed just outside the sanctuary, cracking the stone beneath its clawed feet. Large, leathery wings flapped in the darkness. The terrifying, nightmare creature hissed, drawing a flail and stygian sword, scraping its talons menacingly.

The two groups faced one another. Then it howled to the darkness.

Its fellow demons stampeded from the gloom and poured into the shrine.

They rushed in; clawing up the sides and leaping while others scurried straight at them. Dink and Bouden fired into the crowd. The demons collided with the front ranks of defenders.

Ethan moved in one fluid motion. His foot shot forward, kicking the blade up off the ground with one slap to start his swing. His first strike was upwards, connecting with the first wraith; the strike so hard it pin-wheeled its upper body back over its own feet. He stabbed down through and killed it. He kept moving, using large, broad strokes to fend off the approaching imps, parrying their black swords as they folded around him. He turned, swiping left and right to back them away while standing back-to-back with Mastema, guarding one another.

The first one to break through, a snaggle-toothed imp, scrambled up the ramp towards them. It swung a large mace at Dani. She ducked. Its swing came around at Nathaniel, who took the blow across his shield and hacked into the back of its shoulder. The demon howled and swung at him again.

An arrow shaft lanced through its shoulder. Dink notched a second arrow and fired again. This time, the bolt smashed through its forehead and it fell. Dink smirked.

But very quickly, superior numbers pushed the defenders back. Two Numen fell screaming under the monstrous wave. A Gatekeeper armed with a spear and shield attacked the leading beast. The winged demon swiped with the flail. Burning tongs lashed away his shield. He stabbed, nearly impaling it before it leapt into the air. Talons slashed across his back and knocked him to the ground. Deftly, the thing spun, bringing the point of its black blade around through the Gatekeeper's back, killing him.

It lashed out with the flail again, hurtling burning gouts of fire at the archers. Dink and Bouden howled as embers sizzled past them. Another archer took the coal to the throat, clutching his neck and falling for good.

"Dink!"

They moved in front of Dink as the creature leapt over the fighting. It's whip cracked again, throwing more fire into the crowd, even wounding some of its own, but it landed before Dani and Nathaniel.

"Round two, harpy." Nathaniel raised his shield and axe.

The demon's mottled, putrid lips curled with a hiss. Flicking its sword to clean off the dripping blood, it ascended the ramp toward them.

Nathaniel attacked from the right, Dani from the left. It blocked and parried his axe, then Dani's empyreal sword. The flail shot out, whipping at her face but she dropped to avoid the sharp spine-tips. She rolled and cut at the wing, but missed. The creature turned, shooting out the opposite wing and striking Nathaniel hard enough to toss him into Bouden a few feet away.

The demon raised the whip to strike but Dani sliced out with her sword, cutting the tongs from the end. It attacked with its other weapon, the glowing and black steels colliding hard enough to shake Dani's bones. But she held her ground.

Bouden drew a short, single-edged straightsword and attacked. He leapt, flying towards it but the demon's wing lashed out again and struck him mid-air. It threw him aside into the lanterns, which shattered harshly under him, eventually rolling a stop and not moving.

Dani screamed, attacking again and again with her blade, fending off one blow and then another. They fought uphill, but the creature was faster and more skilled. She was tired. Her arm ached. She wouldn't last.

She spotted Nathaniel getting up. If she could survive long enough, they could gang up on it.

Unfortunately, her momentary loss of concentration cost her. One bat wing lashed around and tripped her foot. Off balance, the demon kicked her and she fell, weapon falling out of her hand.

"NO!" Nathaniel launched over the lanterns towards them, but stupidly he announced his attack. The demon spun and caught him by the front of his tunic, easily flinging him to the ground hard enough to knock him unconscious.

Dani tried to get back up but a filthy, clawed foot pinned her back down. The smile on its face oozed joy and pus.

"Go to hell." Dani snarled.

Its eerily feminine voice growled back, "From there."

The creature raised its sword, but an arrow bolted through its forearm from behind. The demon howled, turning to find Dink at the foot of Gabriel's statue, wounded but on his feet.

He notched another arrow and fired, missing the head and notching another. "Don't touch her, freak!"

Dink fired once more but the thing dodged. As it turned, its wing whipped Dani across the temple, smacking her head into the stone walkway. Her vision swam. Then it stalked towards Dink.

He fired one arrow after another. The creature dodged or blocked every one. It made its way calmly towards him, growling happily in its throat. Dink reached for another arrow, but they were gone. He dropped his bow and drew his short sword, standing his ground.

Dink struck, trying to decapitate it. The demon blocked and batted away his blade. In one backhanded stroke, it sliced open his chest from collarbone to ribs, then ran him through.

Dani screamed. Vaguely she wondered why her hands weren't burning.

Dink sputtered. His knees gave way, the sword in his chest the only thing keeping him up. The demon pushed the blade in to the hilt and twisted cruelly. He shuddered and the beast cackled joyously, yanking it from his body.

Dink dropped back with a splash into the pool around the statue's feet.

"No!" Dani tried to get up. "No! No! No!"

The demon turned, smiling. Dani snatched up her sword with a blaze of light, limping after it. It wasn't fear fueling her anymore. It was anger. She charged; no tact, no plan. Just screaming in rage.

A wing struck her in the chin. It was too fast to block. Dani tumbled back down the ramp into Nathaniel's unconscious body.

The demon launched into the air, up over the statue. It hovered for a second, wings wide, before dropping onto the head. The shrine of Gabriel shattered, raining stone and dust and debris down around it. Dani shielded her eyes.

Around her, screams and the sounds of battle mixed with the haze of stone-dust. Something shot past her, retreating. Dani drew her dagger, but it was gone. The beast darted from the dust, over the tops of the defenders and into the night air.

"Nathaniel?" she shook his unconscious form. "Nathaniel?"

Bouden pulled himself up from the lanterns, painfully crawling over to them. "Is he alive?"

Nathaniel groaned, coming awake.

"Yes." She breathed, relieved, but dread washed over her. She staggered through the haze towards the rubble of the statue. "No! No! No!"

Her feet splashed into the pool, and then into Dink's body. Dani fell to her knees. Dink lay with his head against what remained of the feet of Gabriel.

"No! Please, God, no!"

But she knew. She knew when she saw his open eyes. She knew when she touched his still-warm, unmoving cheek. She knew when she knelt down next to him.

Dink was dead.

Tears blurred her vision until she couldn't see his face. She cradled his head in her arms; sobbing, shaking, screaming.

"No!" she moaned wretchedly. "Dink! Dink please! Wake up! Wake up!"

A voice behind her, softer than she'd ever heard, spoke. "Daniella." Hands fell on her shoulders, around her arms. "Daniella. Come away."

"Get away from me!"

"Come away." Mastema whispered. "There is nothing more that can be done."

She allowed herself to let Dink go, leaving him in the tranquil pool where he fell; where he saved her. She cried even as she heard Dink's voice in her memory.

I just wanted you to know how sorry I am, he said after their first lesson in the Vale. *If I could take it back, if I could make it up to you, if I could somehow repay you, I would. I'd do it in a heartbeat. I'd do anything to redeem myself for what I did. I want you to know that.*

She collapsed with grief. Around her, Nathaniel and Bouden were crying as well. Those who survived stood in reverent vigil.

Mastema whispered. "We must go."

"I can't..." she sobbed miserably. "I can't leave him..."

"Daniella, we must. The demon fled, but it took someone. We need to alert the guards before it can flee the city."

She tried to swallow her grief, shaking him off. "Wha—What are you talking about?"

When she looked up into her Guardian's eyes, she saw something much worse than grief. She saw fear. Mastema never showed fear.

"Dani, the creature took Ethan."

Chapter Forty-Six

The Throne Room was chaos. Healers and volunteers ran from one wounded Numen to another. The massive glass pool washed out the bloody bandages.

The main doors were open. The battle for the bridge was over. Asaph shouted orders to bring more injured inside, even though black and red blood smeared across his armor and one arm dangled against his side. Among the ones brought in, Dani saw centaurs. Wounded and unwounded, they arrived in time to help the Numen. She spotted Nessus with Caesar perched on his shoulder and she ran to them.

"*Dani!*" Caesar swooped down and nuzzled her friend. "*You're alive! Thank God!*"

"What happened?"

"The demons are defeated." Nessus told her, his sword caked in ash and black blood. "Their ranks broke upon our arrival. Their lives were as meaningless as their deaths."

"It wasn't meaningless. They attacked the Citadel. Oh God—!" she forgot about Ethan.

But Mastema hadn't. Behind her, Elder Asaph shouted over the din of soldiers, "Search party! I need volunteers!" the voices began to quiet. "The filth that led the attack has fled with one of ours! I need volunteers to scour the city! Secure the gates immediately!"

Hands went up. Groups quickly organized.

"*Who's missing?*" Caesar asked.

"Ethan."

"*Oh, Dani!*"

"We just need to find him. He's alive. That thing won't kill him. It took him for a reason."

Her friend exchanged glances with Nessus in a very human-like way. It didn't take a genius to figure out they didn't believe her.

"He's alive. I know it." She insisted. "I have to go."

"*Dani, your arm is hurt badly.*"

"I have to go. I'm glad you're both okay." She left as quickly as she could. She didn't like what Caesar implied. Getting away from her was the only way she could not think about it.

Asaph put men into groups and assigned them parts of the city when she got to him. "I wish to volunteer."

"You may not."

"Ethan is my friend. I want to help."

"On orders of your Guardian you are not." He told her. "You are wounded and in need of treatment."

"So are you."

"For which I am sorely being ordered to stay as well." He scowled. "The monster attacked our city. It does us no service if we die of blood loss while searching for the Guardian. I dispatched as many as I can. The gates are sealed. It cannot escape, even by the way it gained admission. We will find it. We will kill it. If Guardian Ethan is alive, we will find him." He faced her sternly. "You did well today, Novice. The reinforcement by the centaurs turned the tide of the battle. But now, you must rest and heal."

Dani hated it, but she could barely lift her arm. The fight in the Fane drained any use out of it. She shook her head miserably. "The centaurs were Ethan's idea. I didn't do well today. He did. If we don't find him, then there's no point in winning."

"Then I suggest you rely on your brethren to do their job." The battle-hardened Elder sighed regretfully. "Novice, the most difficult part of this life is learning when to do something, and when to wait. I will inform you when we find him."

Asaph left. He wasn't the warm and cuddly type, but at least he wasn't actively looking to have her killed. Bonus points for progress.

A healer sat her by the pool and used salves to treat her maimed shoulder. It stung horribly. In addition to her shoulder, she had claw marks across her chest. The healer was also concerned about a concussion from her smack to the head.

But she was alive. The same couldn't be said for Dink or dozens.

Grief came back like a familiar song. Tears seeped from her eyes, seeing Dink's lifeless face in the pool of the Fane. She replayed the scene over and over in her head, trying to imagine what she could have done differently. She could have gone for her sword again, tried to take the thing down from behind, or used that power in her hands. Why hadn't she?

Even now her hands burned, but not in the way she had needed. She squeezed them so tight it hurt, shaking with anguish. She felt like she would explode.

"It is understandable." said a voice.

She looked up. Dani could barely see Alecto through the tears. She wiped them away. "What?"

"You lost a friend." The gentle Fury knelt before her, her wings folding around them both in a comforting embrace. She took Dani's hands. The warmth faded the moment she touched her skin. "When someone dies, mourning is understandable. And so is anger."

"You know about Dink?"

"I heard." Alecto comforted her, running a hand down her face. "Dani, anger is natural. To lose someone, to mourn, will always cause anger. Do not fight it. Embrace it."

Dani sniffed, wiping her eyes again.

"I have seen many die in battle. Some were friends. Some were family. You cannot allow yourself to lose your resolve. You must be strong."

"How?"

"Use it." The leader of the Hellions told her. "Use that anger. Allow it to fill you. Unleash it on the world and make no excuses for it." She squeezed her hands. "I am the Erinys of Unceasing Anger. I understand rage. And I understand its power."

"The thing that killed him is gone. I won't get revenge."

"You will." Alecto promised. "And in this battle, there is more blame than just with the beast that attacked this city." Her eyes wandered to Heman and a few other Elders. "Do not allow them to break you. You are stronger than they."

"It's not just Dink." Dani shook her head miserably. "Ethan is missing. That thing, whatever it was, took him. I don't know why."

"Ethan? The Guardian you spoke of? I understand he is a friend, but why would his abduction hurt you so...?" she trailed off, seeing Dani's expression. "Oh. I see."

"It's not like that."

"Of course it is. The heart has a will of its own. Numen pretend to not feel as humans, but they do. They pretend not to love, but they do. They pretend that death does not bother them, but it does." She stroked Dani's cheek. Alecto was so nice, so motherly in a way she hadn't expected. Dani was grateful for her presence. The Hellion leader tipped her chin up. "Dani, you are strong. Use your grief. Let it fuel you. Turn it to anger and fight back. This attack is only some of what is to come. Darkness is rising. You must be ready."

Dani looked up into her eyes. A fire burned there, probably hotter than the fires of Hell. It was the face of a warrior. Dani needed that kind of strength.

"I must go." Alecto told her. "My contingent of Hellions and I must return from whence we came. If an attack occurred here, there is no telling what might happen in Dis or Asphodel. I must depart for my home." She stood, still holding Dani's hands and helping her up. "Until we meet again, Novice Dani."

"Until then, Lady Alecto."

The Fury departed with the centaurs in tow. Nessus said something to Caesar before leaving, and then he too joined the departing group. Her friend flew to her side.

"How are you doing?" Caesar asked softly, landing next to her.

"I'll heal."

"That's not what I meant."

Dani shook her head. "I just want them to find him."

"They will. I promise."

Dani tried hard to believe that.

They didn't find him. By morning the patrols returned from every part of Empyrean. The demon fled and somehow took Ethan with it. Every demon was destroyed, but the damage was done. Sixty-three Numen were dead; twenty-five gifted as well. Over a hundred were wounded, and five were missing.

Dani tried not to listen when other Numen said that missing were usually assumed dead.

They moved the bodies to another part of the Citadel; Dink among them. So was Lorcan, Bouden's Guardian and a man named Amadeus, the Gatekeeper who saved Dani and fell from the bridge. Then there was Chase, the Novice that led her into a trap in the Vale. She didn't give a crap about him.

Dani went once to see them, collected into rows of white-shrouded bodies to prepare for burial. Numen, gifted, even two Elders; there were so many.

Bouden was a wreck. He and Dink had become pretty close friends. His best friend and Guardian lost in one night. Nathaniel was with him, comforting him, but even Dani knew he wouldn't be okay. It would be awhile before anyone was.

For the most part, everyone was left to recover. A lot of gifted homes were destroyed. The last vestiges of demon blood were cleaned from the Vale Bridge and washed downriver by the Crystalline, as if purging Empyrean of the evil that came here. The Elders would call a convocation once decisions were made about how to proceed.

Over the next two days, people visited. Roxelana was a wreck after Korë. She and Dani spent time by her fountain next to Dani's house. They just talked, both worrying and both so horrified by what had happened.

Kleos came to the Arn as well. Mastema had just left on an errand. "How are you?" He asked, sitting in the open air pavilion. The skies of Empyrean were clear blue. Sylphs once again danced on the air.

"I'll be better when they find Ethan."

He pursed his lips.

"Don't do that." She warned. "They'll find him."

"Dani, the chances are very slim." Kleos cautioned. "Demons do not hold prisoners long and when they do, you do not want them to. The things they do are horrendous."

"I don't want to think about that." She trailed her fingers across the floor panels just so she had something to look at besides him. "I know he's alive."

"The Council convenes tomorrow. Funeral rites will be done for everyone; gifted included. All of Empyrean will participate."

"Good. Dink and Korë deserve that."

"It is not just they to be buried. Ethan will be as well."

"Ethan hasn't been found yet! They haven't sent scouts to Earth to find that thing!"

"Dani, I told you—."

"Don't tell me jack!" she stood. "Those *pendejos* just decide he's dead? Why aren't they looking for him?"

"The manpower it would take could cost more lives. The attack has seriously shaken the Council."

"So they leave him to rot?"

"Dani," he tried to be reasonable, "he is most likely dead. And if he isn't, he will be soon."

"Well that's crap!" she screamed. Her scream reverberated off the sunny hills around her village. She took a moment to compose herself. "I'm sorry."

"You don't need to be." he told her. "Ethan was a friend. He saved a lot of lives. And it was our fault this happened. We all kept quiet about the ladder. We are all to blame. I don't even know how it was able to use it."

"Of course we know! Everyone knows!" Dani shouted, and then quickly quieted herself again. "Sorry...again. What I meant was we do know: someone opened it for them. Someone on the inside opened the ladder; someone working for the demons."

"But who? Demons are monsters. No one would work for them."

"Maybe they got to someone."

The Guardian shook his head. "Even if that were possible, demons kill on sight. None of them would try to talk to one of us, or a gifted, much less one of us try to bargain with them."

"You don't know that."

"I do." He said darkly. "I've been fighting them for centuries. They're killing machines born out of fire and darkness and created for one purpose: killing. They don't plan like that."

"They sure as hell did two nights ago. We should tell the Council what we suspect."

"No, we shouldn't."

"Why? I'm sure I'm not the only one to think of this."

"You're right. So drop it."

The sudden harsh tone took Dani aback. Kleos was always so even-keeled. Why suddenly so confrontational? "What's going on?"

Kleos sighed, shaking his head. "Dani, of course the Council thought someone inside Empyrean allowed them in, even if the idea is ludicrous. Once they discovered the ladder, it was the natural first suspicion. They began to question Numen and gifted about it. If you go to the Council, only one name will come to mind for them."

"Who? Me?"

"No. Mastema."

"Mastema? Why?"

"Think about it: he came back without his charge years ago, leading to his disgrace. He broke the Guardian cardinal rule. He was the only witness to what happened that night. And Mastema is a well-known fighter. He would never have allowed his charge to die, yet he came back without one. So what do you think the Council will surmise when his newest charge comes to them asking about an inside man?" he didn't wait for her to answer. "They will question whether you, his closest confidant, saw him that night."

"But I didn't."

"Exactly. Wherever a charge goes, the Guardian goes. So why wasn't he with you?"

She knew, without having to ask, that Mastema was not the person who opened that portal for the demons. No way.

"You don't believe he had something to do with this, do you?"

"Of course not." Kleos said. "I've known Mastema for lifetimes."

Dani couldn't believe it. She stood, stalking off.

Kleos asked. "Where are you going?"

"To get answers."

"You cannot talk to the Council!"

"I'm not."

"Then where?"

"The same place I got the idea that someone is working for demons."

He followed. "I'll go with you."

"No. I need to go alone."

"Why?"

"Because I'm not sure he'll talk to me if you're there."

Dani flew the first half of the journey towards the Dalles, but then landed as her power faded in the magical mist. She trekked on foot up to the falls, then down behind them into the cave.

"Gabriel!" she called out. "Gabriel! It's me! Dani! We need to talk!"

She didn't know if the Archangel would still be here. Why would he? But he was able to sense evil in the city. Maybe he could give her further clues. Maybe he could tell her if Ethan was alive.

"Gabriel! Archangel! Angel of Truth! Trumpeter of Judgment! Show yourself!" Still nothing. She stomped her foot. "You arrogant, self-centered child! I need your help! If you actually care about fixing your mess, then show yourself!"

"You come more a warrior than before." She heard his voice behind her. "And you wear anger like armor."

Gabriel formed inside the falls, muddled by the rushing water. He descended, the water creating wings around him as parted from it and touched down on the stones. The water wings, glistening and shining, gushed around him like feathers, extending outward in a glorious display before dissolving.

He wore an ancient tunic with no sleeves and belt at the waist. His skin and eyes glowed. He seemed more an angel now; terrifying, more than the man-child who attacked her.

"You have changed, Daniella."

"No I haven't."

"You hold more resolve within you. I can feel it."

"Almost dying will do that to you."

"What do you wish to speak to me in regards?" He asked. "Your destiny?"

"Screw that. A demon attacked Empyrean. Did you know?"

"I felt them, yes." His eyes narrowed. "But I sense that that is not why you are here."

"It killed a lot of people and it took a friend of mine. Ethan. I need help to find him. You were able to sense evil in the city before. Could you find him?"

"Of that I am not sure." Gabriel said. "Many angels hear prayer, but with so many, we cannot always find one particular person unless they pray directly to us."

"Can you try?"

He nodded. He closed his eyes briefly, as if waiting a second, and then opened them. "I do not feel his prayer."

"That was, like, five seconds."

"My kind could once cross the universe in less than a blink of an eye. We are not what we once were, but we are not powerless. I do not feel him."

"Then he's dead?" her heart twisted.

"No. I have not felt the death of the person you speak. I simply cannot find him."

She felt relieved, but at the same time, frustrated. She was no closer to finding Ethan this way. "What about the person in the city who helped the demons get inside? You sensed evil. Can you tell me who that might be?"

"Again, no. I only can sense ill intentions, not the person who holds them."

She was getting less and less impressed by angels. "Then I wasted my time."

"Do you know the demon that attacked you?"

She shook her head. "No. It was some creature with wings, black skin and red eyes. Do you know it?"

"No, though demons come in many forms and have many offspring. Did it carry weapons or was it more of a beast?"

"Weapons. It used a flail, a sword and a cup."

"A cup?"

"A goblet or chalice or something. The Elders called it a 'dark grail.' It poisoned a friend of mine and turned him into an angry killing machine. He tried to kill me. "

"A goblet? Truly?"

"Do you know it?"

"Yes. It is a cup of poison, meant to torture victims with their worst desires and turn them upon themselves and their closest friends."

"Do you know a demon that might use it?"

"It was used in ancient times, but not by demons."

That piqued her interest. "Not by demons? Then by who?"

"Well," Gabriel thought, "if I remember correctly, it was once carried by the Erinyes."

Dani felt a shiver of cold dread creep up her spine. "Erinyes?"

"Yes." The Archangel said, nodding. "I believe we called them the Furies, leaders of the City of Dis."

Chapter Forty-Seven

"Alecto is the demon?" Nathaniel couldn't wrap his head around it. "But that thing looked nothing like her."

They were in the Arn. Nathaniel and Bouden were there when she returned from the Dalles, only to find her retrieving her weapons.

"Dani, slow down." Bouden cautioned. "How do you know Alecto is that thing?"

"I just do, okay? Trust me on this." She didn't tell them about Gabriel. It was too bizarre and they wouldn't believe her. *Oh don't worry, my source is an ancient archangel. What? You want me to wear a strait jacket? Sure! Crazy white is totally my color!* She needed proof.

Nathaniel shook his head, "But it doesn't make sense. How can Alecto be our inside man—er, person?"

"Think about it!" She belted on her sword. "That thing knew how to get into Empyrean. It knew about the ladder to Judah's club. It also knew how to attack us so it could sneak past our defenses <u>and</u> it knew how to sneak out. Only someone from here could know all of that."

"But how did it," he bit back his contempt, "how did she get Ethan out of the city?"

"Since no one suspected her, no one thought to look at her. There are a million ways she could have taken him."

"But it looked nothing like her." Nathaniel repeated.

"Then she can transform! She's a Fury! There's no telling what she can do!" She slid her dagger on in its sheath across the small of her back, then retrieved her gauntlets and greaves before heading out into the square to join them.

Bouden was the first to ask the question even she didn't want to answer. "Dani, I get you trust this person who told you this, but do you really believe Alecto is the one responsible?"

It was difficult to answer. The winged woman, who comforted her after Dink's death, just didn't seem to match the monster that led took Dink's life.

But she's not a woman, she reminded herself. *At least, she's not a human woman.* Dani knew very little about the Erinyes. There was no telling what they were capable of or why.

She shook her head. "Honestly? No. But I don't doubt my source."

"So where are you going?" Nathaniel asked. "Even if it's all true and she's the demon, there's still something we don't know: why the hell would she come to Empyrean? She could kill more Numen in so many different ways. Hell, she has already! Why risk fighting us on our home turf? All the demons did was attack and flee."

Another unanswerable question. She attacked, she killed, and then... It dawned on her. "And they attacked the Fane."

"So?"

"What did she do there?"

"She killed Dink."

"Right." Dani nodded. "And she destroyed the statue of Gabriel."

Smashed lanterns cleared away, blood washed off the stone; the Fane looked more like it used to, but the destroyed statue of Gabriel still lay in ruins with only its feet intact.

Elder Jeduthun oversaw the remaining clean up. When he noticed Dani's swords, his voice was as cynical as she ever heard him. "Novice Dani, to what do we owe the pleasure?"

"Why did you send us here?" she asked sharply.

"Pardon me?"

"Why did you send us to the Fane that night?" she asked. "The demon came here. Why? What is so important about the Fane?"

The question took him off guard. "It is the center of our worship to Gabriel, our founder. We told you this."

"But what else? That thing came here for a reason. Why?"

"I assumed it wished to hurt us where we feel most connected to our forbearers. This is the focus of our beliefs."

"There's no other reason?"

Confused, he shook his head. "No. From our inception, the Fane has stood as our bastion of faith. Every Numen learns to respect and protect it from evil. It is our holy place. Even the Song of Sacrifice speaks of it."

"It does?"

"Yes. The Song says that the Fane, a place of reverence, will be set aside in every city. We do not know why, but it was created by they who came before and we are beseeched to protect it."

Protect it. It was too much of a coincidence that Alecto came here. *That means there's something worth protecting.* Dani assumed, like everyone else, that the Fane was just a shrine, but looking at it now she couldn't help but notice other things: built into Empyrean's rocky crater, only one entrance and only able to be assaulted if an enemy came across open ground; it was the most fortified part of the city.

This wasn't just a shrine. It was a vault.

"Is there anything missing from the statue?" she asked, walking past him.

"Missing?"

"The statue was destroyed by the demon," she didn't want to say who she suspected the creature was, "but is there anything missing from what's left? Anything not destroyed?"

"We have not looked. Why would the demon take a part of a statue?"

"That's a good question."

Everyone searched. The sculpture was in a million pieces, both large and small. Some were the size of baseballs and some were the size of rice grains. It was the world's worst jigsaw puzzle. Dani sifted through the debris, examining what was left, but it was hard to recognize what part of Gabriel she was looking at, much less if anything was missing.

"Hmm." Bouden squatted next to a large piece of the face. He frowned, looking around. "Does anyone see part of the trumpet?"

"Trumpet?"

"Gabriel's Horn. It's sometimes called the Horn of Truth or the Trumpet of Judgment. Gabriel is always depicted carrying it."

They all looked. Nothing.

"I don't see it." Nathaniel said.

"Me neither." Dani sighed. "I never thought much about the horn. Why do you ask?"

"Gabriel is God's messenger and herald." Bouden told her. "It's said when the final battle for Earth commences, Gabriel's Horn will blow. It will 'reveal the truth and unbind the bound.'"

"And that means?"

"It frees those kept in confinement and loosens their bonds."

"It is a myth." Jeduthun told them. "Gabriel is depicted in iconography with a horn due to his role as herald. It is only a legend. Gabriel is gone, like all the angels."

But he's not, she knew.

Dani kept looking, but try as she might she couldn't find it. The trumpet was missing. "What if his horn was here?"

"Here?" Jeduthun shook his head. "You must be joking."

"Why? What if Gabriel, who built this city, hid his horn here? He left with the rest of the angels, so what if the reason the Fane exists is to contain something that actually belonged to Gabriel himself?"

"Then the angels would have left some allusion to it within the Song."

"But what if they didn't want us to know about it?"

"Why would they do that?"

Nathaniel picked up on Dani's line of thought. "What if the clues are there, but hidden in a language we can't understand? Maybe Gabriel didn't want his horn falling into the wrong hands and feared what would happen if Numen or demons used it. Then the best way to protect it would be to hide it somewhere safe, but secret. The Fane hides it in plain sight."

Dani's memory flashed back to her conversation with Gabriel in the cave: *It is where my heart, my truth, still lies. Within its walls lies something special to me. A symbol of who I was.* She assumed he was speaking metaphorically, but what if he wasn't?

...my truth, still lies. His Horn of Truth, the Trumpet of Judgment, was here. Or had been.

For the first time, Elder Jeduthun took the idea seriously. He looked horrified.

"What would demons want with it?" Nathaniel asked. "Bouden, what does it do?"

He shrugged. "I don't know. The horn is just supposed to reveal the truth and sound Judgment Day. That's it."

"That is not it." Jeduthun spoke softly. His face, characteristically closed and hard to read, now read only fear. "If what you suggest is true, then it is much graver."

Dani turned on him. "You know what this thing does?"

"As Novice Bouden told you, it loosens bonds, reveals the truth and unbinds those that were bound."

"And?"

"It would unbind anything the angels bound. Namely, it could undo the bindings that cast all demons into Hell."

The Elders gathered. Two seats remained empty for the those who perished in the attack. When Jeduthun told them what Dani suspected, the same fear was in their eyes. Everyone understood.

"This cannot be." Castus's voice threaded with terror. "How could a demon know the location of the Horn, but not this Council?"

The Elders looked to Dani who stood with everyone else. Kleos, Nathaniel, Bouden, and of course Mastema; everyone there to back her up.

"The demon isn't a demon. It's a Fury." She barely got through before they erupted into argument. "It's Lady Alecto. She led them inside."

"Impossible!" cried Elder Berith. "Lady Alecto is a servant of this Council. She would not side with demons!"

"It's true." Dani insisted. "The cup that poisoned Nathaniel was used by the Furies in ancient times. It is their weapon."

"Lies!" of course Elder Heman added his own two-cents worth, even if it was worthless. "We should expect these foul deceits from you! Lady Alecto is a fierce warrior. She holds the reverence of many. It is simple to see your jealousy."

"Jealousy? Are you serious?" But from the looks the Council gave her, they were.

"This Council sees your treachery," Heman declared, "and now you attempt to undermine one our greatest and most beloved supporters. Unlike you, Lady Alecto knows her place. She does not seek to encourage sedition and you wish to subvert her. I call on every honest man to stand with me against this treason."

Castus stood. "Elder Heman, you speak out of turn."

But where Heman backed down before, he didn't now. "No! We have lost many. Our borders were penetrated. The gifted question whether we can protect them. It did not happen until this," he angrily pointed at Dani, "was allowed to enter."

He pointed at Dani and Dani wanted to snap that finger off, but Mastema stepped forward before she had a chance. "That is a lie, Elder. How dare you level such an accusation without merit!"

No one was more shocked by Mastema speaking up for her than Heman. "I would expect such vileness from none other than a traitor, a failure and a coward! She corrupted you, Guardian Mastema. Her ilk spread vile lies. We broke our laws and moral code to allow her entry. Now we pay the price. I will not stand by and allow the punishment of God to rain upon us for turning away from Him."

Her eyes widened. "You think all of this is my fault? God's punishing you because of me? Are you high?"

Heman scowled. "What insult do you imply?"

"I'm sorry." She snarled sarcastically. "Allow me to speak your language: have you imbibed large amounts of cannabis to the point you no longer control your mental faculties, you dim-witted, moronic codpiece?"

"That is enough!" Castus roared, trying to bring them both under control and failing.

"No longer, Elder Castus." Heman wouldn't back down. "If you will not act, than I will. And I encourage all my fellow Elders to do the same. Gatekeepers!" the doors behind them swung open. A contingent marshalled in. "Arrest the Novice Daniella for subversion! Arrest her Guardian as well." He turned on Castus. "We will get to the bottom of this."

The Gatekeepers encircled Dani and the others. Castus looked at a loss. His power was gone. Heman was taking over.

Mastema stepped between her and the guards, drawing his khopesh. With a wave of his hand, he summoned Fyre around them, creating a ring of flames. A dozen spears leveled in his direction.

"Stay yourselves, brethren." He warned. "I do not wish to spill blood."

Heman leapt from his throne to the floor, drawing his adamantine blade. "Do you not see their treachery? Elder Asaph! Summon your men! If she will not stand down," he raised his sword, "she will be put down like the dog she is."

Her anger flared. Her hands burned. In that moment, she could have done it: she could have summoned the destructive light and burnt him to ashes. She would have enjoyed it, too.

But she couldn't. Her hands lost their warmth. The small, unnoticeable glow faded. She wouldn't kill him. If she did, Mastema and most her friends would be dead for supporting her.

Dani expected to hear the call for more arms, but she did not. Asaph said nothing. He sat silently on his throne.

Heman noticed, too. "Elder Asaph!"

He stood, drawing his scimitar. He stepped down, flanking Heman. He looked ready to carry out the order. But then his sword came up and pressed against Heman's neck.

"Stay your blade." Asaph warned him. "Gatekeepers! Lower your weapons!"

"No!" Heman yelled. "Do not!"

But the Gatekeepers quickly snapped to, their spears withdrawn.

"Did you not hear me?" Heman cried.

They had, but they also heard Asaph. He was Head Gatekeeper. Ethan said they all respected him most. They wouldn't disobey.

"Our laws state," Asaph said to Heman, "that the Council makes decisions. Elder Castus and Elder Jeduthun are our Co-Consuls. They have the final word."

"You cannot earnestly side with her!"

Asaph glanced at Dani, and then turned back to Heman, his sword staying where it was. "No. But whatever reserves I have, I will maintain fealty to this city and to this Council. I will not bring forth a kangaroo court to judge and hang us all. Now stay your blade, Heman."

The lack of title was explicitly clear. Similarly, the look in his fellow Elder's eyes was enough. Heman withdrew his sword, sheathing it. When

Asaph extended his hand, he gave it over. Only then did the Head Gatekeeper withdraw his own.

Asaph looked again at Dani. There was no love loss there. He didn't trust her, but had some sense of code that stopped him from killing her. Small victories and whatnot.

Heman returned to his seat, shamefully staring at the ground. His supporters quickly sidled away from him.

Asaph turned to Castus. "Elder, I believe that all suspicions must be looked into. Elder Heman was," he glared briefly at him, "foolish, but we must be prepared for all possibilities. Lady Alecto should be summoned."

"Very well."

"Guardian Mastema should also be put in shackles."

Castus glanced briefly at Elder Jeduthun, who said or indicated nothing. The white-haired Elder nodded. "Guardian Mastema, Novice Daniella, do you acquiesce?"

Before Dani could give a biting comeback—possibly a Pirates of the Caribbean reference—Mastema withdrew his sword and offered it to the nearest Gatekeeper. "I do."

"Mastema!"

He shushed her with one gesture. "I will submit myself before this Council."

"Elders," Kleos rushed forward, "Novice Daniella was with the rest of us when the attack occurred. She is innocent of the attack on this city."

"We will see." Castus said solemnly. "Everyone will be confined to quarters. Elder Jeduthun? Do you agree?"

The other Elder looked briefly at Dani. She silently pleaded for him not to do this, but instead, he nodded. "I do. We must be cautious, but she may keep her weapons. Take Guardian Mastema to the cells for drawing his blade. Return Novice Daniella and the others to their homes. I will go with them to ensure their safe return."

The Elders left. Gatekeepers placed Mastema in shackles. Dani glared at Jeduthun has he stepped from the thrones. "How could you? You and I both know Mastema and I aren't in the wrong here."

"Do not speak as if we are equals, Novice." Jeduthun's voice was warning.

But all he did was piss her off. Dani went to Mastema. "I'm sorry. It's all my fault."

"It is not. I raised my sword gladly in your defense." He leaned down to her ear as a Gatekeepers put on his bindings. "Find Ethan. Lady Alecto took him. In this I know you are correct."

"But I don't know where to look."

The Gatekeepers pulled him from her. He murmured. "The idols." Then he was gone.

Dani watched them take him. *The idols.* What the hell did that mean?

"Novice Daniella," Jeduthun called, "it is time."

Jeduthun led the column of friends and soldiers from the Keep. He walked next to Dani. She could barely look at him.

"I know we aren't friends," she said with her eyes forward, "but I thought we at least weren't enemies."

"We are not." The Elder replied.

"Funny way of showing it."

"If your Guardian had not surrendered, you would have died." They descended toward the Vale Bridge. "You do not understand when it is time to struggle and when it is time to yield."

"Well you're such an expert, aren't you?"

For the first time, Jeduthun faced her as they walked. "Yes. I have had much practice."

"So tell me: what's the point of detaining us? You know Mastema is innocent. You know Alecto is the demon."

"Of course I know. The investigation will clear him and you of the charges eventually."

"And in the meantime, Ethan is out there somewhere with Alecto, dying."

"Yes. I realize. But the Council is a bureaucracy. It is hostile towards you, as you saw today. If Asaph had not intervened, you would be facing execution. Even I would have been powerless."

"You don't sound like you trust the Council."

"That is because I do not." They were halfway across the bridge. "Do not mistake me, Novice Dani. I would never work against the Council, but I am no fool. I trust my instincts, both about myself and about certain others." He put weight behind the last few words of that sentence. "I know when something needs to be done, but I am a patient man. I know when there is an opportunity. Just as I know Lady Alecto took the opportunity gain entry into our city."

They just crossed over the Crystalline River.

"I also know when fortune spreads its arms for me." Kleos and the others started to notice his tone. They exchanged quick glances. "Fortune such as traveling with one who knows the incantation to open that ladder," his eyes flicked briefly to Kleos, "and being within reach of the very bypass to our wards. All I would need is one who is unafraid to defy the Council and willing to risk everything to find Guardian Ethan."

She blinked. Did he just suggest what she thought he suggested?

"Of course, I could only offer you the briefest of chances."

"Like what?"

"Guardian Kleos," Jeduthun asked, "did you know I have a moniker, just as Guardian Ethan does?"

Kleos's mouth slightly tugged at the corners. "The Lord of Shouting."

He stopped. "Do you know why I am called that?"

Everyone came to a halt. As Elder Jeduthun turned, Kleos's fingers went to his ears. It took Dani a second to do the same. Her friends were right behind her.

Jeduthun opened his mouth and the sound that came out shook her bones. It was like the Tigris's roar times ten. Her knees buckled. It was if she stood in front of a two-story tall subwoofer. It reverberated on her body like waves. Her friends cried out, but protected themselves in time. Unfortunately, the Gatekeepers were not so lucky. Most collapsed, passing out in the seconds it took to fall to the ground. Dani got only a fraction of what they did and even she felt ready to black out.

Jeduthun stopped. Dani staggered back up to stand, staring at him. Cautiously, she unplugged her ears.

Her hearing returned slowly. "What the hell was that?"

Kleos moved his jaw like popping his ears. "Elder Jeduthun has a very rare, unique gift over sound; like your power to speak to birds or Ethan's to call lightning to his sword. It is why they call him the Lord of Shouting."

Jeduthun held out his hands. Ethan's sword, Stormthrower, shimmered into existence. He held it out to Dani. "When you find him, Guardian Ethan will need this."

She didn't take it. "You believe me?"

"Of course."

"But," she tried to think, "why are you helping me?"

"The Council's investigation will take time. Alecto will kill Guardian Ethan if she does not get what she wants: you."

"Me?"

Jeduthun nodded. "Alecto came to Empyrean under the guise of watching the Trials. We know her true motive now was to gain access to

Gabriel's Horn, but she also took an interest in you. And she took someone special to you."

Dani's ears burned. "Ethan isn't special to me."

"We all know otherwise." He held out the sword again. "That is why he was taken. She knows you will come for him. The Council would never allow you to go, so I was forced to improvise. Have Kleos take you to the river gate. Find him."

She took the sword. "Thank you."

"Do not thank me. If Alecto truly took Ethan, then she will expect you. And she is still the fiercest warrior in existence." He stepped back. "Now go. Good luck."

Chapter Forty-Eight

Dani landed on the pavement and a hand caught her arm. Kleos opened the ladder for her, but didn't follow. He stayed as Numen Gatekeepers pursued them, hoping to give her time.

Now she looked up to the kind smile of Judah. "Thanks."

"Of course, my dear." The barkeep said. "Come. We should go. You will have pursuers."

He led her inside. The club looked like it was under remodel. It was a wreck of overturned and broken furniture, smashed glass, and torn curtains. But it wasn't a remodel. It was a demolition.

"What happened?" she asked.

"Demons." He grunted. "They destroyed most of my golems and my establishment."

"Judah, I'm so sorry."

"It is nothing that cannot be fixed. It is also not your fault. As I have been informed, the traitor Alecto brought them through my protective spells, not you." He came around the bar caked with golem clay. "Jeduthun sent me word you were coming. He assumed you would need these." He handed her two vials. Panacea. "For you and Ethan."

"Thank you, but I don't know where he is. I don't even know if he's in Los Angeles."

"I do not know, either. I cannot think of a place she would take him."

Dani remembered Mastema's words. *The idols.* "Judah, what direction is the Wholesale District?"

"The one near the Los Angeles River? It is not far by flight, I suppose." He pointed west. "You would need to fly. Could you manage it and to keep behind the veil?"

She nodded. "I can try."

"Then go. Good luck."

"Thanks Judah." Dani ascended the steps and headed to the front. She walked out into the bright daylight and shimmered behind the veil as soon as she stepped onto the pavement.

Dani fantasized about being Supergirl as she flew over the city. A nice little daydream distraction from her messed-up reality.

The Wholesale District looked different from the air in the daylight. At first she couldn't discern which building was the storage warehouse where they found the demon idol. She eventually recognized the street. This time of day, the warehouses bustled with workers or shoppers or the casual truck. She landed in the alleyway, her sword in one hand and Ethan's sheathed in the other. She quickly strode down the empty street, looking for the entrance.

She found it and two waiting wraiths seconds later.

Two demons dressed as delivery truck drivers guarded the door. Dani appeared from the veil, not caring whether they saw her or not. Her blade ignited as she strode across the parking lot. The two monsters leapt forward like feral dogs.

She cut them down in seconds.

Blade wiped clean, there were no more in sight, so Dani tried the side door. Unlocked. It was stupid to try to sneak in. Alecto took Ethan on purpose. If she wanted Dani to come, she'd be expecting her. There was no element of surprise.

She crept softly into loading bay, sword up. No demons lay in wait. Her footsteps barely registered in the deafening silence. Dust-caked windows cast gray blue hues across the floor. She moved softly across the open space, keeping a nervous eye out.

It was empty except for Ethan, who lay in the middle of the floor with his hands and feet bound by bolted-chains to the floor.

A new demonic graven image stared at Dani from a table behind him. Now, it wasn't some harmless sculpture. The hairs on the back of her neck stood on end. The air smelled acrid, like a car battery exploded. Underneath that was the stench of demons. Sulfuric brimstone. She kept her sword ready as she made her way towards Ethan.

He heard footsteps and turned in her direction. "Dani!" he hissed. "Dani, what are you doing here?"

"I'm here to rescue you. Duh." She knelt next to him. "Are you okay?"

"Dani, it's not a demon! It's—!"

"Alecto. I know." She put down his sword and sheathed hers. The chains on his wrists and ankles were not metal, but black steel. Stygian. "Where is she?"

"I don't know." He shook his head. "You shouldn't be here. Alecto wants you to come."

"Yep. I know that, too." She touched the black metal and yanked her fingers back. She expected hellish metal to burn, but instead it was so cold it stung like needles. Ethan's bound wrists bruised with frostbite.

"Leave Dani." Ethan warned quietly. "Please. I don't know why you're here or why she took me, but go!"

"I'm not leaving." She had to cut these chains off. "And you know why I'm here."

His eyes met hers. He did. Even if neither of them was going to say it, they both knew.

He shook his head. "I'm not letting something happen to you because of me. Go. Get the others and tell them what's happening. Tell them to kill Alecto. You don't know what she's planning."

"Let me guess: free demons with Gabriel's Horn?"

"Well, I never did take you for a fool."

Dani spun, sword drawing in one fluid motion. Alecto stood a few feet from the tip of her pointed blade. She looked as heavenly as ever, but wore her armor; black stygian laced into a silvery adamantine battle-dress, breastplate and bracers. Her flail and stygian sword hung from her belt, but she kept her hands innocently folded. She looked harmless. Beautiful.

Almost. Even tigers looked beautiful if you ignored the claws and teeth.

Dani swallowed her fear, keeping her sword up. "You look a lot prettier than the last time I saw you. I got to say: when you have a bad hair day, you _really_ have a bad hair day."

"Bravado. I always admired that about you, Dani. Yes, my more," she licked her lips, "monstrous side is hard to stomach, but it is very well at home in Hell. Demons fear my other visage. I've never shown it to the men of Empyrean. Tugging on their heart-strings is easier when I appear as this."

"You're ugly to me either way."

Alecto chuckled. "You've always had such courage in the face of your enemies."

She raised her blade a little higher. "I'm facing one right now."

"Are you?" The Fury asked. "Are you really? Am I your enemy, or is it those in Empyrean that sought to undermine, threaten, and kill you? Tell me: is your life worth theirs?"

Dani gripped her sword tighter. She said nothing.

Alecto's wings hissed along the floor as she paced around her, speaking in an even, innocent tone. "I knew you'd come for him. It is no secret what is between you. Love, much like anger, has a particularly telling energy. It leaves its mark. You would come for no one else."

"I would." She insisted. "The people in Empyrean are my friends."

"Friends? Really? Do friends cower behind you and avoid conflict as Bouden? Do friends fly into a jealous rage like Nathaniel? Do friends wish to imprison, or worse kill you, as the Elder Council attempted? Or not stand with you like the gifted?" she smiled knowingly. "And what of your attackers in the Vale? What would they have," her lip curled in disgust, "had of you if not for the intervention of your caladrius and centaur companions?"

"Don't pretend like you care about Caesar or Nessus. Or me." Dani put herself between Alecto and Ethan.

"I do care for Nessus. He is like I: a creature cast aside by humanity and the Numen. Left for dead by God's supposed special species. We are monsters to be feared and reviled, except when we fight the demonic for them. Then, we are cannon fodder. I've seen my kind slaughtered because Numen wish not to stand against Hell's fires with us. I would seek to save Nessus, the bird and you. I would save all who are forgotten by the misogynistic tyranny of God."

"God's a misogynist? Really? Have you ever met the Man?"

"I do not need to. His evil is evident."

"I find that funny since last time I checked, He wasn't the one attacking and killing my friends." She shook her head. "You remember all my friends, right? You forgot one. His name was Ailbe. We called him Dink. You killed him and left him choking on the floor in a pool of his own blood. You want to talk evil?"

"He was a cog in the machine that continues the slaughter of my kind for their benefit. He stood in the way of my vengeance."

"Is that why you're doing this?" she asked. "To get back at God and the Numen? You infiltrate and then take them down from the inside? That's very *Mean Girls* of you."

"There's that infamous wit of yours, Dani. Have you not seen what they are like?" Alecto shot back. "I have. I was an honest servant once. I tried to ignore what I knew in my soul, until I could ignore it no longer. How are such vile creatures part of a divine plan? Numen are as fallen as the angels of old." Dani flinched. Alecto smiled. "Yes. I watched the angels destroy most of Creation. I saw those impudent children rip apart the galaxy, decimate species you've never heard of, destroy worlds full of God's other creations; my kind along with it. Other Hellions, before there was such a word, had their lives wiped from existence. And for what? Because God created you."

The emotion in her voice made Dani's skin crawl. She heard anger plenty of times. This wasn't anger. This wasn't even rage. It was fury.

"Humanity. You were His perfect creations; a symbol of greatness for billions upon billions to admire. You, a bunch of mud-slinging apes, given an honor you've squandered. When the seeds of your existence evolved, when the first *Homo sapiens* came from the creatures that preceded you, you were promised to be greatest amongst the flock. The whole of Creation felt God's love for you. And all you've done since then is fight and fornicate yourselves to death. And the Numen? They are the worst of your species. Haughty. Arrogant. Self-centered and self-serving. You believe yourselves to be the inheritors of His angels?" She shook her head. "You are more right than you can imagine. You are just like them."

Dani found her voice. "And you think siding with demons is a better choice? Their god was—as my kind would put it—an immature, self-destructive, putrid scum. And, I remind you, he was an angel. He started everything that led to your species' destruction."

"Is that so?" Alecto's voice was full of contempt and mirth. "You believe the angel Lucifer is to blame?"

"Well, obviously, you don't, but you drank the demonic Kool-Aid."

"You know nothing, Daniella del Lucio!" Alecto seethed. "You know nothing of Lucifer, his children or the angels. You have been fed a lie. You are on the wrong side if you stand with the Numen."

"I'm not going to argue that. Hell, I'd like it stick it to half the Elder Council, pointy-end of the blade first. And the one angel I met has some growing up to do. But just because I may not be on the right side doesn't mean you are, either. A choice between scum and sewage doesn't make one better than the other." She raised her sword again. "Where's the horn?"

Alecto raised her hands. The air shimmered and it appeared between them. Dani never paid attention to the statue of Gabriel. She didn't remember what the horn looked like. She imagined a modern jazz trumpet or a long-stemmed flute, but what appeared in Alecto's hands was something more like a ram's horn than a _horn_ horn. It was made of spiraled white bone and shone in the gloom of the warehouse. Tapered at one end and a large mouth at the other, if someone held it to their lips it would angle above their head. Gabriel's Horn radiated energy unlike anything Dani ever felt. She was drawn to it. It called to her.

"You can feel it, can't you?" Alecto marveled, running her hands across the marble surface. "The Horn of the Archangel Gabriel. With the power to call forth the truth of Creation, unbind that which was bound and herald the beginning of Judgment Day."

"Don't count on Judgment Day starting any time soon. Gabriel won't blow that kazoo."

"The legend says the Horn of Gabriel will signal the end of times. Who said Gabriel had to be the one to do it?"

Dani felt a tremor run down her spine. "What have you done?"

The Fury played the horn through her hands, caressing it lovingly. "Such a remarkable weapon. Imagine it: the gift of an angel to undo the power of angels. You know," she said casually, "the first demons were terrifying creatures. They were created to oppose God and His angels. Lucifer made them the perfect opposites. They were fearsome. When the War was over, angels bound them to Hell with their creator to torment him. Their children lived on, or escaped Hell, but the originals could not until now."

Dani already knew. "The idols. They're like some sort of worship beacons."

"All holy objects are. They take on the power of their worshippers. Demons worship their ancestors. With enough power, they can influence this world. With more, could be raised. But that kind of faith is difficult to come by. This," she raised the horn reverently, "speeds up that process."

"Dani," Ethan warned, "she's used it already."

Dani glanced at the idol, which radiated dark energy. "What did you summon, Alecto?"

"I've summoned many. Hell is coming to Earth and the Numen will know what it is like to stand on the frontlines. The demon lords have risen." The cruelest smile crossed her lips. "But in particular? That idol? He was the one I truly wanted. He can unite Hell against the Numen. They call him Belial. And he is very glad to be free."

She placed the horn down. She faced Dani, only a few paces away. Then she drew her sword. The black, double-edge blade shone with purple and blue hues, so deep she could barely see them. The stygian glinted, but instead of light, it reflected the darkness of its surface.

"You cannot stop them, Dani. This is your last chance. Do not side with the corrupt Numen or their God. Join us."

Dani glanced at Ethan. The Council, Michael, Andreas, Lester; all of them were horrible human beings. But Ethan? Her friends? Mastema? She was not a fan her new people as a whole, but there were a few worth fighting for. And the gifted needed protection. If there were a few, she was ready to lay it down to protect them.

"Only my friends call me Dani," she told her, raising her sword again, "and hell no."

"Then your choice is death."

Alecto transformed. Her skin turned black. Her eyes became blood red. Her feathers melted into bat wings and her hands and feet morphed into claws. Her demonic form surged to life. Twisted, sharp teeth spewed saliva as she screeched and leapt the short distance, sword slashing.

The first blow was so hard it shook Dani's bones. She blocked and parried, slicing out and cutting across Alecto's armor, but it protected the Fury from the edge. Alecto struck, smashing the pommel of her sword across Dani's unprotected wounded shoulder. The wound was healed almost completely, but it was enough to stagger her.

Alecto thrust her double-edged stygian blade at Dani's gut. She turned her body sideways to avoid it, using her adamantine bracer to fend it off before slashing again with her blade, this time to stop Alecto's attacking bat wing. Her glowing empyreal blade caught flesh and tore a gash. Alecto screamed.

Dani went on the attack, cutting and hacking, forcing Alecto away from Ethan. She drove her back. When the Erinys countered, Dani brought up her forearm and used the bracer to block. Pain and numbness shot down her right arm. The adamantine armor caught it, but taking the full force of blow probably fractured something underneath.

Alecto screeched with an unholy battle cry, attacking with one of her clawed feet. Dani caught it along the greaves, then jumped and landed on the same foot, delivering a practiced kick to her midsection. Again, Alecto was forced back. Dani was winning.

But just like her attack on the city, everything the Fury did was misdirection. Dani was too slow to see it.

The stygian sword sliced open Dani's thigh as soon as her kick landed. With a sudden fury, the demonic Hellion charged forward, one strike after another so quick Dani could barely stop them before another came. Her sword absorbed the blows along the glowing steel, but as her confidence waned and cold pain coursed through her injured leg, she began failing.

Their blades connected, hilts crossing. Alecto used her free hand to claw into Dani's left shoulder. She nearly lost her sword, screaming in agony as her flesh rended from her arm. Alecto spun and struck with her other wing, throwing Dani across the room into a pile of refuse.

"You should have joined us!" Alecto's voice was as hideous as her appearance.

Dani got up, limping, left arm barely able to hold her sword. Her claws tore through the protective Arachne-weave and sliced the flesh underneath. Blood streamed down her bicep.

She raised her hand. Light burst from her palm. Alecto raised her sword, but the heat and pure white light thrashed into her, burning her clawed hand and forcing her sword from it. As it poured over her, her stygian and adamantine armor melted under the intense heat.

But Dani couldn't make it last. The pain was too intense. She curled her fingers, pulling it back. Groaning, she raised her hand to strike again, but Alecto summoned the Horn of Gabriel to her hand. When the blast of light struck, it hit the Horn to no effect.

Alecto grinned. "Even your lightbringing cannot destroy an artifact of the Archangel!"

She pulled her flail from her belt, the tongs flickering with fire as she drew back and whipped. Balls of flames lashed out and Dani threw herself sideways. One of the fireballs sliced by her ear and singed her hair, exploding behind her. Others decorated the walls, pulverizing small holes in the concrete. She landed hard and her empyreal sword clattered from her grasp.

Alecto yanked her armor from her body, the metal reduced to smoldering slag by Dani's power. Dani summoned Aer to pull her sword to her, but Alecto leaped and closed the distance between them with a single flap of her wings. She landed and kicked, the blow breaking something inside Dani's ribcage and spinning her up off the floor. Pointyend flung uselessly away. Dani flew through the air and struck the wall, falling back to earth hard and painfully.

She whimpered, barely able to get up. She watched through blurred, painful tears as Alecto retrieved her stygian blade and dropped the Horn, stalking towards her. Dani got to her feet, barely able to stand.

"Why do you bother?" the beast demanded.

Alecto lashed the whip, this time to wound. Embers cut across her arms and legs, carving her to her knees. The pain was unbearable.

Dani had to do something. She was not going to let this thing kill her without a fight. But with nothing left, with no weapon and agonizing pain, she felt darkness roll up around her. Alecto would kill her. Fight or not, she was going to die.

"I will take you quick." Alecto promised, leaping onto the loading ramp.

And as her death stalked towards her, Dani heard Mastema's words:

Let no man, woman or creature take your life from you. Let no other stay your blade but you. Give no quarter unless earned. Give no mercy unless needed. Let your heart and your mind guide you and keep you. Let the light shine upon you.

She got to her feet again, huddling against the wall for support. *Live selflessly so others may live by your example. Die so others might take up your cause. Welcome death and in death, conquer it.*

Ethan watched on as Alecto came for her. He strained against the shackles. He wouldn't be able to help her.

And should you die, and they find your body in the streets come morning, may the blood of your enemies be upon the palm of your hand, And your last words be:

I am Numen

I am Earthborn

"I am the light in the darkness."

She summoned her power again and as Alecto came at her, she struck. The powerful blast of energy exploded towards the Fury. Pain radiated up her arms with the intense, blinding light. Dani screamed as she poured herself into it.

Alecto, seeing the attack at the last second, dodged and it shot past her. She rolled, wings flapping once and flipping her back onto her feet. She spun as the light dissipated and Dani's last stand failed.

With a single bound, Alecto landed in front of her and seized her by the braids with one clawed hand, yanking Dani's head back. She pressed the tip of stygian sword against her throat.

"You failed. You failed yourself, you failed your boyfriend and you failed your kind. And all because you chose the wrong side."

She glared back up at her without fear. "Screw...you...!"

"Defiant to the last. What did you hope to accomplish?" The Fury demanded. "You think I would not see your desperate, final attack?"

"No. I figured you'd see it." Dani grinned bloodily. "I also figured you'd think it was aimed at you, you self-righteous freak!"

The blade of Ethan's Montante sword burst through Alecto's exposed chest. Her voice cut off in a wet choke. Behind her, Ethan stood, sword in hand. Dani's blast of light did its job: heal him. Dani didn't use anger. She didn't use fear. She used her hope. The frostbite was gone. The weakness was gone. Her light melted the chains like Alecto's armor, allowing him to break free.

He twisted and yanked the blade out. Alecto stumbled, tar-like blood spilling freely from the wound. She dropped Dani from her grasp.

Dani rose, grabbing her by the front of her tunic.

The Fury laughed, thick black blood spittling from her twisted teeth. "You," she coughed, "chose wrong."

"I didn't choose anything." She said, her hands beginning to glow. It hurt, but Dani enjoyed the pain. It meant she was still alive. "You did this. You killed my friend. You killed a little girl. But you wanted revenge, so you murdered them. You expect me to be like you? Fine. I'll happily send you back to Hell where you belong. Enjoy your revenge there."

"Kill me then." She grinned, her skin and tunic burning as it made contact with Dani's hands. "It matters not. I told you: change is coming. Terrible change. The fires of Hell burn brighter than ever before. Demonkind's progenitors have returned. And you are a part of it."

Light balled around her fists as Dani yanked her closer. "I'm not part of anything." Fire erupted around them. Alecto's body began to burn. "Tell me what the demons are planning and I'll make it quick. How did you get into the city?"

Alecto's bloody laugh nearly drowned her. She kept laughing, even as she caught fire. "We are inside Empyrean. We are coming for you." Alecto's teeth bared in a wide, ugly grin. "We are legion, Daniella del Lucio, for we are many. For we are everywhere. For we are death."

Then she leaned in. As light and fire consumed her, she whispered one last word into Dani's ear.

"Vespertide."

The light twisted around her, violently breaking apart her body. Dani's hands burned but she pushed that pain, and anger, and grief into the creature. The Fury screamed and flailed as she incinerated. Dani let her go and she fell to her knees, the light writhing around Alecto.

She transformed, morphing from the demonic figure back into the lady Dani met. Her eyes were wide, glowing from the inside. Her screams crescendoed and her body seized. The light flared. Dani shielded her eyes.

Alecto vanished with a scream.

Dani didn't remember dropping. She didn't remember falling into Ethan's arms as he caught her. She didn't remember a thing until she stared up into his eyes.

"Dani!" his voice was far off; distant. "Dani! No! Dani, wake up!"

She could see him over her. He uncapped a vial of panacea, putting it to her lips. She wouldn't drink.

"Dani! Come on! Don't do this to me! Wake up!"

It all seemed so distant; like she floated over her body. She could see herself, collapsed in the arms of a boy with cherub curls and honey eyes, with a good heart and a kind face. She watched him try to save her. But she was dying. And she was okay with it.

422

Dani felt her life slide away. And slowly, she drifted blissfully into oblivion.

Chapter Forty-Nine

She hated passing out. It happened so many times it was a running joke by now; in the Vale, in her first sparring session with Mastema, in her fight with Gabriel, in her last Trial. Now in her battle with Alecto. She was a regular fainting fair-lady.

Except this time, she died. That was less of a joke.

Her heart stopped. Ethan used CPR, something very modern for the very un-modern Numen. The panacea could heal her, but only if her blood was pumping. He wouldn't let her die, at least no longer than the whole two and half minutes she wasn't breathing before reviving her.

They told her all of this when she awoke in the Ward under armed guard. This would make her second stay and this time, it wasn't a voluntary stay. Her "escape stunt" caused "considerable ire" amongst the Elder Council. They didn't know how Dani subdued the Gatekeepers on the bridge, all of whom had no recollection of what happened. And they were equally unsure how a Novice could overpower an Elder like Jeduthun.

Jeduthun told her all of this when he came to see her.

"You didn't tell them?" Dani asked when the healers released her to the Elder.

"Of course not. I am not a fool." He gave her a playful smile.

"So what's going to happen? Is the Council angry with me?"

"Of course they are. Would you honestly expect anything less?"

"Not really."

"But they cannot harm you, at least not for the time being." He promised. "After Guardian Ethan's rescue, he corroborated your story about Alecto; though I have questions about how her body could be destroyed to the point that not even ash was left."

He looked pointedly at Dani. She gave away nothing.

"And your victory was a victory for Empyrean." He continued. They left the Keep, descended the steps and walked into the Citadel. "You are renowned amongst Numen and supernatural alike. To kill you, or let anyone else kill you, would be an embarrassment. Your fame protects you."

"What about Kleos and Mastema? Are they in trouble?"

He shook his head. "No. As with Ethan, they have been cleared of any wrongdoing, though it was begrudgingly. My fellow Elders would have questioned Guardian Ethan's account if not for the artifact he brought back with you."

They approached the Fane. Dani felt the familiar resonance. The white Horn of Gabriel, now under guard of Gatekeepers, lay on a pedestal in the middle of the rebuilt shrine.

"You retrieved a very powerful artifact." Jeduthun acknowledged. "Very few can question your explanation of events. Alecto was corrupt. She betrayed her oath and turned to a traitorous pact with demons. The Council accepts that, so you and your companions are free."

Dani hesitated to say anything. They gave her a free pass. But she also knew she couldn't _not_ say anything. "Elder Jeduthun, that's not true."

"How so?"

"Alecto didn't get in bed with demons because she was corrupt. She was angry." She faced him nervously. "The Hellions are her people. She blamed the Numen for their deaths because we won't help them. I'm sorry, but I agree with her."

"You do? Really?"

"I'm not ungrateful for being rescued and I certainly am not siding with Alecto, but if they're dying en masse and we stand by and do nothing, then how much good are we? It's not just humanity in danger. So are they." She glanced at Gabriel's Horn. "You told me once that the Horn reveals the truth. What if it did? What if it's not a coincidence that the Horn popped up in Alecto's hands?"

"Are you suggesting the Horn willed itself to be stolen? Why?"

"To show us what we were doing was wrong and the consequences if we keep doing it. Alecto's rebellion came from our mistake. If the Horn is some powerful symbol of truth, then maybe this shows us what will happen if we turn our backs on the Hellions. We'll face more than demons if it comes to that."

Jeduthun frowned, but considered it thoughtfully. He stared long and hard at Gabriel's Horn. "Are you claiming there may be a divine plan?"

"I don't know about divine." She said. "I'm still not sold on that, but if the Horn is magical, then it certainly could have a mind of its own. There's a lot we don't know about it."

"Like its owner?" The question caught her off guard. Clearly, he wasn't asking. He knew. "You leave Empyrean, go off into the Dalles and three days later you return with a purpose; a mission. I know angelic intervention when I see it. I can assume which angel came to you during your journey. Most of the Council is aware that angelic presences still exist in our world."

"Then why haven't you said anything?"

"There are secrets the Council guards; secrets about the angelic that Numen do not know. I suspect some of them you know now." His expression turned very serious. "And I suspect you know what would happen if the rest of our kind discovers what our angelic founders really were. The Earthborn fight with the belief we are on a mission by our forefathers. If they discovered the scope of destruction and untold mass of lives lost during their war, then our very existence would be brought into question."

Dani said what she suspected for some time. "You haven't had problems translating the Song of Sacrifice, have you? You've known this whole time why the angels left."

"Some. Certain prophecies are not as clear as they should be."

"Prophecies?"

Jeduthun just shrugged. "For another time, perhaps."

"And Gabriel's Horn? Did you know about that, too?"

"No, but we suspected there was another reason for the Fane."

"So other than not causing mass panic, what's my motivation for not telling everyone?" She folded her arms. "Because from where I stand, the Council sold everyone a bag of goods and you put us in the line of fire that got a friend of mine killed."

Jeduthun put a finger to his lip, frowning behind it. "The Council may not know what secrets you figured out, but should they, it would endanger your life."

"Are you threatening me to keep quiet?"

"I simply suggest that this stay between us."

"You seriously expect me to keep that kind of a secret?"

"Yes. For your sake and ours." The Elder looked once more at the artifact of Gabriel, now in its place of honor in the shrine, and said, "Do you remember our first conversation, Dani? Why it was that I put my confidence in you and I allowed you into Empyrean?"

She nodded, quoting, "'I believe most of all that everyone should be vigilant and watchful.' You said you thought I was good at heart, but even the good at heart cause bad things to happen."

"That has not changed." Jeduthun told her. "You have done a great many things your short time here, and may do more in the future, but I still have concerns to allay about you. You are at the center of very worrying omens and I do not know what those omens mean yet."

Every time she thought Jeduthun was on her side, the rug pulled out from under her. "I don't get you. You helped me save Ethan."

"And I did so to learn what could not be learned another way. Alecto took special interest in you and I have yet to figure out why. Your existence is an enigma."

"You're a complicated man, Elder Jeduthun."

"And you are a complicated woman, Novice Dani."

She smiled tightly. "Please, call me Daniella."

"I thought you preferred Dani?"

"I prefer my friends to call me Dani. I have the not-so-sneaky suspicion we're not friends."

Elder Jeduthun smiled, then walked off. And just like first day, she knew whole-heartedly that any hope of him as an ally, friend or someone to trust was completely gone.

He was as dangerous now as he had ever been.

Funerals were the following day. With hoods raised and masks on, Dani and the other Numen bore the bodies of the fallen to their resting places within the Hypogeum. Gifted were in attendance as well. The Numen allowed the fallen gifted to buried as well; a good sign. The skies darkened and rain drizzled, as if Empyrean itself mourned their loss. Dani was one of Dink's pallbearers. She gladly carried the person who saved her to the tomb beneath the city, reveling the rain as if it were Korë's gentle hand on her cheek.

After the funeral, life proceeded on as normal. Sanctuary Hill's market reopened and gifted returned to their life. For Dani, the Trials were over, but training was not. She was back at it, but now more accepted by her fellow Numen. Word of what she did spread. She was semi-famous as opposed to semi-infamous.

Of course, not everyone was as accepting. Andreas, Michael, and Lester still antagonized her. And they had friends who felt the same way. Some things didn't change.

Mastema, now free and cleared, returned to Dani's tutelage. Even though she defeated a number of demons, helped save the city and killed a Fury, he found ways to critique her. She suspected he would always be a hardass, but at least now she was okay with it.

But a return to lessons meant a return to Studies. The Anthenaeum had many books on demons and she had a few things she wanted to check. She stayed in the library after Studies ended that first week.

Ethan found her as she was looking over some tomes. "What are you up to?"

She smiled warmly. "Nothing much." They hadn't spoken since Alecto and now, more than ever, a tense awkwardness passed between them. "How are you feeling since, well, everything?"

"Good." He took a seat across from her. "I feel amazing, actually. The healers told me I had no ill effects or lasting wounds. Even a few old scars disappeared." He looked a little concerned by that. "What are you looking up?"

Dani turned the tome towards him. Each of the books in front of her had one subject. Drawn in dark black ink and described in detail, was the image of something she wished she could unsee.

"Belial." She said. "It was the name Alecto used. He's an ancient demon, referred to as the Wicked One, the King of Demons but more importantly," she pointed to the text, "he is said to be the very first demon ever created. He's the first of them all, Ethan. The oldest monster in existence. Alecto released him using the Horn and that idol." She felt cold inside. "If what she said is true about the Horn's power, then he's out there now. All these books describe him differently and none can agree on how powerful he is or what he can do. All they do agree on is that his rising his very, very bad." She shook her head. "I'm scared."

"I am too." He reached out and took her hands. "But being scared is part of being us. Dani, you took down Alecto. If you can fight someone as powerful as her, you can fight anyone."

"You're the one who actually stopped her."

"You gave me the power to do it."

She squeezed his hands and sighed. "Yeah, well, that's the other thing I've been looking for, but there aren't any books on it."

"Books on what?"

"'Lightbringing.' That's what Alecto called this power I have but," she held up her hands, "I can't find anything in here about it. Some mention power over sunlight, but not one that destroys the demonic or heals people. There is nothing about it in these books." She looked up into his eyes. Something in them made her pause. "What?"

"I need to show you something." He said. "Can you come with me?"

Holding her hand, he led Dani out of the Anthenaeum. They slipped past soldiers and Novices in training and walked to the Hypogeum. He was taking her to the Song of Sacrifice.

"Ethan, what's going on?" she asked as they descended the stairs.

"Dani, you can't talk to anyone about what you can do."

"What? Why? This power can help me fight demons. I could save lives!" They arrived at the bottom, descending to the wall of the Song and decorated caveside. She stopped him, spinning him around. "You know what this is, don't you? Lightbringing. All this secrecy is because even though it's not in the books, you know what it is." She searched his eyes. That much was true. What surprised her was the other part. "And it freaks you out."

"Dani—."

"No lying, no sugarcoating. You're afraid of it, even though I used it to saved your life."

"Then maybe you shouldn't have!" he shot back harshly.

Dani tensed. She didn't want to fight, but his anger and fear were scary. It wasn't like him to be that scared and that told her she needed to know more.

Ethan bit his lower lip hard, as if wanting to stop himself from telling her. "Dani, I know what it is. I've known for a while. So has Mastema."

"Then I should know too. Ethan, please. You brought me here, so tell me."

He sighed heavily. Then, raising the torch, he pointed to a section on the wall. Dani recognized the same section—the one that stood off by itself—that she asked about the first night he brought her here.

"This part is about Lucifer. Do you remember him?"

"Of course."

"Lucifer was known by many names. He was the eldest and most powerful angel. They gave him all kinds of names: the Morningstar, the Son of Dawn, the Angel of the First Daylight."

"Okay, fine, he was the Chuck Norris of angels. So?"

"He had one other moniker: Lightbringer. He led the fight against the darkness at the beginning of Creation. It was said when God spoke light into existence, that was Lucifer. He was the first angel." He looked into Dani's eyes. "The myth goes that he could call forth the very first light of Creation and that he could shine brighter than any angel. He could heal with that light and dispel darkness with a touch of his hands, just as God did in the beginning. In his name, that ability is called 'lightbringing.'"

Dani felt a cold chill run down her back.

"This part of the Song isn't about the ability, though. It's a prophecy. It speaks of a coming war. It's where the myth of Gabriel's Horn is mentioned. It says Gabriel's Horn will blow to announce the beginning of Judgment Day; the final battle between the forces of Heaven and Hell. And it forewarns of a time where demons will rise and a 'lightbringer' will lead the forces of Hell. It says this person will command the demons in the final battle. Lucifer is the only thing in existence with that moniker, but now—"

"But now," she finished, "I'm a lightbringer."

A long silence passed between them. Ethan put the torch down and took her hands, squeezing them comfortingly. "I don't think you're going to lead the forces of Hell, Dani."

"But you're scared anyway."

He didn't want to say anything, but nodded. "I'm a little scared, but _for_ you than _of_ you. If the Council found out there was another lightbringer, I don't know what they'd do. I don't want anything to happen to you, but if people find out, they may not understand." He squeezed her hands. "I know you are a good person. I care about you. Even Alecto knew that."

He leaned forward. When his lips brushed hers, they were sweet and tender. It wasn't the kiss they shared before Alecto's attack. This was different. Dani leaned into him, felt his warm mouth on hers and savored the feeling as she slipped her arms around him and held him close. An eternity stretched between them.

And then immediately ended.

"Am I interrupting?"

They jumped apart. Mastema stood at the top of the stairs with his own torch, his scowling features highlighted by orange flame.

Ethan backed away sheepishly. "No, Mastema, you're not interrupting anything."

Dani was less sheepish. "Jeez. Knock first."

"There is nowhere to knock."

"It's an expression!" How was it that she, living in a celestial city, suddenly had a chaperone? She killed demons! That earned her at least five minutes of privacy, right?

Her Guardian flicked his eyes to Ethan, then to the Song and back. "You told her?"

"Yes. Even though I didn't want to do it."

"She deserves to know. She is no longer a child. She can handle the responsibility. But," he lectured Dani, "you must keep your gift a secret until we determine how best to protect you; until we know who to trust."

"Trust?" Ethan shook his head. "What does that mean?"

He and Dani shared a look. She may not have known about lightbringing, but she was the first to point something out to Mastema. "Ethan, there's someone in Empyrean working for the demons."

"What?"

"Alecto knew how to get into the city because of 'vespertide.' Someone who goes to it allowed her in."

"That's crazy."

"Kleos said that the ladder could only be opened from the inside. He shut the ladder after I came up from Hellfire. That means someone had to reopen it."

"You think Kleos did this?"

"I think someone did. It could be Kleos, or a gifted, or a Numen; I'm not about to rule anyone out."

"You believe Alecto? Dani, she was in league with demons. We can trust nothing she said and anyone who does is a fool."

"I'm a fool?" she asked.

"If you believe her, then yes." And just like that, all the warm and fuzzies were gone. Ethan could tell he insulted her. He tried to explain. "Dani, Alecto threw her lot in with demons. That proves she can't tell the truth."

"She did that because we didn't help her people." He still didn't look convinced. "Ethan, she told the truth. I looked into her eyes as she died. I believe her. She had no reason to lie. Why don't you believe me?"

"I know everyone who goes to vespertide. They are the best men I've ever known. I trust them."

"Yeah," she said cynically, "because they're so trustworthy. It's not like they've done anything to make my life a living hell."

"Dani, I have to trust the people I fight with. There are some bad seeds, sure, but that doesn't mean they're all bad. Mastema, you can't really believe this."

"Contrary to your opinion, I do." Her Guardian told her. "I was imprisoned under suspicion. I do not share such blind faith."

"It's not blind faith!" With an angry shake of his head, he said, "I thought you were smarter than this."

She couldn't believe it. Ethan, of all people, was walking the party-line? He didn't doubt the others and what's worse, he doubted her.

"It's a Guardian's job to have faith in the man next to him," he told her, "and I'd rather trust the men I serve with than trust the word of a traitorous Fury."

"Or me?" she cut back. "Or trust me?"

"That's not what I meant."

"No, it's not, but that doesn't make it any less true."

Seeing no other option, he picked up his torch and with one last look back, ascended the stairs and disappeared. Mastema and Dani watched him go.

"I trust you." Her Guardian told her.

"Thanks." But it didn't change her mood. "I don't understand why he doesn't."

"He is conditioned to put his faith in Empyrean no matter the cost."

"So were you."

"My opinions changed of late. Imprisonment will do that to you." He placed a comforting hand on her shoulder. "You made the right decision. We both know what you said is true: someone turned traitor. Ethan may not believe us, but it changes nothing."

"No." she shook her head, looking to where he disappeared. "It changes everything. At least, it does for me."

Together, they ascended the stairs to the platform overlooking the Hypogeum. She could see the tomb where Dink and Korë and so many others laid at rest. Because of Alecto and whoever allowed her in, they were gone. She followed Mastema up the stairs.

"You told me once that I'd be alone," she said to him. "You told me I wouldn't have anyone there for me. I guess you were partly right. At least you believed me. You're here."

He stopped her as they crossed into the light at the mouth of the stairs. "And one day, I may not be. A time will come when you will face an enemy alone. I know that whenever that may be, your decision will determine the fate of more than yourself." He put a hand on her shoulder. "There is a reason this gift came to you and no one else. Remember: we are forced down a path for a reason. Whatever happens, I know only you are capable of walking this one."

"It doesn't make it any less lonely."

"No, it doesn't."

Mastema, the Archangel Gabriel; they said she had a destiny to fulfill. She assumed she had when she killed Alecto—that the rising darkness was destroyed—but she suspected there was more to come.

And whenever it did, she'd fight it. She didn't care how; she would stop it.

They started walking again. The light spilled down around her as she ascended into the daylight and Dani left the darkness behind her.

About the Author

Spencer Helsel was born in Culpeper, Virginia. He earned his Bachelor's Degree from Christopher Newport University and has spent the last decade as a middle school and high school teacher.

He currently lives with his wife Jessica and sons Adam and Sammy wherever the military sends them.

www.ingramcontent.com/pod-product-compliance
Lightning Source LLC
Chambersburg PA
CBHW070615260626
47161CB00007B/2441